I0779671

REQUIEM

by

Keshaune Hatchett

WORKBOOK PRESS LLC
187 E Warm Springs Rd,
Suite B285 Las Vegas NV 89119 USA

Website: https://workbookpress.com/
Hotline: 1-888-818-4856
Email: admin@workbookpress.com

Ordering Information:

Quantity sales. Special discounts are available on quantity purchases by corporations, associations, and others. For details, contact the publisher at the address above.

Library of Congress Control Number:

ISBN-13:   978-1-965732-46-5   Paperback Version

REV. DATE: 05/09/2025

Contents

CHAPTER 1

Lightning strafed the sky, followed by loud claps of thunder as inclement weather ravaged an impoverished village in Colombia. At the end of a wet, muddy road off a dead-end street sat a small, dilapidated hut on the right side. The structure's rusted tin roof was being battered by the heavy winds and rain. Drops of water leaked through dime-sized holes in the roof, but that was ancillary compared to what was transpiring inside.

Six members of the Diaz family congregated in the hovel's only bedroom, surrounding a meager old crib. Loud cries and chatter filled the room, but one specific cry stood out from the rest, not because it was the loudest but because it was one of pain and suffering.

A small, beautiful infant named Carolina lay helpless, suffering from childhood leukemia. She was surrounded by her family, which included her young mother, Rosa, who held her daughter's hand, and the matriarch, Sofia. Some in the room prayed and tried to make bargains with God to spare the infant's life. The others comforted the distraught mother, who was inconsolable as her daughter endured great pain.

Meanwhile an unexpected and certainly uninvited guest stood inconspicuously by the rear wall of the room, observing the activities. Samael—a.k.a. the angel of death—remained in the shadows, wearing a stoic expression. He yawned, numb to the pleas and histrionics of humans when a loved one was close to death. He just rolled his eyes and waited patiently for his signal so he could move in, perform his duty, and then move on to his next mission.

His outward appearance was the complete opposite of what one would expect when envisioning the angel of death. Absent were the cloak and boney hands holding a sharp hooked scythe. The entity that was present was of medium build and dressed in a black suit. His matching long, stringy, shoulder-length hair slightly covered his eyes and parts of his face.

He received a slight jolt at the base of his stomach; that was his signal. He calmly brushed the raindrops from his sleeves, adjusted his tie, and then slowly made his way toward the crib. With each meticulous step he took, the temperature in the room endured a precipitous drop. He stood at the foot of the crib and peered down at the child. The baby's loud screams echoed in his ears as she writhed in pain. It was a scene that would pull at anyone's heartstrings, but he was immune to such feelings and remained focused on the task at hand.

As he held the tip of his right index finger in the air, his eyes turned completely black, as if they were two lumps of coal in his head. The tip of his finger glowed white. With one touch, the infant would be put out of her misery. He leaned over and extended his hand, but just before making contact, Samael stopped abruptly. He was flummoxed by Carolina's actions. The baby had stopped crying and smiled while staring in his direction. It was as if she could see him and appeared to be happy to be in his presence. He had never experienced that type of reaction and was at a loss as he quickly retracted his finger and stared at the child.

Bewildered, he moved slightly to his left and then to his right. Her eyes followed his movements. It was all the proof he needed. She could see him. His eyes returned to their alternative state—white with blue iris—as he continued to gaze at her.

He had become mesmerized by her beauty and the glimmer in her big brown eyes. He marveled at her curly black locks. But it was her joyous smile that captured his heart. For the first time, he did not want to carry out his duty as an unfamiliar emotion was unmasked.

Angels of his making did not have the luxury of feeling sympathy, but he could not ignore the emotion as it ran rampant through his body. He had been ambivalent because he was sent to take this child's life, but now he wanted to find a way to save her. However, that ability was beyond the scope of his powers.

In the interim, the family had rejoiced the moment Carolina had stopped crying. They thought their prayers had been answered. As they embraced and shouted the word *miracle*, Sofia stood silent, knowing different.

She noticed that something or someone had captured her granddaughter's attention. She knew that, coupled with the sudden chill in the room, it could only mean one thing. She fell to her knees and in her native language began to beg and plead, offering her life in place of Carolina's—an act that confused the other members of the family.

Seeing her mother in distress, Rosa left Carolina's side and knelt beside Sofia. She questioned her mother and implored her to rise to her feet. She tried to convince Sofia that all was well and the worst was behind them, but Sofia vehemently refused, even shoving her daughter aside. While Sofia continued to make bargains, the rest of the family checked on Rosa and then went over to Sofia, which left Samael alone with Carolina.

Samael leaned over the railing of the crib and began to speak to the infant. He reveled when she returned his words with a gum-filled smile. He felt another jolt, this one more violent in nature. He clenched his fist as the pain reverberated through his body. Even though he was torn between carrying out his mission and sparing the child's life, he knew there would be severe repercussions if he disobeyed an order. He was left with no choice.

He grazed the child's cheek with the backs of his fingers as a single tear fell from each of his eyes. He exhaled heavily and lifted his index finger into the air once more. He looked down at her innocent face and took in her smile one last time. He swallowed the massive amount of saliva that had accumulated in his mouth, and his eyes turned completely black. He watched as Carolina's eyes lit up at the sight of his glowing finger. With a heavy heart, he reluctantly extended his right arm and closed his eyes. More tears fell the moment the baby reached up and made contact with her little finger.

At that moment, the pain and suffering were no more, but the cries from the family were deafening as they gathered around the infant's lifeless body. Samael took a step back. His job was complete, but he stayed for a few minutes and watched the family. He shared in their grief and leaned against the wall as he felt his heart breaking. He approached the crib once again and gave Carolina a soft kiss on the cheek before finally departing.

A short time later, Samael was perched high above the clouds, staring down upon the earth with his angel eyes. His attention was focused on the Diaz household. His heart remained heavy. He heard their cries as if he were still in the room and watched as Rosa held Carolina's body next to her bosom.

"Well, look who we have here," a voice rang out from behind him.

Samael's eyes shifted back to their alternative state as he spun around to see his friend, the archangel Michael, approaching with a huge grin sprawled across his face.

"To what do we owe the pleasure?" Michael asked before giving Samael a welcoming embrace.

"I am just taking in the sights," Samael replied in a dry tone.

"It is quite a sight, if I do say so myself." Michael placed his arm around Samael's shoulder and then looked down upon the earth with his angel eyes. Unlike Samael, whose eyes were completely black, Michael's eyes were completely white. "Are you looking at anything in particular?"

"I am looking at a house in Colombia." Samael exhaled heavily as his shoulders sank and his head dropped. "I took their beautiful daughter not too long ago." He shook his head. "It was the hardest thing I have ever had to do."

Michael's eyes returned to their normal shade of blue. He could not believe what he had just heard. He took a step back to observe Samael's body language and noticed something he had never seen from his friend before: defeat.

"You have taken countless lives over countless years." Michael placed a hand on his chin. "What makes this little girl any different than any other child you have taken?"

"She had her whole life ahead of her. She had not spoken her first word or taken her first step." A tear formed in Samael's eye. "But what really got me was when she looked at me." He turned away. "She actually smiled … at me." He took a deep breath before turning to face Michael. "You do not know what it is like for me. All I see on a daily basis is pain and tears coupled with hopelessness and despair." He strolled away, creating space between them. "You are loved and revered while I am feared and despised."

Michael attempted to console the angel of death, but his gesture was quickly rejected.

"I do not need or desire your pity," Samael said, staring at Michael with jealous eyes. "Your wings are a thing of beauty. Everything about you exudes grace and perfection, while I am the complete opposite."

Michael nodded as Samael's words resonated with him. "I fully understand what you are saying and empathize with your plight, but we are two very different angels with two very different purposes." He stepped forward, eliminating some of the space between them. "Even though you do not have wings, you have the ability to teleport. No other angel can do that, not even me, so you are unique in that manner."

"Powers have nothing to do with my point, old friend." Samael shook his head. "I am viewed as some kind of monster in the eyes of the humans while you and your brethren are viewed as bastions of everything that is good and holy."

"You cannot change the humans' perception of you," Michael said. He walked over to Samael and placed both hands on his shoulders. "What can be done to make you happy?"

Samael took a step back and peered down to earth, at the Diaz household in particular.

He suddenly knew exactly what he wanted. When he turned his attention back to Michael, his expression was serious and his resolve was absolute. "I want to know what it is like to feel happiness and experience joy instead of constant pain. I want to live among the humans and have my slice of happiness, even if only for a short period of time."

Michael was not surprised by his friend's reply, but he took a moment to search for the right response. Just as their conversation was about to resume, a loud voice rang out from behind them, drawing their attention.

Gabriel, Michael's fellow archangel, landed just a few feet away with his beautiful white wings spread wide. He retracted his wings as he approached, but not before giving Samael a glare laced with disdain.

"What is he doing here?" Gabriel inquired, rolling his eyes as if Samael was not worthy of his presence.

Samael returned Gabriel's glare with just as much venom. It was safe to say that no love was lost between the two celestials. "We are in the middle of an important conversation, and your presence is not required."

The two rivals exchanged some bitter words, followed by veiled threats, but before the two could come to fisticuffs, Michael stepped between them, grabbed Samael by the arm, and pulled him to the side.

"What you ask for I do not have the power to grant. I am sorry old friend."

"But the one you serve does wield such power," Samael retorted.

As he waited for a response, he watched Michael's facial expressions intently and noticed the conflict that stirred within his friend. He knew his request could not be granted without Michael's help, so he took the opportunity to attempt to persuade the archangel over to his side. He made his case, each word filled with passion, all the while taking slight glances in Gabriel's direction. Just as his monologue came to its conclusion, Samael noticed Gabriel had become antsy and was heading in their direction.

Gabriel abruptly forced his way between the two, and Samael found himself face-to-face with his nemesis. The hulking archangel glared at Samael, his body the epitome of perfection with not an ounce of body fat to be found. He retrieved the mace that hung from his belt and held it with a grip so tight that the veins on his forearm and bicep stood out. He gave the weapon a slight turn, and with that action, spikes appeared from the sphere that rested on top of the steel-like handle.

"Now," Gabriel said, "I asked a question. For your sake, an answer should be given before you experience the very thing you dole out."

Tired of the archangel's pathetic attempts at intimidation, Samael shoved him and prepared for the altercation that was long overdue. He displayed his dark, lifeless angel eyes and tightly clenched his fists, ready to unleash countless years of frustration and pain upon the truculent archangel.

He hurled insults toward Gabriel, baiting him to attack, but was met with taunting laughter instead. Itching for a fight, Samael decided to take matters into his own hands. But just as he made his move, a hand on his arm stopped his advance.

"I need you to calm down, my friend," Michael said in a soothing tone. "If you want me to go to him and make your request, engaging in an altercation with an archangel would not endear him to grant it."

Hearing those words, both angels stopped and gazed at Michael, but with two different expressions. Samael's was one of elation while Gabriel's was filled with bewilderment.

Samael's eyes returned to their alternative state as a huge smile graced his lips. "You will do this for me?"

"He will do nothing of the sort," Gabriel responded in a very deep tone. "You do not speak for me, Gabriel," Michael replied. "We are all angels.

We are supposed to be above such petty actions, and it is very disappointing that a fellow archangel continues to behave so petulantly when in the presence of the angel of death." He turned toward Samael. "You have duties to perform."

"Yes, you have duties that you cannot walk away from, death boy," Gabriel said with a tone that exuded arrogance.

"Speaking of duties, I am sure that you have your own duties to perform." Michael turned his attention back to Samael. "Go perform your duties, and when they are complete, I want you to return to this exact spot. I will go speak with him at once and formally submit your request."

Gabriel's disgust was evident in his scowl; he did not even attempt to hide his contempt. He turned his hand to the left—the one that was holding the mace—causing the spikes to retract.

He then returned the weapon to his belt and phased, exposing his wings. Before taking flight, he gazed at both Samael and Michael but did not utter a word. Then he simply flew away.

Hope permeated Samael's being as he hugged and thanked Michael numerous times. But after breaking the embrace and departing from his friend, the hope that had seemed to spring eternal quickly dissipated. He had to go perform his duties, which meant more lives had to be taken. After his encounter with Carolina, he looked at the reason for his existence through a different lens, and he knew he would never be the same.

CHAPTER 2

A short time later, Samael returned to the same spot as instructed. It had only been a few hours, but to him it seemed like centuries had passed as he eagerly waited for his friend to arrive with the answer to his request. He paced the area as a myriad of thoughts ran through his mind. What if his request was denied? How could he manage to continue doing his duties not knowing what it felt like to be loved and happy? He recollected every duty he'd performed. The screams from the families as he'd taken their loved ones' lives and the tears in each of their eyes. Those images were etched in his mind. But lastly, Carolina was never far from his thoughts. At the end of each task, he thought of her. The way she had smiled when she saw him, even though she had endured unspeakable pain. He could not imagine how someone so small and young could show him how to care about the human race.

Through his trying time, a swell of joy engulfed the somber angel when he saw wings flapping in the distance, heading his way. The moment had arrived. He was nervous. His heart raced, knowing there was a good chance that his request would be denied, but the suspense was too much and he had to know one way or the other.

He continued to focus on the wings, but as they got closer, Samael noticed something was off. This angel's body type was drastically different than Michael's. The smile that spread from ear to ear quickly dissolved when Samael realized it was Gabriel rapidly approaching.

He cursed under his breath as Gabriel landed just a few feet away and frowned as the archangel approached with a smirk.

"This is the most I have seen you in centuries, and let me inform you that it is entirely too much," Gabriel spouted.

"No one is asking you to stay, so if you do not wish to be in my presence, feel free to depart," Samael replied.

Gabriel chuckled and continued to come forward, closing the gap between them. His eyes displayed scorn as he lightly grazed the handle of his mace that rested on his belt. Using his higher stature, he looked down upon Samael in an attempt to impose his physical will, but it was futile, as Samael refused to be intimidated. Gabriel then turned his back on Samael to show disrespect and to rub some salt in the wound by displaying his wings, which he knew Samael yearned to have.

"I wanted to be here when Michael returned." He turned to face Samael once more. "From what I understand, he has some information that you are dying to have."

"You do not have better things to do with your time than to concern yourself with what is going on with me?" Samael shook his head in disgust. "You are truly a pathetic creature."

The archangel quickly turned to face Samael, his angel eyes on display and his mace held firmly in his hand.

"Ahh," was the noise that escaped Samael's lips as he saw Gabriel's reaction to his words. He continued his barrage of demeaning words and took pleasure knowing that he was responsible for exacerbating Gabriel's anger. "Enough!" a voice shouted from a distance.

Samael took a step back and smiled when he noticed the angel that had arrived this time was the one he wished to see. He went to approach his friend but was stopped by Michael's firm hand to his chest.

"Your behavior is deplorable." Michael shook his head at Samael.

"You come to me asking for my help on making a request on your behalf and this is how you act?"

"He has some nerve. He is beneath us," Gabriel interjected. "Silence!" Michael shouted.

Gabriel paused for a second and then slowly turned his body to face Michael. "You are no better than me, so I suggest that you lose the tone."

"What should be lost is this notion that you are better than anyone and everyone." Michael said. "Why are you even here in the first place?"

"I am not the outsider here." Gabriel turned to Samael. "Give this cretin what he desires so he can leave at once."

Samael just sat back patiently while the two archangels worked out their differences. When they were finished, his insides quailed when Michael turned in his direction. By the expression on the archangel's face, the news did not appear to be good. He looked down, purposely avoiding eye contact as he felt a hand on his shoulder. In his peripheral vision, he could see Gabriel standing with his arms folded, looking smug, but he refused to give him joy by showing his disappointment.

"I presented your request to him, and in no time I had the answer," Michael said very slowly and deliberately. He took a step back, purposely drawing out the process. The archangel tried to maintain his serious expression, but he could no longer contain his enthusiasm. A huge grin appeared on his face, which drew Samael's elation and Gabriel's fury. "Your request was granted. You will be allowed to take human form and live among them for a period of time."

"This is blasphemy!" Gabriel shouted.

"Do you dare question him?" Michael inquired.

Gabriel looked down and his shoulders slumped as if he were an admonished puppy. "I would never question him." He quickly turned his attention toward Samael. "But why would he give the likes of him anything?"

"If answers are what you require, feel free to go to him and demand them yourself," Michael said.

Gabriel knew he had to choose his next words very carefully but decided silence was the best option. He phased, stood for a few seconds glaring at Samael with contempt, and then, with a powerful swoop of his wings, took flight, leaving a gust of wind in his wake.

Seeing Gabriel's disgust brought delight to Samael, and watching his adversary fly away angry brought out a smile followed by a chuckle. But the time for basking in the glory of his victory soon came to an end, for he needed answers.

He turned to Michael. "How long will I be able to be on earth?"

"The time period could be indefinite. It could be one day or thirty days or maybe thirty years." Michael approached Samael, placed his arm around his friend, and gave him a hug, sharing in Samael's happiness. "I want you to relax and have some fun but learn some things about the humans and their way of life."

Samael closed his eyes and let out a sigh of relief. His nerves had been on edge as he waited for a response to his request. But even though everything had gone his way, his heart continued to pound as tears formed in his eyes. Once he wiped his eyes, the tears were replaced by a sparkle—a sight that was unusual for an entity that was known to be dark.

"When do I go?" He was antsy, shuffling from side to side and rubbing his hands together like a kid waiting for his birthday present. "Will I be some sort of successful businessman or a healer?" He raised his chin as if he were displaying regality. "Or will I be a person of more importance?"

"Calm down," Michael said, laughing. "For someone that is universally feared among the humans, your actions are like a kid in a candy store right now."

"What?" Samael questioned with a perplexed expression.

"If you are going to congregate with the humans, you must learn to speak like them." Michael shook his head and chuckled at the expense of his friend. "Now to your questions." His expression turned serious. "Your venture to earth will begin after we cover the rules and you have a full understanding of them."

"How many rules are we talking about?"

"Just a few, but they must be followed or there will be severe consequences."

At this point, Samael would have followed any rule or condition given to him as long as he could be on earth. He shrugged and held his hands in the air nonchalantly, wearing a sly smirk. "Lay them out. I am ready for anything that is given."

"Rule number one!" Michael shouted in a stern voice while holding his index finger in the air. "You will keep your true self a secret and under no circumstances make it known who you truly are." He paused. "If you do, your time on earth will come to an abrupt end." He took a step back and gazed into Samael's eyes. "Rule number two: you are not to commit the act of murder."

"Why would I want to murder anyone?"

"Well, when in Rome you tend to act like the Romans."

Samael's perplexed expression returned once again, but unlike the last time, he did not question the analogy; he just sat and waited for further instruction.

"That is it for the rules, but there are a few more things to cover before you are off to earth."

"Only two rules?" Samael asked, shaking his head. "I will not have any problems following the rules."

"It may seem simple now, but once you are with them and fully involved in their world, it may not be so easy." Michael took a deep breath. "I love the humans, but they are very flawed, and being a higher form of life, you may find it very difficult to be patient with them at times."

Michael walked over and took a seat on a cloud that was shaped like a bench. He invited Samael to join him. "Do not underestimate their innate ability to drive someone to kill or maim." He placed his hand on Samael's arm. "I need you to be above reproach and take the high road when they go low." He looked down upon the earth and then back at Samael. "Since you will be with the humans, you will be stripped of your abilities. That means you will be unable to teleport, your telekinetic ability will certainly be gone, and that creepy thing you do with your index finger will be out of commission."

Samael held his index finger in the air and smiled when it radiated white light. "Are you talking about this?"

"You are such a show-off," Michael said, and they shared a laugh. "The only ability you will have is your angel eyes, and please be discreet when you display them. The last thing we need is a human to see a man with eyes that look like two lumps of coal in his head." He turned and placed both hands on Samael's shoulders and looked in his eyes. "Listen, because this is very important. You will be stronger than the humans. You will wear their skin but will be far from a human being. But that does not mean that you are invulnerable."

Michael stood and took a few steps clear of Samael. "It will take a lot to do you harm, but harm can be done, and if you die as a human, you will not return as the angel of death; you will cease to exist altogether."

The smile that could not be displaced from Samael's face quickly disappeared when he heard Michael's revelation. Fear and concern replaced his joy. He took deep breaths while thoughts of his possible demise ran rampant through his mind.

"If you have had a change of heart, now is the time to make it known," Michael said.

"No!" Samael stood. "It just threw me for a second." He nodded, trying to shake his apprehension, but it was futile. "For countless millennia, I have taken lives; I just find it ironic that mine could be taken by the same ones that I have taken from."

"Not to change the subject," Michael interjected, "but you asked what you will be when you are on earth. That answer is simple." He smiled. "You will be a student in high school."

Samael broke out in uncontrollable laughter and then shook his head. "He shows that he has a sense of humor." His laughter stopped and his expression turned serious. "So how am I supposed to support myself if I am a teenage boy?"

"You will be living with a man named Riley Marks. He will pose as your uncle who is taking care of you after the tragic loss of your parents."

"Am I taking over the body of some kid that is already on earth?" Samael asked.

"No. You will be an original, but memories will be implanted in Mr.

Marks's head as if you have been in his life the entire time." "Why this guy? What makes him so special?" Samael asked.

"He is an earth angel of sorts. Riley is a good-hearted man who has a very good chance of becoming an angel once his time on earth has come to an end."

"So when my time on earth has concluded, how will my disappearance be explained to everyone I have interacted with?"

"When you leave earth, it will be as if you never existed. No one will remember anything about you, not even a conversation," Michael said and then placed his hand on Samael's shoulder before looking him in the eye. "I will be watching over you personally. If you need me for anything, all you have to do is say my name and I will appear."

Samael hugged his friend and thanked him once again for everything he had done for him. After breaking the embrace, he peered down at the Diaz family home and simply watched them for a few minutes. He saw the love they had for one another and their close bond after the loss of Carolina. He turned back to Michael and informed the archangel that he was ready to embark on his journey.

The two took a short stroll as Michael stressed the importance of following the rules and reiterated the importance of optimizing his time as a human. After everything was clear, Samael stopped Michael because he had one final question: "How will I transform into a human?"

"Ah," Michael said before displaying a devious smile. "You will receive a slight jolt, and once you awaken, you will be human." He led Samael to his left. "Seeing that you are a teenage boy, it might be best to be called Sammy instead of Samael, and your last name will be Angel." He chuckled. "That sense of humor that you spoke of earlier is rearing its head once again."

"This jolt that you speak of?" Samael asked with a confused expression.

Suddenly, Michael punched Samael in the jaw, knocking him unconscious and propelling him down to earth.

CHAPTER 3

S amael felt discomfort as a ringing noise filled his ears. It was as if someone was ringing a bell right next to his head. With one quick swat of his hand, he smashed the source of his pain into pieces; it was an alarm clock. He sat up in bed, rubbing his jaw and then his head, still feeling the residual effects from the right cross Michael had administered. He opened his eyes, startled, and slid back against the headboard. He surveyed his foreign surroundings and realized it was someone's bedroom. He was disoriented at first but then quickly realized the transformation had taken place. He was human.

He smiled as he touched his face, then his neck, and finally his torso. He let out a celebratory yelp and threw his arms in the air. He was ready for his first day on earth as a human. He did not know what it would entail, but he was looking forward to it nonetheless. He threw back the covers on the bed and prepared to take his first steps in his new body, but something unexpected happened: he fell. His legs were weak, as his muscles had not been acclimated to his human form. Every time he tried to stand, he fell like a newborn foal.

He was confused about what was happening and decided to be patient instead of allowing panic to ruin his moment. After falling to the floor repeatedly, he leaned against the bed to rest for a few seconds. He placed his fingers against his temples as a minor discomfort began to surface. Within a few seconds, it quickly grew to an immense, unbearable pain. He clutched his head and screamed at the top of his lungs; he felt as if his head were in a vice and being squeezed. His senses had not dulled; a bombardment of noises seared through his ears, ranging from a car crash ten miles away to a door slamming in the next city.

Blood began to seep from his eyes, nose, and ears. He clutched his head as the pressure mounted to the point that he thought it was about to explode. With every breath he felt the heat of a raging fire in his nostrils. He crumpled to the floor. The pain was too much. He began to regret his request to become human and yearned for death so his misery would come to an end.

After what seemed like an eternity, but in reality lasted only ten minutes, his senses dulled and the pain subsided. He was relieved as he leaned against the side of his bed, taking deep breaths to calm his nerves. Just as he was beginning to relax, dread reared its ugly head once again as he noticed that his shirt was saturated with blood and a pool of the same substance rested on the hardwood floor. He removed his shirt, wiped the residual blood from his face and ears, and then tossed it to the side. Just as he began to rise to his feet, he was startled by a loud knock on the door.

"Are you all right in there?" a voice asked from the other side of the door. He stood silent in hopes that the person talking to him, who he surmised was his uncle Riley, would simply go away if he did not supply an answer, but that thought was incorrect. The pounding and voice became louder, which pained his still sensitive ears. A massive lump developed in his throat, and his heart began to pound as he looked around the room. If Riley were to enter, how would Samael explain the shattered alarm clock and the massive pool of blood on the floor? He leaned against the door just in case Riley tried to enter.

"Everything is fine. I am just trying to wake up."

"You wake up by screaming now? You sound like someone is killing you in there!" Riley shouted.

"Ah, I … I … I …" Samael searched his room and mind for an answer that would appease Riley enough that he would not feel compelled to enter and check on his well-being. "I kicked my bedpost and hurt my toe." He closed his eyes and hoped his answer would suffice.

"Well, be more careful next time. Breakfast is on the table, so hurry up, and remember that I have to take you to school today."

Samael listened at the door to make sure Riley had departed. When he heard the steps creak under his uncle's feet as he descended the stairs, he breathed a sigh of relief. A smile appeared. It was inspection time; he could not contain his curiosity any longer and could not wait to see what he looked like. With haste, he raced into the bathroom.

At first glance, he was very pleased with his appearance. His skin tone was very high yellow, and his hair was short on the sides but had loose curls on the top. Two curls hung over his forehead and rested just above his eyes. Samael was very impressed with his muscular definition, but he was curious about one last thing. He grabbed the waistband of his shorts and gave it a slight tug to inspect down below. The huge smile that appeared indicated that he was very pleased. Now he was ready for his day.

Just as he was about to exit the bathroom, he stopped. He wanted to take one last look before departing. He gently ran his fingers along his face to feel the texture of his skin. He tugged at his nose and his earlobes and finally ran his tongue over his perfectly white teeth, but one last thing caught his attention: his eyes remained blue.

"I take it everything is to your liking?" a voice rang out from behind him.

Samael turned to find Michael standing in the doorway. "I really could have used your assistance a little while ago."

Michael turned and noticed the shattered alarm clock and the pool of blood. "I see that your time on earth has been very eventful thus far."

"I wish you would have told me how much pain I had to endure and warned me about the punch to the jaw." Samael shook his head. "Some friend you are." He picked up a washcloth, turned on the cold water, and after dipping the cloth, wiped his face and neck. He placed the cloth on the sink and then turned back to Michael. "Where exactly on earth am I?"

"You are in Virginia Beach, Virginia," Michael answered before taking a step to the side to allow Samael to exit the bathroom.

"What are we going to do about all this blood?" Samael asked as he grabbed the bloody shirt from the corner of the room and tossed it at Michael.

Michael winked and then placed the shirt on top of the pool of blood. He knelt down and placed his hand just above the blood. A white glow began to illuminate, and within seconds, all the blood had disappeared. "I cannot help you with the rest of the mess in here, but at least the bodily fluids are gone." He walked over to the desk that was located against the wall just to left of the window. "You are going to need these items to survive on earth as a teenager."

Samael approached Michael with a raised eyebrow and noticed three items. "What are these?"

"Oh, Samael." Michael shook his head. "This is a cell phone and a laptop computer."

"What do I need these for?" Samael asked with a shrug.

"Teenagers cannot live without their electronic devices, in particular their cell phones, and even though the phone can do all the functions of the computer, you need it also."

After applying the finishing touches to his wardrobe, Samael grabbed the phone and placed it in his back pocket, but as he turned to leave, Michael stopped him.

The archangel retrieved a trinket from his waist belt and handed it to Samael. "I want to give you something." He watched as Samael held the chain necklace with an angel with its wings spread as the centerpiece. "This is just a reminder of who you are when things become tough on earth and when the humans become a little too much to handle."

Samael smiled as he gazed at the necklace. The moment he placed it around his neck, his angel eyes appeared for a few seconds before turning back to blue.

The two exited the room and made their way down the stairs, exchanging playful banter. Michael added a few more instructions about how to act the part of a teenage boy. Once Samael reached the kitchen door, he stopped and looked back for Michael, who had disappeared, which brought a smile to Samael's face. "Figures," he whispered.

He opened the door and saw Riley standing by the kitchen sink with his back turned to the door, sipping a cup of coffee. Samael's eyes bulged out, and he quickly closed the door. Confused, he called for Michael. Then he ran back to his room and closed the door.

"What is the problem?" Michael asked after appearing.

"Am I in the right house?" Samael asked, looking at his own arm. "Riley is white, and I clearly am not."

"You have been around people before to know that there are mixed races." Michael shook his head. "Riley's sister was white and her husband was black. Are there any other questions or concerns?"

"No." Samael chuckled, feeling somewhat embarrassed. "I do need to get down there before more suspicion is raised."

Samael raced down the stairs and slowly opened the door once again, only to find Riley in the same position. He used his angel eyes to view Riley's aura and get a feel for what kind of person he truly was. The aura was white, which was to his liking. It indicated that Riley was good and pure of heart. Just as he was about to enter the kitchen, he felt a hand on his shoulder. He turned and saw Michael wearing an expression that read of disappointment.

"The whole point of you coming to earth is to have life experiences. You cannot do that by using your angel eyes. You have to be around the humans, get to know them, and find out things organically."

He unbuttoned the top two buttons of Samael's shirt. "You cannot be so stuffy and proper. You cannot go around using big words that even grown- ups have to look up to find out their meaning." He handed Samael his book bag. "And remember to go by Sammy instead of Samael. It is less formal."

Samael placed the bag over his left shoulder and then placed his hand on the kitchen door. He paused for a few seconds, allowing his nerves to settle. Then, after taking a few shorts breaths, he entered the kitchen. "Hey, Uncle Riley," he said in a chipper tone.

Hearing his nephew's voice, Riley spun around with a plate in each hand containing eggs, bacon, and toast. He walked over and placed the two plates on the table, one in front of Samael and the other where he was going to sit. He handed Samael a fork and a glass of orange juice before refilling his cup with coffee. Lastly, he adjusted his black tie, which matched his suit, before taking his seat. Riley was a slender man in his late forties, though he looked younger because of the deep dimples that were prevalent when he smiled. His hair was completely gray, and he wore it slicked back. He also had a mole just to right of his nose.

Samael watched as Riley began to devour his food. He grabbed his fork and surveyed the utensil. Then he looked down at his plate and turned up his nose at runny eggs, but the aroma was intriguing, so he decided to give them a chance. He imitated his uncle by taking a hearty bite of his eggs but immediately frowned, not liking the bland taste. With each chew, he made a face as if he were in agonizing pain. Then he forced down the eggs, almost choking in the process. He snuck a glimpse at Riley's plate and wondered how he managed to shovel the food down his throat without regurgitating.

He turned his attention back to his own plate and the strips of bacon that rested beside the eggs and toast. He reluctantly grabbed a piece and slowly took a bite, but his reaction was the total opposite than with the eggs. It was the best thing that had ever crossed his lips, though he had only the eggs to compare it to since it was his first time eating food.

He quickly grabbed the other three pieces and scarfed them down within seconds.

Riley watched with an astonished expression. "I see you really took a liking to the bacon this morning," he said before taking a sip of coffee. He looked at his watch and then took one last sip before folding the newspaper and placing it under his left arm. "We have to get going."

Samael sat back in his chair as Riley gathered the dishes. He noticed his uncle had left two slices of bacon on his plate and quickly grabbed them before he could place the plates in the sink.

Riley returned to his seat, smiling, his dimples on display. He held some papers in his right hand and his coffee mug in the other. "Why don't you go brush your teeth so I can fill out this paperwork before I take you to school?"

Samael nodded as he licked the bacon grease from his fingers. He hoisted the bag over his shoulder, departing the kitchen, and headed to his room to brush his teeth. He stopped at the threshold of his room, looked down at the kitchen door, and smiled. He knew he was going to enjoy his time on earth if he had to spend his days and nights with Riley. He was pleased they had chosen Riley to look after him during his time as a human.

A short time later, they were driving through the city. Samael was nestled comfortably on the passenger side of the car. He admired the beautiful sights of the city and found solace in the simple things like people walking down the street with their dogs or couples holding hands. He smiled as he observed nature: the sound of birds chirping, the smell of the air, and the feel of the breeze against his face and hair. A butterfly landed on his hand, which hung out of the car window; even that brought him joy. He leaned back in his seat as the soothing sounds from the radio penetrated his ears. *It cannot get any better than this*, he thought, feeling so relaxed. He knew things could get a lot worse or a lot better, but he would always have that moment in time to reflect back on if the former should occur.

Minutes later, they arrived at Princess Anne High School. Sammy exited the car and looked around in awe at the students, taking notice of their clothes and how they interacted with one another. The sheer number of people outside was becoming overwhelming. He could not take more than three steps without bumping into someone. He was nervous and began to look for Riley. When he turned forward, Samael was knocked to the ground by a very large student.

He was on his hands and knees, taking deep breaths, but was put at ease when he felt Riley's hands on his arm, helping him to his feet. He brushed the dirt off his clothes while Riley retrieved his book bag.

"You are a good man, Uncle Riley," he said, feeling touched by his uncle's concern.

"Thank you." Riley gave him a hug. "You're a good kid, Sammy, but you have to watch out for the other kids." He winked and gave him a kiss on the forehead.

"Sammy," Samael said under his breath. "I have to get used to using that name."

CHAPTER 4

Registration was complete. Sammy emerged from his counselor's office with his school schedule in hand, sporting a huge smile. Just as he and his uncle were about to exit the main office, a voice rang out from behind them.

"Who do we have here?"

Sammy spun around and was surprised yet appalled by the person standing a few feet away. The assistant principal stood before them, smiling, displaying his coffee soaked brown teeth. His gray sports jacket was a size too small, his black tie only reached halfway down his torso, and his white shirt had a red stain on the collar that one could only surmise was a dessert filling of some kind.

Sammy's eyes quickly focused on the principal's stomach, which hung over his beltline. The three bottom buttons of his shirt were undone, and upon closer inspection, the fine brown hairs that protruded from his navel area were visible.

The secretary rose to her feet and made her way over to Sammy and his uncle. "Mr. Rogan, allow me to introduce you to our new student, Samuel." Before she could finish the introduction, Samael interrupted. "The name is Sammy."

"I'm sorry," she said with a shocked expression. "Let me introduce you to Sammy Angel."

The assistant principal walked over and extended his hand to Sammy and then to his uncle. "It's a pleasure to have you here at our school."

Riley noticed the look of disdain on Sammy's face and quickly nudged him. He eyeballed the office and admired the scenery. "I like this school, and I think my nephew will like it also." He looked at Sammy. "You think you will like it?"

Sammy could barely manage to take his eyes off the assistant principal, feeling nauseated at his appearance. He could not believe a person of authority would show up to work looking so sloppy and obviously not caring. He let his contempt be known by rolling his eyes and shaking his head before finally turning his attention to the other sights in the office like the paintings on the walls.

"I am just ready to get started," Sammy replied skeptically.

"That's what I like to hear, a student that is ready to learn," Mr. Rogan said. "Don't let us stand in your way, Mr. Angel."

"You will not," Sammy replied in a dry tone.

He departed the office without uttering another word, but his uncle tracked him down and lectured him about his callous behavior. With the image of the assistant principal engraved in his memory, Sammy simply ignored his uncle and continued on his path to homeroom.

He wandered the halls, feverishly looking at his schedule and the room numbers, trying to find his destination. The task was frustrating and drew a few unsavory words from his lips, language that was beneath a higher life form such as him. After a few wrong turns, he finally found room 102, which brought out a grin and a sigh of relief. He was so excited until he opened the door. In an instant, those good feelings disappeared. He was stunned that the students were doing what they pleased while the teacher sat behind his desk with his face plastered in a magazine, immune to their antics and the profanity that flowed freely from their mouths as if they were hanging at a party.

The jocks were easy to identify because they wore their letterman jackets, even though it was still warm outside. The cheerleaders were in the front corner of the room, applying makeup and teasing their hair. Sammy's gaze wandered to the back corner of the room where the outcasts mustered, reading, reviewing flash cards, and highlighting sentences from notes they took in prior classes. Sammy gently closed the door, trying not to draw anyone's attention, but his act was futile. The teacher glanced up from his magazine, and a handful of students turned their attention to the door at the back of the room.

Sammy made eye contact with each student that stared at him. Then he looked at the teacher, who motioned for him to approach, rolling his eyes, annoyed that he had to do some work. Sammy swallowed the saliva that had amassed in his mouth. He could feel the gazes of his fellow students burrowing through his skin as he walked down the center aisle toward the teacher's desk. His apprehension grew with every step. After arriving at the teacher's desk, he handed over his schedule along with his papers and cupped his hands behind his back, squeezing very tightly.

The teacher skimmed over the items, barely taking the time to read Sammy's name, nonchalantly tossed the papers in Sammy's direction, ordered him to take a seat, and then returned to his magazine.

Astonished at the educator's attitude, Sammy snatched the documents off the desk, which earned him a gaze over the top of the teacher's glasses. Sammy whispered the word *pathetic* before turning and finding an empty desk in the very back of the room—the perfect spot for him to get away from the imbeciles that littered the enclosed space. He thought back to the moments of tranquility he'd had in the car on the ride to school. What he had seen so far from the students and people of authority inside the school made him think being human was not what he had expected. A small glimmer of regret began to resonate deep inside.

Minutes later, the bell rang, signaling it was time for the first class of the day. Sammy retrieved his schedule from his pocket and saw that he was headed to algebra. He rose to his feet and gathered his books. Just as he prepared to exit the room, he felt a forceful bump to the back of his left shoulder, which caused him and his books to tumble to the floor.

"Watch where you're going!" a strong, deep voice belted from behind him.

Sammy turned and spotted his assailant. He was an imposing specimen with broad shoulders and muscles that were practically busting out of his tight letterman jacket. Veins protruded from the jock's tightly balled brown fists, so Sammy knew he lusted for a confrontation. Sammy's eyes diverted from the jock to his friends, who stood just behind him, praising him and goading him to do more.

Sammy glimpsed in the teacher's direction, hoping the educator would intervene, but to his dismay, the teacher never took his eyes off his magazine, despite the ruckus occurring in his classroom. Sammy closed his eyes and took a deep breath. It took everything inside him not to jump to his feet and take the jock down a few notches in front of everyone who worshipped him. Instead, he remained docile and slowly rose to his feet, only to be shoved back to the floor.

"Did I say you could get up, boy?" the jock said with a frightening intensity in his eyes. "I don't think you know who you are dealing with, so it's time you learn before you get hurt." The jock took a few steps forward to stand over Sammy and looked down on him with a slight grin on an otherwise serious face. "My name is Slade Connors. I'm the best football player in this state, better yet the country. I'm the man here, so if you want to stay in one piece, you should stay outta of my way."

Sammy rolled his eyes and went to gather his books, but before he could, they were kicked out of his reach. He glared at Slade but did not say a word because he knew it would only exacerbate the situation, and he could not take the chance of doing serious harm to a human. So he endured the ridicule and mocking laughter and remained on the floor, avoiding eye contact, until Slade and his friends exited the classroom. He knew what it felt like to be embarrassed as the remaining students looked down at him while he sat on the floor. Some chuckled; others just shook their heads. He gritted his teeth and pressed down on the floor with such force that his finger impressions remained after he departed.

Hours later, Sammy had moved through his listless day, listening to his fellow students' vulgar jokes and obtuse answers to simple questions during class. He rolled his eyes as he noticed that his next class was history; he thought it was an exercise in redundancy since he had lived through and been with every person or event he was about to hear about. He was on the cusp of entering the room when he was met by an outburst of laughter. He examined the room and noticed that a majority of the students had been in his homeroom. He took a deep breath, lowered his head, and began to make his way to the rear of the classroom while enduring finger-pointing and jokes.

Halfway to his destination, he looked up and noticed the most beautiful sight he had ever seen. She was breathtaking. The young lady wore a cheerleading outfit, and the garter that rested on her right thigh signaled that she was the captain of the squad. Her long blond hair hung to the middle of her back, and she possessed the most beautiful gray eyes that he had ever seen. He clutched his chest as his heart fluttered; he had never experienced such a feeling. It was concerning, but that quickly ceased. His pace slowed, but his eyes remained fixated on the beauty. For a split second, he closed his eyes and enjoyed the alluring fragrance that emanated from her.

The moment he opened his eyes, he saw an extended foot from one of the football players that sat behind the head cheerleader. He tried to avoid it, but it was too late. He tripped and tumbled to the hard cement floor. The class' raucous laughter rang loudly in his ears, and Sammy had enough. He clenched his fists and began to pound them on the floor. As the laughs continued to sear through his ears, his anger began to overtake him.

His breathing began to intensify. He was ready to exact vengeance for being the butt of their jokes. He quickly lowered his head, feeling his eyes shift from blue to all black. But just as he was about to rise to his feet and dole out his wrath, he heard the teacher's voice as she entered the room and ordered everyone to be quiet. The teacher's authoritative tone cut through Sammy's anger, causing his eyes to return to their alternative state. He rose to his feet and turned to face the portly teacher, who stood behind her desk with a perplexed expression.

"Who are you, and what were you doing on the floor?" she asked, shaking her head.

"I can be clumsy at times." Sammy shrugged and then peered at the boy who had tripped him. "I just know my clumsiness better not be a habit."

"What's your name, son?" the teacher inquired, looking at her class roster. "My name is Sammy, Sammy Angel."

She smiled and nodded when she found his name on the roster. "It's a pleasure to meet you, Mr. Angel." She looked at him. "My name is Mrs. Stevens, and I have the pleasure of being your history teacher."

Her words and smile were refreshing to Sammy as he waved and took his seat. But that smile disappeared when he saw his fellow classmates' faces as they snickered and stared at him. He opened his book bag, retrieved his history book, and then exhaled. This is not what I wished it to be, he thought.

CHAPTER 5

When the final bell rang, it was music to Sammy's ears. He closed his eyes and pumped his fist, knowing his first day of school had come to an end. Armed with the books necessary to complete his homework, he exited the building and headed straight to the school bus. Just as he was about to board, he heard voices coming from the right of the building, so he decided to investigate. He walked a short way over to a fence that encompassed the football field, where the players and cheerleaders were practicing. Within seconds, he spotted her—the girl who had caught his attention in history class. He decided to take a seat and watch their practice for a little while.

He paid close attention as she went through her routine, mesmerized by her beauty. He admired her curves, which could not be concealed by the skimpy outfit. Everything about her was perfect, from her smile to her flawless pale skin.

"I hate to burst your bubble, but she isn't a nice person," a voice said softly from behind him.

Startled, Sammy spun around and saw a tall, slender boy dressed in black from head to toe standing a few feet away. He was taken aback by the boy's outward appearance. Aside from his wardrobe, he wore heavy black eyeliner and piercings on every part of his ears and four in his nose, two in each nostril.

Once the two made eye contact, Sammy found it peculiar that the boy had a strange expression on his face. "Is something wrong?" Sammy watched the boy take a few steps back and point in his direction.

"What are you?" the boy asked with a petrified expression.

The question threw Sammy for a loop, and he could not come up with a suitable answer. He broke eye contact and watched as the school buses passed, wishing he was sitting on one instead of dealing with the person that stood before him. He knew he had to address the subject with the boy because it would look suspicious if he simply walked away, so he displayed a fake smile even though his heart was pounding in his chest.

"What do you mean what am I?" He walked a circle around the boy, who stood motionless. "If anyone should be asking that question, it would be me."

He listened while the boy fumbled and stuttered, trying to reply. Sammy decided to try a different approach. "How about we start by you telling me your name?"

The boy gulped as he stared at the ground, refusing to make eye contact. "My name is … is … is …"

Sammy stood directly in front of the boy and lifted his chin, forcing him to make eye contact. "Have you forgotten your name?"

The apprehension the boy had once exuded vanished as he stared into Sammy's eyes. It was as though he were looking past Sammy's human shell to somewhere deeper; it was like he could see into his soul. Their roles had reversed. Now it was the boy who exuded confidence and Sammy was the one who felt uneasy.

"My name is Jonathon Franks." The boy surveyed Sammy from his forehead to his toes, trying to figure out the enigma. "People call me names like freak, but it's easy for myopic minds to dismiss things they don't understand."

Jonathon walked a circle around Sammy, rubbing the strands of wild hair that protruded from his chin. "My mother has a gift for witchcraft and spotting supernatural beings, and that gift was passed down to me. Even though I'm not as strong as my mother, I can spot a supernatural." His eyes narrowed. "I don't know what you are, but I do know that you're pretending to be a human."

"Pretending?" Sammy began to chuckle, but it stemmed from fear instead of humor. "Do you know how ludicrous you sound right now?" He shook his head. "You are standing here talking about witchcraft and supernaturals while walking around wearing a Halloween costume."

"You're resorting to insults?"

"I am calling it like I see it." Sammy walked back to the fence and watched his newly minted crush as she practiced her routine. "I do not remember asking for company, so if you are going to talk crazy, you can be on your way."

Sammy acted like he was focused on the cheerleader but continued to watch Jonathon out of the corner of his eye, hoping he would take the hint and leave. Much to his chagrin, Jonathon not only stayed but also approached and stood beside him at the fence.

"Her name is Emily Keele. She's the captain of the cheerleading squad and the former girlfriend of the school meathead, Slade Connors."

"Why am I not surprised?" Sammy replied, rolling his eyes as his anger spiked at the mere mention of the football star's name.

Noticing the knuckles on Sammy's hand turning white where he clutched the fence, Jonathon began to talk about ancillary things like the weather and the beach, but his rambling fell upon deaf ears because Sammy's thoughts were filled with doing harm to Slade.

Sammy knew he could not allow Slade to consume him, so he turned his attention back to Emily. Just as she was about to perform an acrobatic move, he felt a slap on his left shoulder.

"Why did you assault me?" he asked, turning his attention to Jonathon. "Assault you? Who talks like that?" Jonathon asked before breaking out into an overembellished laugh. "You haven't heard a word I've said."

Sammy had his fill of Jonathon and his antics for the day, so he grabbed his book bag, hoisted it over his shoulder, and started to depart. Jonathon stopped him with a hand on his arm.

"I was wondering"—Jonathon avoided eye contact by looking at the ground—"if you aren't doing anything …" He paused as his eyes slowly rose to make contact with Sammy's. "I would like for you to come hang out at my place."

Even though Sammy was new to earth and naïve to human ways, he knew Jonathon's invitation was nothing but a ploy to get him in front of his mother to satisfy his supernatural theory. He looked down at Jonathon's hand on his forearm in such a manner that Jonathon knew to remove it at once. "I do not wish to entertain your hocus-pocus conspiracies, so I will be declining your invitation to come to your residence."

He turned to walk away but felt bad about being rude to Jonathon. He stopped and took a deep breath, as he could not help but notice the disappointed expression on Jonathon's face. "Excuse me for being uncouth. Today has been a very long day, but I would gladly accept a rain check to hang out another time, my friend."

Joy filled Sammy when he saw the broad smile that graced Jonathon's lips. He was delighted to know that someone desired to be in his company. It dawned on him that he had made his first friend. Before departing, he shook Jonathon's hand and then waved as he made his way down the sidewalk, hoisting his book bag higher on his shoulder.

Later that day, Sammy arrived home. The moment he walked through the front door, he was greeted by Riley, who had a huge grin plastered on his face.

"How was your day?" Riley asked as he took Sammy's bag and placed it just inside the front door.

"It was very tedious and trying," Sammy answered.

He was about to make his way into the kitchen, but an unexpected sight stopped him in his tracks. He saw Michael sitting in the lounge chair in the corner of the living room. He watched as the archangel walked past him and through Riley and headed up to his room. But before he went through the doorway, he motioned for Sammy to follow. Sammy was clearly thrown off by Michael's presence, something that did not escape Riley.

"What's wrong, kid?" Riley asked.

"Ah, nothing, Uncle Riley. I just have a lot of homework to do." Sammy grabbed his bag. "I am going up to my room to get started."

"You're acting very strange." Riley looked at Sammy with a raised eyebrow. "Did you get into any trouble today?"

"Actually, the complete opposite. I made a friend today," Sammy replied and then raced to his room. He wanted to end the conversation, so he hurried and closed the door before Riley could come back with any follow- up questions.

Sammy leaned back against the door and then tossed his bag on the bed before turning his attention to Michael, who was sitting at his desk with his legs crossed, twiddling his fingers. "Something must be wrong for you to be here waiting for me."

"Actually, the opposite." Michael stood. "I want to commend you on keeping your cool after the mishaps that occurred today with those boys."

Before Michael could continue his praise, Sammy interjected, "There might be a problem." He walked into the bathroom to splash some cold water on his face and then dried himself with a towel. "There is this boy at school who claims to know I am not human. How is that?"

Michael stood and began to pace the room with his hands clasped behind his back. "Some humans are in tune with the spiritual side. It is said that they can see things that the normal person cannot, which includes spotting a celestial being." He stopped. "What did he do or say?"

"We were talking and he looked into my eyes, and I must say it made me feel uneasy." Sammy sat on the bed. "It was as if he could see past the human form and could see me, but he did not know who I really was." He leaned back against the headboard and took a deep breath. "He mentioned his mother being versed in witchcraft and able to recognize supernatural beings."

"Witchcraft hmm?" Michael rubbed his chin, deep in thought. "Do not worry about this. Everything will be just fine."

At that moment, there was a very loud knock on the door. Before Sammy could respond, it swung open. Riley scanned the room but only found Sammy. He looked at him, thoroughly confused. "I heard you having a full- fledged conversation but you are the only one in here." He sat beside Sammy. "Are you sure everything is all right?" He placed his arm around Sammy, exuding concern. "If anything is wrong or you need to talk about anything, I am here."

Sammy chuckled and shook his head. "Everything is perfectly fine, but I am getting hungry. Are we going to have some more of that delicious bacon?"

"Bacon?" Riley laughed. "I guess we can have breakfast for dinner. Let's go, son. I want you to tell me all about your day. Don't leave out any details."

Sammy gazed at Riley with admiration as the two exited the room. He told his uncle about his day, the first words out of his mouth being Emily Keele, as they went down the stairs and entered the kitchen.

The next day, time seemed to go by very slowly because Sammy constantly watched the clock, counting down the minutes until history class and the next time he would see Emily.

He waited with great anticipation for the final minutes to elapse in one of his elective classes. When the bell finally rang, Sammy grabbed his bag and ran out of the room like the building was on fire. As the hallways filled, his sprint became a fast-paced walk, but with each step, her beauty occupied his mind. He thought about and rehearsed what he would say to her to break the ice and how would he convince her to spend time with him. He was nervous because he did not have smooth pickup lines to bestow upon her and was clueless about how to talk to a beautiful young lady.

Once he reached the classroom, his heart began to pound. He knew that just a few feet away was the girl of his dreams and when he entered the room, the moment of truth would be at hand. His eagerness had turned to fear, a feeling he could not understand because she was just a girl while he was the bringer of death. He should not be afraid to talk to a mere mortal. As he inched toward the door, his heart rate increased with each step. His palms began to sweat, and his mouth became dry. He stopped just short of the classroom's threshold and took a few deep breaths in an attempt to calm his nerves.

Here goes nothing, he thought and then entered the room. There she was, a sight for longing eyes. Emily sat in her chair, wearing a tight pair of jeans and a beautiful white blouse. Her hair was pulled back in a ponytail, and her makeup had been applied to perfection. He cautiously approached her as a myriad of words permeated his mind. He wanted to make a great first impression but did not want to come on too strong. He stood before her desk, and when she looked up, their eyes made contact. His moment had arrived. She sat back in her chair, giving him her undivided attention, but just when he was about to speak, the bell rang.

The opportunity had passed, but luckily for him there would be others. He had time. So he simply waved and flashed a smile before making his way to his desk at the back of the room. He continued to watch Emily, but his attention was soon diverted to the door as Mrs. Stevens hustled into the room. She was out of breath, and her skin was flushed. When she bumped into her desk, the books she carried fell to the floor. As if on cue, the students erupted in laughter.

"I guess when all that girth gets moving, it's almost impossible to stop without hitting something," Emily said with attitude while twirling her hair, which only induced more laughter and mocking from the students.

Sammy could not believe his ears as he glared at Emily. He remembered Jonathon had said she was not a nice person, but the level of her disrespect was appalling. He was sickened by the blatant disrespect she had shown toward a person of authority. As he scanned the room, he noticed all the students pointing and making lewd gestures about Mrs. Stevens's weight, with the exception of one student, who sat in silence. He turned his attention back to the teacher and watched in horror as she began to crack emotionally. Tears welled in her eyes, so she turned her back to the class in an attempt to hide her grief, which only fueled their enjoyment.

Mrs. Stevens slowly reached for and grabbed a book without turning to face her hecklers. Then she slammed it on the floor, sending an awful thud resounding through the room, which caused the laughter to come to an immediate halt. All eyes focused on the educator as she slowly turned to face the class. Sammy was intrigued to find out how she would handle the situation.

She removed her glasses, wiped the tears from her eyes, and then returned the spectacles to her face without uttering a word. She leaned over, placing her fist on the desk, and gave Emily a scornful glare, which was met by a snide grin from the head cheerleader.

"How dare you speak to me that way?" Mrs. Stevens shouted. "You think because you are the captain of the cheerleaders that gives you carte blanche to do whatever you please?"

"Curt what?" Emily tossed her hands into the air. "Who in the world is this Curt and what does he have to do with you being fat?"

Sammy could not stand the disrespect any longer and wanted to teach the ungrateful students a lesson they would never forget. Having witnessed the vitriol that was said and the vile way in which it was delivered, he lost hope for the human race. He wanted to show who he really was and instill fear in every soul in the room. The worst that would happen was he would be admonished and would go back to his duties. He could not wait to see most in the room again but in a very different form. His eyes shifted to their celestial state, and even though he could hear Michael's voice in his ear begging him to stop and think about his actions, the decision had been made. The miscreants needed to be taught a horrifying lesson about being kind and respectful to their fellow man.

He looked up, but all the students' eyes were on the teacher and Mrs. Stevens's attention was focused on Emily, so no one saw death's eyes gazing upon them. Just as he began to stand to make his true presence known, he stopped as a fellow student intervened. To his surprise, it was to aid the teacher.

"You need to shut your mouth, Emily," the girl shouted.

Sammy covered his eyes as everyone's attention shifted to the right side of the room. Even though he was ready to show everyone his true identity, he wanted to see how things materialized. Once his eyes returned to their alternative state, he looked over at the student who had spoken up in defense of Mrs. Stevens. He was surprised that it was a fellow cheerleader, who just happened to be Mrs. Stevens's daughter, Cathy.

Emily rolled her eyes and then exhaled before turning her attention to Cathy. "You better learn your place if you value your position on my cheerleading squad."

"You have the nerve to tell me that I need to learn my place after you sit there and insult my mother the way you did?" Cathy shouted.

Mrs. Stevens soon had enough of the girls' bickering. Enough of the class's time had been wasted. She wanted to show professionalism, so she took a deep breath, swallowed her pride, and addressed the two girls. "If you both don't stop interrupting class, I'll send both of you to the principal's office." She turned to Emily. "If you address me in such a manner again, I will see to it that you are thrown out of this school." Her eyes red from tears and her voice trembling, she then instructed the students to open their books to page 20.

Sammy sat back and looked at every student in the class. He heard whispers from some and faint snickering from the jocks. His eyes finally made it to Emily.

The girl of his dreams had turned out to be a nightmare. He was astonished by the depth of her cruelty. It was safe to say that the strong crush he had developed for the beautiful cheerleader had disappeared. He was dumbfounded at how quick humans were to belittle one another without remorse for simple amusement. He turned his attention to the teacher and watched as she battled her emotions by wiping her eyes and nose with a tissue while her back was facing the class. He hoped that one day the youth in the classroom would realize that their cruel words could have a lasting effect on a person's life, and that in some cases, their words could cause a person to end it all.

CHAPTER 6

Later that day, Sammy entered the locker room for gym class. The moment he sat down on the bench and removed his shirt, a loud ruckus erupted from the right side of the room as the locker room doors abruptly opened. Slade and his best friend and school quarterback, Alex Martinez, entered laughing and conversing with profanity-laced language.

Sammy rolled his eyes and turned his back to the duo, but he could not help but notice that the room fell silent. He knew that his presence had been discovered.

"Look. It's the new boy," Alex whispered, tapping Slade's forearm.

A sinister grin crossed the superstar's face as he decided to approach Sammy. "If it isn't the new kid on the block." Slade slapped the back of Sammy's head. "Is there a problem?" He repeated the action. "If so, you should do something about it."

Sammy closed his eyes tightly and clenched the bench with such force that the wood cracked. Violent thoughts flowed through his mind as his anger began to rise. He lowered his head, feeling his eyes start to turn black. Michael's voice in his head, encouraging him to turn the other cheek, was Slade's saving grace; it kept Sammy calm. He took a few deep breaths and, once he was confident that his eyes had not phased, finally opened them and gazed upon his harasser. He slowly rose to his feet and stood face-to- face with Slade, peering at his arrogant smile.

"Are you going to do something this time, or are you going to cower on the floor like before?" Slade chuckled, never breaking eye contact.

Sammy glanced over Slade's shoulder and noticed that every boy in the room waited with bated breath for his response. He wanted nothing more than to break Slade in front of everyone, but he knew that was not an option, so he took a step back and turned away before the situation could escalate to the point of no return.

"I'm talking to you!" Slade shouted, grabbing Sammy's arm aggressively. "Don't you dare turn away from me when I'm talking to you."

Sammy snatched his arm away and then approached Slade so he stood within inches of his face. "You really have no idea who you are messing with. If you did, you would refrain from trying to engage me in combat."

"What did you just say?" Slade asked with a confused expression. "You sound like my grandpa."

Sammy heard the boys' laughter and saw their pointing fingers, which took him back to his first day of school and his encounter with Slade in homeroom. He could not take the embarrassment again, so he clenched his fist, preparing to show Slade what he was capable of. But just as he was about to take action, he saw Jonathon standing in the back corner of the room, watching with great interest. He took a step back, despite the mocking. Sammy did not want to give credence to Jonathon's suspicions, so he simply returned to his bench and finished getting dressed for gym.

Minutes later, the students gathered and ventured outside for class. The majority of the boys rushed to the middle of the field and began to choose sides for a game of flag football, while small groups of girls mustered on different parts of the field to converse. Sammy was not interested in mingling with the same boys who had ridiculed him minutes prior, so he decided to enjoy the weather and take a stroll on the track.

As he passed the bleachers on the right side of the field, Jonathon caught his eye. The odd young man sat and continued to closely watch Sammy's every move, searching for the slightest clue to validate his theory. Sammy chuckled as he passed.

Halfway around the track, Sammy spotted Cathy standing near the goalpost on her own, more than twenty feet away from her fellow cheerleaders, as if she were a lone wolf exiled from its pack. He noticed that every few seconds she would glare in Emily's direction and then turn away and mumble something to herself, so he decided to make his way over to her in the hope of making a new acquaintance and to stop anything bad from possibly happening.

He approached slowly, noticing that her eyes were looking toward the ground and her arms were crossed as she continued to mumble. Once he reached Cathy, he took a deep breath. "Hey. How are you doing?" He extended his hand. "My name is—"

Before he could finish, she interrupted, "I am well aware who you are." Cathy looked up with a stare that was as dry as her tone. "You're the new boy, Sammy Angel."

Sammy smiled as he gazed into her big brown eyes and then at her stringy dark hair. His eyes examined her thin frame, which didn't possess the curves that Emily had, but he recognized that not every girl was blessed with the same endowments.

"I just wanted to say hello and commend you for sticking up for your mother."

"Someone had to put the goddess in her place." Cathy glared over at Emily. "She may be pretty on the outside, but she is very ugly on the inside." She turned her attention back to Sammy. "I see how you look at her. I've seen you standing outside the fence, watching us practice, or should I say watching her every move." Her eyes narrowed and the corner of her mouth turned upward. "I know you would rather be over there talking to her just like every boy in this school." She chuckled. "Well, almost every boy."

"What do you mean by that?" Sammy asked, rubbing his chin with his thumb and index finger, his curiosity piqued.

"She's helplessly in love with Slade, but he doesn't want anything to do with her, which is so funny." Cathy laughed and then looked over her left shoulder at Emily. "The girl that everyone wants, but the one boy she desires refuses to give her the time of day."

Sammy noticed the disdain that Cathy exuded and wanted to defuse the situation, so he decided to change the subject and also fish for some answers to his questions. "Do all new students get treated like this, or am I a special case?"

"There was a major buzz about you around school. I mean, look at you.

You're gorgeous."

Sammy was perplexed by her reply, and his facial expression did very little to hide his confusion. "If my arrival has garnered all this buzz, as you say, then why am I being treated like garbage?"

"You were punked out within the first few minutes you stepped into a classroom, and this is high school." She smiled, displaying deep dimples. "News spreads around this school like wildfire."

"Punked out?" Sammy shrugged. "Forgive me if I am not aware of your meaning."

"Have you been under a rock or something?" Cathy shook her head and then rolled her eyes. "It means that someone challenged you to a fight and you backed down out of fear." She walked over and placed her hand on his arm. "I thought it was smart of you not to fight him because you would have been suspended."

"Me?" His eyebrow rose. "You meant we, because we both would have been fighting on school grounds, which is against the rules."

"They would not have suspended him." She shook her head. "He makes this school too much money and brings a lot of exposure through his exploits on the field." She turned her attention to Slade. "They let him get away with anything he chooses because he is such a good football player. So no. I said it right the first time. They would have suspended you for fighting, and he would have just run extra laps at practice."

Sammy also turned his attention to Slade and watched as the superstar caught a touchdown pass and rubbed it in his classmates' faces. "So what was the purpose of this boy challenging me to a fight? I do not even know this boy and have not wronged him in any way."

"Oh, that's an easy one." She turned to face Sammy again. "He sees you as a threat."

"A threat?"

"Yes. He is the man in this school and wants every girl to fall at his feet, but when you arrived and he saw how great looking you are, he knew the girls would look your way. His massive ego can't handle that." She shook her head. "So he challenged you, and you backed down. Now every time a female talks about you, one of his lackeys will quickly bring up the fact that he punked you out. So that brings you down and casts you in a bad light with the girls."

"And the boys?"

"They all want to be around him, so basically they just go along with anything he does, except for that boy." She turned and pointed at Jonathon, who was still seated on the bleachers, watching Sammy.

Sammy looked at Jonathon, who was giving him a creepy wave. "He definitely walks to the beat of his own drum, and that is not a bad thing." He turned his attention back to Cathy. "Would you do me the honor of taking a walk with me?" He smiled. "And I am asking because I want your company and no one else's."

Sammy noticed the sparkle in her eyes and the broad, beautiful smile that graced her lips, which put her dimples on full display. After she graciously accepted his invitation, the two were on their way, and their conversation and laughter flowed as if they had known each other for years. As the two turned the curve and headed toward the school, Emily and Slade took notice of the newly minted union. Without a doubt, mischievous thoughts entered their minds, and actions were soon to follow.

After gym, Sammy and his new friend met up and walked the halls en route to their next class. They laughed and conversed along the way as if they were the only people in the school. When they had to go their separate ways, they stopped at the corner. Sammy leaned against the wall while staring deep into her eyes.

"We're friends, but the way you look at me." Cathy blushed as she broke eye contact, looking toward the floor.

"Does it make you uncomfortable?" He leaned in close and placed his hand on her forearm. "If so, I sincerely apologize."

She backed away and took a deep breath. "I feel very comfortable with you, and that's the problem." She paused for a few seconds to collect her thoughts. "I know you have a crush on Emily, and I just don't want to be a fill-in until you're able to get next to her."

Sammy closed the space between them and took her hand in his. "I do not wish to be with her. I am where I want to be." He lifted her chin with his bent index finger. "I do enjoy your company and would like to have more of it."

"Let's be friends for now and see how things go." She winked at him, turned, and made her way to her next class.

Sammy smiled as he watched Cathy strut down the hall and waved each time she turned to see if he was looking. He had made his first friend. For the first time, he felt that all humans were not lost causes outside of Riley. The concern that he had made a mistake by requesting to become human had been put to rest. The only thing on his mind now was what he and Cathy would do next to build upon their friendship. That contemplation brought a huge smile to his face.

Hours later, the school day was almost at its end, so Sammy decided to head to his locker and drop off his excess books and only take the one he needed home. He decided to take a detour, hoping to run into Cathy. With a smile, he descended the stairs and walked down the ramp toward the locker area, looking in every direction for his new friend.

Once he reached his locker, he was disappointed that the only person in the vicinity was a male student talking on his cell phone. No sign of Cathy. Just as he opened his locker, Sammy heard some laughter accompanied by some loud chatter just around the corner. His first instinct was to ignore it and mind his own business. But as the commotion became louder, he felt compelled to investigate.

He cautiously walked to the end of the row of lockers and then peeked over his shoulder to see if anyone else was coming, but he was alone. He took a deep breath and looked around the corner to find the people responsible for the uproar. Three huge members of the football team surrounded Jonathon, pushing him to the floor while verbally abusing him.

Sammy stepped out of sight, leaned back against the lockers, and closed his eyes. *This is not my problem or my fight*, he thought and then turned and took a few steps in the opposite direction, intending to vacate the area. He stopped when he heard the mocking laughter grow louder, which took him back to the moment when he'd been on the floor in homeroom with Slade standing over him. Even though he was not helpless, Jonathon was clearly outnumbered. After taking a deep breath, Sammy felt compelled to come to the outcast's aid. He peeked around the corner one more time to assess the situation, and what he saw was disturbing. One of the linemen stood behind Jonathon with his arm wrapped around his neck, rendering him helpless, while another player punched Jonathon in the stomach. The third player watched and laughed.

The time had arrived and action needed to be taken, so Sammy nonchalantly stepped around the corner and cleared his throat to get the players' attention. He was successful.

"What do you want?" one of the burley football players asked.

"It don't matter what he wants. If he don't want to end up like this freak, he better go to class before it's too late," the second player added.

Sammy ignored their remarks and made his way past them, over to Jonathon, who had fallen to the floor and was clutching his stomach while gasping for air. Sammy helped Jonathon to his feet and brushed dust from his shirt. "Are you alright?"

He accepted Jonathon's nod to mean he was fine, despite him wincing in pain before sliding back to the floor, still unable to catch his breath. Sammy assured Jonathon that everything would be fine, but the moment he turned to face the three players, Sammy was greeted with a huge hand that engulfed his face and shoved him backward.

"You made a huge mistake sticking your nose where it doesn't belong, punk," the biggest of the three players shouted. "Now we have to give you the same medicine that this freak was taking." He shoved Sammy by the face once again. "Do you see how big we are? We're football players. You don't stand a chance against us, dummy."

"You are a very truculent person if I do not say so myself," Sammy replied.

Everyone, including Jonathon, stared at Sammy with a bewildered expression. The leader of the trio stepped forward, his face contorted in anger. "What did you call me?"

Before Sammy could respond, the lead bully punched him in the jaw. The blow did not faze Sammy at all, though the punch was thrown with such force that it would have broken a normal high school student's jaw. He remembered Michael's words about him being tougher than humans, and he knew he could not just shake off the punch without drawing suspicion, so he collapsed to the floor, holding his face. He slowly turned his head and glared at the linemen as they laughed. He'd had enough. He slowly rose to his feet and clenched his fist as bad intentions entered his mind. He had no thoughts of holding back. They were big tough guys; they could take the punishment. He motioned for the players to come at him, a request they quickly obliged.

The tussle lasted only a few minutes as Sammy unleashed a vicious attack that displayed his supernatural strength. He landed debilitating shots that were too much for the linemen to endure. He was gracious enough to allow them to land one punch each, but in the end, he stood over their fallen, battered, groaning bodies like a conqueror. He turned his attention to Jonathon, who returned his stare with awe. Sammy stood with his shirt torn, exposing his chiseled physique and chest glistening with sweat.

"That was awesome!" Jonathon shouted as he ran over to his newly crowned hero. "You destroyed them with ease."

Sammy ignored the comment and tried to repair his shirt to no avail. "I have to go to biology class." He lifted the torn fabric off his shoulder. "I cannot go to class like this."

Jonathon quickly removed his thin black jacket. "I know this is too small for all those muscles, but you can try to cover up with this."

Sammy chuckled but took the jacket knowing it was at least two sizes too small. He expended more energy trying to don the garment than he had fighting the three bullies. After a few minutes, he managed somehow get it on, but breathing was a huge issue. He took one last look at the football players, who were still lying on the floor, and thanked Jonathon for his jacket. Then he turned and made his way to class, struggling to breathe with each step as the jacket zipper dug into his diaphragm. He entered his biology class long after the late bell. All eyes were immediately on him because of his attire. He apologized to the teacher for his tardiness but got a flummoxed expression in return as the educator was at a loss for words.

Sammy was elated that this was his last class; he did not want to endure the same stares throughout the day and the whispers that were sure to follow.

A short time later, the bell sounded, signaling the end of the school day. The noise brought Sammy great joy. He grabbed his bag and rushed out of the building, unzipping the jacket along the way, which allowed him to take comfortable deep breaths. Amid stares from males and females alike, he exited the building and spotted Jonathon standing by the fence where they had watched the cheerleaders a few days earlier. He smiled and breathed a sigh of relief to know that his friend was safe and unharmed. He also knew he was lucky to have arrived on the scene when he did. He shuddered to think what Jonathon's fate would have been had he not taken that detour and been there to stop those Neanderthals from unleashing their wrath. He removed the jacket and adjusted his tattered shirt in an attempt to conceal his torso from the onlookers, which included Cathy and Emily.

Once he reached Jonathon, he handed him the jacket and thanked him again. After a few jokes dished out by Jonathon at Sammy's expense, the two shared a laugh. A loud disturbance from behind them grabbed Sammy's attention. When he turned to seek the source of the ruckus, he saw Slade rapidly approaching with an expression filled with bad intentions. He was flanked by the three linemen Sammy had battered earlier, and Alex Martinez was pulling up the rear.

Sammy smiled as they continued to march his way, knowing this was the perfect opportunity to knock Slade down a few notches in his followers' eyes and to get retribution from their earlier encounters.

He pulled away from Jonathon, who had grabbed of his arm and was begging him to retreat. That was not an option. He ripped off what remained of his shirt, aggressively threw it to the ground, and balled his fist. "This is going to be fun," he mumbled as his eyes fixated on his unknowing prey.

CHAPTER 7

Abuzz filled the air, and a crowd quickly gathered around the combatants as Slade came to a stop within a few feet of his opponent. The smile remained on Sammy's face as he blocked out the noise from the other kids and remained focused on the task at hand: pummeling the superstar and his friends, if they were courageous enough to join the fray. He did not step back but instead encouraged Slade to advance, planning to attack the moment his adversary was within arm's length. As the five players continued forward, Sammy prepared to strike. The moment he was about to unleash his fury, the crowd suddenly parted and the head football coach, along with Mrs. Stevens, emerged.

"What's going on here?" the coach asked, looking at his players. "Why aren't you guys getting ready for practice?"

Slade nodded as the crowd groaned, disappointed that they were not going to see a fight. "This ain't over by a long shot," he said while backing away.

"No truer words have never been spoken, superstar," Sammy countered.

Sammy's eyes never wavered from Slade as he departed. After the crowd dispersed, he noticed that Cathy and Emily stood their ground, admiring his physique from different areas of the property. He bent over, grabbed what was left of his shirt, and tossed it over his shoulder. Then he grabbed his book bag. He smiled and waved at Cathy before nudging Jonathon. The two boys made their way down the street to their respective homes.

As they strolled, Sammy could not help but notice that Jonathon was staring at him. He tried to ignore it, but it continued for more than two blocks, so Sammy stopped and made eye contact. "Why are you staring at me?"

"Man, you're really jacked. Do you spend all your time outside of school working out?" Jonathon was awestruck as he studied Sammy's body from head to toe. "There isn't a speck of fat on you, dude."

Sammy shrugged, unsure of the question. "When I am not at school, I spend my time with Uncle Riley just doing regular things." He began to walk. "I do love bacon, though; it is scrumptious."

"If all you did to get a body like that was eat bacon, millions of people would look like you." Jonathon shook his head. "Among the dozens of girls that were about to faint when you ripped your shirt off, there were two I noticed who became huge fans." He smiled. "One was Cathy, and the other was the object of your admiration, Miss Emily Keele."

Upon hearing Emily's name, Sammy instantly frowned. He turned up his nose and shook his head. "She is no longer a person of interest to me. I do not care that she is a fan."

"You can't mean that." Jonathon grabbed his arm, stopping Sammy with a surprised expression. "She's the dream girl of every boy in that school. You cannot pass up the chance to come across her radar."

"Is she the girl of your dreams?" Sammy asked with a raised eyebrow. "No. Because I'm a realist. I know that she is way out of my league, so there's no need to even dream about getting a girl like that." Jonathon dropped his chin. "I wouldn't stand a chance with a girl like her."

"You are wrong." Sammy placed his hand on Jonathon's shoulder. "You are a great guy and any girl would be lucky to get someone like you. If anything, you are out of her league, my friend."

A huge smile appeared as Jonathon's eyes illuminated. Those words meant the world to him and instilled much needed confidence. He thanked Sammy and pulled him into an embrace as tears escaped his eyes. Even though they received awkward looks from people passing by in their vehicles and others in their yards, Sammy returned the hug, not caring what others thought. He felt elated that his words had made Jonathon's day.

A short time later, Sammy arrived home after parting ways with Jonathon. He entered the kitchen to grab a bottle of water before dropping his book bag by the front door as he prepared to head to his room. Just as he took his first step onto the staircase, a knock at the door halted his plans of relaxation and a quick nap before Riley arrived so they could enjoy a meal and discuss each other's day.

Curious, he placed the water on the floor. Not knowing if the person on the other side was friend or foe, he had to be prepared for anything. He slowly reached for the doorknob with his right hand, his left clenched tightly into a balled fist. When he finally opened the door, he stepped back with a huge grin plastered on his face. "How did you know where I lived?"

Cathy returned Sammy's smile, but her eyes were glued to his shirtless torso, which caused her to blush. "When you almost got into that fight, I went to my mom and expressed my concern. I begged her to break the rules and give me your address so I could check on you." Her gaze then turned to the ground, but her smile remained. "I needed to know that my friend was okay."

"Where are my manners?" Sammy stepped out of the doorway. "Would you like to come in?"

Cathy did not utter a word; she just nodded and entered the house, avoiding eye contact, clearly nervous about staring at Sammy's torso.

Sammy grabbed his bottle of water and then led Cathy into the kitchen. After pulling out her chair so she could be seated, he grabbed another bottle of water from the refrigerator and, ever the gentlemen, opened it, wiped the condensation from the outside of the container, and presented it to her.

"I am going upstairs to grab a shirt and will return shortly." He winked at her and then departed the kitchen.

As he exited, she watched every step, biting her lower lip. She fanned herself, took a sip of her water, and then rubbed the cold bottle against her forehead. "He really didn't have to go get a shirt," she whispered and then snickered just before taking another drink.

Sammy smiled as he entered his room, but that expression quickly disappeared when he found Michael sitting in the chair at his desk with his legs crossed. He could not help but notice the look of dismay etched on the archangel's face. He chose to ignore his guest and walked toward the dresser to grab a shirt.

"You are coming dangerously close to angering him with your deplorable actions," Michael said, his voice elevating with each word. "What were you thinking?"

"What am I supposed to do?" Sammy donned a blue T-shirt and then exhaled heavily. "Am I supposed to allow these kids to bully everyone and capitulate when they come after me?"

"No!" Michael shouted and rose to his feet. "You are supposed to conduct yourself like you are the superior being instead of reducing yourself to lower human acts."

"I refuse to be those kids' punching bag, and I will not sit idle while Jonathon gets beaten up for being different than those meathead jocks."

Sammy was sick of the lecture and waved his hand in the air, dismissing Michael as he walked toward the door, but before he had a chance to grab the doorknob, he felt Michael's hand on his arm, forcefully pulling him backward. Sammy had had enough and snatched his arm free. He turned to face the archangel as his eyes turned completely black and his hands balled into fists as if he were preparing for a confrontation.

"I am not one of those high school boys that think they are big and bad," Michael said calmly. "I suggest that you infuse some white in those eyes." He leaned in close. "You do not have any of your powers, and without those, you do not stand a chance against me."

Sammy grunted, exited the room, and returned to the kitchen, where Cathy was patiently waiting. He slowly opened the door and saw that she was drinking her water and checking her phone for messages, so he decided to ignore Michael's wishes and use his angel eyes to check her aura. He saw that it was white but faded, which indicated that she was a good person but not pure. He was satisfied with his findings because she was still a good person and he had not met many of those during his time on earth. He returned his eyes to their alternative state and made his presence known by coughing, as he entered the room.

He apologized for keeping her waiting before taking a seat across from her. He leaned back in his chair, grabbed his bottle of water, and flashed a huge smile. "So you wanted to check on me?"

She smiled and brushed the hair from her face. "Yes. I saw those guys, the marks on their faces, and your torn shirt." She made eye contact and then placed her water on the table. "It didn't take a genius to realize that you had been in a fight."

Sammy felt the energy developing between them, but just as he leaned forward to touch her hand where it rested on the table, the kitchen door flew open and Riley entered, causing the two teenagers to jump apart.

"Hey guys." Riley stared at Sammy, noticing the horrified expression on his face. "Am I interrupting something?" He looked at Cathy. "Who's the pretty girl?"

Embarrassed, Sammy stood. After making brief introductions, he rushed Cathy out of the room to spare her the interrogation that was to follow. He walked her to her car and watched as she drove away, his stomach fluttering as her perfume tickled his nostrils and her smile lingered in his mind. He returned to the kitchen, where Riley was seated at the table, looking concerned.

"Have a seat," Riley requested. "I want to talk."

"Did I do something wrong?" Sammy asked, sitting across from Riley. "Whatever I did to offend you, you have my sincerest apology."

Riley quickly dismissed that notion, putting Sammy's mind at ease, but his uncle's mannerisms—the rubbing of his neck, accompanied by the shaking of his head and the deep breaths followed by loud exhales—indicated that something was clearly bothering him.

"After your parents' death, I was given the pleasure of raising you." Riley paused and took another deep breath. "I know that I'm not your father, but I've always thought of you as my son." He stood and began to pace the room, searching for the right way to articulate his thoughts. "Time has gone by so fast, and I've been so busy lately that I never had the talk with you."

"The talk?" Sammy asked with a raised eyebrow.

Riley nodded and returned to his chair. "I know this is embarrassing, but with your lady friend coming around, I think it's time to talk about the birds and the bees."

"What birds are you talking about?" Sammy leaned forward. "There are so many beautiful birds, and they are so graceful." He smiled. "As for bees, I see them flying around all the time. One of my fellow students got stung by one the other day; it really looked painful."

Sammy noticed a familiar lost expression etched on Riley's face, the one everyone expressed at some point when engaging in conversation with him, so he knew he had misspoken and needed to dial it back and stay on subject.

"I am not clear what you mean about these birds and bees you speak of, but I do remember you mentioning Cathy, and since her presence triggered this conversation, I cannot help but surmise that this is about her." Sammy smiled. "We are just friends. I really enjoy her company and her conversation, but that is all that is transpiring."

"The way you talk." Riley laughed. "You talk better than I do, and I'm your elder." He stood and placed a kiss on Sammy's forehead. "I know you're responsible, but you're a very good-looking kid, and I know that girls line up to spend time with you." He winked and then departed, leaving Sammy alone at the table.

Sammy remained seated, reviewing the conversation that had just occurred. He took a few sips of water, but no matter how hard he tried, he could not get one thought out of his head: He never told me what bird he was talking about and his thoughts about those dreadful bees.

The next day at school, as Sammy stood at his locker, gathering his books for class, he could not help but feel excited. He was going to see Cathy soon and was eager to be in her presence once again. After placing the last of his four books in his bag, he tossed it over his right shoulder and closed the locker. At that moment, he was pleasantly surprised by who he saw standing next to him when he closed the door. "Cathy," he said as a huge grin appeared. "You are a sight for sore eyes."

She blushed, running her fingers through her long dark locks. "I just wanted to stop by and say hello." She looked down and then back up at him. "I really enjoyed spending time with you yesterday, even though it was a short visit."

"I did not want to subject you to my uncle." He shook his head. "He means well but can be a bit overbearing."

"I wouldn't have minded." She moved closer. "If talking to your uncle meant I got to spend more time with you, it would've been worth it."

"I will keep that in mind next time." He smiled as they began to walk. "He started to talk to me about some things that were confusing."

"What did he say?" she asked, intrigued.

Just as he was about to answer, Sammy thought back to Riley's expression when he spoke about the birds and bees, so he decided that not divulging the information was best. "He was just talking about grown-up stuff."

"Okay," she said and then stopped. "I want to ask you something, and before I do …" She paused for a brief moment. "You're not obligated to say yes. If you have other things to do, I fully understand."

He took her by the hand and caressed it softly. "Please feel free to ask your question."

"There's a game Friday night at seven thirty, and I was thinking that you could come and afterward we could hang out and do something. Maybe we can go get something to eat or something." She looked away, fearing his answer would be no.

"There is nothing I would rather do on Friday than spend time with you," Sammy said.

Cathy's eyes gleamed, and her smile was broad, exposing her deep dimples. "If you can get a ride to the game, I'll take you home. I would pick you up, but I have to be there early. The life of a cheerleader."

"I will be there even if I have to walk." He winked.

The two made their way to homeroom. Along the way, joy radiated through Sammy as it dawned on him that he would have his first date in just a few days.

CHAPTER 8

After parting ways with Cathy, Sammy headed to homeroom with a huge grin on his face. His mind began to focus on his date on Friday. Thoughts of what he would wear and what they would do occupied his mind. A few minutes later, he reached the entrance to the classroom and heard the usual chatter from the students, but once he entered, all conversation came to an immediate halt and all eyes focused on him, including the teacher's.

Sammy stopped and peered at every student in the room. There were no snickers or demeaning jokes, just stares filled with curiosity, which brought a sly grin to his face. He went to take his seat at the back of the room, but a disturbance caught his attention. Slade had risen to his feet and kicked his chair in the process, causing it to slam into the desk behind him. Sammy became excited when he saw Slade's glare—a look that promised bad intentions were to follow. Sammy stood his ground and watched intently as his adversary rapidly approached. The moment he had been waiting for had arrived. Just when Slade was within striking distance, Sammy clenched his fist and drew back, preparing to strike, but then the unthinkable happened.

The homeroom teacher intervened, grabbing Slade by the arm and pulling him away from Sammy. *Where was this responsible act when I was on the floor and you were reading your magazine?* Sammy thought as he stared at the teacher in disbelief.

"If you get into a fight, I'll be forced to send you to the principal's office," the teacher said to Slade in a soft, calm tone. He dropped his head. "That would mean you'll be suspended and won't be able to play in the game Friday, and no one wants that." Then he turned his attention to Sammy, and in an instant, his demeanor changed from tranquil to hostile. "You need to take your seat and stop causing trouble, new kid!"

"What!" Sammy shouted. "All I did was enter the room. He came at me with hostile intentions."

"I said sit down before I send you to see the principal!" the teacher yelled. Sammy could not believe his ears, but then he remembered what Cathy had said about Slade and his importance as an athlete to this school. He shook his head and looked from the teacher to Slade; they both glared at him. He gave Slade a mischievous wink, taunting the football star and exacerbating his anger, before finally taking his seat.

A short time later, homeroom came to an end and Sammy was off to his first class of the day. He adjusted the bag on his shoulder and noticed something perplexing. Two cheerleaders, neither of whom were Cathy, were approaching him. Rose Vazquez, a petite Latina with long black curly hair, perfect olive skin, and beauty on par with Emily, was accompanied by Joanne Thomas, a tall thin girl with shoulder-length dirty blond hair and looks that were average at best. They were quickly closing in, which piqued Sammy's curiosity. After locking eyes with the two, he stopped and leaned back against the wall, waiting for their arrival.

"We heard about what happened yesterday," Rose said with a thick accent while staring at him with her piercing brown eyes.

"Yeah, we heard how you beat up three of our biggest and best football players," Joanne added.

"Ladies, ladies, ladies, give the new guy some space," an alluring voice said from a distance.

Sammy looked past the two girls in front of him and spotted Emily approaching with a devious smirk.

"I don't care about the fight whatsoever." She moved past her friends and stood directly in front of Sammy. "But when you ripped off that shirt"—she ran her fingers across his chest—"that's what I enjoyed the most."

Sammy swallowed the excess saliva that had accumulated in his mouth. His heart began to race, and his palms became slick with sweat. It was her; the most beautiful girl he had ever laid eyes on was standing a few inches away with her hands on his torso. He became lost in her eyes and mesmerized by her sweet-smelling perfume. He stared at her as though in a trance, but snapped out of it when he remembered how she had spoken to Mrs. Stevens. Just as he was about to speak, he noticed Cathy standing in the distance with tears in her eyes. When she turned to leave, he quickly broke away from the trio and ran after his friend, who obviously in pain.

Sammy reached her just before she reached the stairs. Even though she tried to break away and shield her tears by refusing to make eye contact, he managed to calm the situation by apologizing and assuring her that the encounter had been innocent. Seeing tears in her eyes and knowing her sadness was because of him brought a somber feeling to Sammy. He wiped at her tears with his thumbs and apologized one more time. Then he offered to walk her to her next class, a request she reluctantly accepted.

Rejection did not sit well with Emily. She had a scornful look in her eyes as she watched Sammy and Cathy depart side by side. She looked at her two friends and shook her head. Then the trio walked away without uttering a word, but the disdainful feeling was shared by all three.

Meanwhile, standing in the distance, Slade had watched the entire situation unfold. His blood began to boil because he realized Sammy was starting to garner the attention of the girls in school, which meant all eyes weren't on him, and that was something he refused to allow.

Another school day soon concluded. Instead of going home, Sammy decided to sit beside the fence that overlooked the football field and watch the cheerleaders' practice, Cathy in particular. He smiled each time he made eye contact with her and gave her a wave, actions that did not go unnoticed by Emily, which sparked an argument between the two cheerleaders. Just as Sammy was about to stand to try to find a way onto the field to defuse the budding altercation, Jonathon sat beside him.

"You are quickly becoming the man around here," Jonathon said and nudged him with his elbow.

Sammy tried to acknowledge Jonathon's words, but his attention was focused on the two ladies who were arguing and on the precipice of a physical confrontation. Once the argument was stopped by their coach, Sammy was able to relax and turn his attention to Jonathon. "I am just a high school kid. I am not a man here or anywhere else."

"What?" Jonathon asked and then shrugged. "You know what, never mind." He shook his head. "Hey, if you aren't busy, I was thinking we could go to my house and hang out."

Sammy turned and stared at Jonathon for a few seconds, very skeptical of his invitation. He sighed, rolled his eyes, and remained silent, giving Jonathon an uneasy feeling. Sammy stood and began to circle his friend, rubbing his chin, but his eyes never wavered from Jonathon's.

"Are you trying to get me in the vicinity of your mother?" Sammy returned to his spot by the fence. "It is killing you to find out if I am this supernatural being that you proclaim. I do not wish to have some strange woman trying to peer into my soul to satisfy your curiosity."

Sammy was clearly annoyed. When Jonathon tried to make a joke and place a hand on his shoulder, Sammy quickly brushed it off, grabbed his book bag, and began to walk home.

"Please wait," Jonathon begged as he ran to catch Sammy. "I'm not trying to trick you; I just want to be your friend." He paused for a few seconds. "The way you stood up to those guys … No one has ever done anything like that for me, and I just think you're cool."

Hearing those words struck a chord in Sammy. His heart softened and a smile appeared. It made him feel good that people actually wanted to spend time with him instead of running away or making bargains, hoping he would spare their lives. He became overwhelmed by his emotions and pulled Jonathon into an embrace.

"I would love to hang out with you. Not today, but very soon."

"Anytime you want, my friend," Jonathon whispered.

Sammy broke the embrace with tears in his eyes. He was too choked up to speak. He wiped away the tears as Jonathon watched closely. He managed to flash a smile before turning and waving at Cathy, who returned the gesture, and made his way home.

Friday night finally arrived, but not soon enough for Sammy. After being dropped off at the game by Riley, Sammy sat in the bleachers behind the cheerleaders. His eyes never strayed from Cathy as he watched every move she made and smiled each time they made eye contact between routines. After giving her a quick wave, he was joined by an unexpected guest.

"Hey, buddy. *Que pasa?*" Jonathon took a seat beside Sammy, holding three hotdogs in his right hand and a soda in his left. He took a bite of one and then turned to Sammy with ketchup in the corners of his mouth. "I see Cathy is really *diggin'* you."

"I see that you are really hungry." Sammy motioned to the condiment on Jonathon's face. "What are you doing here? A football game is the last place I thought I would see you."

Jonathon shoved the last half of his third hotdog into his mouth and then washed it down with his drink. He wiped his mouth and then took a deep breath while rubbing his overly full stomach. "Mom and Pops were having their usual argument over money, and I didn't want to be around when they made up, if you know what I mean."

"No, I do not know what you mean," Sammy said with a lost expression. "Seriously?" Jonathon asked, shaking his head. Instead of taking the time

to explain his statement to Sammy, he looked around the stadium and marveled at the mass of humanity that filled the seats. "It amazes me how all these people come together to watch high school kids run into each other for two hours."

"What is the point of this contest anyway?" Sammy asked.

"I have the slightest idea; I just wanted to get out of the house."

The two quickly diverted their attention from the football field back to the cheerleaders. Sammy enjoyed spending time with his friend as the two exchanged playful banter and shared some laughs. The night felt so easy and free for Sammy, and it was much needed. To be out and not have to worry about getting into a physical confrontation was priceless.

After the game, Sammy waited for Cathy at the far gate near the parking lot. He said his goodbyes to Jonathon, and when he turned and saw Cathy approaching, his eyes lit up and his heart fluttered. He was nervous. His legs trembled when he walked over to greet her, but all those feelings disappeared when he took her in his arms and squeezed her tight.

"You look beautiful," he whispered. "I am so happy that we are going out tonight."

She kissed him on the cheek, took him by the hand, and then led him to her pearl white convertible Mustang.

After they got into the car, Sammy looked around as she dropped the top, confused about what was happening. But then she placed her hand on his and put all his angst at ease.

He leaned back in his seat and then turned to her and smiled. "So where are we going?"

"I thought we would go down to the strip, grab a bite to eat, and then hang out at the beach," she replied and returned his smile. "Is that okay by you?"

"That sounds perfect." He rubbed her hand and noticed something had changed. The feelings he had for her were growing stronger, and he was beginning to see her in a different light. He would have agreed to go anywhere with her as long as she was willing to spend time with him.

A short time later, they arrived at the boardwalk. After parking the car, Cathy took Sammy by the hand once again and led him to a pizzeria that served pizza by the slice. Upon entering the restaurant, Sammy was enticed by the aroma of the food and intrigued by the ambiance.

"What is that delectable smell?"

"Who says delectable?" Cathy playfully punched Sammy on the arm. "Your vocabulary is so cute. It's one of the many things I like about you." She displayed her effervescent smile and deep dimples and then led him by the hand to the last booth at the rear of the restaurant. She handed him a menu, still holding his hand. "I'm so glad that you agreed to spend time with me."

Sammy caressed her hand and rubbed the inner part of her wrist with his thumb. "I am so glad that you suggested it." He leaned in close. "You looked amazing tonight." His heart began to pound in his chest as their eyes met. His mouth went dry as a nervous feeling coursed through his body. He saw her lean forward, preparing to make contact of some kind, but he was unsure what to do next, so he decided to follow her lead, watching her movements very closely.

He saw her eyes close and her lips pucker slightly, but just before they could finish the deed, the waitress arrived and abruptly placed two glasses of water between them.

Sammy leaned back in his seat and gazed angrily at the waitress, who was chomping on her gum and standing there with her hand on her hip. She rolled her eyes as she waited for their order, as if she had better things to do, but Sammy held back his words, knowing she was the one who would bring out their food and beverages. He did not want their meal tainted in any way.

They ordered a couple of slices of pizza with the works and two sodas. After the waitress departed, they engaged in conversation; the moment that had mesmerized them earlier had passed.

Within minutes, their food and drinks arrived. Sammy's mouth watered and his eyes bulged as he gazed down at his plate. The aroma that filled his nostrils was like nothing he had experienced. Despite Cathy's warning to wait a moment or two because the food was extremely hot, he grabbed one of the slices and took a huge bite. He immediately regretted his hasty decision. He dropped the food back onto his plate and fanned his mouth as the heat from the pizza burned his tongue and the roof of his mouth. He grabbed his drink and took a huge gulp as Cathy laughed hysterically at his antics.

"Did you find my anguish pleasurable?" Sammy asked, placing his empty glass on the table.

"I tried to tell you to wait, but you wouldn't listen." Cathy continued to laugh. "You should've seen the look on your face. Your eyes were huge." She placed her hand over her stomach and continued to laugh even harder.

Despite his torture, he found the taste of his dinner delicious. He gathered the pizza in his hands once more and blew on it for a few seconds before indulging. He closed his eyes and moaned with pleasure. "This is the best tasting food I have ever had." He took another bite as the waitress placed a refill of his drink next to his plate. "I could eat this every day for eternity."

"For eternity?"

Sammy froze midchew and looked around with a lost expression, knowing he had misspoken. He chewed slowly, trying to figure out what to say next. "Yes. I could eat pizza every day forever." He smiled, took another bite, and immediately looked away, breaking eye contact.

Cathy simply shook her head, accepting his strange vernacular. "You act as if you've never had pizza before."

"I have never had pizza before," he answered, shoving the rest of the slice into his mouth. "My parents kept me on a very strict diet, and even though my uncle has loosened the reigns a tad, there are certain foods I have yet to experience."

"Is that why you have a body like that?" Cathy asked with a devilish look in her eye.

"You know what they say: milk does a body good," he replied before sinking his teeth into his next slice of pizza.

Cathy returned her food to her plate, and her expression changed from jovial to serious. She reached across the table and took his hand. The moment he placed his food back on his plate, she took his other hand in hers. "I've never heard you speak about your parents before. I'd like to hear more about them."

Sammy sat back, pulling away as a lump developed in his throat. He knew he had to sell his hurt because he had not actually lost his parents, so he drew on the pain he had felt on that rainy night in Colombia when he had to take Carolina's life. As he thought back to her smile and her pain, tears welled in his eyes and ran down his cheeks. He grabbed a napkin and wiped his eyes and face. The desired effect was successful, but old, somber feelings that were buried made their way back to the surface.

He shook his head as the baby's cries rang loudly in his mind. "I do not wish to talk about it at this time."

He saw the disappointment in her eyes and knew sympathetic words were about to follow, so before she could utter a word, he grabbed his food and took a bite before cracking a joke to lighten the mood. They shared some laughter; though it was uneasy and somewhat forced, it was the perfect opportunity to change the subject. Their conversation reverted back to the food as Sammy continued to gorge himself with pizza, ordering two additional slices.

After they'd consumed their food and drinks, the two decided to take a walk along the boardwalk. They stopped at different shops, looking at clothing items and trinkets, before making their way to the beach. They removed their shoes and socks and placed them by the sidewalk. When Sammy took his first few steps on the beach, he smiled as he felt the unusual yet satisfying sensation of the sand meshed between his toes.

They sat down just out of reach of the waves washing up onto the shore but placed their feet on the wet sand and allowed the water to wash over them. It felt a little odd to Sammy but delightful.

He looked around and noticed that they were the only two on the beach. Then he turned his attention to the calm water of the Atlantic Ocean. He looked up at the bright stars and thought about how perfect the night was going.

Then he stared into her big brown eyes and become lost. "I am having the best night of my life."

She moved in close. "I was thinking, since you've never had pizza, is there anything else you've never done?"

Unlike the time in the restaurant when he noticed that look in her eyes, he was not nervous; instead, he felt a swell of confidence. He wrapped his arms around her, pulled her close, and gave her a very deep, passionate kiss. Feeling the heat of her body and the softness of her skin awakened his desires, and certain parts of his body were ready to express how he felt. Swept away by the moment, he moved closer, but the instant she felt his eagerness to go further, she pulled back, even though every fiber of her being wanted to capitulate to her lust.

"I think we should call it a night," she said, breathing deeply.

In his mind, he disagreed completely, but he had no choice but to respect her decision. He helped her to her feet and then gave her a hug before kissing her softly on the forehead.

"I really don't want to stop, but I think it's best if we take things a little slower." She smiled. "I hope you aren't mad at me."

He brushed the hair from her eyes. "I could never be mad at you."

"That's good because I can't wait to go out on another date with you, if that's what you want."

"I would not have it any other way," he replied, taking her by the hand and leading her to the car.

Sammy wrapped his arm around her shoulder and then pulled her close as they continued their journey, but he could not help but think of what might have been.

CHAPTER 9

It was almost three o'clock in the morning by the time Sammy arrived home. Before exiting Cathy's car, he made sure to pepper her with tender kisses and gentle touches. By the time he walked through the front door, four o'clock was rapidly approaching. After closing the door, he leaned against it and closed his eyes, replaying the events of the night. Before he could make his way to his room, Riley met him at the bottom of the stairs, looking angry.

Sammy endured the berating from his uncle, but the words fell on deaf ears as he entered the kitchen to grab a bottle of water with Riley in close pursuit. The admonishing lasted for about fifteen minutes, but the louder Riley's voice became, the more frequently Sammy's eye rolls and the sneers were given. He leaned against the sink and watched how exasperated Riley had become. When his uncle gave up and threw his arms into the air before exiting the kitchen, Sammy simply shook his head and finished his drink before heading to his room.

Sammy's thoughts returned to Cathy. The mere thought of her had him on cloud nine, so much so that he could have floated to his room instead of ascending the stairs. The moment he opened the door, his smile disappeared. He found Michael sitting patiently at the desk with his legs crossed, twiddling his fingers.

"You have become very disrespectful." Michael shook his head. "Why would you disrespect Riley by coming home at such a late hour?"

"I was unaware of the time." Sammy removed his shoes and tossed them by the foot of his bed. "I am sure you are aware of the adage time flies when you are having fun."

Michael nodded and then stood. "So what is your reason for dismissing Riley when he was speaking to you?"

"That human is beneath me," Sammy barked out, standing up straight. "He is lucky that I did not put him in his place like I did those pissants at that high school." He began to remove the rest of his clothes. "It is late. We can continue this discussion another time."

"You will not dismiss me," Michael shouted as he made his way over to Sammy and grabbed him by the arm. "You are changing, and it is not for the better. I suggest you clean up your act before I step in and treat you like you treated those young men at that school." He shoved Sammy's arm. "I suggest you apologize to Riley for your appalling behavior at once."

At that moment, the door swung open and Riley entered the room. "Is everything all right in here?"

Sammy noticed the concern that Riley exuded for his well-being and simply smiled. "No matter what, it seems you will always come running to check on me."

"No matter what." Riley took a breath and then grinned. "You have been acting strangely lately, but I do remember what it's like to be a teenager." He approached Sammy and gave him a hug. "I just worry about you, and when I didn't hear from you by midnight, I became worried." He shook his head. "Walking through the door at close to four in the morning is unacceptable."

"I understand, Uncle Riley, and I do apologize." Sammy hugged Riley. "I am truly sorry for the disrespect that I showed. I do not know what came over me."

"Apology accepted." Riley tapped Sammy on the chin. "You need to get some rest. As your punishment for coming in so late, you have extra chores tomorrow, which includes washing my car and cleaning it out."

"I will be happy to," Sammy replied before lying down in bed as Riley departed.

A few days later, Sammy was sitting in his class with his face in his palms, listening to his classmates struggle with the questions posed to them by Mrs. Stevens. He wondered about the future of the world, because the stupidity of the kids around him was mind-boggling. The bell finally rang, signaling the end of class. He quickly grabbed his books and began to make his way out the door, but he was stopped by the teacher. He had felt like being in those kids' presence was torture enough, but being made to wait while they exited seemed like cruel and unusual punishment.

"Why are you making me stay?"

Mrs. Stevens waited until every last student exited and they were alone. She sat behind her desk and took a deep breath, equally as frustrated with the level of intelligence of the students as Sammy was.

"You're a very bright young man, and you have an undisputed knowledge of history." She retrieved her coffee thermos from her bottom drawer. "That being said, I'd like to ask you for a favor."

He looked at her with a raised eyebrow. "What can I do for you?" He took a seat across from her and waited with bated breath for her response.

She poured a cup of coffee and then took a drink, but before answering, she looked over and saw her daughter waiting just outside the door for Sammy. The sight brought a smile to the proud mother's face. She took another sip of her beverage and then placed the cup on the desk before standing and wiping the chalkboard clean.

"I have some students that are struggling in my class." She turned to face him. "I'd love for you to tutor one person in particular."

"Who is that person?" Sammy asked.

Mrs. Stevens glanced again at her daughter before returning to her seat. She paused for a few seconds, collecting her thoughts. Then she slowly looked up and made eye contact with Sammy. "I'm going to cut to the chase, Mr. Angel." She leaned back in her chair. "Emily Keele is struggling big time in this class, and if she doesn't turn it around very soon, she will fail." She gasped and then took another sip of her coffee.

"Even though I consider myself to be the utmost professional, I don't want that girl back in my class."

Sammy was unclear about what being a tutor entailed, but the tone in Mrs. Stevens's voice told him it was very important to her. He trusted that she would not place him in an adverse situation, so he reluctantly agreed to assist her even though he noticed the disappointed expression on Cathy's face. He accepted the teacher's gratitude, along with late slips for him and Cathy, and rushed out of the room to catch up with her, noticing she was visibly distraught.

He jogged to catch her, as her pace had quickened. The moment he reached Cathy, he heard her sobbing and saw her wiping her eyes and nose, which was confusing.

"What is the problem?" he asked, placing a hand on her shoulder, slowing her progress. He slowly turned her and noticed that tears were flowing down her cheeks and her beautiful brown eyes were outlined with red. "Please tell me what is bothering you."

She tried to turn away, but Sammy would not allow it, shifting to whatever side she turned. He refused to let the issue simmer; he wanted to address the matter in the moment and not let it linger. He took her by the hand, softly stroked it, and then gently kissed her palm.

"Please tell me what is on your mind."

"I know we're friends or whatever that's going on between us, but there's still a part of me that thinks you still want her." She wiped away newly formed tears. "I love that you want to spend time with me, but I can't help but think that you really want her but don't want to hurt my feelings."

His heart broke to see her in such a vulnerable state. He pulled her into an embrace and squeezed her tightly. "I do not want her. I only want to spend time with you." He broke the embrace and wiped the tears from her cheeks. "If tutoring her bothers you this much, I will go back to your mother and tell her to find someone else to do it."

Cathy rejected that idea and assured Sammy that all was well, even though her claim was not fooling either of them.

He handed her the late slip and watched as she made her way down the hall to class. He sighed. Dealing with human emotions was tougher than he thought it would be, but because it was Cathy, it was all worthwhile.

Few hours later, school mercifully came to an end. Sammy made his way through the crowded halls en route to his locker, but with each step, Cathy occupied his thoughts. He could not shake the image of her crying because he had agreed to tutor Emily. Even though he had done his best to reassure her that his infatuation with the head cheerleader was in the past, Cathy's insecurities had surfaced, and he did not know how to rectify the situation.

After the quick stop at his locker, he exited the building and headed to his spot near the fence, hoping to catch Cathy's attention just to let her know she was on his mind. But much to his chagrin, he spotted Emily waiting out front, leaning against the flagpole, waving at him.

The moment she made her way toward him, he shook his head and exhaled heavily. He looked around, searching for Cathy. He did not want her to see this impromptu meeting, which would further exacerbate her anxieties. He lowered his head as Emily approached, but no matter how hard he tried, he could not keep his eyes off her. He could smell the sweet scent of her perfume, which drove him wild, so he closed his eyes and leaned against the building, trying not to show what was really on his mind. "I understand that you are my new tutor," Emily said softly. She turned to her right and saw Cathy watching their interaction from a distance. She decided to give her voyeur a good show. She leaned in close and ran her fingers lightly over his chest. "I really appreciate your help." She retrieved a pen and a piece of paper from her purse, scribbled down her number, and then slipped it into his front pants pocket. She turned and looked at Cathy, recognizing the pain in her eyes, which drew a smile from the vixen.

She turned back to Sammy, whose eyes were still closed. His intense breathing and reluctance to make eye contact gave her the impression that she was his guilty pleasure. "Call me when you're ready to get together; I'm at your beck and call," she whispered.

Emily leaned back and then turned her attention to Cathy, whose stare exuded bad intentions. The head cheerleader loved every second of her enemy's misery. She gave her a wink, followed by a seductive wave. Then, with a snide smirk, she departed and made her way to the locker room to prepare for practice.

Sammy opened his eyes just in time to see her depart and loved the view. He watched closely as she sauntered away, especially her butt as it moved gracefully in her tight blue jeans. He admired her figure and remembered what had attracted him to the beautiful specimen.

As he began to fall into a trancelike state, he felt an arm around his neck, pulling him to the side. Startled, he grabbed the person's wrist and pulled him forward so he could identify who it was. To his surprise, it was his friend Jonathon, who was equally startled by Sammy's quick and aggressive action.

"I'm sorry if I scared you," Jonathon said, rubbing his wrist. "I know not to sneak up on you, man!"

Sammy chuckled and then shook his head. "Yes, you should announce your presence before placing your arm around a person's neck. It could have been a whole lot worse, my friend." He looked around once more, searching for Cathy. "What do you want anyway?"

"I just wanted to know if you had plans today."

Sammy slowly turned his eyes from the crowd to Jonathon. He knew what question was coming before his friend could even ask, but he did not want to be presumptuous, so he decided to play along. "Cathy has cheerleading practice, and Riley is working late, so my evening is free."

"Well, since you're free, why don't you come and hang out with me and eat dinner at my house?" Jonathon smiled. "I'm sure you can take a break from watching Cathy jump around." He nudged Sammy. "Come on."

Sammy knew there was more to Jonathon's invitation than dinner and hanging out, but he also knew that the more he continued to put off his invitations, the more suspicious he would grow. So Sammy took a deep breath and simply nodded, which garnered an enthusiastic hug from Jonathon. He returned his friend's embrace, and the two began to make their way down the street. Sammy's demeanor was upbeat, but it was a façade because his insides were in knots. He was nervous at the thought of coming face-to-face with a person who could see past his human shell and identify what really lie beneath the surface. Even though he heard Michael's voice imploring him to remain calm, that was not an option. Facing his fear was soon to be a reality.

Meanwhile, on the football field, most of the cheerleaders had exited the locker room and were split into separate groups, conversing among themselves as they waited for the remaining few to join so practice could commence. Suddenly, the locker room door flew open, slamming against the brick wall of the school building. Cathy emerged with a stern purpose to her walk.

Focused on finding Emily, she bumped into a few of her teammates strolling ahead of her and did not even bother to apologize as she made her way past. Once she reached the field, she spotted Emily off to the side laughing and joking with Joanne and Rose. She made a beeline for them, ignoring some of the other girls who called her name and spoke pleasantries once they saw her. Emily's back was to her, and even though the other two were turned to their sides, they were not paying attention and did not see her advancing toward them.

The moment Cathy was within a few feet of her adversary, she grabbed Emily by her shoulder and aggressively spun her around so that they were face-to-face. Cathy saw the shock and dismay on the trio's faces. Their conversation and laughter came to an abrupt end. She pushed Emily so hard that the head cheerleader fell to the ground. When Joanne tried to intervene, she experienced the same fate as her friend. Cathy stood over Emily with her fist balled, hoping the captain of the cheerleaders would retaliate or even appear as if she was about to so that Cathy could unleash her pent-up fury.

"I know what you're trying to do, but I suggest that you stop right now!" Cathy said.

Shocked and appalled, Emily slid back, creating some space between her and Cathy. She rubbed her shoulder, wincing in pain once she hit the spots where Cathy's fingers had dug into her flesh.

"Have you lost your mind?" She made her way back to her feet. "I don't know what you're talking about, but I suggest you calm down or you'll come to regret it!"

As Cathy went to advance toward Emily, Joanne quickly joined Rose in making a barrier between the two girls.

"I have no problem beating the hell *outta* both of you," Cathy said.

Emily chuckled and then moved closer but remained behind her friends. "I know what you're talking about." She wrapped her arms around Joanne and Rose's shoulders. "You're talking about that gorgeous hunk that has you in the friend zone." She laughed. "Look at him and look at you. Sorry, honey, but he is way *outta* your league."

"Yes, we're just friends," Cathy replied.

"Then why are you so mad that another girl is talking to him?" Emily smirked and then shrugged. "Unless you want more than friendship with my new tutor."

Cathy did not know how to respond. She took a few steps back and noticed that everyone's eyes—football players and cheerleaders alike—were fixated on her. She knew every word of Emily's statement was true.

She did feel jealousy, which had led to anger, when she saw her talking to Sammy. She wanted to disappear, wanted to run back into the locker room and leave the property. Just as she was about to do so, she heard the blaring sound of the coach's whistle, followed by orders for them to start practice. Her anger was replaced by embarrassment as she fell in line, avoiding eye contact with Emily but feeling her gaze. She ignored her teammates' whispers but heard every word. Her only thought was to find Sammy and let him know how she really felt.

Meanwhile, Slade stood on the fifty yard line and watched the entire interaction, seething over what he'd heard. Seconds later, Alex joined his friend, tugging at his shoulder pads.

"We have to get back to practice, bro." Alex looked over at the cheerleaders. "What's wrong?"

"I'm sick of that punk Sammy Angel." Slade spat on the ground and with a cold, calm demeanor turned to his friend. "Does your brother's friend still hurt people for money?"

"Chavo would hurt his parents for the right price." Alex shook his head. "There're two things he loves in the world. That's money and the thought of making more money."

Slade removed his helmet and stared at Emily. Even though he was not involved with her, the thought of her being interested in another boy drove him crazy. "The moment practice ends, I want you to get ahold of Chavo." He tightened the grip on his facemask. "Tell him there's a big payday for him if he can do a job for me."

Meanwhile, a few miles away, Sammy and Jonathon had just turned the corner and were approaching Jonathon's house. Sammy stopped and took notice of the beautiful homes that lined the street.

"You live in a very nice area." He nodded in approval. "I am not surprised." His words did not match the thoughts circling in his mind as he glanced at the house and then at his friend's attire.

Once the two stepped foot onto Jonathon's front yard, Sammy continued to admire the two-story white brick house with red shutters on every window. He watched as his friend dug into his pocket for the key to the front door and questioned his decision to come here. He looked around at the other houses, avoiding eye contact. As his nerves were getting the best of him, Jonathon found the key and unlocked the door. Sammy took a deep breath and followed his friend into the house with his gaze pinned to the floor.

Jonathon shouted for his mother and tossed his bag on the floor. He turned toward Sammy and offered him a cold beverage. After Sammy accepted, they began to make their way to the kitchen but stopped when Jonathon's mother, Lola, emerged from that very room.

Sammy was pleasantly surprised by her appearance. He had expected her to share the same look and attire as her son, but it was the total opposite. She had long blond hair that was slightly curled and brown eyes, and she wore very little makeup because she was blessed with stunning natural beauty. He also noticed her curvaceous figure, along with her vivacious smile that lit up the room. The moment she turned her attention to him, Sammy quickly looked back down at the floor, remembering Michael's words about some people's ability to sense supernatural beings. It made him feel uneasy.

"You must be Sammy." Lola approached and extended her hand. "I've heard so much about you. Nothing but great things, of course."

Sammy forced a smile, feeling Jonathon's eyes watching his every move and facial expression. He made eye contact, took her palm in his, and kissed the back of her hand.

"I was not expecting an old-fashioned greeting from such a young man," Lola said and then began to chuckle like a schoolgirl. She smiled and turned her attention to Jonathon. "Your father needs your help out back. Go help him finish up before dinner is ready."

Jonathon's shoulders slumped and his excitement dissipated. He'd been expecting a different reaction from his mother. He was disappointed that his assertions were wrong and that Sammy was just a normal kid and not some mystical being in disguise. He tapped Sammy on the arm and motioned for him to accompany him out back, but Lola intervened.

"Sammy is a guest in our home; he isn't going out back to do manual labor." She turned her attention to Sammy, displaying that beautiful smile.

"Plus, I want to hear all about how he fought off those huge football players." She lightly stroked his arm. "We'll be here waiting for you guys to finish up."

She watched as her son rolled his eyes and mumbled under his breath as he pushed through the kitchen doors and slammed the back door after he exited. She walked over and peeked out the back window. Once Lola was sure that she and Sammy were alone, she turned and faced him. Her expression had changed dramatically. Gone was the beautiful smile. In its places was a serious scowl.

"What are you doing here, and why are you hanging around my son?"
"Jonathon invited me here. I thought that my presence was welcomed,"

Sammy said.

"Don't play games with me." She moved in close. "I know who you really are under that skin. You're death, and I want to know why you're here and taking such a liking to my son!"

Sammy swallowed the excess saliva that had accumulated in his mouth.

He noticed the fear in her eyes and the frantic tone of her voice that hinted at desperation. Michael's words were true.

CHAPTER 10

Shocked, Sammy stood silent for a few seconds, searching for the proper words that would satisfy Lola. As he walked over and stood by the couch, her eyes followed his every move.

"I am not here to do any harm." He sat down on the couch. "I am just here finding out about humans and what makes them tick."

He noticed her expression change once again; horror was now present. He knew she was studying him, looking past the human shell to the real entity as if she were trying to find some answers. He saw the beads of sweat that developed on her forehead and the tears that formed in her eyes. But when he went over to comfort her, she pulled away, retreating to the other side of the room.

"I just want to talk," Sammy said, holding his hands at waist level, palms facing the floor. "There is no need to fear me. I just have a couple of questions, and in turn"—he moved a few steps closer to her—"I will answer any questions that you have as well."

"What questions do you have?" Lola asked, her voice trembling.

"I hear you have a gift for witchcraft. How is that possible?" Sammy returned to the couch and sat with his legs crossed.

"My great-great-grandmother was a witch, and her abilities are passed down from generation to generation through the daughters." She reluctantly sat beside Sammy but kept a safe distance between them. "She was very powerful from what I understand and was murdered because of it." She began to feel at ease and managed to make eye contact. "Can you do something for me?" She paused and then took a deep breath. "I would like to see your real eyes."

Sammy was apprehensive about granting her request. He thought back to one of the rules Michael had given him before he plummeted to earth, but since she already knew who he was, that warning was null and void. He leaned back and glanced toward the kitchen door. The last thing he needed was to expose his angel eyes and have Jonathon or his father come through the door. Once he was assured that the two were busy and would not interrupt, he could not think of any reason not to grant her wish. So he took a deep breath and closed his eyes. The moment he opened them again, his celestial eyes were visible.

Silence filled the room as Lola gazed into his eyes for a few seconds without uttering a word. She leaned forward, rubbing her chin, clearly deep in thought. "You're eyes are so bold, dark, but the rest of you seems faded." She leaned back with an inquisitive expression on her face. "It's like you are trapped in limbo."

"I do not possess all my abilities. Since I am among the humans, I do not have my powers, so I am not complete." Sammy leaned back in his seat as his eyes returned to their alternative state.

"So how does an angel whose purpose is to take lives go on vacation from his duties?"

"You take vacations from your job, I am sure, so why is that any different for me?"

"I see what you're trying to say, but to compare my job to your job is laughable."

"Touché, Mrs. Franks." Sammy chuckled. "Touché"

Lola ventured into the kitchen, and when she returned, she carried a steaming pot of tea and two mugs. She poured two cups and then returned to her seat on the couch.

"Are you being honest that you're here to mingle among the people and not here to take my son?" She took a sip of her hot beverage and closed her eyes, hoping the answer was positive.

"Everyone dies, Mrs. Franks, but I assure you that I am here for pleasure and not duty." He smiled, took his own sip, and then complimented her on the tea. "It surprised me that Jonathon had an inkling that I was not human." "He has my gift but does not know how to harness it." She shrugged before indulging in her drink again. "It comes naturally for the daughters but is clouded in the sons. It's a gift that he will never figure out, no matter how hard he tries."

Before another word was spoken, the kitchen door swung open and Jonathon, along with his father, entered the living room, sweaty and out of breath.

Sammy rose to his feet and snickered at Jonathon, poking fun at his friend, who had engaged in some sort of physical labor. He approached the patriarch of the family and made a proper introduction—a gesture that was appreciated by Mr. Franks. After all the pleasantries were given, Sammy helped Lola set the table for dinner while Jonathon and his father cleaned up. Within half an hour, everyone sat down and enjoyed great conversation and a meal.

After dinner, Sammy began to make the journey home. He refused a ride from Jonathon's parents because he wanted to enjoy the weather and nature as it happened around him in the moment. And, last but not least, he wanted to entertain his thoughts of Cathy, as she had continually crossed his mind most of the evening.

As he strolled the streets of the city, images of her smile and sounds of her laughter permeated his thoughts. He longed to hear her voice. He wondered how her day went. He could not wait to listen to her talk about even simple things, as long as he was able to be in her atmosphere. Countless cars passed him as he walked; he paid no attention to any of them. But one person who sped by paid close attention to him.

Slade parked his expensive sports car across the busy street from where Sammy was walking. The moment his hated rival turned down a back street that was a shortcut to his house, a sinister grin crossed the star athlete's face. He retrieved his cell phone from his pocket and called his friend Alex. Then he smiled as he turned the key in the ignition.

"He's in place. Deploy the package." With those words, he abruptly ended the call. Then he donned his sunglasses and, with a snide smirk, drove into traffic, disappearing among the multitude of cars.

A short time later, the sun had set and dusk had turned to darkness. Sammy continued to make his way down the back streets as the streetlights flickered, illuminating dim light. His thoughts remained on Cathy, but the sound of glass breaking from behind him caused him to stop suddenly and quickly turn to investigate.

At first glance, he saw nothing, but he knew the noise had not been a figment of his imagination, so he decided to use his angel eyes to see things that his other eyes could not. Alas, there was nothing in sight. He slowly turned and continued on his path, but seconds later, another noise radiated from behind him. This time it sounded as if sticks were cracking. He knew someone or something was on the street with him, and his concerns grew at a rapid rate.

"You are in danger," a voice whispered.

When Sammy turned, he saw Michael standing there with a concerned expression on his face. "What is going on?" Sammy asked.

"Your high school nemesis hates you so badly that he hired someone to do you serious harm or even kill you."

Sammy gritted his teeth as his angel eyes appeared. His tolerance for Slade had reached its limit, but he had to deal with whoever was stalking him first. He saw Michael's eyes, so he knew his possible assailant was very close. He shifted his eyes back to their alternative state, and when Michael disappeared, he turned and came face-to-face with the hired goon.

Standing a few feet away was a young Latino man, short in stature but very muscular. He wore a sleeveless shirt, exposing bulging biceps covered in tattoos, but his left arm caught Sammy's attention. It had miniature knives with drops of blood on the tips. These markings started from the top of his shoulder and extended down his entire arm, ending at his wrist; they were a clear signal of the jobs he had performed and the lives he had damaged or ended.

"Looks like you're getting on the wrong person's nerves, *ese*," Chavo said with a maniacal grin as he tightened a thick chain around his right hand. "They called me to take care of their headache." He allowed a portion of the chain to drop to the ground, causing a loud thud. "This *ain't* personal for me, but it'll be personal for you."

Sammy took a step back and avoided Chavo's vicious strikes. His angel eyes returned as his anger rose. He slapped away a wild punch, grabbed Chavo by the throat, pulled him close, and gazed into his eyes. He wanted his attacker to see that he was dealing with something otherworldly. After a few seconds, he shoved Chavo to the ground, but his eyes never wavered.

A steady stream of urine flowed down Chavo's leg. He dropped the chain and scooted away from Sammy. "Please don't hurt me, *ese*." His breathing intensified as his eyes bulged. "Just let me go and we can forget about this whole thing." He cowered in a fetal position as he begged for his life.

Sammy relented and took a step back. His eyes returned to their alternative state, and his fist unclenched. But, unbeknownst to him, as Chavo pleaded, his left hand was behind his back, retrieving a knife from his belt.

Sammy made an effort to show compassion by leaning over and extending his hand to help Chavo to his feet. At that moment, Chavo took advantage of Sammy's kind nature and savagely thrust the ten-inch blade into Sammy's stomach until it was stopped by the hilt.

Chavo took almost orgasmic pleasure in hearing Sammy's yelp of pain. He closed his eyes and repeated the action several times before breaking out into a sinister laugh. The moment Sammy fell to his knees, clutching his stomach, Chavo buried the knife in his back and then kicked him to the ground. He circled Sammy a few times and then ripped the knife from his back. He kicked his prey in the face and then nudged Sammy onto his back. Sammy gasped for air for a few seconds, but the sounds of Chavo's laughter began to fuel his rage. He took one last deep breath and snarled as his angel eyes returned. The wounds on his stomach and back began to close as he made eye contact with Chavo, who became terrified once again when he looked at the knife and saw that the blood covering the blade had suddenly disappeared.

When Chavo tried to run, Sammy grabbed his ankle with such force that the bone shattered. He rose to his feet and stalked Chavo, who was trying to crawl away while yelling and crying in pain. Sammy reached down, grabbed Chavo by the back of his neck, and hurled him back ten feet. The man landed on his backside. Sammy approached slowly, rubbing his hands together as his anger continued to build. Once he reached his attacker, he stood over him for a few seconds, snarling. He saw Slade's face as he stared down at Chavo; the image sent him over the top. He quickly reached down, grabbed Chavo by the throat, and lifted him into the air.

"What are you?" Chavo struggled to ask as his throat was being squeezed. "The last image you will ever see," Sammy replied in a deep, dark voice.

Then with one motion, he broke Chavo's neck.

CHAPTER 11

A short time later, Sammy turned onto his street. As he reached the front steps of his house, the events that had occurred a few blocks away ran through his mind. He touched his stomach where the knife had entered and rubbed the hole in his shirt. He thought of the knife and the feeling he had experienced as it pierced his abdomen. He stopped just short of the door and fought the feeling of anger at knowing Slade had set into motion events that had caused him to take a human's life, even if that human had been a vile person. He removed his shirt, not wanting to alarm Riley or to answer the litany of questions that were sure to follow. But one more thought entered his mind: *If I were a mere human, I would be dead right now, and for what? Because a boy feels jealous that his status is threatened in high school?*

"Ridiculous!" he said and then entered the house.

He placed his bag on the floor by the door as he usually did and noticed his uncle was sound asleep on the couch. He entered the kitchen, grabbed a bottle of water, and then headed to his room. Once inside, he tossed the tattered shirt on his bed and stared at it for a few seconds, particularly at the holes. Once again, his thoughts went back to Slade. He began to pace, trying his best to retard his anger, but all the football star's actions toward him since he entered that school began to play in Sammy's mind like a broken record. He debated his next move. Should he just stay home or go out and find Slade and put an end to this once and for all?

He took a sip of water, but when he glanced at the shirt, his decision was made. He retrieved a black T-shirt from his drawer and then headed for the door but stopped when he saw Michael.

"I know you are angry, but I implore you to calm down before you do something that you cannot take back." Michael slowly approached his friend. "You were justified with your action toward that man earlier, but you will not be justified if you walk out that door and kill someone else." He placed his hands on Sammy's arm. "I need you to sit down and take a few deep breaths."

Sammy held the tattered shirt in the air, displaying the holes. "Do you see what could have been if I was not who I am?" He threw the shirt to the floor in disgust. "This Slade boy needs to be dealt with once and for all before someone else less fortunate feels his deadly wrath."

"You cannot be his executioner, Sammy." Michael placed his hand on Sammy's shoulder. "It is not your place."

Sammy nodded in reluctant agreement. He walked back over to his dresser, grabbed his nightshirt, and prepared for bed.

"There is a reason for my visit." Michael stood and faced his friend. "I need to have a word with you; it is of the utmost importance."

"Not tonight." Sammy donned the nightshirt and then lay on his bed. "It has been a very long and eventful day, and all I want to do is go to bed. It will have to wait until tomorrow."

"Okay, but we should not put this off for much longer." Michael paused as a somber expression came over his face. After taking one last look at Sammy, he vanished.

At that moment, Sammy sat up and looked around the room. He immediately regretted the decision to delay the talk with Michael, but for now their discussion would have to wait.

The next morning, Sammy arrived at school a few minutes late so that the halls would be almost empty before he made his way to homeroom. He did not want Slade to know he had safely survived the attack he orchestrated, so he took a different route through the halls to avoid anyone that might tip off the superstar. Once he reached the classroom, he stood just outside the door, peeking around the corner at Slade and his friends as they gathered in their usual spot. He watched as the boys laughed and joked, speaking in code so no one else would know what they were talking about as they basked in their glory of pulling off a heinous coup.

Sammy decided it was the perfect time to enter the room, so he adjusted his book bag on his shoulder and nonchalantly stepped across the threshold.

In an instant, all laughter and joking came to an abrupt stop when the jocks saw Sammy standing in the distance, healthy and unharmed.

Slade slowly stood and swallowed hard, staring at Sammy as if he had seen a ghost. "Impossible," he uttered under his breath.

"Why are you staring at me as if you did not expect me to be here?" Sammy asked, looking at Slade. "It would be a crime if I missed school for no reason at all."

The bell rang, interrupting the uneasy silence that filled the room. Sammy watched with great pleasure as Slade grabbed his books and ran out of the room, avoiding eye contact as he passed.

Slade frantically ran down the halls, shoving people out of his path. The second he arrived at the locker room area, he stopped when he spotted Alex talking to a pretty girl. He rudely forced his way between them with such force that the girl fell to the floor.

He did not even bat an eye or bother to check on the girl because his needs usurped everyone else's needs, wants, or well-being. He shoved Alex against the lockers, grabbed him by the collar of his shirt, and then yanked him close.

"Where you been?" He pushed him back against the lockers once more. "Are you just getting here?" Before Alex could respond, he interrupted, "Have you talked to Chavo?"

"No!" Alex pulled away and went to check on the girl, but she had gotten up and left, which was frustrating. "What's your problem, dude?"

Slade moved in close with scorn in his eyes. "Sammy Angel walked into homeroom just a few minutes ago. He did not have a scratch on him." He backed away and then paused and took a deep breath. "I thought you said that Chavo was the man for the job. I gave him a lot of money to take that punk out."

"I have no idea, but I'll make a few calls and find out," Alex said in a low tone, clearly surprised to hear that Chavo had failed.

Frustrated, Slade punched the lockers and then shouted a few threats in Alex's direction before storming off. He ignored his lackey's pleas for him to return. He just continued making his way to his first class as his fellow students whispered and stared with confused expressions.

Meanwhile, on the other side of the school, Sammy was enjoying Cathy's company. They exchanged flirtatious smiles and tender touches as they gazed into each other's eyes.

Because of the unforeseen and equally unfortunate events that had happened in the back streets and resulted in a person's death, Sammy had lost out on the opportunity to speak with Cathy the day before, so he yearned to make up for lost time. He pulled her close and placed soft kisses on her cheek, which brought on giggles. He lightly ran his fingers along her right arm, which caused goose bumps to develop.

"I was wondering if you would like to spend some time together later?"

"I was thinking the exact same thing." She moved in very close. "I have practice, but afterward we can go enjoy a slice or two of pizza."

The mere mention of the delectable cuisine brought a huge smile to Sammy's face. He moaned in delight, but just before he could confirm their outing, they were interrupted by Emily and her friends; she seemed to have a talent for bad timing.

"I just stopped by to set up an appointment with my handsome tutor." Emily looked at Cathy, noticed the disdain written on her face, and took great pleasure in knowing she was the cause. She chuckled and then turned her attention to Rose. "I guess we were interrupting a tender moment between the so-called friends."

Sammy sensed Cathy's anger and knew the situation could quickly get out of control, so he stepped forward and extended his right hand, palm out, toward Emily. "This is not the best time to discuss the matter, so I am requesting that you contact me at a later time."

Emily ignored Sammy's request, took him by the hand, and pulled him close, which incensed Cathy. Emily caressed his hand and examined him from head to toe. Then she turned her focus to his face. "You have some of the most beautiful blue eyes."

She leaned in close, put her lips next to his ear, closed her eyes, and whispered, "I could spend the entire day just looking at your gorgeous face while getting lost in those dreamy eyes."

The disrespect Emily displayed sent Cathy into a rage. She pushed Rose and Joanne to the side, grabbed Emily by her perfect blond hair, and yanked so hard it sent the head cheerleader tumbling to the floor. "If it's a fight you want"—Cathy clenched her fists tightly—"I can give you what you're looking for, bitch."

Sammy was in shock as he stared at the two girls. It dawned on him that they were fighting over him, which brought a small feeling of delight. But before he could bask in his glory, he knew he had to take action as Emily made her way to her feet. By the expression on her face, he knew she was not in the mood for talking. He managed to step between the two combatants before a punch was thrown and barely kept them separated. Their sole purpose seemed to be to tear each other apart.

He turned his attention to Emily. "I will get with you another time so we can set up a date. I do have your number, remember?" Then he turned his attention to Cathy, who was struggling as she tried to get free. "You know she is trying to get under your skin." He hugged her after releasing his grip on Emily. "Do not let her win."

He continued to hold Cathy in his arms, but his eyes never wavered from Emily, who stood in the middle of her two friends with a huge grin plastered on her face and a seductive gleam in her eye.

Later that day, school had come to an end, but Cathy's rage had not subsided. She made her way to the locker room to change for practice, but the thought of Emily touching Sammy filled her mind. She could not focus on anything else but doing bodily harm to the head cheerleader, so she decided to pace the room and think of Sammy's tender touch and lips on hers, hoping it would finally calm her nerves. She went to get a drink of water and headed to the restroom. At that moment, she heard the locker room door open and Emily's voice, along with her friends', flooding the room. She gritted her teeth and abruptly stood, ready for a confrontation with her sworn enemy, but at the last moment, Cathy decided to listen in on their conversation since they were unaware of her presence.

"Can you believe that girl?" Joanne asked with a laugh. "Who does she think she is?"

Emily walked into the restroom and teased her hair while looking into the mirror. "She thinks she owns Sammy." She chuckled. "It is clear as day that she wants to be more than friends with him, but why would he want her if he could have me?"

Emily looked at the restroom partition and noticed someone was using the facility. She surmised it was Cathy because her shoes were black instead of the white low-top gym shoes the other cheerleaders wore. A devious smile crossed her face as she decided to add more fuel to the inferno. She retrieved her makeup kit from her purse and added the finishing touches to her appearance. Then she took another glance at her eavesdropping visitor.

"I don't know what makes that average-looking girl think that she can compete with someone like me." Emily shook her head while laughing. "She needs to accept the fact that it's only a matter of time before he's mine."

She knew her comments had struck a chord with Cathy because she saw her feet tapping on the floor. The damage was done, so she went back into the locker room area and finished changing clothes. As the trio departed, she stopped in the doorway and belted out one last laugh before closing the door.

After the coast was clear, Cathy exited the restroom stall and walked slowly toward the mirror. Emily's cruel words played in her mind, and she started to doubt herself as her self-confidence began to sink. She questioned whether she was good enough for Sammy and if he was just spending time with her out of pity instead of having feelings for her. She looked at her face and thought that she was pretty. But Emily was beautiful. She placed her hands on her breasts and pushed them up. They were a good size, but Emily's breasts were bigger and perfect. In the end, Cathy knew she did not measure up to the goddess of Princess Anne High School. She hung her head because, adding to her mounting troubles, Emily and Sammy were going to be spending a great deal of time together alone. Even though Sammy would not admit it, Cathy was not blind to the fact that he had eyes for Emily.

She took a deep breath and then headed toward her locker to change for practice. Despite all the negative thoughts creeping through her mind, she took solace in the fact that she would spending time with Sammy, and that brought a smile to her face.

A short time later, the cheerleaders were practicing. Cathy's absence went unnoticed by everyone except the captain. Never one to let an opportunity to sully Cathy's name slip by, Emily marched over to the coach to inform her that Cathy had skipped practice. But the desired outcome she was hoping for—Cathy's dismissal from the team—was dashed when the coach pointed out that Cathy was making her way toward the rest of the team.

Emily rolled her eyes and frowned as she walked back to join her team. The moment she was in Cathy's presence, she turned to her foe and shouted, "It's about time." She snarled and made her way to the front of the group so practice could continue.

Cathy stared at Emily for a few seconds, and when she saw the snide grin on her face, it was the last straw. She could not take any more as her anger usurped her rationale. Her breathing intensified, and her eyes narrowed. When Emily gave her a mocking wink, Cathy marched straight toward her. Once Cathy was within a few feet, she unleashed all her frustrations, punching Emily in the eye and knocking her to the ground. A feeling of euphoria radiated throughout Cathy, and she took perverse pleasure in watching Emily writhe and scream in pain, clutching her face. Cathy's head snapped back, looking at her fellow cheerleaders, but no one moved an inch for fear of repercussion, so she decided to move in and inflict more punishment. She pounced on her fallen foe and began to pepper her with violent blows to the head and neck. As blood flowed from Emily's nose, Cathy put even more fervor into her strikes.

The fact that Emily began to plead for help was music to Cathy's ears, and she did not let up on her attack until the coach arrived and pushed her off Emily. Cathy lay on the ground, feeling immune to the trouble she was in. She just focused on Emily's bloody face with a disturbing glare that shook everyone in the vicinity of the confrontation.

She was admonished for her heinous acts, dismissed from the team, and informed that her mother would be called, but all that meant nothing. She was feeling too good as she made her way to her feet and stared down at Emily, who was in tears. She turned her attention to Rose and Joanne and winked before departing the field without uttering a word as others rushed to the scene to check on the fallen cheerleader.

Meanwhile, a few blocks away from the school, Sammy and Jonathon were walking home. They were discussing the day at school, and then the conversation quickly turned to the evening at Jonathon's house. As Jonathon delved into the praise that his mother had heaped on Sammy about his manners and kindness, a car pulled up beside them and stopped abruptly, causing the tires to screech.

Sammy instinctively pushed Jonathon away from the street and into a nearby yard and then jumped back away from the road. Feeling threatened, he rose to his feet, preparing for a fight, thinking it was Slade and his friends seeking retribution. He was pleasantly surprised when he saw it was Cathy. He began to make his way toward the car as Cathy exited, rushed over, and wrapped her arms around him, squeezing him tight.

Her chest was pressed against his torso, and he could feel her rapid heartbeat, accompanied by her heavy breathing. He knew something was amiss. "Is everything okay?"

"Everything is perfect now," she replied, forcing a smile. "I'm just happy to see you."

Sammy took a step back, trying to read her facial expressions and body language. "I thought you had practice?"

"It ended early." She turned and greeted Jonathon and then turned back to Sammy. "I'm hungry. Do you want to go get that pizza?"

Sammy asked Jonathon to tag along, but he declined, not wanting to be the third wheel, but accepted a ride home instead.

After Jonathon's departure, Sammy reached for Cathy's hand but was horrified when he saw small traces of blood on her knuckles. "Is there something you are not telling me?"

She snatched her hand away, retrieved a tissue from her glove box, and wiped the residual fluids from her hand. She gave a flimsy explanation for it, but he was incredulous as he listened to her story. Instead of interrogating her about the holes in her tale, Sammy just sat back in his seat and hoped their friendship was strong enough that she would trust him with the truth, no matter how bad it was.

Minutes later, they arrived at their favorite pizzeria and took a seat at their favorite booth. They ordered a couple of sodas and a few slices of pizza and engaged in casual conversation.

Sammy peeked at her knuckles every few minutes but refused to ask her about the blood. Instead, he reached across the table and held her hands, and they stared into each other's eyes as if they were the only two people in the room.

Just outside the pizza shop, Slade parked his car. He was about to enter the establishment to pick up a few large pizzas for dinner, but just as he reached for the door handle, he stopped when he saw Alex approaching out of the corner of his eye.

"I need you to come with me right now," Alex said with a disturbing panic to his voice. He grabbed Slade by the arm and led him down a side street next to the restaurant. He began pacing, his body visibly shaking. He repeatedly wiped his eyes and face while mumbling some inaudible words. Then he wiped his hands on his pants before rubbing them together.

Slade grabbed his friend by the shoulders and shook him. "What's your problem, dude?"

"I talked to my brother, and he told me why Chavo didn't take care of Sammy." He broke free of Slade's clutches and began pacing once again.

Annoyed, Slade pushed Alex against the wall and slapped him across the face. "I don't have all day, so tell me what your brother said."

"He's dead!" Alex shouted as tears streamed down his face.

"What do you mean dead?" Slade countered, the machismo that he exuded dissipating.

"They found him lying in the street with a broken neck." Alex wiped the tears from his cheeks, and his voice quivered. "Something doesn't seem right about this guy. He beats up three of our biggest linemen and came out of the fight without a scratch on him. We don't know a thing about this dude. Whatever the issue you two have, I think you should bury the beef before something bad happens to us!"

Slade took a step back and remained silent for a few seconds. He rubbed his chin and then looked at Alex with disgust. His anger grew with each passing second until he could not contain it any longer. He stepped forward, drew his right hand back over his left shoulder, and backhanded Alex with such force, it knocked Alex to the ground.

He seethed as he stood over his so-called friend, staring down at him. "I can't believe you uttered those words to me. You showed your true colors. You're afraid." He kicked Alex in the stomach. "I see your boy wasn't man enough to finish the job, so I'll have to do it myself." He kicked him once more, spit on Alex's back, and then left him cowering on the ground.

He walked with purpose to the front of the restaurant and then violently swung the door open. He headed straight to the counter, ignoring the praise of the people in the establishment, and grabbed his food. On his way out, he examined the room, searching for a familiar face, but was unsuccessful. Seething over Chavo's failure and the perceived lack of courage his friend had exuded, he shouted expletives, hoping someone would take exception and challenge him to a fight so he could blow off some steam. He waited for a few seconds. When there were no takers, he pushed past some onlookers and made his way to his car, thoughts of Sammy exacerbating his anger.

Meanwhile, on the beach, Sammy and Cathy walked side by side, enjoying casual conversation as they sipped virgin margaritas while basking in the sun.

Cathy abruptly stopped and took Sammy by the hand. She looked toward the ground and took a couple of deep breaths, trying to muster the confidence to engage in a serious conversation.

"I know we're friends." She ran her bare toes over the sand. "But I want to know how you feel about me." She gazed into his eyes. "I want to know if we can be more than friends."

Sammy was new to this type of interaction and did not know how to properly answer the question. He smiled as he noticed the sun reflecting off her dark hair and brushed the stray strands away from her eyes. Afterward, he gently ran his fingers along her cheek, leaned in, and gave her a soft kiss on the forehead. Even though he lacked experience, he decided to speak from his heart. He took her by the hand and gave it a gentle squeeze.

"Yes, we are very good friends, but when you are not around, I yearn for your presence. When we end our conversations on the phone, I look forward to our next dialogue." He pulled her close. "I know I like being with you and look forward to spending any time with you, even if it is only a few seconds."

His response brought a huge smile to her face, but as quickly as her elation appeared, it vanished. "I need to know one thing before we take the next step."

"Anything," he replied.

"Will that skank Emily be a problem?" Tears formed in her eyes. "I wouldn't be able to handle the heartbreak if you leave me for her."

"She means nothing to me." He kissed her on the cheek. "I only have eyes for you."

Sammy leaned in, and the two shared a deep, passionate kiss, but a few seconds into the intimate moment, he stopped when he heard a deep, sinister laugh in the distance. He took a step back and looked around, but the only people in sight were two kids around the age of ten playing in the sand a few feet away, accompanied by their grandparents.

"Is everything all right?" Cathy asked.

"Yes," he said and then turned his attention back to her. "For the first time in a very long time, everything is as right as rain." He leaned in to give her another kiss, but just before their lips met, he heard the creepy laugh again. He looked up to survey the area, but only the same four people were in the vicinity. An uneasy feeling coursed through his body, and it took everything he could muster to refrain from using his angel eyes to investigate further. He placed his hand over his stomach and then took a deep breath as his facial expression exuded disappointment and discomfort.

"I think I ate too much. I am not feeling well."

Without uttering a word, Cathy retrieved her keys from her purse, took Sammy by the hand, and led him to her car.

CHAPTER 12

Minutes later, the two arrived and parked alongside the curb in front of Sammy's house. He directed his attention to her purse because he could not ignore the constant vibrating any longer.

"Someone is trying very hard to get ahold of you." He looked at her. "Are you going to answer it? It might be of the utmost importance."

"The only one that matters is sitting right next me." She leaned over and gave him a kiss. "Everything and everybody else can wait."

After exiting the vehicle, Sammy watched as Cathy looked at her phone and then promptly closed it. Her expression signaled that something was awry, so he decided to ask, but she quickly dismissed his concern.

They walked with their hands intertwined toward his house. Just as they reached the front door, Cathy stopped him and requested a kiss, which Sammy happily gave her. He opened the front door and realized that Riley was not home, so he invited her in and led her to the couch. He gave her one more passionate kiss before they took their seats. Afterward, he gazed deeply into her brown eyes as his heart fluttered.

He excused himself and made his way to his bedroom. Upon entering, he was surprised by an unexpected visitor: Michael. He noticed that the archangel was patiently waiting, sitting with his legs crossed, but Sammy did not have time for small talk. Cathy was waiting downstairs.

He searched for his cologne, ignoring Michael, and when he sensed the archangel was approaching from the rear, he quickly cut him off before he could speak. "Not now. I have a lady friend waiting for me." He found his cologne in his second drawer beside his socks. "Whatever it is that you want to talk about, it will have to wait."

"No, it cannot wait, my friend," Michael said in a low, somber tone. "We need to talk right now."

Sammy turned to face his friend. Just as he was about to refuse his request, he stopped. He noticed the anguish etched on Michael's face and returned the bottle to his dresser. He sat on his bed and gave Michael his undivided attention. A lump developed in his throat as he saw the pain in Michael's eyes. Now he needed to know what the issue was, even if Cathy was waiting for his return. His palms began to sweat as Michael paced the room. He swallowed the excess saliva that had accumulated in his mouth. Just as Michael opened his mouth to speak, Cathy shouted Sammy's name, interrupting the conversation.

Sammy rose to his feet, torn over his predicament. He took a step toward the door and then looked back at Michael. He wanted to hear what his friend had to say, but Cathy wanted his company, and her needs usurped Michael's conversation.

"Give me a few minutes," Sammy implored and then made his way to the door. He exited despite Michael's pleas for him to remain.

He hustled down the stairs to where Cathy was waiting at the bottom step with tears in her eyes. Sammy rushed to her side and tried to take her into his arms, but she pulled away.

"My mother has been blowing up my phone." She wiped her eyes. "I have to go."

"Are you going to tell me what is wrong?" Sammy asked.

She cracked a smile, followed by a nervous laugh. "I promise I'll tell you all about it tomorrow." She wiped her eyes once again. "I have a feeling that I'll be getting yelled at all night, so I won't be able to call you." She leaned in and kissed his cheek. "I miss you already."

He pulled her close, and she hugged him more tightly than usual—something he noticed. After the two shared another deep, passionate kiss, they exited the house and walked to her vehicle. Sammy stood on the front lawn and waved as she drove away. Just as she turned the corner, he remembered that Michael was waiting in his room with something important to say. He turned to go back into the house but came to abrupt stop when he heard that deep, dark, creepy laugh he had heard at the beach earlier. He quickly displayed his angel eyes to survey the area. Unlike before, he did not care who was around to see his celestial gift.

Horrified, he took a step back as he saw a black aura following Cathy's car. His heart began to pound so hard that it felt as if it were about to burst from his chest. He ran to the middle of the street and tried to teleport but only managed to fall to the ground. He rose to his feet and ran back into the house to grab his phone. He frantically dialed her number, but his calls went straight to voice mail. Distraught and helpless for the first time in his infinite existence, he knew there was only one entity that could help him: his friend Michael. He turned toward the stairs but stopped because the archangel was standing at the bottom of the staircase with his head lowered.

Meanwhile, a few blocks away, Cathy was driving down the street as her phone rang.

Tired of the constant noise, she decided to answer it and face whoever kept bugging her. She reached into her purse and retrieved her phone. She had more than fifty missed calls and just as many text messages. She rolled her eyes when she saw they were from her cheerleading teammates. Joanne and Rose had been doing the bulk of the calling and texting, but she had some things to get off her chest, so she could not resist answering the next call from Joanne.

The conversation quickly became heated, filled with a lot of threats and expletives from both sides. After a few minutes, she slammed the phone down on her passenger seat and then squeezed her steering wheel so tightly that her knuckles turned pale. She tried to change the tenor of her mood by thinking of Sammy—the tender kisses, the tight hugs, and the passion-filled moments. But, despite her valiant efforts, she could not because her phone continued to ring, which interrupted her pleasant train of thought.

She'd had enough; her anger got the best of her. She prioritized her anger over common sense and decided to lean over and retrieve her phone, which had fallen to the floor. She took her eyes off the road for a few seconds while maintaining her forty-five mile per hour speed. After patting around on the floor, she finally found her phone and sat upright, only to find a car stopped at the traffic light only a few feet ahead of her. She did not have time to perform any evasive maneuvers; the only thing she could manage was to let out a blood-curdling scream as she drove into the rear of the car.

Back at the house, Sammy pleaded with Michael to help him, feeling that his friend was in mortal danger, but all Michael could do was drop his head and apologize.

Sammy raced over to Michael and grabbed him by the collar. "Why are you sorry?" He jerked him back and forth as tears streamed down his face. "Tell me why you are sorry!"

"She is gone, old friend," Michael replied in a low, somber tone.

Sammy could not believe what he had just heard. Pain ripped through his chest. He struggled to breathe as he fell to one knee and closed his eyes tightly. He had always been on the other side of death, ignorant to how humans dealt with loss, but now he was experiencing the full brunt of sorrow, and it was crippling. He became dizzy, and his body went limp, causing him to crumple to the floor.

"I was just with her," he whispered, placing his fingertips on his lips.

He could still feel her kiss and smell her aroma and see her beautiful smile, but now all that was gone. He could not contain his emotions any longer. He tilted his head back and let out a spine-chilling scream just as Riley walked through the front door.

Concerned, Riley dropped his coat and briefcase and rushed over to Sammy, who was now curled in the fetal position. He gathered his nephew into his arms, consoling him, allowing him to cry without asking what happened because that was not important at the moment. Seeing Sammy in so much pain caused Riley to break down into tears. They continued to hold one another as their emotions flowed freely.

As the days passed, Sammy lay in his bed silent, just staring at the ceiling while Michael stood in the corner, keeping vigil over his distraught friend. Riley did his part by sitting by Sammy's side, showing his love and support like a father figure would in a time of need.

For the past three nights, Sammy had only managed to get a total of four hours of sleep because when he closed his eyes, he often saw Cathy's face, which caused him to wake up screaming, followed by weeping. He had not eaten since the tragic accident, which concerned Riley, but his inability to handle grief and the way it debilitated him concerned Michael. The archangel questioned if Sammy would ever fully recover from the tragedy and if it would hinder him from carrying out his duty once his time on earth had come to an end.

Sammy turned to lay on his right side and peered at Riley, who was sitting a few feet away in a chair. He noticed his uncle's hair was a mess, and his mood was more somber than usual, so he decided to engage him in conversation.

"What seems to be the problem?" Sammy asked.

"I'm very concerned about you." Riley stood, made his way over to the bed, and sat beside Sammy. "You haven't eaten a thing in three days and have barely had two sips of water." Riley took Sammy's hand. "I don't want you to get sick."

Sammy sat up on the bed, grabbed the bottle of water that sat on the nightstand, and took a huge drink. "Thank you for being by my side and helping me through this tough time."

"You're my family, my responsibility, and I would do anything for you." Riley placed his hand on Sammy's leg. "I remember the last time I had to do this." His eyes welled with tears as he turned away.

"Please, Uncle, tell me what is on your mind."

Riley stood and took a very deep breath as grief racked his body. He paced the room for a few seconds in silence, running his fingertips along the dresser and lamp that sat on the desk near the window.

"I remember the day your mother died like it was yesterday. It tore me apart." He returned to sit beside Sammy. "I had to hide my grief because I made your parents a promise that I would look after their most prized possession: you." He chuckled. "Your mother and I were thick as thieves. Everywhere I went, she wasn't too far behind." He lowered his head as tears flowed. "I protected her from any and everything, but when she died, I felt responsible because I wasn't there to save her."

"She died in a car accident, Uncle Riley. There was nothing you could have done."

"I knew that deep down inside, but that didn't take away the pain." Riley turned away and took a deep breath. "I endured some dark days, some very low times. I even contemplated suicide because the pain seemed as if it would never end." He turned to face Sammy, and through his tears, a light illuminated in his eyes. "You saved my life. You gave me something to live for. And slowly, the pain eased because I had a very special boy to raise who I loved like he was my very own."

A huge grin appeared on Riley's face as he wiped the tears from his eyes and cheeks. "I don't know about you, but I'm starving. I think a large pizza with the works is in order with plenty of soda to wash it down." He tapped Sammy on the leg. "Be ready to eat in about thirty minutes, even if it is just a slice or three." He winked, leaned over, and gave Sammy a hug. "I love you, son." He kissed Sammy on the cheek and flashed a smile before departing the room.

Sammy's heart swelled with love and even more admiration for Riley as he watched him depart. For the first time since Cathy's death, he managed to crack a smile, even if it was only half of one. He lay back on the bed, but just before he closed his eyes, Sammy spotted Michael standing in the corner. "How long have you been there?"

"I have not left your side since that tragic day." Michael lowered his head. "I could not abandon my friend during this trying time."

"Friend?" Sammy sat up with fire in his eyes. "How dare you call yourself my friend. You did nothing to stop Cathy from dying. You did not tell me the events that were about to occur."

"I tried to tell you on a few different occasions, but you never had time." Michael shook his head. "And you know I could not do anything to stop it." "Who came for her?" Sammy asked through gritted teeth. "I saw his dark

aura behind her car and heard his laugh as he was going after her."

Michael paused for a few seconds and stared into his friend's eyes. He saw the undeniable pain and anguish there and knew the answer would only further Sammy's agony. "It is not important."

"It is important to me!" Sammy shouted as a single tear fell from his eye, but no matter how demonstrative he was, Michael would not capitulate and give him the answer he wanted so desperately.

"You need to cope with your loss and find a way to find meaning and hope during your time on earth." Michael approached Sammy but was shoved away.

"I do not want to go on with my life on the planet." Sammy took a deep breath as his resolve set in. "I am ready to resume my responsibilities. I cannot take the heartache."

"*Ah*, I see." Michael rubbed his chin while shaking his head. "The moment you face some adversity, you are ready to run away and quit." The archangel let out a sarcastic chuckle. "I went to him and begged for you to become human and this is how you repay me?"

"I do not need your pity party or lecture; I need you to go to him and tell him that I am ready to resume my duties."

Angered by Sammy's curtness, Michael reared back and slapped his friend so hard across the face with his open palm that he sent Sammy tumbling to the floor. "You wanted this, so you will take the bitter with the sweet, the good with the bad" He reached down, grabbed Sammy by the arm, and abruptly lifted him to his feet. "You are going to dust yourself off and continue to plow forward. You wanted to be human; you will endure the pain of loss like humans."

A light knock on the door interrupted the intense conversation. The moment the door opened, Sammy was standing in the middle of the room with his eyes full of tears.

He smiled at his uncle and took a deep breath. "Is the pizza here?" He rubbed his stomach. "I am starving."

CHAPTER 13

After their quiet dinner concluded, Sammy needed some air, so he politely excused himself from the table and went out the front door. He sat on the top step and gazed at the spot where Cathy's car had been parked during her last visit. Just as he was about to break down into tears, he spotted Jonathon cautiously approaching through the front yard.

"I didn't mean to intrude," Jonathon said as his stride shortened and his pace slowed. "I just came to check on you and see how you were doing."

Sammy was touched by his friend's concern. He wiped the tears from his eyes and stood. Then he approached Jonathon and gave him a hug. "Thank you for thinking of me."

"You're my best friend. Of course, I'm thinking of you during this rough time," Jonathon replied. After breaking their embrace, he shook his head as tears gathered in his eyes. "I can't believe she's gone." He took a deep breath. "I know how much she meant to you."

"How has school been?" Sammy asked, needing to change the subject because his emotions were becoming too hard to control. He felt his celestial side beginning to take over. His angel eyes flickered, appearing and then turning back to their alternative state. He put a few steps of space between him and Jonathon as sorrow began to take over and the tears continued to flow.

"Who cares about school? I'm here to check on you," Jonathon said, making sure to respect Sammy and maintain his distance.

Without warning, Sammy walked to the end of the driveway and then came to a stop. He turned to face Jonathon as he rubbed the back of his neck while shaking his head. "I need to get out of here for a little while." He took a deep breath. "Forgive me for being rude, but there is a place I need to be."

"Do you want company?" Jonathon asked with a tone that reeked of desperation.

"No!" Sammy answered, extending his hand, palm first, toward Jonathon. "I need to make this trip alone." He appreciated his friend's gesture and smiled as he made his way toward him. He hugged him and thanked him for visiting, wanting to leave things on a good note. He waited until his friend was out of sight and then looked to the sky and begged for strength and courage as he began to embark on his next journey—a visit that was long overdue.

A short time later, he stood a few feet away from his destination. The trip had been trying as he reminisced about Cathy and the great times they had shared. Many times he had wanted to stop, return home, head straight to his room, and lock the door. But every time he had stopped, he had heard Michael's voice in his head, imploring him to be strong and to face the inevitable. So, with each step tougher than the last, he finally stood on Cathy's doorstep.

Nervous, he swallowed hard and took a few deep breaths as he went to knock on the door. But just before he made contact, he retracted his hand. He paced for a few seconds, doubting if he could face Cathy's mother, but after a few minutes, he finally mustered the courage to ring the doorbell instead of knocking. He closed his eyes and wiped his sweaty palms on his pants. When the door opened, he was shocked at the sight before him.

Mrs. Stevens emerged wearing a dingy white robe and a matching bandanna on her head. A half-smoked cigarette hung from the right corner of her mouth, and she held a glass of whiskey in her right hand.

"Having a student at my house is extremely inappropriate." She stepped to the side. "But I really don't care at this point."

Sammy cautiously entered the house and immediately noticed pictures of Cathy hanging on the walls and sitting on every table in sight. His heart sank as he slowly approached the photo on the coffee table. He picked it up and traced her lips with the tip of his index finger as he gazed at her beautiful smile. He gently returned the picture to the table and then turned and faced Mrs. Stevens.

"If this is a bad time, I could return another time."

"Nonsense!" She removed the cigarette from her mouth and then finished her drink. "I was just about to refill my glass. Would you like a drink?"

Sammy politely declined and looked past Mrs. Stevens to the front door, wondering if his impromptu visit had been a mistake. He excused himself, apologized for intruding, and made his way toward the door but was stopped.

"I would like it very much if you stayed," Mrs. Stevens said as a tear appeared in her eye. "My daughter cared for you very much, and I would like it if we could have a conversation outside of school." She closed her robe to cover her nudity. "I'd like it very much if you would stay and talk."

Despite feeling uncomfortable with what he had just seen, Sammy agreed to stay. He took a seat on far right side of the couch and kept his gaze fixated on the far wall. After refilling her glass with alcohol, Mrs. Stevens took a seat on the other side of the couch and took a healthy sip before placing the glass on the table.

"You're such a good young man." She crossed her legs. "For you to think of me in this trying time speaks volumes. I see why my daughter was crazy about you." She retrieved a picture that rested beside her. She gazed at the photograph as her emotions got the best of her. "To lose a child … words cannot describe how I feel."

Sammy looked over at her and saw her quivering while clutching the picture to her heart. He reached for her, wanting to console Mrs. Stevens, but he knew there was nothing he could do or say to take away her pain. So he retracted his hand, closed his eyes, and listened to her cries as his heart broke one more time.

He felt the need to make himself useful, so while she was sobbing, Sammy grabbed her glass and headed into the kitchen. He poured the alcohol down the drain and filled the cup with coffee. He returned to the living room, handed her the beverage, and then took the picture from her shaking hands.

"I do not want to delve into your personal life, but I was wondering, where is your husband during your time of need?"

"My husband and I haven't been together in years." She wiped the tears from her eyes. "I just wear the ring for appearances because I had troubles facing my failures." She took a sip of her coffee and winced at the heat. "Since we're asking questions, have you returned to school yet?"

"No," Sammy said in a soft, somber voice. "There are too many things in that building that would remind me of Cathy." He swallowed hard as his tears began to flow. "Without her, there is no need for me to ever go back."

Disgusted by his response, Mrs. Stevens slammed her cup on the table, causing the liquid to splash everywhere. "You are one of the brightest students I've ever had the privilege of teaching, but the words that just came out of your mouth were the dumbest I've ever heard."

She stood abruptly, which caused her robe to open, partially exposing her nude body. She quickly closed her garment as Sammy turned his head, but the sight could not be unseen. She made her way toward him and stood in front of him. Then she kicked his leg to get his attention.

"My daughter's life came to a premature end, but you have plenty of years in front of you. Don't stop living your life and remain stuck in time."

"When are you returning to work?" Sammy asked in a calm voice. "Touché, Mr. Angel." She took a deep breath and managed to smile

despite her pain. She strolled over and stared at the various pictures that littered the wall. "I still can't wrap my head around the fact that I have to bury my baby in a few days." She turned to face Sammy. "I'll make you a deal." She paused. "I'll return to work after the funeral as long as you do the same." She approached him and extended her hand. "Do we have a deal?"

Sammy rose to his feet and looked at her hand. As a single tear rolled down his cheek and fell harmlessly to the floor, he gazed over her shoulder at Cathy's picture, marveling at her beautiful smile. He turned his attention back to Mrs. Stevens, bypassed the handshake, and pulled her into an embrace.

"We have a deal," he whispered and then closed his eyes and let the tears flow.

A short time later, after sharing painful memories and some laughs, Sammy departed but not without a portrait of Cathy. He looked at the picture, softly placed his lips over hers, and then closed his eyes. His thoughts returned to their first date, the time they had shared in the pizzeria and the long walk on the beach. He imitated Mrs. Stevens's action, holding the picture to his heart, as he began to make his way home. His legs trembled with each step. He was barely able to make it to the end of the driveway before having to stop. With a heavy heart, he slowly turned and stared at the house where Cathy had once resided. He began to weep. Even though he knew she was gone, being inside that house had made it real. His love was no more.

A few days later, the day of the funeral had arrived. Sammy had been up all night staring out the window at the sky, trying to make sense of the death of someone who had been so full of life and destined for something great. He sat on the bed, holding her portrait as a lump developed in his throat. Finally, he began to have conversation with her, asking for the strength to get through the toughest day of his young human life. After finishing, he placed a tender kiss on her forehead and placed the picture on his pillow. As he made his way into the bathroom, he heard a knock on his bedroom door.

Riley entered the room and did not say a word. He just greeted Sammy with a hug and assured him that all would be okay—words that neither of them believed to be true. After breaking the embrace, Riley retrieved the picture.

"She was a beautiful young woman." He returned the picture to its place on the pillow and put his hand on Sammy's shoulder as he prepared to depart. "Take it one day at a time." He gave Sammy a slight squeeze. "I'll be downstairs waiting for you so we can go to the funeral."

Sammy stood still, focused on the picture, until he heard the door close. He was alone once again and made his way over to his bed. He smiled as he stared at Cathy's face.

"I knew Riley liked you, and I know you are looking down at me smiling right now." He paused for a few seconds, but his eyes never wavered. "You will always be in my heart."

A short time later, Riley and Sammy arrived at the church. The parking lot was clear, as the people were gathered in front of the church, but something odd happened the moment Sammy exited the car. His eyes shifted to angel without him consciously doing it, and as hard as he tried to shift them back to their alternative state, he could not. He noticed how all the statues that lined the outside of the church turned to stare at him, which caused him to pause. In his moment of panic, his eyes shifted back to their alternative state just as Riley reached his side.

"Is everything all right?" Riley asked.

Sammy nodded, assuring his uncle that all was well, but he knew something was amiss. He was hesitant to go any further, not wanting what had just happened to occur in front of all the people who were standing just a few feet away. As he continued on his path with Riley close to his side, he felt a swell of emotions, and his eyes shifted once again. He looked away and then closed them tightly, trying to make them change back. After a few seconds, he reluctantly opened them and was relieved that his alternative eyes had returned.

Confused, he looked off to the side and saw Michael standing at the entrance to the parking lot. The archangel was shaking his head, discouraging Sammy from proceeding, but Sammy did not know what the message was. Sammy turned the corner and saw Jonathon and his mother standing by some of the well-wishers. The minute Lola laid eyes on him, she rushed over and gave him a hug, placing her hands over his eyes.

"It's not a good idea for you to be here. All will be revealed later, but for right now, you need to get out of here as soon as possible," she whispered in his ear. "I'll make up an excuse to explain your absence to your uncle, but you need to go right now."

Sammy did not question her; he simply nodded and departed. He avoided Riley, who was quickly grabbed by Lola, allowing Sammy to walk away without being stopped. As he crossed the street, he turned and glanced at the entrance of the church. What he saw sent him into a frenzy. He could not believe his eyes as he witnessed Emily and her friends dressed in tight black dresses entering the church with members of Cathy's family, hugging and crying with tissues in their hands. He wanted to go back and give them a piece of his mind, but he knew that was not possible. What pained him even more was the fact that the ones responsible for Cathy's death would be able to attend the funeral service but he could not.

CHAPTER 14

The next day, all classes at school were suspended to give the students a day to mourn. Sammy spent his day at the beach, staring out at the waves of the Atlantic Ocean while drinking virgin margaritas. He endured Riley's scorn for missing the funeral and the gathering at the school that followed, but he had not had a choice in the matter. Instead, during the ceremony he had sat perched in the highest tree a few blocks away and wept as Michael consoled him while reciting verbatim what was said by everyone inside the church during the proceedings.

He finished his drink and decided to head over to the pizzeria to grab a slice of pizza, but he stopped in his tracks when he saw Slade and his minions standing outside the restaurant, joking and laughing as if nothing tragic had occurred. He knew his presence would cause a scene and would probably end in a physical confrontation. He knew Cathy would not want that, so to honor his friend, he decided to head home and listen to more of Riley's scolding.

School resumed the next day, and just as promised, Sammy returned. He entered the building and headed to his locker. At every turn, he expected Cathy to appear, hoping he'd just had a bad dream, but of course his wish was dashed. He entered homeroom and the chatter came to a sudden halt. Every student and the teacher stared at Sammy, but he just took his usual seat in back of the class.

The teacher and a group of students approached Sammy and gave him their well-wishes. He thanked them, but he couldn't keep his gaze from wandering over to Slade, who was staring at him with bad intentions from across the room. Once he saw a smile creep across Slade's lips, Sammy quickly diverted his attention elsewhere. He knew his adversary was taking pleasure in his misery, so he was not going to give the punk the pleasure of allowing his words to provoke him into something he would not be able to take back. The bell rang and not a second too soon. Sammy grabbed his bag, raced out of the classroom, and thought about heading to the exit. He could not fathom spending the day in that school without Cathy. Knowing she was somewhere in the building had gotten him through most of the tedious days, but now that was not the case.

He raced down the back stairs and was just a few steps from the door when he felt a hand on his shoulder. His heart jumped and hope filled his body because the touch was soft against his skin. A smile graced his lips because he was sure it was Cathy. He quickly turned and extended his arms, but the moment he laid eyes on the owner of the hand, his smile and arms retracted.

"I'm sorry if I scared you," Emily said in a soft tone. "I know this may not be the right time to ask, but I was wondering about our tutoring sessions."

"The unmitigated gall!" Sammy shouted, drops of his saliva pelting Emily. "How dare you come asking me to help you with anything?" He dropped his bag and approached her with hatred in his eyes. "One of the last conversations I had with Cathy was spent on you." He slowly shook his head. "I was assuring her that she was not a consolation prize. I had to convince her that she was the one I wanted and not you, and now she is dead."

His voice grew louder with every word. Curious students began to gather around them, but their presence did not deter Sammy from delivering his message.

"Your arrogance and flaunting of your looks made Cathy doubt herself; you made her feel like she could not measure up to you." He looked at her feet and drew his gaze up her body. "She did not have to feel less than, because she was beautiful. You are the one that is ugly and should feel less." He took a few deep breaths. "I refuse to help you with anything, so go find someone else to help you. I do not care if you spend the rest of your life in this damn school."

Sammy reached down and snatched his bag off the floor. He turned toward the door but paused as he thought of the promise he made to Cathy's mother. Even though he did not want anything to do with Emily, he had given his word and felt a need to fulfill his obligation. He placed his hand over his heart and thought of Cathy. He knew she would want him to do the right thing even if he did not approve. He turned to face Emily, but his disdain would not let his kindness win. The right thing to do would have been to wait a little longer, but he made his way to his next class, leaving Emily ashamed and embarrassed in his wake.

Later that day, Sammy arrived at the door of his history class, but instead of entering, he stopped and stared at the threshold. He could feel a strong presence radiating from inside the room and managed to smile, knowing Cathy was with him in spirit.

He adjusted his book bag on his shoulder, lowered his head, and entered the room. But as much as he wanted to keep his head down and head to his seat, he failed; his gaze immediately made its way to the empty chair that had belonged to his loving friend. He stopped as his heart dropped, and his legs began to shake. Out of the corner of his eye, he noticed Emily staring at him. He did not want anyone to see him cry, especially her, so he gathered his composure and took slow steps because his legs felt unstable. He managed to make it to his desk in the back of the room.

He lowered his head, wanting to avoid the stares from the rest of the class, but when a sudden hush fell over the room, he looked up and was pleasantly surprised when he saw Mrs. Stevens enter. She had honored her promise to him. He gave her a slight wave, which was returned with a small smile before she took her seat.

"I want you to open your books and review chapters three through six," Mrs. Stevens said before she removed her glasses and rubbed the indentions on her nose. "There will be a pop quiz in fifteen minutes, so you better be ready."

Sammy smiled, but what came next was dumbfounding. He watched as Emily stood and slowly made her way to Mrs. Stevens's desk. While the other students riffled through pages, combing the material, he watched the front of the room with intrigue.

"I want to extend my condolences to you," Emily said with her head lowered.

Mrs. Stevens rolled her eyes and then returned her glasses to her face. She exhaled heavily and looked up at Emily, visibly annoyed. She muttered, "Thank you," and leaned back in her chair, grabbing the quiz from her desk.

"If there's anything I can do, don't hesitate."

"Let me stop you right there, Miss Keele!" Mrs. Stevens interrupted. She removed her glasses once again and flung them onto her desk. "I don't know where all this fake concern is coming from." She stood and gazed into Emily's eyes. "You and my daughter were far from friends." She shook her head. "I used to listen outside Cathy's door at night as she argued with you and your friends. It used to pain me knowing that she was envious of you." She thought back to those nights and tears began to flow as her daughter's voice rang in her head. Anger and sorrow began to fight within Mrs. Steven's heart as she pounded her desk. "You need to return to your seat right now."

Visibly fighting with her emotions, Mrs. Stevens buried her head in the palm of her hands. She thought back to all those nights Cathy had spent crying after talking on the phone with Emily, and then the moment she had received the phone call about her daughter being in an accident. She slumped in her chair, thinking of how her last words to her loving daughter had been in anger. Then her mind envisioned Cathy's casket being lowered into the ground. She clutched her glasses and then slammed them on her desk as she glared at the bane of her daughter's existence. She slowly stood, seething as small clumps of saliva gathered in the corners of her mouth.

"Cathy was on the phone with your lackeys at the time of her death." She slammed the papers down on her desk and pointed at Emily. "If it weren't for you and your followers, my daughter would be sitting in her seat right now." Her anger had gotten the best of her, and she was past the point of no return. She rushed over, slapped the book out of Emily's hands, and then leaned over and stared into the head cheerleader's eyes. Saliva dropped from the points of her teeth and onto the desk as she squeezed the sides of the wooden desk. Tears streamed out of her red eyes as she breathed heavily.

"You said if there was anything you could do. There is something you can do." She exhaled. "While you darken my classroom, I don't want to hear a peep from you unless it's school related. And by looking at your pathetic grades, you shouldn't have a word to say." She slapped the middle of the desk, startling Emily and every student in the room with the exception of Sammy. "Now pick your book up off the floor and read over the material so you can fail another test."

As Mrs. Stevens nonchalantly strolled back to her desk, leaving Emily a quivering emotional mess, Sammy reveled in the outburst. He gazed over at the empty seat that had belonged to Cathy and thought, *You would have been so proud of your mother.*

After class ended, Sammy made his way toward the door with a huge grin on his face, but Mrs. Stevens stopped him before he could exit.

"Before you leave, I want to speak with you," she requested. She patiently waited until every student had departed. "First, I want to apologize for my unprofessional outburst."

He brushed off her comment with a wave of his hand followed by a chuckle. "If anyone deserved to be put in their place, it was Emily Keele."

"Second, I want to thank you for coming to see me. But there was something I was wondering." She rubbed her chin. "I didn't see you at my daughter's funeral. Why?"

Sammy was shaken by the question but quickly came up with a response. "The moment I got there, I was so saddened that I became physically ill. I could not go through with attending the funeral."

"I understand," Mrs. Stevens said and then gave Sammy a hug. "There is something else I want to talk to you about."

"Anything."

"I hope you still intend on tutoring Emily like we discussed."

Sammy broke the embrace and strolled over to the window. He watched as cars drove down the public street in front of the school and then diverted his attention to the school parking lot, searching for Cathy's car.

"I could not believe my eyes when I saw Emily at Cathy's funeral. I was shocked and appalled, and even though every fiber of my being wants to deny your request, I will honor my commitment."

He walked over to Cathy's seat, kissed his fingertips, and then placed them softly on top of the chair. He then pulled Mrs. Stevens into an embrace, and the two shed tears. Afterward, he grabbed his bag and, with a heavy heart, exited the classroom.

He traversed the hallways, having a full conversation with himself about how to handle Emily. Despite the odd stares and whispers from his fellow students, he did not care as he continued on his path.

He reached the locker area, where he spotted Emily with Joanne and Rose on both sides. He remained quiet and just stared at the trio from a distance. Hatred filled his thoughts, but he knew he could not allow those feelings to consume him, so he took a deep breath and approached them.

Just as the three shared a laugh, Sammy rudely interrupted by placing himself in the middle of their triangle. He stood directly in front of Emily. "I will remain your tutor. We will meet at the library after school, and do not waste a second of my time by being late."

She attempted to express her gratitude, but Sammy was not interested. He rolled his eyes the moment she opened her mouth and left before she could utter a word.

When the final bell rang, it was music to Sammy's ears. The day had been long and extremely taxing, but mostly he was elated that he did not have to sit through another tedious class. He walked out the front door of the school and immediately retrieved Cathy's picture from the front pocket of his book bag. Just as he was about to tell her how his day went and how much he missed her presence, Jonathon approached from the rear and placed his arm around Sammy's shoulders but regretted the action once he saw what was in Sammy's hand.

"I'm sorry, bro." Jonathon took a step back. "I'll leave you alone and give you some privacy."

"Do not be silly." Sammy returned the picture back to his bag. "I was just about to find you."

"I don't think you should be alone any longer." Jonathon closed the space between them. "You should come to my house and hang out."

A smile appeared on Sammy's face as a swell of emotion radiated through his body. He pulled Jonathon into an embrace. "You are a true friend." He took a deep breath and then exhaled, feeling like a huge load had been lifted from his shoulders. "You seem to have appeared just when I needed you the most."

"Funny!" Jonathon said and began to chuckle. "Most people say I appear when I'm not wanted."

They shared a much needed laugh. It was cathartic for both of them because Sammy was in pain and needed a friend, while Jonathon also endured pain and was glad to be a friend to someone instead of a hindrance. A short time later, they arrived at Jonathon's house. Before he could open the door, Lola beat him to the punch and greeted them with a huge smile.

She saw through the façade of Sammy's fake smile and stopped both boys before they entered the house.

She hugged her son and then took his book bag. "Why don't you go into the kitchen and prepare some snacks"—she turned to Sammy— "while your friend and I take a walk around the block."

Sammy watched Jonathon enter the house, and the moment the door closed, his smile disappeared because he knew he could be his true self around Lola. As the two strolled to the end of the block, Sammy thanked her for coming to his aid and saving him from everyone seeing his celestial side at the church.

He stopped and looked up to the sky. "I have taken millions of lives over countless millennia, and I have witnessed countless humans crying when I did so." He paused and then shook his head. "I could not empathize with them, but I have learned a very painful lesson."

She took him by the hand and pulled him close. "Anytime you need to talk, just let me know. I will always be here to listen."

Just as Sammy was about to respond, he looked back and saw Jonathon standing in the middle of their street, waving his arms in an attempt to get their attention. "I think the snacks are finished and Jonathon wants us to return to your house."

"We will go only if you are alright."

Sammy gave her hand a slight squeeze and then kissed the back of it. "I am not all the way fine, but I will be one day." With a genuine smile, Sammy motioned for them to return to the house, where they enjoyed milk and chocolate chip cookies while engaging in delightful conversation that took his mind off his sorrow.

Later that evening, after a pleasant, much needed visit with his friend, Sammy returned home. He hugged Riley, who was waiting patiently for him to come home, and then grabbed a bottle of water before retiring to his room. He sensed that Riley wanted to talk about his feelings, but he was tired and assured his uncle that all was well.

Upon entering his bedroom, he slowly closed and locked the door, but his eyes never strayed from the picture of Cathy that sat on the nightstand. He sat down on the bed, took a huge drink of water to wet his parched throat, and then told his friend about his trying day. He explained the challenges he faced and once again begged her for strength to forge through his coming days, weeks, and months. He placed an endearing kiss on her forehead before placing the portrait on his pillow and lying beside her. Tomorrow presented a new set of challenges, and he needed all the rest he could get, so he turned off the light and retired for the evening.

The next day after school, Sammy sat in the public library off campus, waiting for Emily. He looked at his watch, seething because she was three minutes late. Just as minute four arrived, Sammy was gathering his belongings to leave when Emily rushed into the building.

"I'm so sorry." She stood before him, dropping books out of her bag. "There was an accident and I got held up in traffic." She begged for his forgiveness and promised it would never happen again.

Unpersuaded and showing apathy for her excuses, Sammy rolled his eyes and continued toward the door. Just as he was about to exit, Emily grabbed his arm.

"Please don't go." She moved in close so no one else in the library could hear their conversation or, more importantly, her begging. "I need you." She paused as tears welled in her eyes. "That is hard for me to admit, but I need you, so I'll get down on my hands and knees and beg you to stay if that'll change your mind."

Sammy took a deep breath. Even though he wanted to walk out the door and leave Emily humiliated, he had a promise to keep. So he snatched his arm away and turned to face her.

"Next time be prompt. My time is valuable, and I will not waste it waiting for you." He exhaled heavily and gazed at her with a cold stare. "If you are late again, I do not care if it is a traffic accident or a death in your family, this unholy union will come to an end." He adjusted his bag on his shoulder. "Now take your seat and open your book so we can get to work."

"Why are you being so nasty to me?"

"You have not seen my nasty side, so I suggest you do as I tell you or you can find someone else to help you with your studies." He rolled his eyes.

"Now go take your seat and open your book while I go get a drink of water."

As their session began, Sammy watched as Emily read over her notes. Mrs. Stevens's words that Cathy's accident had been caused by an argument instigated by Emily's friends played over and over again in his mind. His anger grew, and he had no problem displaying his emotion. Emily could not do anything right. He berated her each time she got an answer wrong, dismissed her when she got one correct, and pounded on the table when she took too long to answer, which caught the attention of other students.

Unbeknownst to Sammy, one student in particular took interest in the manner in which he spoke to Emily. A male friend of Slade's who was not a member of the football team went into the restroom, called Slade, and informed him of Sammy's antics but embellished the story by claiming physical contact was made.

A short time later, as the session came to its end, Sammy's anger toward Emily had eased. He had even managed to crack a smile and dole out a compliment after she got an answer correct, which made her smile as well.

They were conversing and making plans for their next session when a loud ruckus at the front of the library caught their attention. Sammy's eyes narrowed and his fist clenched when he saw Slade rapidly approaching flanked by five of his teammates. Their demeanors radiated bad intentions. Sammy rose to his feet and watched as the football star violently removed his jacket and slammed it to the ground.

He chuckled as he stared into each of their faces. "You guys are clearly lost. This is a place filled with books, and we all know that is not your forte."

"I heard how you have been talking to my girl, and it's time that you are put in your place and taught some manners, tough guy," Slade shouted, spit flying from his mouth.

Sammy nonchalantly wiped the spittle from his cheek. "Are you going to teach me this lesson?" He turned his attention to Alex. "Or are you going to have someone else do it for you?" He chuckled once again but this time in a menacing tone. "I heard about your friend that got killed. It looks like he was in the wrong place at the wrong time." Sammy turned his attention back to Slade. "And the brutal manner in which he died … He clearly had no idea what or who he was messing with." He winked at Slade, which exacerbated the football star's fervor.

The moment Slade went to lunge at Sammy, Emily stepped between them. She placed a calming hand on Sammy's chest and then glared at Slade with contempt.

"Why are you even here?" she asked with attitude in her tone. "I'm not your girlfriend. You've made that perfectly clear. So don't use me as an excuse to start something with him." She turned to Sammy and apologized for Slade's petulant actions.

"Why are you apologizing to this punk?" Slade asked harshly. "He disrespects you, treating you like gum under his shoe, and you apologize to him?"

"I don't need you to come to my rescue. Next time you feel the need to do so, do us both a favor. Don't." Emily turned to Sammy and apologized again before excusing herself to go to the restroom.

Sammy laughed mockingly and gathered his belongings. He stopped and gazed at Slade and his minions. "It looks like someone does not bow at your alter any longer, superstar." He smirked and made his way past Slade, bumping his shoulder with his own. He strolled away slowly, knowing they were watching him and basking in the knowledge that they could not do anything about it.

Days and nights passed, each one playing out like the one prior. Sammy sat on the back porch, enjoying a refreshing glass of orange juice. The cool night air brought a chill to his skin, but he found it invigorating as he gazed at the sky, which was littered with stars and a full moon. He took a deep breath and smiled as he experienced something unfamiliar: boredom. He did not mind the experience. After dealing with the constant hustle and bustle of everyday life as a high school student, he found that some time alone with nothing to do and no one around was quite satisfying. He took the opportunity to use his angel eyes and see things that his other sight would not allow.

His eyes pierced the darkness and focused on two spiders mating in a tree in the neighbor's yard. He took the last sip of his beverage and placed the glass next to the swing, but a noise a few blocks away caught his attention. It was a bat's squeal as it had the unfortunate luck of crossing the path of an owl and becoming its evening meal. He watched nature take its course, though the ferocity of the owl made him squeamish and he had to turn away. He sat back and closed his eyes, running his fingers through his curly locks. Just before he was about to enter the house, he heard the door open.

He kept his eyes closed and switched his vision back to its alternative state. Then he opened them and saw Riley emerge from the house.

He sat up, grabbed the glass, and slid over to his left to make room. "Hey, Uncle Riley. To what do I owe the pleasure?"

"Do I need a reason to spend time with my nephew?" Riley smiled, but his grin was not genuine, and Sammy knew as much.

"What is on your mind?" Sammy moved closer with an expression of concern.

Riley chuckled as his gaze made its way down to his hand. "You are very wise beyond your years." He reached into his pocket and pulled out a small black box. He swallowed hard and then softly caressed the box, silently collecting his thoughts.

"What seems to be the problem?" Sammy asked.

Riley wiped his eyes and took a deep breath before turning his attention to Sammy. "When your mother was days away from giving birth to you, we were out at the mall." He looked into Sammy's eyes. "We were doing some last-minute shopping, preparing for your arrival, but something caught her eye." He opened the box and pulled out a silver necklace with a heart- shaped sapphire encased in a diamond halo. "She thought it was the most beautiful thing she had ever seen." He paused. "That is, until she saw your face for the first time." He placed the box on the swing between them but held the necklace in the air and smiled as it sparkled in the moonlight. "She was going to give this to you when the time was right." He shrugged. "She never said when that was, but I think the time is right, so here it is."

Sammy hesitated, not knowing what to do. He stared at the trinket and then looked at Riley, who met his gaze. He was in the midst of a conundrum. On one hand, he did not want to disappoint his uncle by turning down the gesture. But on the other hand, he was not the rightful receiver of the gift and did not want to accept something that did not belong to him. He stuttered and turned away. As the necklace came into his personal space, he stood up abruptly, which upset Riley.

He walked to the edge of the porch, ignoring Riley as he called his name, each time louder than the previous one. Sammy needed Michael's guidance and wisdom but could not call for him in the presence of a human. Many thoughts ran through his mind as he strolled to the middle of the yard. His heart broke for Riley because he loved his sister so much. It was evident that he was still in pain even after all these years. Sammy could not accept the gift. When he turned to face Riley, he was surprised to see him standing directly in front of him.

"What is your problem?" Riley asked with anger in his tone. "I offer you a gift from your mother and you act like you don't want it."

"Uncle Riley, it is not that I do not want it." Sammy looked at the necklace and then back at Riley. "I feel like you should keep it."

Riley was incensed by Sammy's response and called him scathing things like ungrateful and self-centered. He then focused on the angel necklace that hung from Sammy's neck and tried to snatch it off but was surprised and confused when it would not budge, let alone break.

"What in the world is that thing made of?"

Sammy pushed Riley's hand away. "How dare you try to break my property!"

"How dare you refuse something from your mother!"

"Do not put your hand on my belongings again!" Sammy shouted.

As soon as those words left Sammy's mouth, Riley reared back and slapped Sammy across the face. Sammy was stunned by Riley's action. He placed his hand against the left side of his face. The blow had not hurt him, but it took all he could muster inside not to retaliate against the man who had watched over him since he arrived on earth. He waited for an apology, but instead more harsh words followed. He closed his eyes as his breathing intensified. His fists clenched as he felt his eyes shift to their celestial state.

His anger built as the words continued to flow. Just as he was about to erupt, he felt a hand on his shoulder, followed by Michael's voice in his ear, pleading for him to calm down and display restraint instead of giving into wrath.

The barrage of words finally came to a stop and not a moment too soon. Luckily for everyone involved, Michael's words were able to soothe the savagery that was growing inside. Without a word, Sammy walked past Riley, who tried to apologize for his actions, but his words rang hollow. Instead, Sammy remained quiet, not even looking over in his uncle's direction. He grabbed the glass and walked through the back door and up to his room. He closed the door and rubbed his face once more. Then he crushed the glass in his hand. The cuts were multiple and deep, but they closed within seconds, leaving no sign of trauma. Despite the evening being young, Sammy lay down in his bed, grabbed the picture of Cathy, and began to tell her about his day, ignoring the knocks on his door and the pleas and apologies that came from the other side.

Meanwhile, across town Slade and his friends were devouring a platter of cheeseburgers at a popular fast-food restaurant. After taking a huge bite of his eighth burger, Slade heard Emily's laughter from the front of the restaurant and quickly turned to see if she was with Sammy. He then thought back to the confrontation in the library.

"I can't believe how she sided with that punk over me." He grabbed his burger and quickly finished it. "My patience with him is at its end."

"The way he threw Chavo in our faces. It was like he was telling us he killed him," Alex added.

"Don't make me laugh," Slade said, rolling his eyes. "Dude is a wannabe tough guy but is soft as tissue." He stood up after finishing his soda and then grabbed the last cheeseburger on the platter. "I need some air." He took a few bites of the sandwich and then tossed the small piece onto the table. "You guys clean this mess up and pay the bill. I'll be outside."

CHAPTER 15

A few weeks passed and nothing much changed in Sammy's life. Despite Riley's attempts to make things right, Sammy could not get over the fact that he had crossed the line by slapping him in the face, and all because Sammy had respectfully turned down a gift. Their relationship had suffered immensely because of that moment. The two had gone days without uttering a word to one another. But one thing that had changed was Sammy's treatment of Emily. Early on in their tutorial sessions, Sammy had harshly admonished her for giving wrong answers and berated her about wasting his time; now he took the time to correct her and even gave her encouragement instead of demeaning words.

It was a Monday. Sammy was in the library with Emily, and it was nearing the end of a long, successful session. He clutched his stomach as it growled from hunger—a sound that did not go unnoticed by Emily.

"Was that your stomach?" she asked with a chuckle.

"Yeah. The meal they provided at lunch was less than desirable. So needless to say, I have barely eaten all day." He stretched and began to place his books in his bag. "I will go home and find something to eat, if my stomach will wait that long."

"Well," Emily looked down at her books and then back at Sammy, "you've done so much for me, maybe I can do something for you."

Sammy's interest was piqued. He leaned forward. "What do you have in mind?"

"I can take you to get a bite to eat."

Sammy smiled and leaned back in his chair. "I appreciate the sentiment, but I will get something to eat when I arrive home."

"I know you have every reason to hate me, but I really like being around you." She placed her hand on his arm. "You're so smart and mature, unlike the juvenile boys I'm around every day." She gazed into his eyes. "I just want to pay you back for everything you've done for me."

"You know who else liked my company?" Sammy snatched his arm away as his demeanor and tone changed. "Cathy liked my company, but because of you, she is not around anymore." He grabbed his bag, hoisted it over his shoulder, and abruptly stood. "I will see you tomorrow at school and not a minute before."

Sammy made his way toward the door as his anger began to rise, but before he reached the exit, Emily stepped in his path.

"Before you leave, please hear me out." She took a deep breath. "I wasn't on the phone with Cathy that day. It was Joanne and Rose." She broke eye contact and then paused for few seconds. "Cathy hit me that day and was kicked out of practice. So my friends called her and things escalated from there." She shook her head. "We had our differences, but she was still a cheerleader; she was one of us."

"The differences that you speak of were brought on by you." He turned away. "You disrespected her mother in front of her and the rest of the class, and it was not the first time I am sure."

"Yes. I will accept my part in this whole thing, but what happened to her made me see the error of my ways and makes me want to be a better person," Emily said passionately as tears gathered in her eyes.

"I have been around a lot of people in my lifetime, and in my experience, people do not change." He looked her up and down and then smirked in disgust. "I will see you at school tomorrow, Ms. Keele."

Sammy exited the library and stopped just outside the door. He felt bad after the exchange with Emily. Even though he did not want to admit it to her or himself, he had seen the change in her attitude. He just could not bring himself to admit it out loud because then it would be real.

As darkness fell upon the city of Virginia Beach, he began to make his way home. He was halfway down the block when he noticed a car approaching on his left, which made him wary. Because of the tension between him and Slade and his friends, he could not be too careful.

When the car pulled up next to him, he jumped to the side with his fists clenched, prepared for a confrontation. The moment he saw it was Emily behind the wheel, he relaxed and breathed a sigh of relief. "I thought our business had concluded at the library."

"It's dark out here. The least you can do is let me give you a ride home since you refuse to let me buy you dinner," she said, displaying that beautiful smile.

He wanted to turn her down, but he was facing a three-mile walk and when he gazed over his shoulder, he saw the clock read nine. He smiled as he reluctantly approached the car and shook his head. "I will allow you to give me a ride this one time." He entered her car and stared into her face, admiring her beauty.

"Are you sure I can't entice you to grab a bite to eat with me?" Emily asked while twirling her hair.

Again, he wanted to say no, but the pain that permeated his stomach, coupled with her striking beauty, made the offer too difficult to refuse. "Okay, you win." He smiled. "Can I use your phone to call my uncle to inform him I will be late? My phone is dead."

"Of course," she said, handing him her phone and giving him a playful wink.

"Where are we going to dine?" Sammy asked as he dialed his uncle's number.

"I was thinking Marty's. They have wonderful cheeseburgers."

A short time later, Sammy arrived home with a full stomach and a smile after having a delightful evening with Emily. He had not laughed in the company of a female since Cathy's passing, and for the first time since then, he had not thought of her when around students from the high school. After entering his room, he quietly shut the door. When he turned on his light, he was surprised to find Riley sitting in the chair that Michael usually occupied when he made his unexpected visits. Sammy stared at his uncle before tossing his book bag onto his bed and asking Riley to depart because it had been a long day, but his request fell on deaf ears.

Instead, Riley approached Sammy, wrapped his arms around him, and squeezed tightly.

"My actions were inexcusable, and I do apologize." Riley kissed the top of Sammy's head. "I just wanted you to wear your mother's necklace that she picked out for you, and when you denied it, I lost it."

Sammy broke the embrace and took a few seconds to collect his thoughts before responding. He did not want to let his anger cloud his judgment, so he tried to cleanse his mind and be thoughtful of his next words. "I understand your frustration, but for you to strike me just because I wanted you to keep the necklace a little while longer ..." Sammy shook his head and turned away as he felt his emotions stirring.

"I'm sorry, son." Riley cautiously approached. "Words cannot express how truly sorry I am."

Sammy knew in his heart that Riley's apology was sincere, and he could not harbor ill will toward the person who had been assigned to look over him. He turned toward his uncle and smiled. "If you get a large pizza tomorrow with everything on it, then maybe I will forgive you."

They shared a laugh and then an embrace. They promised to communicate better so there would be a better understanding. When Riley departed, it felt as if a huge weight had been lifted off Sammy's shoulders. He felt that he was growing as a human, and that made him feel better about the conversation.

After returning from the bathroom a few minutes later, he found Michael sitting in his usual spot. "To what do I owe the pleasure?" Sammy asked.

"I just came to check on you." Michael replied as he crossed his legs. "I am glad to see that you are forgiving. You have stopped being so nasty to that young lady, and the way you handled the unfortunate situation with Riley ..." He began to slow clap. "Bravo." He made his way to his feet. "You have to understand that you are dealing with teenagers while also being a teenager being cared for by an adult. That is something new for you."

Sammy smirked. "I think I am doing a pretty good job considering." He walked to the bed to take a seat.

"I commend you on your efforts." Michael smiled. "I will leave you to tend to your affairs."

"Before you go"—Sammy stood with an inquisitive expression on his face—"I need you to answer a question."

"Anything," Michael quickly replied.

"Who is taking my place while I am here on earth?"

The joyous smile Michael had displayed quickly disappeared. His expression turned serious. He stood silent as Sammy waited with bated breath for a response.

"Well?" Sammy asked. "Are you going to answer my question?"

"No!" Michael answered with a deep tone. "I want you to focus on being a thriving teenage boy in high school, not worry about celestial business."

Sammy objected, but Michael did not acknowledge his words. Instead, he simply disappeared without saying another word, which frustrated Sammy to no end.

The next day, Sammy arrived at school and found Emily standing by his locker. He tried not to smile, but it was futile, as she was sight for sore eyes. "I'm sorry if I overstepped my bounds." Emily bit her bottom lip. "I just wanted to thank you for spending time with me last night. I had a great time."

Sammy felt a spark in his chest and butterflies in his stomach as he gazed into her beautiful gray eyes. He debated whether he should move in closer or keep his distance, but when he noticed Slade watching their every move from the end of the row of lockers, the choice was easy.

He leaned against the locker, standing very close to the head cheerleader, and rubbed her arm. "Thank you for treating me to that delicious burger and giving me a ride home." He leaned in so his mouth was next to Emily's ear. "I am looking forward to seeing you later."

He cut his gaze to Slade, who was visibly seething, and that brought joy to Sammy. He knew Slade's imagination was running wild because he was not privy to their conversation, but their flirtatious mannerisms were enough to send the superstar into a jealous frenzy. Sammy took Emily's hand in his and kissed the back of it. He smiled at her before departing.

He walked past Slade, who was barely able to contain his anger. The moment Sammy was past him, he heard Slade punch the locker. When Sammy turned to investigate the noise, he saw Slade storming off as his friends approached. It was a sight to behold.

CHAPTER 16

Later that day, Sammy sat in the back of history class, waiting for Mrs. Stevens to arrive to administer the big test. While others studied and exuded concern, he did not have a care in the world because he had lived through every event that was printed in the book sitting closed on his desk. He turned his attention to Emily, who was frantically reviewing her notes, trying to absorb as much last-minute information as possible. He knew she needed to calm down, so he whispered her name. The moment she turned around and flashed that smile, his heart fluttered.

"You will do just fine," he whispered and crossed his fingers, wishing her luck.

Just as she was about to respond, all conversation ceased and Mrs. Stevens rambled into the room with her belongings clutched next to her bosom. She dumped her things onto her desk and ordered everyone to close their books and put their notes away.

Sammy watched Mrs. Stevens slowly move up and down the aisles, handing out the test and wishing everyone luck. When she reached Emily, her demeanor quickly changed. Her smile turned into a scowl. She slammed the paper onto Emily's desk and rolled her eyes before moving onto the next student, for whom her smile reappeared.

Once she reached Sammy, he tried to get her attention and ask her about her actions toward Emily, but she ignored him, placing the paper on his desk and returning to her seat. Sammy knew something was bothering the teacher, but a classroom filled with students was not the place to spark a conversation. He knew it would have to wait.

When the test started, Sammy examined the paper, which had fifty questions. Five minutes later, he was finished. After handing in the test, he made his way back to his seat but slowed once he reached Emily. He tapped her on the shoulder and tried to whisper a few words of encouragement, but Mrs. Stevens stopped that by harshly ordering him back to his seat. He was confused by the treatment he received from Mrs. Stevens, and the cold stare he endured was puzzling, but he kept quiet and bided his time.

A short time later, the bell rang and all the students stood and made their way toward the door, where Mrs. Stevens was waiting. She handed each student their graded test as they exited her room, but when Sammy passed, she avoided eye contact and her face was devoid of emotion, which puzzled him.

He made his way down the hall to his next class, but his thoughts remained with his teacher. He questioned what he could have possibly done to draw her ire and contemplated a few times about circling back and discussing the matter with her, but he decided to give her some time. He would address the matter later. He was not too far down the hall when he heard his name bellowed over the other students' banter. When he turned, he saw Emily rapidly approaching. He stopped to allow the head cheerleader to reach him but quickly noticed the trepidation etched on her face.

"What seems to be the problem?"

"That test was really hard, and I'm afraid to see what I got." She held the folded paper in her hand. "What did you get on the test?"

"I got a perfect score." He smiled. "I am sure you did fine as well."

"I'm not as smart as you," she said as her confidence plummeted. "I need to pass this class to graduate on time." She shook her head as tears began to well in her eyes. "Do you know how humiliating it'll be not to graduate on time and to have to go to summer school?"

"You do not know what you scored on the test." He pushed her hand that was holding the test toward her chest. "At least look before you make arrangements for summer school."

She tried to open the test a few times but was crippled by fear. "I want you to do it." She shoved the paper against his stomach. "I can't do it."

Sammy laughed and took the test from her loose grasp. The moment he opened the paper, his expression turned from happy to sad. He gazed at her and shook his head. "I am so sorry that I failed you." He looked at the paper and then back at her once again and saw the sadness in her face. "You got an 85 percent."

Her eyes widened as she ripped the paper from his hands. She let out a loud shriek the moment she saw her test score. Then she turned her attention back to him. "Why would you do that to me?" Elation overcame her, and she playfully punched his arm. "The look on your face made me believe I failed the test."

"You did not get a perfect score on the test, so I feel that I failed you," he replied seriously.

"Are you kidding me?" She gave him a hug and a kiss on the cheek. "I would've gotten a 55 percent if it weren't for you." She hugged him again. "I owe you everything."

"No!" he said quickly. "You did all the work; you committed to learning the mundane material, so this accomplishment is yours and yours alone."

She placed her hand on his forearm. "You're something else." She paused and then gazed deeply into his eyes. "These boys in this school are so quick to pound their chests and take credit for everything, even if it isn't deserved, but you're so modest, so humble." She was amazed as she stared at him with a gleam in her eye. "You'll deflect the credit and place it on others when you're the reason for the success." She moved in close. "I want to show my appreciation. I would love to take you out to dinner and to see that new horror movie that I've heard so much about. What do you say?"

Sammy swallowed the massive amount of saliva that had accumulated in his mouth. His heart skipped a beat as he was mesmerized by her beauty and seduced by the smell of her perfume. He wanted nothing more than to spend an evening with Emily. She was his crush, his unattainable trophy, but his emotions were torn. He felt he still owed Cathy his fidelity. Even though they had just been friends, they had been on the cusp of so much more. He took a step back as Emily waited for his answer. Just as she moved closer and touched his chest, which sent a shock wave through his body, the bell rang. For him, it came not a moment too soon.

"Can we discuss this matter at a later time?" "Yes." She smiled. "I'll hold you to it."

Later that day after school concluded, Sammy made his way to Mrs. Stevens's classroom for a discussion that was overdue. He stopped just outside her open door, reluctant to enter because he did not know how he would be received. He went to knock but stopped just short of it. Then he turned to leave. But he knew it had to be done at some time, so he took a deep breath and entered, only to find Mrs. Stevens sitting behind her desk, staring at a small green box.

"I do not mean to interrupt, but I would like to have a word with you if it is the right time."

Mrs. Stevens wiped tears from her eyes and motioned for Sammy to enter with a wave of her hand. "To what do I owe the unexpected pleasure?"

"Earlier you were not yourself when it came to your interaction with me, and I also noticed the hostility toward Emily, so I decided to stop by and see what was going on." Sammy took a seat at a desk across from her. "Was there something I did to make you mad?"

Silence filled the room as he stared at her, waiting for an answer. As she stared at the box on the desk, he approached her. Then he picked up the box slowly, his eyes never wavering from the teacher. "What is in this box?"

She stood, took the box from his hand, and then walked over to the window and stared at the bright sun while tears streamed down her cheeks. "Today is Cathy's birthday, and I bought her a pair of diamond earrings to celebrate her turning eighteen." She turned to face Sammy. Her eyeliner had run because of her tears. "I received this earlier this morning." She wiped her eyes. "The company made a mistake and delivered this to me and my gift to my house." She opened the box, exposing the diamond earrings. "Cathy saved up some money and bought me a pair of earrings so she would have a gift to give to me to thank me for giving her life." She wiped her eyes once again and then returned to her desk, as the grief was becoming overwhelming. "Can you believe that? She bought me a gift for her birthday."

Sammy rushed in and wrapped his arms around Mrs. Stevens as she began to crumble. He stared at the box as she placed it on her desk. He closed his eyes as his heart began to break once again at the unbelievable story he had just heard. He did not attempt to say any words to ease her grief; he knew none could. So he just provided her a much needed shoulder to cry on and an ear to listen.

After the commiserating had ended and an apology was given and accepted, Sammy needed some advice, so he walked over to the door, closed it, and then returned to his seat. "I need to have a word with you. Do you have time?"

"Of course I do," she answered with a smile.

"Emily asked to take me to dinner for helping her with her studies." He looked away. "I do not know what to do."

"I thought this would happen." She smirked and then rolled her eyes. "What do you want to do?"

"I would like to go, but I do not want to besmirch Cathy's memory." He lowered his head. "I want to respect her always."

Mrs. Stevens walked over and placed her hand on Sammy's shoulder. "I think you and my daughter would have fallen in love and been together forever. It would have been like a romance novel, but unfortunately life had other plans." She took a deep breath and exhaled. "You need to live your life and not be stuck in this moment. She would not have liked your choice of girls to spend your time with, but she would want you to have fun and be very happy." She gave him a hug. "You're a very special young man, so you go on that date and be happy."

He closed his eyes as a tear fell from each. A slight smile graced his lips as he thanked Mrs. Stevens for understanding. He stood as she made her way back to her desk. He pulled her into an embrace and squeezed tightly as his tears continued to flow.

"You are a wonderful woman and an even more wonderful mother. Thank you."

After the emotional conversation, Sammy had gotten the answers he needed. As he headed toward his locker, his heart was heavy and his emotions were raw, but his conscience was clear. School had long since let out, so Sammy was surprised to find Emily leaning against his locker, holding her books close to her chest, patiently waiting.

"What are you doing here?" He approached her with a huge grin.

"We had a conversation earlier, and I wanted to have the answer before we parted ways for the day." She moved in close and rubbed his cheek with her hand. "Will you go out with me Friday night?"

"I would love to go out with you, but I am sorry to say that I cannot." He turned away in shame.

"May I ask why?"

"I do not have a vehicle and cannot pick you up for a proper date."

She took him by the hand and gently stroked it. "I have a very nice car, and I'll pick you up. And since I asked you out, I'll pay for everything. I just want to spend some time with you outside the library and this school." She moved in close. "So will you do me the honor of letting me take you out on a date?"

"No!" He gazed into her beautiful gray eyes. "It will be my honor to go out on a date with you, Ms. Keele."

Later that afternoon, Sammy stood on his back porch, staring into the distance as the sun was about to set. He thought about his upcoming date with Emily, but his mind could not help but think about his time with Cathy, especially since it was her birthday. He reminisced about the time they had shared—the conversations, the laughs, and the fact that she was the one who had introduced him to pizza. He closed his eyes and pictured their long walks on the beach. He touched his lips when he thought about the soft, tender kisses they had enjoyed. He could still smell her sweet scent and smiled at the thought of her beautiful dimples.

Just as a tear escaped his eye, he heard the door open. He turned to see Riley exit the house and join him on the porch. He wiped his eyes in an attempt to conceal his emotions and turned his head away when his uncle tried to investigate.

"Are you all right, son?" Riley asked.

Sammy turned to face his uncle, refusing to hide the tears that had gathered. "Today is Cathy's birthday." He looked to the sky. "I would like it very much if you would take me to the cemetery so I could visit her."

Riley placed his arm around Sammy's shoulders and pulled him in tightly. "I'd be more than happy to take you to see her. I think it would be therapeutic if you sat and talked to her for a while." He kissed Sammy on the side of his head. "Whenever you're ready, just let me know."

"I am ready now, Uncle. I am ready now."

Minutes later, they arrived at the cemetery. Sammy felt the enormity of the situation, to see Cathy's tombstone, her final resting place, for the first time. His insides began to churn. He sat in the passenger seat for a few minutes, just staring out the window at the other headstones and taking deep breaths. In the back of his mind, he knew he had seen most of these people in their last minutes on earth. He lowered his head because he felt that he could not endure seeing Cathy lying under a pile of dirt. Just as he was about to tell Riley to drive away, he felt his uncle's hand on his leg.

"You're a strong young man, and I know that you can do this," Riley said. "If you need me to come with you, just say the word and I'll be right next to you."

Sammy wanted to take Riley up on his offer, but he knew this was something he had to do alone. He closed his eyes, thought of Cathy's smile, and found the strength to forge through. "I can do this, Uncle. I am strong like you."

He opened the door and exited the car but did not take a step. He gathered his thoughts, trying to figure out what he wanted to say to his best friend and potential love, but in the end, he wanted it to be natural, so he slowly made his way toward her grave.

After reaching his destination, he stood and stared at her headstone for a few minutes. He kissed his fingertips and placed them on her name before kneeling. "I am not sure what the proper protocol is in this situation, but from what I gather, I am supposed to talk to you." He smiled as tears raced down his cheeks. "So we are going to have a conversation, if you do not mind."

He talked to her nonstop for about thirty minutes. He laughed a few times and cried a few more times. He spoke about school, and toward the end, he made it to the subject of going out on a date with Emily.

Just as he was about to leave, he apologized about not being honest about who he really was and why he could not tell her. Then he used his angel eyes to look beyond the earth and into her coffin to make sure she was intact and everything was perfect.

"I am glad you came to see her," a voice said from behind him.

Startled, Sammy quickly returned his eyes to their alternative state and then turned to find Michael standing a few feet away. "What are you doing here?"

"I just wanted to come and check on my friend," Michael replied.

"Is she all right up there?" Sammy approached the archangel. "Tell me she is doing fine."

"You know I do not have any contact with them once their souls exit their bodies." Michael knelt beside his friend. "But I think she is doing just fine." Sammy leaned forward and gave Cathy's headstone a kiss. "I think we are both doing fine." He turned to Michael. "I think I can finally move past this and begin to fully enjoy my time on earth again." He stood, shook Michael's hand, and flashed a smile before heading back to the car, where he spotted his uncle waiting outside the passenger door. He greeted Riley

with a hug and took a deep breath.

"I see the talk you had with her helped. Are you okay now?" Riley asked. "I am right as rain," Sammy replied, displaying a huge grin.

CHAPTER 17

The big day had arrived. It was date night, and Sammy was very nervous. He nibbled on his bottom lip as he paced the room, staring at five outfits he had laid out on his bed, hoping the perfect one would stand out from the rest. He turned to Jonathon, who sat at his desk, eating potato chips and drinking orange soda. He wanted to ask his opinion but was reminded that all his friend wore on a daily basis was all black and black eyeliner, so he thought better about seeking his advice where fashion was concerned.

Sammy was at his wit's end. He could not decide on an outfit. Just as he was about to grab his hair and yell, his door swung open and Riley appeared with a huge grin.

"Hey, son." Riley approached Sammy, placed his arm around his shoulders, and pulled him close. "How's your preparation coming along?" As the final word escaped his lips, Riley's gaze paused on the fifth outfit.

"I thought you were just going on a simple date." He made his way over to the bed. "Why do you have a suit and tie laid out?"

"I just want to look nice." Sammy shrugged. "Do you think that is a little too much?"

"Yes!" Riley said and then laughed. "There's no need to be so uptight. Just keep it simple and be yourself, and everything will be just fine."

A sense of calm settled over Sammy after hearing Riley's words, and his decision on an outfit became easy. He chose outfit number three, which consisted of an all-white polo shirt and a pair of black slacks.

After Riley and Jonathon departed, Sammy began to prep for his big day. After taking a shower and applying the right amount of cologne, he got dressed. He stood in front of the mirror and smiled as his stomach fluttered. This, in essence, was the girl of his dreams. Even though it was their first official date, it was a day he knew he would remember for the rest of his existence. He put the final touches on his hair and made his way downstairs to where Riley and Jonathon were waiting. The moment they saw him, huge smiles appeared on their faces, so Sammy knew he looked good.

"What time will she be here?" Riley asked.

"Seven," Sammy quickly answered. He looked at the clock on the wall and smiled when he realized she would be there in less than twenty minutes.

"What are your plans tonight?" Riley asked.

"Well, we are going to a fancy Italian restaurant and then to a movie." Sammy glanced at the clock once again, and his smile widened when five minutes had passed. "To tell you the truth, we could be going to watch flowers grow and it still would not matter."

"Do you have everything you need? Do you need some money?" Riley asked.

"Wait!" Jonathon intervened, stepping between them. "I thought she was paying for the entire date, so why would he need money?" He playfully slapped Sammy on his shoulder. "She got this."

"Oh my gosh," Riley uttered as he rolled his eyes, disgusted at Jonathon's comment. After shaking his head and then pausing, trying to extricate Jonathon's words from his memory, he turned his attention to his nephew. "I want you to be the perfect gentleman tonight, so when the check comes"— he retrieved his wallet from his back pocket and handed Sammy a one hundred dollar bill—"I want you to insist on paying."

Just as Sammy graciously accepted the money, he heard a loud beep from a car horn outside. He looked at the clock and then smiled. "She is early."

He raced to the front door but stopped just before exiting. He took a few deep breaths to collect his composure, not wanting to appear too excited. He removed the smile that stretched from ear to ear and took the time to straighten his clothes. He turned to his uncle and best friend and thanked them for being there for him. Finally, he opened the door but quickly stopped before leaving the house. His huge smile returned as he was pleasantly surprised to see Emily standing in front of him holding a single red rose while gazing at him with her alluring gray eyes.

It took all the restraint he could muster to keep from taking her into his arms and giving her the kiss he had wanted to give her the moment he first laid eyes on her. Instead, he turned his attention to the lovely rose in her hand. "I was under the impression that I was supposed to give you beautiful flowers."

Emily slowly approached and gave him a tender kiss on the cheek before presenting him the rose. "You're out of the ordinary, so I decided to do something out of the ordinary as well."

Sammy graciously accepted the rose and placed it in front of his nose. He closed his eyes as the delightful aroma filled his nostrils. He looked at her and then placed the palm of his hand against her cheek and gently stroked her face. "Thank you very much, Ms. Keele." He turned and handed the gift to his uncle. Then he took Emily by the hand and led her to her vehicle, which was parked in the driveway.

Hearing the car start, Riley rushed over to the living room window to get a glance of the car Emily drove. He could not believe his eyes as he turned to Jonathon. "You mean to tell me that a girl her age drives a convertible BMW?"

"You're aware that her father is the owner of Keele Textiles?"

"What!" Riley shouted, dropping the rose onto the couch. "The bank I work at handles their corporate account." He nodded in approval before turning to Jonathon. "Get your stuff together so I can have you home for dinner."

Meanwhile, as Sammy and Emily drove down the street, heading to their first destination, he could not help but admire her beauty, especially the way she looked in her blue form-fitting dress. Every time she looked in his direction, he would look away, trying not to let on that he was staring at her, but she knew differently.

"You look very handsome tonight," she said.

"Thank you," he replied and then turned in his seat to face her. "I know you wanted to pay for the date, and that is commendable, but I would not feel right if I did not contribute." He went to place his hand on her leg but stopped, feeling it was not appropriate at the time. "The least I can do is pay for the meal, and I will not take no for an answer."

"I do appreciate how you want to pay, but this was my idea." She placed her hand on his leg and gazed at him, batting her eyelashes. "You did so much for me, helping me out with my history class, so even though you won't take no for answer, you'll have to take no tonight because this date is on me." She slowly stroked his thigh, never breaking eye contact. "Besides, the next date can be on you if you feel that strongly about it."

"Next date?" He looked at her with a raised eyebrow. "You may not want another date with me after tonight."

She smirked and then winked at him. "Trust me. I want several dates with you, and nothing you will do tonight will change that."

A warm feeling permeated through Sammy's body at her words. He watched her as she drove, her hair blowing in the wind, and relished the sweet smell of her perfume. He admired how strong she was and the fact that she would not back down from his pseudo demand. He remembered the feelings that had radiated through his body the first time he saw Emily. Now those feelings had returned in full force. He was ecstatic that the nasty attitude she had once exuded had disappeared and her inner beauty finally matched her stunning outward splendor.

They arrived at their destination. The moment Sammy entered the restaurant, he was impressed by the ambiance. Soon, he was impressed by the cuisine. After stimulating conversation and a delectable dinner, they headed to part two of their date.

Sammy was all smiles as he sat back in his seat in the car, taking in the cool night air, but all that changed the moment they arrived at the movie theater and he saw the title of the show on the marquee: *The Reaper's Revenge!*

He turned to face her. "I hope you have something else in mind for us to see."

They exited the car, and she rushed to his side and took him by the hand. "I really love horror movies, and I heard this was really good." She kissed him on the cheek and then moved close to his ear. "I would love to share this with you."

He could not deny her even if he wanted to. He sighed deeply and then rolled his eyes. "What is this movie about?"

"It's about the grim reaper going around killing people." She shook as though she were scared. "I heard it was a bloody gore fest and the graphics are incredible."

Listening to the description of the movie made his blood boil. But even though his anger began to rise, he could not let his contempt show. To hear that a movie had been made suggesting that he would go on a murderous rampage sickened him to his core. He did not want any part of the untrue, deplorable depiction of his existence.

"I have a better idea. How about we go see that new French documentary?

I heard it was well made."

She quickly burst into hysterical laughter as they approached the ticket booth. "You're the total package. Not only are you a sight to behold, but you're a very funny guy." She reached into her purse and retrieved the money to pay for the tickets. Then she glanced over her shoulder at Sammy. "Trust me. You're going to enjoy this movie."

I know for a fact I will not, he thought but reluctantly made his way into the theater with a look of disdain etched on his face.

The movie lasted two hours and thirty minutes, and every second was hell for Sammy. The only solace he took was when the ending credits appeared on the screen, but then he had to listen to Emily's banter about how great it was for the entire walk to the car. He tried his best to hide his displeasure, but her constant raving and exuberance appalled him, and he could no longer hide his anger. Emily took notice.

"Is something wrong?" Her laughter stopped as concern replaced her joy. "You didn't enjoy the movie?"

He looked at her over the top of her convertible and noticed that the joy had dissipated from her face. The last thing he wanted to do was cause her unhappiness. He walked around the vehicle and joined her on the driver's side. Then he placed both palms on her cheeks.

"Why did you love this movie?" he asked in a calm, low voice.

"I love horror movies." She gazed into his eyes. "The way the grim reaper was stalking and killing those people and the way it all ended—I thought it was great."

A slight frown appeared on Sammy's face as he took a few steps back, contemplating how he wanted to approach the subject at hand. He turned back to her and then paused for a few more seconds as she waited patiently and intently for the next words from his lips.

"What are your opinions on the grim reaper?" He moved in close. "Do you think he is some evil monster that goes around killing people?" He placed his hand on his forehead, exasperated just thinking about the movie. "To even think that the angel of death wears this black cloak and goes around wielding a scythe is ludicrous."

"Why are you taking this to heart?" Emily placed a hand on Sammy's forearm.

"Can you answer my question please?"

Emily removed her hand, noticing the intense look in Sammy's eyes. "Anyone who goes around killing people is evil."

"He is not killing anyone."

A perplexed expression appeared on Emily's face as she wondered where the hostility was manifesting from—an expression Sammy knew all too well.

"I know for a fact that the angel of death is not evil and is not killing people. He was created to take souls from this life and send them to the hereafter." Sammy lowered his head and turned his back on her as tears flooded his eyes. "He does not take pleasure in his purpose and desires to be loved, not hated or feared or depicted as some psychopathic killer that levitates in the air and chases teenagers around to cut their heads off."

She wrapped her loving arms around his waist. "It's just a movie, babe.

Why do you care so much about the angel of death?"

Sammy slowly opened his eyelids, displaying his angel eyes. He thought it was time to come clean about who he was before they got any closer; he wanted her to know everything about him instead of the facade he had been portraying. His heart raced because he knew that in a few seconds, she would either be running away from him, screaming at the top of her lungs, or wrapping her arms around his neck and pulling him into a passionate kiss. The moment of truth had arrived, but just as he was about to turn and face Emily, a frightening streak of lightning flashed across the sky, followed by an ear-popping clap of thunder. The sound was so horrific that Emily scurried to the front of Sammy then threw herself into his arms.

Sammy felt Emily trembling, so he squeezed her tightly to provide comfort. He surveyed the parking lot and saw a multitude of people on the ground next to their cars, but a single entity caught his eye off to the far left. Michael stood with his wings spread and his sword in his right hand, preparing to attack. Since there was no sign of inclement weather, Sammy knew the histrionics had been a warning, and he got the message. He nodded, and his eyes returned to their alternative state.

He kissed the top of Emily's head and rested his head on top of hers. "The worst is over now, but I want you to know that I will always protect you."

"Promise?"

"Yes, I promise."

A short time later, they arrived at his uncle's house at the conclusion of their date. After he exited the car, Sammy looked up at the stars and admired their beauty.

He walked around to her side of the car, took her in his arms, and gave her a deep, passionate kiss. "I had a great time tonight and would love to see you again."

"I've got a game tomorrow, but I'm free on Sunday." She returned his kiss. "I would love to go on a picnic. I know this nice wooded area on the outskirts of town."

"That sounds lovely. I will bring the food."

"I can't wait." She gave him one last kiss. "I'll see you Sunday."

CHAPTER 18

The next night, as the autumn season lent a chill to the air, thousands of people filled Princess Anne's football stadium to watch their beloved team, and the city's favorite sports' star, perform. He did not disappoint. After scoring his third touchdown of the game, Slade sat on the bench while his teammates celebrated, listening to the crowd chant his name, feeding his already massive ego.

Alex approached his friend with a cup of water in each hand. He handed Slade his refreshment and refused to take a drink until Slade drank first. When Slade gave his nod of approval, Alex sat and then quenched his thirst with a huge drink. After he was finished, Alex crumpled the cup and threw it on the ground. He went back for a second helping, but during his journey, he noticed the cheerleaders in their tight, skimpy outfits, so he decided to take a few seconds to watch them perform their routine. Pleased at what he saw, the quarterback grabbed his refreshment and turned to return to his seat. Out of the corner of his eye, he saw Emily and Rose conversing, so he decided to eavesdrop on their private conversation.

"So you and Sammy have been spending a lot of time together lately." Rose nudged Emily's shoulder with hers. "How did the date go yesterday, and will there be another?"

Joanne leaned in on their conversation by looking over Rose's shoulder. "Yes, inquiring minds want to know."

The mere mention of Sammy's name produced a huge grin from Emily. She twirled her hair, shook her head, and let out a school-girl giggle that dumbfounded her friends. "He's amazing. We had a wonderful time on our date last night." She closed her eyes and thought back to their evening. "We had a fantastic dinner and then went to a movie; he did not like the movie that much, but when that loud clap of thunder hit, he held me in his strong arms." She wrapped herself in her arms and imagined it was Sammy holding her as she closed her eyes. "Words can't describe how he made me feel, and then he kissed me."

"He kissed you?" Rose shouted.

"Yes, and it was magical," Emily replied.

"I know you are excited and that's fine, but how does the whole Cathy thing play into this? They were very close, and you two were not friends," Joanne said.

"I don't think he's over her death and won't be anytime soon, but the way he looks at me, the way he kisses me, and the tender moments we share lead me to believe that he wants me and only me." Emily smiled once again. "We have a picnic planned for tomorrow, and I can't wait."

The three cheerleaders continued their banter, but Alex had heard all he needed to hear. He grabbed two more cups of water and returned to the bench, once again waiting for Slade's approval before taking a drink. "You won't believe what I just heard."

Slade finished his drink, focusing on the game and dismissing what Alex had to say. But when the quarterback repeated his statement, he reluctantly gave his attention to his friend. "Tell me."

"Evidently, Emily went out on a date with Sammy last night, and from what I heard, he could not keep his hands or lips off her."

For a few seconds, Slade did not say a word; he just peered at Alex with cold, dead eyes. Then, without warning, he abruptly stood and crushed the empty cup in his hand. Then he turned to face the three cheerleaders as they continued their conversation. He did not attempt to hide his disdain as he slammed his helmet to the ground, which garnered the attention of a few of his teammates in the vicinity, along with all the cheerleaders. His eyes focused on Emily, but just as he was about to make his way over to her, Alex grabbed his arm.

"If you go over there, all you will do is cause a scene," Alex whispered. "We have a game to play, and we need your head in the game. She can wait."

Alex's words seemed to temper the beast growing within him, and not a moment too soon, because when he looked around at the people in the stands on his side of the field, they had their eyes glued on him. He reached down, grabbed his helmet, and aggressively placed it on his head. He took one last scornful glance at Emily before jogging out onto the field.

A short time later, the game concluded in another impressive victory for Princess Anne. The team celebrated in the locker room, with the exception of their star player, who stood by his locker, sulking. Slade did not utter a word to anyone, often shrugging off attempts by his teammates to draw him into the celebration.

The thought of Sammy's hands all over Emily's body angered Slade to no end. As the images flowed through his mind, he could not contain his emotions. Without showering, he quickly got dressed, grabbed his jacket, and then stormed out of the locker room in search of his former girlfriend.

He burst through the locker room doors and surveyed the parking lot, looking for Emily. He spotted her about fifty feet away conversing and laughing with her friends. Thoughts about her conversation surged through his mind. He wondered if she was talking about Sammy and their date the prior evening, which only exacerbated his anger. Wearing clothes saturated with sweat and emitting a foul stench from playing four quarters of hard- fought football, he pushed his way through the crowd of well-wishers, ignoring their adulations as he focused on Emily. He shouted her name when he was within earshot and smarted when she rolled her eyes and broke away from her friends to make her way to her car.

His arrogance was not going to allow her to ignore his presence. His paced quickened when she arrived at her car door and searched her purse for her keys. He arrived the moment she opened the door slightly. He placed his hand on top of the door and forcefully pushed it closed.

"What is your problem?" she shouted. "I have things to do, and that does not include talking to you."

"How could you do this to me?" His demeanor reeked of desperation. "How could you go out with this punk?" He clenched his fist and then closed his eyes before glaring at her with contempt. "You're my girl, and I demand that you stop seeing that clown."

Emily stood silent for a few seconds, taking in Slade's words. Her facial expression went from surprise to disbelief to complete disgust. She placed her hand on her hip and then set her purse on the top of her car. "First, I'm not your girl and haven't been for a long time."

She pointed her key in his face to get her point across. "Second, who I see is none of your business." She laughed, but it was not derived from humor. "I could've had any boy in this school, but I wanted you. I turned down tons of dates from boys from around this city, hoping you would come to your senses and come back to me, but instead you screwed other girls who only wanted to be with you because of your football prowess. Yet I was still willing to take you back." A tear ran down her cheek as her emotions turned to sadness. "I loved you and wanted to be with you. I looked like a fool chasing you around like a puppy, being laughed at by your followers."

She snatched her purse off the top of her car and pushed him away from her door. Tears flowed freely down her cheeks as she thought back to the tumultuous time in her life when he had rejected her for other girls. She got into her car and turned the key in the ignition, but before departing, she rolled down her window.

"Who I see is no longer your business, so I suggest you go find those other girls that you wanted so badly and pay attention to them and leave me alone." She put her car into gear and sped off, leaving him standing in the middle of the dust her car kicked up while her friends and others watched and snickered at his expense.

The next day, Sammy woke early to prepare for his picnic with Emily. He made a few turkey sandwiches and gathered fried chicken from the refrigerator, along with chips and sodas. He finished the meal off with slices of cherry pie for dessert. He placed them neatly in a brown wicker basket. The moment he finished, he headed upstairs to shower for his outing.

Unlike their prior date, he did not haggle over his wardrobe. He just selected a sweatshirt and a pair of jeans. When his preparation was complete, he returned to the kitchen and sat, waiting for Emily's arrival. He did not have to wait long. He soon heard a slight knock on the front door, which brought a huge grin to his face. He rushed to the door, and when he opened it, his eyes widened, as her beauty was a sight to behold. He pulled her into a passionate kiss and then took her by the hand and led her into the kitchen. He did not procrastinate; he stayed just long enough to grab the basket and wave at his uncle, who was standing at the top of the stairs, and the couple made their way to her car.

He placed the basket in the back seat and then gave her one more kiss before they got in her car to begin their date. They drove for miles with the top down, allowing the wind to blow through their hair. He took in the scenery as they left the city and approached the rural part of the area.

"Where are we?"

Emily placed her index finger over her lips and winked at Sammy. Despite his many inquiries, she would not divulge a word of their whereabouts or their impending destination, which only added to the allure.

A short time later, they finally arrived at journey's end. After grabbing the basket, they walked hand in hand through a patch of woods.

They made their way to the middle of a grassy hill where a stream flowed at the base and set up camp. She spread a huge red blanket on the ground, and Sammy unpacked the basket. The two shared one last tender kiss before indulging in the food.

After the meal, they cuddled as they fed each other small bites of pie. Their conversation was pleasant, but they could not refrain from indulging in playful moments, tossing leftover pieces of bread from their sandwiches at one another. They shared tender kisses while gazing into each other's eyes and listening to the calming sounds of the flowing stream. They could have stayed there all day, but soon it was time to get back to the city. They slowly packed everything and began to make their way back to the car.

The hour had grown late, and the temperature had dropped as they made their way through the woods. Sammy held Emily close, providing warmth against the brisk autumn air while also giving affection as he peppered her cheek with loving kisses. The couple's banter was light as they made plans for their next date, but amid their conversation, Sammy heard a peculiar noise behind them. It sounded like sticks breaking. He quickly turned around to investigate but saw nothing. With apprehension, he faced forward while Emily rested her head against his chest and continued on his way. He remained quiet, looking around with every step as Emily continued to talk, but the moment they reached the middle of the woods, Sammy heard two more sticks break, which caused him to come to an immediate stop.

"Is something wrong?" Emily asked. "Why did we stop?"

Sammy did not answer. Instead, he searched for the perpetrator responsible for the noise. Unfortunately, he did not have to search long, as the culprits soon came into sight. Four wolves slowly emerged from the trees. Within seconds, they were just a few feet away.

A single black wolf, presumably the alpha, stood firm while the other three fanned out to the right and left. Their movement was deliberate yet concise, as if they were synchronized. Before the couple knew it, the wolves had them completely surrounded. Emily was terrified to the brink of hysteria. Sammy tried to keep her calm even though his heart was beating three times its normal rate. The wolves were positioned and primed for attack. Sammy knew he had to do something, and quickly, because time was not a luxury. As the animals inched closer, Sammy could feel the heat from their breath and saw the saliva dripping from their sharp teeth. It was now or never. He pressed Emily's head against his chest and displayed his angel eyes.

Immediately, the apex predators stopped in their tracks as they gazed into the cold, dark eyes of death incarnate. They backed away slowly because they recognized him. Death touched all living things; it was not just limited to humans. The predators had either seen him as they devoured their prey or when a member of their own had passed on. Either way, they did not want to be in death's presence. So the wolves backed away slowly and then turned, tucked their tails, and vacated the premises.

Once they were gone, Sammy breathed a sigh of relief as his eyes changed back to their alternative state. He held Emily tightly as she cried and assured her that all was well and they were safe. He closed his eyes and rested his head on hers as she continued to weep.

He had looked certain death in the face without blinking, but all he had been able to think of was Emily's well-being, even though his own existence had been in serious peril. He felt her tremble in his muscular arms, and as her legs gave way, he scooped her up and carried her to the car as she rested her head on his shoulder.

A few minutes later, the couple emerged from the woods. The car was finally in sight. With each step, Emily's grip around his neck got tighter and her whimpering grew louder. The moment he reached the vehicle, he retrieved the keys from her purse because her hands shook so badly that she could barely unzip the handbag. He unlocked the driver side door and tried to place her behind the wheel, but he was met with an objection.

"What are you doing?" She looked around in search of the predators. "We should be dead right now." Her breathing intensified as panic set in. "Where are they?" She maneuvered until she was in the back seat. "You have to get in the car and drive us out of here before they come back."

"Um …" He looked down at the keys in his hand and then back at her. "I do not know how to operate this vehicle."

She looked down at her hands, which were still shaking. "I can't drive down the street, let alone drive us back to town." She wiped her eyes and then looked at him as new tears replaced the old ones. "I think we'll spend the rest of the day teaching you how to drive."

"I do not think that is a good idea." He stepped back to examine her car and saw that it was in pristine condition; it did not have a mark or a dent anywhere. "I do not want to cause any harm to your vehicle."

She leaned forward and placed her hands on his. "I trust you with my life.

You can do this."

He shook his head, looked back at the trees, and saw something that startled him to his core. A pair of eyes stared back at him from the forest, but they did not belong to the wolves. They were mysterious and very ominous. Even more confusing, they were black like his. A chill washed over his body, and fear coursed through his insides. He wanted to know who the owner of those eyes was, but he could not risk Emily's safety. He turned away and closed his eyes tightly, but when he turned back toward the woods, the eyes were still staring at him. When Emily called his name, it broke his trancelike focus on the trees. He diverted his attention toward her and then glanced back to the woods, but the eyes had disappeared.

He took a deep breath and then entered the car. After fastening his seatbelt per her instructions, he started the car. He was nervous as he placed the vehicle in gear, and with great trepidation, he began to drive. He swallowed the access saliva that had accumulated in his mouth. His anxiety began to subside, but the moment he reached the intersection, he slammed on the brakes as another car sped past. He placed his hand over his heart. It was pounding so hard that it felt as if it were about to burst out of his chest.

"You have to relax." She winked at him. "You got this."

"I disagree with your assessment." He looked over at her while reaching for his seatbelt. "I cannot do this and would appreciate it if you drove."

He implored her to take over, but she remained steadfast and refused, leaving him no choice but to drive. He looked in both directions and finally turned right onto the road. He giggled as he took great joy in his simple accomplishment. Considering all he had done during his existence, this should seem miniscule, but his smile showed otherwise. His confidence began to grow as he pressed down on the accelerator, driving slowly down the narrow road. He drove cautiously and pressed hard on the brakes when they came to a stop sign, jerking them both forward, but Emily did not mind because she saw the joy etched on Sammy's face.

After about an hour, Sammy pulled over and allowed Emily to take the wheel. He gave her a kiss in passing and then sat in the passenger seat and watched as she fastened her seatbelt.

"You did great." She brushed her hair away from her eyes. "Next time, we'll try the city."

CHAPTER 19

One more class, Sammy thought as he stood in front of his open locker, exchanging books for his final class of the day. Just as he finished, he was surprised by the person approaching him out of the blue.

"May I have a word with you?" Joanne asked in a soft voice.

Sammy brushed her off and continued to adjust the books in his bag. Even though he had been spending time with Emily, he had gone out of his way to avoid Joanne because he still blamed her for her part in Cathy's untimely demise. He did not want to give her the time of day, so he slung the bag over his shoulder and went to walk past her. She stepped in his path. He rolled his eyes, clearly annoyed. When Emily did that to him, Sammy found it endearing and cute, but those feelings didn't extend to Joanne.

"What do you want?"

"I would like to clear the air between us," Joanne replied.

"Just because I am seeing your friend does not mean that we have to be friends, and I do not see any reason to continue this conversation." Sammy tried to make his way around her once again, but her hand against his chest stopped him.

"I know you don't like me because of Cathy."

Incensed, Sammy slapped Joanne's hand away. "You do not speak her name in my presence." He moved in close. "She was full of life; she had dreams and aspirations, and all that is gone because you injected yourself into something that did not concern you."

He gritted his teeth, but just as he was about to continue, Sammy stopped. His anger was causing his true nature to take over, so he quickly turned away as his eyes flickered between angel and alternative states. He closed his eyes tightly and began to back away, but Joanne wanted to continue the conversation. She placed her hand on his shoulder and spun him around to face her.

"I need to get some things off my chest," Joanne said with attitude. "I'm not going to listen to you and let you go without hearing me out."

He kept his eyes closed as he felt her hands shoving his chest. She was making demands, but he needed to get away before something happened that he would regret later. His breathing intensified as her voice rang in his ears. Despite the fact that he was visibly distraught, she would not let up. His anger was beyond his control. He felt his angel eyes take over. Just as he was about to reveal them to her, the late bell rang.

"I need to get to class," he said in a deep, dark voice.

Sammy's tone sent horror surging through Joanne's body and down her spine. She feared that something was not right about him and needed to inform her friend before something bad happened.

Despite the late bell, Sammy rushed to the restroom because he could not switch his eyes back to their alternative state. Upon entering, he called out to see if anyone was occupying any of the stalls. When no one answered, he locked the door and stood in front of the mirror. His eyes opened slightly, and when he saw his angel eyes staring back at him, Sammy lost his composure and punched the sink, breaking it into pieces.

"Luckily for you, no one else was in here," Michael said as he leaned against the far left wall of the restroom. "We need to have a talk."

Sammy's slowly turned his head as his eyes opened wide. The expression on his face displayed the fact that he did not care what Michael had to say; he was facing bigger problems at the moment. He gazed into the mirror once again. When he was unable to make his eyes change, his anger increased, and he punched the mirror, shattering the glass and causing a massive gash on his hand.

"You need to calm down," Michael said as he approached to extract the shards of glass from Sammy's flesh. "Whatever it is that has your anger at high levels, it has you out of balance. You need to let it go so you will be able to control your eyes."

Sammy took a few deep breaths and then closed his eyes. Thoughts of Joanne and their conversation at his locker flowed through his mind. He continued to take more deep breaths as thoughts of Cathy and Joanne entered his mind, along with the last conversation he'd had with his friend. The negative energy was released, and when he opened his eyes once again, they were back to their alternative state.

He turned to Michael and thanked him. Then his thoughts turned to the impromptu visit. "Why are you here?"

"Like I stated before, I need to have a word with you," Michael reiterated. Sammy grabbed his bag but paused before placing it over his shoulder. "I remember the last time you needed to talk to me. I lost my dear friend." A somber expression came over Sammy's face. "Is this a matter of life or

death?"

No!" Michael replied in a serious tone.

The archangel's demeanor made Sammy skeptical. He tossed the bag over his left shoulder, but his eyes never wavered from Michael as he slowly moved toward the door. "When are we going to have this talk?"

"I will be waiting for you after school on the corner just beyond the buses." Michael approached the door with his hands clasped behind his back. "Do not keep me waiting long."

Sammy nodded as he watched Michael exit the room and walk down the hallway as if he were a member of the faculty. It was strange watching the archangel walk through teachers and his fellow students, who were none the wiser. Any other time, he would find humor in what he had just witnessed, but Michael's mysterious appearance and his serious tone had stripped him of his joy as he walked to his next class.

Later that day, after school had concluded, Slade and Alex stood by the quarterback's locker, watching Sammy and Emily engrossed in a very pleasant conversation filled with laughs and light touching.

Slade took the last bite of his green apple and threw the core to the floor. Just as he leaned back against the locker, he became angry as the couple flaunted their relationship. Out of disgust, he smashed his elbow into the locker but managed to block out the tingling sensation that surged through his arm as he glared at Sammy.

"I'm sick of that punk. He walks around here as if he owns the place." He shook his head. "He needs to be reminded who the man is in this city."

"Don't worry. He'll get his," Alex replied.

As they were about to concoct a plan for a sinister act against Sammy, they were bumped by another student named Marlon Smith, who happened to be the school's resident party animal. He had a huge grin on his face as he handed both football stars a piece of white paper.

"I'm having a party at my house, a Halloween party even though it'll be in November."

Slade accepted the invitation and then nodded and watched as Marlon moved on to the other students at their lockers. He looked down at the flier and then slowly looked at Sammy with a maniacal grin.

"This party is the perfect place for us to teach that punk a lesson he will never forget."

Minutes later, after parting ways with Emily, Sammy exited the building and closed his jacket as he felt a gust of autumn air. He surveyed the area and quickly found Michael standing in the exact spot he had described earlier. After a few words with Jonathon, he made his way over to the archangel. After reaching Michael, he nodded, acknowledging his presence, and the two began to walk, but Sammy remained quiet because he knew he was the only one who could see Michael. He did not want to appear like he was walking and talking to himself.

They turned the corner and were halfway down the block, clear of the school. Sammy looked around to make sure no one was standing outside. Once he was satisfied, he turned his attention to Michael.

"Your demeanor and tone suggests that what you wanted to talk about was of the utmost importance." Sammy's heart began to pound, as he feared what Michael had to say. "So please, do not keep me in suspense."

Michael's hands were clasped behind his back as he remained silent. He took a few deep breaths before finally looking in Sammy's direction.

"You were in the midst of a conversation with a young lady earlier, Ms. Joanne Thomas." He paused for a few seconds. "You were getting very upset, so much so that you actually were about to show her who you really are underneath that boyish exterior."

"Yes I was," Sammy said. "She is responsible for Cathy's death, and I will never forget that."

"Well, she suspects something is not right with you and will be running to tell Emily." Michael stopped abruptly. "I know the humans can be infuriating, but you cannot go around showing them who you are just because they make you upset."

"I will heed your advice." Sammy shook his head. "I have a question before you leave." He looked around as confusion swirled in his mind. "I had a nice picnic with Emily over the weekend, and while it was quite delightful, something happened on the way back to the car." He took a breath. "Wolves surrounded us." He stared at Michael, his expression perplexed. "I talked to Riley, and he told me that there are no wolves in this area. Can you explain this?"

"That is very simple, my friend." Michael continued to walk with his hands clasped behind his back. "When a supernatural being descends to earth and lives among the humans for a period of time, things break their natural order." He placed his hand on Sammy's shoulder. "So animals that are not indigenous to this area will suddenly appear, and when you leave, they will leave. Balance will be restored."

"One more thing struck me as odd about that day." Sammy's confusion turned to curiosity. "When we were about to leave, I looked back and saw a strange pair of eyes staring back at me. They were dark like mine, and they did not belong to those wolves. Who was the owner of those eyes?"

Before Sammy could get an answer to his question, Michael disappeared because they had company. Jonathon approached, waving a piece of paper high above his head. Even though Sammy welcomed his friend's company, he wanted an answer to the question that had been on his mind for days. Now he had no choice but to wait even longer.

"You're a hard person to catch up with," Jonathon said as he gasped for air. "I forgot to show you something when we were at school." He handed Sammy the flier. "There's a party at Marlon Smith's house; it's a costume party."

Sammy examined the paper and handed it back to Jonathon, turning his nose up as if it were beneath him. "I hope you enjoy the soiree, and do not forget to tell me how you enjoyed it."

"Wait! You're going, right?" Jonathon held the paper up in front of Sammy's face. "I've heard about this dude's parties, and they're legendary." A smile appeared on his face. "I don't get invited to that many parties. Heck, who am I kidding? I don't get invited to any parties, so I would really like to go."

"You got invited, so you can go if you please," Sammy said in a condescending tone. "You do not need me to go to that party."

"I would feel lost if you weren't there with me," Jonathon replied in a desperate tone. "Besides, I'm sure Emily got an invite and would want to go."

Sammy stopped in his tracks and lowered his head, not believing Jonathon would stoop to invoking Emily's name to get what he wanted. He slowly turned to face his friend, who had a puppy dog face. He chuckled. "I am not making any promises that I will attend; I will talk it over with Emily."

"*Thank you!*" Jonathon shouted and then rushed in and gave Sammy a hug. "I want to go to this thing and want someone there I can hang out with."

"I am not promising anything," Sammy reiterated.

"Yeah. Once you talk to Emily, we both know how it will end." Jonathon broke the embrace and then slapped Sammy on the shoulder. "I'll see you there."

Meanwhile, on the strip, Emily was enjoying a slice of pizza with Rose at the popular pizzeria. A rush of her fellow students piled in through the front door, and among them were Slade and Alex. She turned her back, hoping to avoid eye contact or a confrontation.

"Is everything all right?" Rose asked.

Just before Emily could answer, the two girls were approached by Marlon Smith, who held two fliers. "You know I have to have the two most popular and prettiest girls at school come to my party." He set the papers on the table, grabbed a slice of pizza, playfully winked, and hurried off before the two girls could react.

They ignored his actions and chalked up his behavior to the typical petulance of a high school boy. Then they turned their attention to the fliers before them. They each grabbed a slice of pizza while scanning over the fliers. After taking a sip of soda in unison, they looked at each other.

"Are you going?" Rose asked.

Before Emily could answer, they were approached by Slade and four members of the football team, including Alex.

"Yeah, are you going?" Slade inquired, taking the flier from Rose and holding it in front of his chest so Emily could read it.

Emily rolled her eyes, took another bite of her pizza, and sipped her soda, refusing to acknowledge his presence. She calmly wiped her mouth and, after a few seconds, resumed her conversation with Rose. She knew how her actions alienated the superstar because he was so used to everyone falling at his feet and giving him their undivided attention. She knew he was seething inside and that her nonchalant attitude toward him had embarrassed him in front of his minions, but neither was a concern of hers.

"Answer me!" Slade shouted, slamming his fist on the table.

Emily remained calm even though the loud thud startled Rose and got the attention of the other students in the vicinity. The room suddenly fell silent. Despite all eyes being focused on her, Emily was unfazed as she took the final bite of her food before leaning back in the booth.

She wiped her mouth again and then sighed as she cut her eyes at Slade. "I guess you forgot about our conversation in the parking lot." She stood, staring the football star down. "Let me remind you then." She grabbed the flier from the table. "What I do is none of your business, and don't ever come up to me again demanding to know anything about me or what I'm doing." She grabbed her cup, which was still half full of soda, and threw the drink in Slade's face. She retrieved a fifty dollar bill from her purse, threw it on the table, and then turned her attention to Rose. "Let's go. I've had my fill of this place."

As the two girls walked out of the restaurant, every student broke out in raucous laughter and pointed at Slade, with exception of his minions, who rushed to wipe the drink and ice from his head, face, and neck.

Slade fumed as people's laughter filled his ears. Their mocking and pointing scarred his eye; Emily's rejection on top of the embarrassing act caused his anger to erupt. He grabbed the pizza the girls had left on the table and threw it, along with the pan it rested on, against the wall. With that, all laughter ceased. The manager emerged from the kitchen, but one scornful glare from Slade caused him to retreat. He turned and saw a smaller boy standing off to the side, and decided to take his wrath out on him by pushing him to the floor. He then looked at his friends, "Let's get out of here. We have some planning to do."

Emily and Rose walked through the parking lot, heading to their cars, beaming after what had occurred in the restaurant. Emily could still see Slade's face dripping with her soda, and the laughter from everyone in the restaurant had been priceless.

She retrieved her keys from her purse. When she looked up, she noticed Joanne leaning against her car, but what was more concerning was the expression on her face; it was one of trepidation. The two girls approached their friend and greeted her with a hug.

"Is something wrong?" Emily asked.

"Can I talk to you alone?" Joanne replied softly, looking over at Rose and then down to the ground.

Emily quickly objected, not wanting to keep anything from her friend, who she considered a sister, but Rose obliged and excused herself to go meet with her boyfriend. Once they were alone, Emily stood beside her friend, but her heart was racing because Joanne's somber expression was scaring her to her core.

"What's wrong?"

"How well do you really know Sammy?" Joanne asked. She paused as her emotions began to rise. She looked at her friend with tears in her eyes. Her uneasy appearance made it no secret that she was shaken.

"I know him well enough. Why are you asking?" Emily's curiosity was piqued at this point, and she wanted to know more.

"I talked to him a little while ago, and he was acting weird, but what frightened me the most was his voice before we parted ways. It was so deep; it was like something took over his body for a second." Joanne wiped her eyes as she began to shake.

Emily's concern turned to annoyance. She rolled her eyes and clutched the keys in her hand. It took all the resolve she could muster not to erupt and lash out at Joanne, who she felt was overstepping, but as Joanne continued on about Sammy, Emily finally had enough.

"Okay. You're my friend, but don't worry about me and Sammy." She took a few deep breaths in an attempt to scale back her anger. "Let me worry about my relationship, and you just worry about getting a boyfriend." After her scathing words, Emily brushed Joanne to the side and got into her car. She did not bother to look at Joanne to see the damage her hurtful words had caused. She just started her car and drove away. Emily was very angry but also hurt. She could not believe that her friend would try to impede upon her happiness by bringing down the one special person in her life.

Later that evening, Sammy was sitting in his room, doing his homework when a loud beep from a car horn caught his attention. He recognized the sound and smiled because he knew who it was. He closed his books and raced downstairs. When he opened the door, Emily was standing in front of him, displaying the same wide smile as him.

"Hey beautiful." He took her in his arms and gave her a kiss. "What are you doing here?"

"Do I need a reason to see the man of my dreams?" Emily replied and gave him a soft kiss on the cheek. Just as she gave him another kiss, she retrieved the flier from her back pocket. She unfolded the paper and presented it to him, never breaking eye contact. "I was invited to a party and was hoping you would be my date." She bit her bottom lip, waiting for his response.

I do not want to mingle with these miscreants. That was the initial thought that surged through his head, but he looked into her eyes and her beauty made it impossible to deny her whim. He took her by the hand and pulled her close. He kissed her on the neck while taking a whiff of her perfume. Then he closed his eyes.

"If you want to go, I would be more than happy to accompany you."

She could not contain her enthusiasm as she wrapped her arms around his neck and squeezed tightly. "I'm so glad you said yes. Now we have to go get costumes."

"Costumes?" Sammy broke their embrace. "What are you talking about?" "It's a costume party. We have to dress up for the event." She looked at

him with a raised eyebrow. "You do know what a costume party is?"

"Of course," he answered but searched his mind, wondering if he had ever seen a costume party before.

"I'd love to stay, but I have to get home." She kissed his cheek, flashed that beautiful smile that made him weak at the knees, then hurried back to her car. She blew him a kiss and winked before departing.

Sammy could not help but smile as he shook his head. "What have I gotten myself into?" he whispered and then ventured back into the house to finish his homework.

The next day after school, Slade leaned against his car in the parking lot, surrounded by his friends. As usual, they hung on the superstar's every word and laughed at all his jokes, which fed into his narcissism. At the end of one of his diatribes, Slade turned to his right as the others laughed uncontrollably. His smile quickly vanished when he saw Sammy and Emily walking hand in hand to her car. At that moment, he felt a nudge on his shoulder from Alex, but it took a second to tear his attention from the loving couple.

"I heard they'll be at Marlon's party," Alex said.

A sinister smile appeared on Slade's face. "That's the best news I've heard all day." He turned to face the rest of his minions. "We'll meet at my house again after practice to put the finishing touches on the plan."

Meanwhile, a few miles away, Sammy and Emily drove through the Hampton Roads tunnel and into the city of Hampton. He took in the sights of the naval ships on the water and was in awe of their size. Even though there was a chill in the air, he rolled down the window and closed his eyes, taking in the smell of sea and marine life before they exited the highway.

Minutes later, they turned onto Mercury Boulevard and then into the first drive on the right for the costume store. Sammy exited the car, placed his arm around Emily's shoulder, and reluctantly entered the store. The two shared a kiss before going their separate ways. He began to walk slowly down the aisles while she bounced around like a kid in a candy store.

He meandered down aisle after aisle, finding the entire process tedious, but he took some pleasure in the fact that she was so excited. The sight of her joy brought a slight smile to his face.

Aisle three was much of the same. It was filled with legendary monsters of lore such as vampires, werewolves, and creatures with bolts in their necks, but he immediately came to a stop when he reached the end of the aisle. His smile quickly disappeared when he saw the grim reaper costume. He stared as though mesmerized. He tuned out everything and everyone in the store, including Emily, who was on the cusp of shouting his name from across the room. He slowly approached the garb that had portrayed him as a symbol of fear. He lightly grazed the material with his fingers and then moved to the skull mask and finally to the plastic scythe that rested in a box just to the right. As if in a trance, he slowly reached for the handle of the weapon. Just as he wrapped his fingers around it, he heard Emily's voice directly behind him.

"Didn't you hear me calling you?" Emily asked.

Sammy's concentration was broken. He slowly turned around and smiled when he saw her face, realizing that only her voice could have brought him out of his state. "I am very sorry. I was dreaming, but that is funny because it is daylight."

"Daydreaming?" She laughed. "You know that's what it's called."

He chuckled and then focused on the costumes in her hands. "What do we have here?"

With a huge grin, she presented the two costumes. She held up her right hand. "This is a maid's outfit." She dropped her right hand and then held up her left. "This is a naughty school-girl outfit." Her grin broadened. "So, which one do you like?"

He took a few seconds to scrutinize each outfit, rubbing his chin as his eyes went back and forth multiple times. He did not utter a word. Instead, he let his facial expressions speak for him, and by the frowns and eye rolls, Emily knew he was not pleased. He turned his attention back to the grim reaper costume and stared at it. His anger began to rise as his eyes shifted back and forth. Out of the corner of his eye, he saw Emily make her way around to stand in front of him. He watched as she placed the two costumes on the rack in front of the cloak.

"Let's go over there and pick out something more conservative," she said, taking him by the hand.

CHAPTER 20

The day of the party had arrived. Guests were arriving at the posh two- story house in Chesapeake, Virginia. Marlon Smith, dressed as Dracula, greeted people at the door with a bag of party favors, which included mints and eye drops, meant to mask the alcohol that was served.

The door opened, and Sammy and Emily, dressed as the Wolf Man and the Bride of Frankenstein, entered arm in arm. Sammy surveyed the house and noticed a bunch of teenagers downing alcohol and dancing lewdly to loud music that was full of heavy guitar playing. It was a typical high school party scene that confirmed what he already believed: it was beneath him and they did not deserve to be in his presence.

"Thanks for showing up," Marlon said and handed them a bag. "Enjoy." Sammy peered inside the bag as they made their way through the crowd.

He ruffled through the items, becoming more annoyed by the second, and sat the bag on a table in passing just before meeting Jonathon, who was standing in the living room, enjoying some appetizers. Sammy greeted his friend with a hug and took pleasure in Jonathon's skeleton costume.

While the two exchanged light-hearted insults because of their costumes, Emily stepped between them and gave Sammy a kiss on his furry cheek.

"I'll leave you guys alone for a little bit. I see my girls just over there." She looked at Jonathon. "Hi, Jonny. Nice costume." She gave him a playful wink and then departed—a gesture that warmed Jonathon's heart.

"Did she just speak to me?" Jonathan asked. "I think she just said a few words in my direction."

Sammy found Jonathon's reaction hysterical, and his laughter did not go unnoticed by Jonathon. He was playfully pushed by his friend, and returned the gesture in kind. "You do not need to place her on a pedestal. She is just a girl."

"She's more than a girl," Jonathon said as a devious grin appeared. "And when I take her from you, you'll realize that."

Sammy nudged his friend, and they leaned back against the wall. As they conversed while watching the other kids and laughing at the costumes, they were unaware that they were being watched. Slade and a handful of his friends dressed in their football uniforms, complete with shoulder pads, watched intently from the staircase while drinking beer. After finishing his beverage, Slade crushed the can and tossed it to the floor. Just as he opened another, he saw Emily across the room and decided to make his way over to her.

He pushed a few people who stood in his path. His eyes were fixated on Emily as his jealously swirled. Once he arrived, he grabbed her by the arm and pulled her away from her friends. "May I have a word with you in private?"

Emily rejected his request and began to make her way back to her friends, but Slade was not going to take no for an answer. He pulled her back once again, but this time with aggression—an act that caused her to lose her balance.

Sammy saw Emily rising to her feet and shoving Slade, so he quickly swooped in to investigate the goings-on between the two. He wrapped his arm around her torso and kissed her on the cheek while Slade watched. "Is everything all right?"

"Everything won't be all right with you if you don't get out of the way," Slade said in a harsh tone.

Sammy took a step forward and placed himself between Emily and Slade. He stood directly in front of his nemesis and stared into his eyes. He wanted to hurt him, to really take him down in front of everyone, but Michael's words resonated in his head. "I think you better go find someone else to talk to. The lady is here with me."

"Last I checked, you weren't her father, so I can talk to her if I damn well please." Slade shoved Sammy. "And there isn't a damn thing you can do about it."

Sammy clenched his fist as he struggled to retard his anger. He endured one more shove from Slade and could not hold back any longer. He grabbed Slade by the throat and drove him to the ground. The thud caught everyone's attention. The music stopped, and all eyes were focused on them. Emily pulled Sammy off Slade as the cavalry arrived. She took him outside to avoid further confrontation. The moment they stepped outside the house, she kissed him passionately.

"You are my knight in shining armor."

"I was not going to stand by and let him treat you in such a deplorable manner."

She smiled, gave him another kiss, and held him tightly as laughter echoed from the house.

A few hours into the party, after cooler heads prevailed, Sammy watched some of the guests engaging in drinking games. He had a few drinks but did not care for the taste of beer or liquor. Furthermore, he did not understand why they were drunk, since alcohol had no effect on a supernatural. Emily grabbed a cup of punch and looked over and saw Sammy sitting in the corner. She sensed he was not enjoying himself, so she walked over and sat on his lap.

"I have an idea. Why don't we go take a drive? Let's get out of here."

Before he could respond, Jonathon approached with a spiked cup of punch. "I'm having a great time."

Sammy smelled the liquor on his friend's breath. "How did you get here tonight?"

"My dad brought me. He was so happy I was invited to a party that he dropped me off. Why you ask?"

"Do you have a ride home?"

"I was hoping to bum a ride with you guys."

Sammy turned to Emily with a disappointed expression. "Can we drop him off before we go?"

Jonathon finished his drink and then intervened before she could answer. "I'm having a blast, and I'm not ready to leave."

"I may have a solution," Emily said. She kissed Sammy on the cheek. "I'll be right back." She strolled over to Joanne and, after a few seconds, returned displaying a huge smile. "Joanne will be more than happy to take you home." She turned to Sammy. "Are you ready to go?"

"I thought you would never ask." Sammy took her by the hand, and they departed.

Slade observed them, still fuming from his encounter. Across the room, Alex was standing by the punch bowl, pouring cheap liquor into the bowl, when he saw Jonathon approach Joanne, who was standing a few feet away talking to Rose.

Jonathon had another drink in his hand. "I hear that you are my ride home." He took a sip, struggling to keep his eyes open. "I'll be around, so text me when you're ready to go." He gave her his phone number before refilling his cup and staggering away, shouting the song that was blaring from the stereo.

Alex immediately ran over to Slade, who was still angry. "Where's that punk?"

"He already left." Slade shook his head while rubbing his neck. "Our plans are shot."

"Maybe not," Alex said and handed Slade a cup of spiked punch. The two took a walk and whispered back and forth while glancing back at Joanne from time to time.

Meanwhile, across town, Emily and Sammy arrived at her house. She rubbed his arm and smiled deviously before giving him a wink and exiting the car.

"Where are your parents?" Sammy asked, following her lead. He admired the massive house, which was located in an immaculate neighborhood, and took her hand as she led him to the front door.

"They went to Florida for the weekend to visit my grandma." She caressed his hand with her thumb. "I told them I was staying at Rose's house, so we'll be alone without any interruptions, if that's okay with you."

Butterflies began to flutter in his stomach. Even though he was nervous, he wanted nothing more than to be alone with Emily. As she opened the door, he took her into his arms and gave her deep, passionate kiss before they could even cross the threshold. He was right where he wanted to be and knew he was in for the night of his life.

Back at the party, Joanne was indulging in the punch, and the alcohol was causing her real feelings of jealousy to surface. Out of the three friends, she was the least attractive. The other two had curves, while she was skinny and often felt like the ugly duckling when her friends were around.

Jonathon approached her and noticed that she was drinking heavily. "Are you all right to drive?"

"Hell yeah!" She shouted after finishing her drink and throwing the cup to the ground. "My car is the blue Grand Am parked by the tree. I'll meet you there in about ten minutes."

Slade watched the exchange, and after Jonathon departed, he gave Alex a slight nod and then descended the stairs and approached Joanne.

Meanwhile, at Emily's house, she and Sammy were comfortable on the couch, entangled in each other's arms, sharing tender kisses and gazing at one another.

Emily nibbled on Sammy's ear, which sent a sensation through his body that ended in his groin area. She cupped his hands in hers and then kissed the back of his right hand before gently rubbing his face.

"Do you want to come upstairs with me?" She removed her wig and allowed her blond locks to fall around her shoulders.

He surveyed her body and then slowly licked his lips before biting his bottom lip. "I would follow you anywhere."

His response was music to her ears. She slowly rose to her feet, never breaking eye contact. She slowly backed up and seductively motioned for Sammy to follow. He quickly obliged. Once they reached the bottom step, she took his arm and wrapped it around her shoulder. Then she led him up the stairs to her bedroom.

Back at the party, Joanne was at a loss for words because Slade was standing in front of her, taking an interest. He complimented her, playing to her insecurities and making her feel as if she were the only girl in the room.

"Where are your friends?" he asked.

"Rose left a little bit ago with her college boyfriend, but I know the only one you're concerned about is Emily." Her head dropped.

"That's not true." He lifted her chin with his index finger. "I don't care where Emily is. I want to spend some time with you." He leaned in close and whispered in her ear, "Alone, if possible"

Her heart jumped as she smiled from ear to ear. "Where do you want to go? Do you want to go get something to eat so we can talk?"

He pulled her close. "Why leave? We can go upstairs to one of the vacant bedrooms and talk." He kissed her on the cheek. "Will you spend some time upstairs with me?"

She reached into her purse and retrieved her phone. "Let me text the person I'm giving a ride home and tell him I will be out later."

He took her phone and returned it to her purse. "I'm sure whoever it is, he's having a good time." He chuckled. "This is the party of the year, so don't worry about him." He leaned in and gave her a soft kiss on the lips, which had the desired effect. She melted like butter. Without giving Jonathon a second thought, she followed Slade upstairs to one of the spare bedrooms.

Outside, Jonathon was staggering down the dirt driveway while finishing his beer and starting on the cup of spiked punch. He heard cans clanking behind him, but each time he turned to check on the noise, the only thing he saw were partygoers drinking and conversing. He walked about a half mile or so, and after finishing his drink, he reached his destination.

It was the only car in the area, parked next to a tree like she said, but much to his chagrin, Joanne was nowhere to be found. "Where are you?" he mumbled and then rolled his eyes. He retrieved his phone from his front pocket and sent a text, but soon after, he heard laughter, which sent a frightening chill down his spine.

He quickly scanned the area and saw nothing, but the situation seemed odd, so he decided to make his way back to the party in hopes of running into Joanne along the way.

A few steps into his journey, Jonathon came to an abrupt stop when he was confronted by two people dressed in the costumes from the horror movie *Scream*. He took a step back and saw another and then another. Before long, he was surrounded. Five people dressed in the same costumes had him boxed in, and no one else was in sight.

"Wh-what's going on?" he asked with a tremble to his voice.

No one said anything for a few seconds. Then one of the ghosts stepped forward.

"You're at the wrong place at the wrong time," he said, his voice distorted like the villain from the movie. "We wanted your friend, but you'll have to do."

At that moment, ax handles emerged from the sleeves of their costumes. Jonathon panicked and tried to find a way out. When he could not find one, he vomited, which caused the assailants to laugh. The five ghosts looked at one another and gave a slow nod, and then they quickly moved in with a vicious assault. Their violent swings landed about Jonathon's torso and some on his head and face.

Jonathon screamed from the pain and begged them to stop, but his pleas only brought laughter and more punishment. They beat him mercilessly. Once they tired, they stepped back to admire their handiwork. The assailants reveled in the bloody mass that lay before them. After giving each other high fives, they quickly departed, leaving Jonathon struggling for his life.

Meanwhile, back inside, Slade was alone in the master bedroom with Joanne. She broke their kissing a couple of times in an attempt to call Jonathon, but each time Slade intercepted.

He snatched the phone from her hand and then rose to his feet. "We're alone in this bedroom and you keep trying to call someone else." He grabbed his shirt. "If you don't want to be alone with me, I'll leave."

She quickly stopped him and begged him to stay. Not wanting to let her opportunity go awry, she removed her clothes and pleaded with him to make love to her. A fiendish smirk appeared on his face because he knew she was putty in his hands. Even though his thoughts were on Emily, he did not mind being with one of her friends.

Back at Emily's house, Sammy lay on the bed in anticipation, waiting for Emily to emerge from the bathroom. A few seconds later, the door opened slowly, and Emily entered the room, wearing a sheer white nightie.

He sat up in the bed, loving the manner in which the negligee hung from her luscious frame. He was breathless as his manhood rose. He could not wait for the moment that he could be with her. She climbed into bed with him and took notice of his naked body. She ran her fingers along his muscular arms. Not able to wait any longer, he lunged at her, and their night of passion began.

A couple of hours later, after sharing an emotional and physical connection with the love of his life, Sammy lay beside her, elated, staring at the ceiling. He turned to her and feathered tender kisses across her cheek and forehead as she inhaled heavily, trying to catch her breath. He felt like he was floating on a cloud as a tingling sensation radiated through his body. After they shared a long, deep, passionate kiss, they fell asleep in each other's arms.

As Sammy's body settled, his mind began to wander and he began to dream. In his dream, the sun was high in the sky as the two lovebirds walked hand in hand through a field filled with beautiful flowers, including lilacs, roses, violets, and lilies. They gazed into each other's eyes, professing their love and admiration, but the moment Sammy turned and faced forward, the sky suddenly darkened to a shade of gray.

He turned to Emily, and fear surged through his heart as she had disappeared. Just as full panic set in, he saw Michael standing before him wearing a somber expression.

"You need to wake up and go to the hospital immediately," the archangel commanded and then lowered his head. The moment he raised it; his angel eyes were on display. He looked at Sammy and shouted, "Now!"

Sammy woke suddenly from his sleep and sat up in the bed. A cold mist of sweat covered his body. He looked over at Emily, who was sound asleep, pushed back the covers, and exited the bed. A cold shiver ran down his spine as he tried to figure out the meaning of his weird dream, but at that moment, Emily's phone rang. His heart began to pound as his gaze shot to the device. He held his breath when Emily answered the phone. A myriad of disturbing thoughts ran through his mind as he tried to figure out what was wrong.

What if something happened to Riley? His heart sank even further. *What would I do without that wonderful man who has shown me nothing but love since I entered his life?* He watched as tears filled her eyes and the call ended.

"What is wrong?"

She lowered her head, tears streaming down her cheeks. Through shock, she managed to utter one word: "Jonathon."

CHAPTER 21

Frantic, Sammy rushed to get dressed and implored Emily to do the same. They rushed out the front door and made their way to the hospital, ignoring all traffic signs and running most stoplights. The entire ride, Sammy's thoughts were focused on his best friend; he silently begged for his well- being as he wiped tears from his eyes. A massive lump developed in his throat as he envisioned Jonathon lying in a hospital bed, in pain. He racked his brain as to who could have done this to his best friend. All signs pointed to one person: Slade Connor.

Minutes later, they arrived at their destination. Sammy quickly exited the car and made his way into the hospital, with Emily following close behind. He rushed through the crowded corridors, bumping people along the way. He was guided by Michael, who stood at the end of each passageway, pointing him in the right direction. When he finally arrived on the eighth floor, his heart sank the moment he laid eyes on Jonathon's parents embracing. Lola was inconsolable as she bellowed at the top of her lungs. It was a sight and sound he would never forget. At that moment, he was taken back to the day of Carolina's passing. Images of the Diaz family crying over the infant's crib entered his mind. He turned to leave because the grief was overwhelming, but the loud shouting of his name stopped him in his tracks.

He slowly turned and saw Lola glaring at him with a hateful stare. She approached him with a purpose to her walk and slapped him across the face. "You told me you weren't here to take him or any of us." She slapped him once again. "You're a liar."

Her husband stepped forward to restrain her, but Sammy stopped him by raising his hand.

"I am here to check on him. He is my friend. You have to believe me."

Lola slapped Sammy once again. "If he was your friend, where were you when this happened?"

"I had already left the party. Jonathon stayed behind because he was having fun." Sammy lowered his head. "I made sure he had a ride home before I left. I swear."

She glared at Sammy with disdain. She raised his head and made him look at her. "You claim to be Jonathon's friend. It really isn't healthy to be friends with you." She paused. "That girl that died in the car accident was your friend, and look what happened to her. My son worships the ground you walk on, and look what happened to him."

Lola turned her attention to Emily. "I suggest you stay as far away from him as possible. Being friends with him will either get you dead or beaten to within an inch of your life." Her husband tried once again to restrain her, but Lola shoved him away. "Then again, you don't mind seeing death. You are used to it."

Emily looked at Sammy, perplexed. "What's she talking about?"

"I see you didn't have full disclosure with your girlfriend, so I guess I will."

Sammy's head dropped. Lola was about to reveal his true identity. His mind was on his friend. At this point, he did not care about anything else.

Just as Lola was about to make her big revelation, the doctors arrived with news about Jonathon. The head doctor's expression told the story. He did not have to open his mouth; everyone knew the prognosis was bad. He removed his cap, took a deep breath, and then looked Jonathon's parents in the eyes as they clutched each other.

"He has multiple breaks in his left arm, and both his legs are broken. He has three broken ribs on his right side and two on his left." The doctor paused. "Both scapulae are broken, and he has a crack in his orbital bone under his right eye and multiple skull fractures. His spleen is lacerated, and his lungs are compromised." He looked at Jonathon's father. "He's going to need surgery as soon as you sign the papers, so I will need you guys to come with me."

Sammy watched helplessly as Jonathon's parents left with the doctor. He sat down and began to cry, as Emily comforted him.

"What was she talking about?" she asked.

"They were ramblings of a mother stricken by grief." Sammy paused. "The better question is where was your friend? I thought she was going to give Jonathon a ride home."

She reached into her purse to retrieve her phone. "I will call her right now and find out."

Meanwhile, at the pizzeria, Slade and his friends were sitting at a table, enjoying two large pizzas and relishing in their heinous act.

Alex took a drink of water and then said, "Slade, that plan was a thing of beauty." He gave Slade a high five. "It wasn't Sammy, but his freak friend will do for now."

"The best part about it is I have an alibi." Slade chuckled. "I was banging Emily's friend until the early morning, so no one can put it on me." He turned toward Alex. "Did you burn those costumes?"

"They've been taken care of."

Slade laughed while holding a slice of pizza high in the air. "The perfect beatdown"

The others joined in the celebration by toasting with their food. They felt untouchable, and their lack of compassion was startling. They had just put a fellow student in the intensive care unit, and they celebrated as if they had just won a big game.

Back at the hospital, after consoling Sammy, Emily called her friend. Her many attempts to reach Joanne failed, so she called Rose and informed her of the situation. She asked her to meet her over Joanne's house. After her phone calls, she returned to the waiting area, where Sammy was sitting with a somber, lost expression on his face.

She sat beside him and hugged him tightly. "He's going to be in surgery for a while. Why don't I take you home so you can clean up, and we'll return later this evening?"

Sammy did not want to leave his friend in such an abysmal state. "I cannot leave." He rose to his feet and began to pace. "What if he wakes up and calls for me? I cannot let him down twice."

"This *ain't* your fault." She rushed over and gave him another hug. "You can't stay in this hospital and worry yourself to death. Your uncle must be worried sick about you." She broke the embrace. "I promise you we'll come back after you get some rest and something to eat."

He knew her points were valid, and the passion in her words was convincing. He simply nodded and allowed her to lead him out of the hospital and, from there, home.

After dropping Sammy off, Emily made her way to Joanne's house. She exited the car, slammed the door, and locked eyes with Joanne, who was sitting on the porch with Rose.

"You were supposed to take Jonny home. Why in the world is he in the hospital?" Emily shouted.

Joanne rose to her feet after hearing Emily's tone. She was unsure of her friend's intentions, so she had her guard up just in case. "I was going to give him a ride home, but I got side-tracked."

Rose stepped in front of Joanne, preventing Emily from reaching her. "Please calm down."

"Who did this?" Emily shook her head. "I already know who did it. This has Slade written all over it."

"Slade's innocent." Joanne quickly retorted. "How do you know?"

"The police came to the party and questioned everyone there. They grilled everyone, and he was inside the whole night."

Emily looked at Joanne with skepticism. "How do you know he was inside the whole night? And why are you so quick to stick up for him?"

Joanne was stuck and didn't have an answer. She turned away, avoiding Emily's stern glare.

Suddenly, a loud screeching noise radiated through the air as the tattered storm door opened and Joanne's mother emerged. "I don't care too much for the way you're speaking to my daughter. I think it's time for the both of you to leave."

Emily gave Joanne one last scowl before turning and walking to her car. A sense of relief flooded Joanne's body, but she knew her mother was not going to be there to protect her when she returned to school.

Meanwhile, across town at Riley's house, Sammy was pacing in his room. Riley attempted to calm him multiple times, but his words fell on deaf ears. After Riley's departure, Sammy locked the door, closed his eyes, and softly called out for Michael. Within seconds, the archangel appeared.

"Who did this?" Sammy asked. "Tell me what happened to my friend."

Michael slowly shook his head. "You are allowing your emotions to get the better of you. If I told you who was responsible, you might go out and do something you will not be able to take back."

"Tell me who did this cowardly act," Sammy said in a deep, dark voice. His eyes turned completely black and his fists clenched. "I want to know right now."

"What are you going to do?" Michael said in a calm manner. "What are you planning?"

Sammy stared at Michael, breathing heavily. "You are my friend, but so is Jonathon."

"No. Jonathon is a human, and you are not." Michael closed in on Sammy. "You are the bringer of death, and somewhere along the line you have forgotten that." He stared intensely into Sammy's eyes. "These people live normal lives, real lives. You, on the other hand, are pretending, and you need to snap back to reality." Michael took a few steps back in an attempt to retard his anger. "I know you are enjoying your time with the humans, but one day you will have to take their lives. You will have to look them in the eye and snatch their souls right out of their bodies."

Sammy was already angry, so Michael's words, though true, were not what he wanted to hear at the moment. His frustration at not being there for his friend, combined with Michael's reluctance to give him the information he requested, sent him over the edge. He grabbed Michael by the collar of his black overcoat and sent him hurling into the far wall.

"Tell me what I want to know right now."

Michael's patience had run its course. He displayed his white angel eyes before rising to his feet. "It is time for me to show you that you are no match for an archangel."

Pounding on the door stopped them from attacking one another. "Are you all right in there? Who are you screaming at?" Riley asked. He tried to open the door. "Why is this door locked?"

Sammy's eyes returned to their alternative state. He turned to look for Michael, but the archangel was gone. "We will finish this," he whispered and then unlocked the door.

CHAPTER 22

The next day, after a night of worrying and pacing, Sammy received a phone call asking him to return to the hospital because Jonathon's condition had taken a turn for the worse; he had fallen into a coma. He rushed down the stairs. Just as he was about to depart, Riley stopped him at the front door, tossed him his jacket, and insisted on taking his nephew to the hospital.

Upon arriving, Sammy met resistance from Lola, who still harbored ill feelings toward him, but Jonathon's father intervened and allowed Sammy to see their son. He took the brunt of his wife's cantankerous attitude, which included a tongue-lashing.

Sammy reached for the doorknob but paused before opening it. Butterflies fluttered in his stomach—an experience that felt foreign. He was afraid for his friend. He would find him lying helpless in a hospital bed, which would be drastically different from the last time Jonathon was in his company.

He lowered his head and, after taking a deep breath, closed his eyes. Lola's continuous ravings as she stood a few feet to his left had become tedious. The more he thought about the task at hand, the more her ranting was reduced to white noise. Struggling to find the courage to open the door, he felt a hand on his shoulder. He turned and saw his uncle.

"I cannot do it." He pulled his hand back. "I … I … I do not want to see him like this."

"You don't have to do anything that you don't want to do." Riley pulled Sammy into an embrace. "But this may be the last chance you get to spend with your friend, and if you don't go in there, it might be a decision that you'll regret for the rest of your life."

Sammy broke the embrace and found clarity as his uncle's words swirled through his mind. He thanked Riley, took one last deep breath, and entered the room.

He took two steps with his eyes focused on the floor. The moment he looked up at Jonathon, he immediately stopped in his tracks. He had seen worse sights in his time, but those people had not held a special place in his heart. He turned away, unable to stomach the grotesque appearance of the battered figure that lay a few feet away.

Jonathon was swollen, and the small fraction of his body that was not covered in bandages was a deep red color, on the cusp of turning purple. His face was marred with stitches, and his left eye was swollen shut, while his right eye was on its way to doing the same.

Sammy's shoulders slumped as a slight breath escaped his body. He slowly made his way to his friend's side and took a seat on the hard plastic chair to Jonathon's left. He leaned forward, and just when he was about to take his friend's bandaged hand, he quickly retracted and leaned back in the chair. A tear escaped his eye as he placed his face in the palms of his hands. He began to make bargains, praying that his friend would recover, which was ironic because he often frowned upon that practice when he heard the futile pleas from humans when he was about to take souls to the afterlife. Just as he finished begging for Jonathon's life, he felt a hand on his shoulder. When he turned to investigate, he found Michael standing behind him.

"I can take you inside so you can spend some time and talk to him."

"Inside where?" Sammy asked, wiping the tears from his eyes and face.

Michael did not respond; he just walked over and placed his hand on Jonathon's bandaged head. "If you want to talk to him and get all the answers you want, just take my hand."

Sammy peered at his injured friend. Then he looked at Michael's extended left hand and then at Michael's right hand, which remained on Jonathon's head. He did not want to accept the offer, fearing that it would mean the end of his best friend's life, but Riley's words from a few minutes earlier played in his head, so he reluctantly agreed.

But just before Sammy could take the archangel's hand, Michael pulled away. "I need to inform you that you cannot lie to him while you are in his domain. You cannot hide your angel eyes, as those are the only eyes that will be on display." Michael extended his hand once again. "Lastly, you need to say everything that is in your heart." He paused. "Are we clear?"

Sammy did not utter a word; he simply nodded, accepting the conditions. He reluctantly offered his hand. The moment their hands were intertwined, Sammy felt a jolt that seared through his entire body. The violence caused his head to snap back and his teeth to clench.

Seconds later, he opened his eyes and was standing beside Michael in a vast room filled with vibrant colors, which was odd because Jonathon always wore black.

"Are we in his head?"

"Yes," Michael replied and then pointed straight ahead to a red door that sat at the end of a long, narrow hall. "He is just on the other side of that door." He looked at Sammy. "I will let you make that journey on your own, my friend."

Sammy turned and stared at the door for a few seconds and then looked back at Michael. He hugged his friend and thanked him for giving him this precious time with Jonathon. When the embrace was broken, he made his way toward the door. He looked around as the colors around him shifted from pink to yellow to orange and then to white with each step he took. When he finally reached the door, he paused again. He gently ran his fingers along the door as he felt his eyes shift. He chuckled, knowing Jonathon would get a kick out of knowing he'd been right all along.

He finally found the courage to open the door, and when he entered the room, he found Jonathon in the middle of an all-white room, sitting on a completely white bed and dressed in all white from head to toe.

Upon seeing Sammy, Jonathon rose to his feet and pointed at Sammy's eyes. "I knew there was something different about you." He approached Sammy and gave him a hug. "I don't care right now. I'm just happy to see you." He abruptly broke the embrace and then smiled. "I've been trapped in this room. Can you get me out of here?"

"No, my friend, I cannot," Sammy replied as a somber feeling settled over him. "I need to know who did this to you."

"I never saw their faces because they wore those creepy masks from that *Scream* movie." Jonathon paused for a few moments, out of breath. "But they said something weird."

"What?"

"They said they wanted you but that I would do."

At those words, it was as if a light bulb went off in Sammy's head. He'd already had a feeling that Slade and his minions were responsible for the attack; Jonathon had unknowingly confirmed his hunch. His anger began to rise, causing him to punch the palm of his hand and then stomp his feet.

"I do need to know something. The curiosity is killing me." Jonathon approached Sammy and stared into his dark eyes. "What are you?"

Sammy closed his eyes and turned away. He knew if he answered the question, it would strike fear in his friend's heart, but he knew he could not lie. He turned to Jonathon as a tear escaped his eye. "You do not need to know the answer to that question." He walked over and hugged his friend. "We do not have a lot of time, so we should focus on other things."

"Okay," Jonathon said and returned to his bed. "I want to thank you."

Sammy turned his head as both of his eyebrows arched. "Why are you thanking me?"

"You never made fun of me. You never treated me like an outcast." Jonathon paused, clutching his head and body, feeling extreme pain. "I feel really bad." His breathing became labored as he continued to wince. "The pain is unbearable at times."

Before Sammy could respond, he felt a significant chill in the room and knew exactly what it meant. He immediately turned and saw Michael and a dark cloaked figure holding a scythe and wearing a hood to conceal his identity. They stood in the doorway.

"No!" Sammy shouted. His heart collapsed, and his eyes became saturated with tears. He swallowed the excess saliva that had accumulated in his mouth. Just as he was about to approach Michael, Jonathon spoke, which broke Sammy's concentration.

"I don't *wanna* die, but I can't live in this much pain." Jonathon extended his hand as he continued to labor for every breath. "I've come to grips with my fate, and I'm ready for the misery to come to an end." He looked past Sammy and saw Michael and the mysterious figure near the door. A slight smile appeared once again. He turned his attention back to Sammy. "It's okay. I see your friends back there, and I know it's time for me to go to another place."

Before Sammy could respond, Michael placed a gentle hand on his shoulder and guided him to the back of the room, but Sammy pulled away when the cloaked figure passed them. He tried to see his face, but the hood prevented it. He quickly went to Michael and made one last plea but was met with a simple shake of the head.

Just as the mysterious figure reached the bedside, Sammy grabbed Michael. "Let me say goodbye to my friend. I did not get a chance to say goodbye to Cathy. Please do not deny me this time around."

After Michael called back Sammy's replacement, Sammy slowly approached, sat on the bed, and gazed into Jonathon's eyes. He witnessed his friend's pain and suffering, and it took him back to that night in Colombia.

"I want you to know that I was the lucky one to have met you. I should be thanking you." He leaned over and hugged his friend. "I love you, Jonathon Franks, and I am better because I had the pleasure of meeting you."

No other words were spoken as Sammy rose to his feet. He shrugged Michael away when the archangel attempted to place an arm around his shoulders and give him comfort. Just as he reached the door, he felt Michael's hand on his shoulder. Within seconds, he was back in the hospital room, standing beside his friend's lifeless body. He exited the room and quietly walked down the corridor, hearing the cries from Lola as doctors and nurses rushed into Jonathon's room.

His heart was broken. He had just lost his friend, his brother, and all he could think about was revenge.

CHAPTER 23

S ammy woke early the next day, as he did every day, and sat in his room, staring out his window, trying to make sense of it all. He ignored the multiple attempts by his uncle to get him to come downstairs and fixated on a sparrow eating bread in the yard. This sight took him back to his first day of school. On his way there, he had taken notice of nature. The simple things in life were beautiful, and he yearned for them instead of the ugly, which were death.

Oh, the irony. He had existed for millions of years and had taken more lives than he could count. His job was death, he was death, and he had heard and ignored humans' cries when they lost loved ones, mankind or animal. He had been immune to their tears, but now he was one of them and his grief knew no bounds.

Sure of his uncle's departure from the hall, Sammy emerged from his room, descended the stairs, and entered the kitchen. He grabbed the bottle of vodka sitting on the top shelf of the refrigerator. He stared at it for a few seconds, examining every inch of it. Before, he'd been ignorant to the reasons humans indulged in such vices, but now he understood.

He returned the bottle to its resting place and grabbed the orange juice that sat in the back. He poured a full glass and then returned to his room, where he found an unexpected visitor waiting. He glared at Michael, not knowing what actions would be taken next. Their last encounter in this very room had not been pleasant, and he was unsure of how to proceed with the archangel.

Awkward silence reigned as both gawked at one another. Sammy knew Michael had not forgotten their last encounter, but he also knew Michael was his friend and knew Sammy was grieving.

"I am so sorry for your loss." Michael stood and made his way toward Sammy. "But I must know what is going through your head at this moment." He stood within a few inches of Sammy. "What are you planning on doing now that you are armed with this treacherous information?"

"You are supposed to be my friend and you kept this from me." A snarl developed on Sammy's lips.

"You wanted to be human. You came to me asking me to plead your case, and you got what you desired." Michael moved in even closer. "Being human is hard, very hard. They have to endure many trials and tribulations. It is not all sunshine, my friend." Michael took a step back. "Now I ask again: What are you planning?"

"I feel it is time for Slade and his lackeys to know just who they are messing with."

Michael nodded and proceeded to clasp his hands behind his back and casually circle Sammy without uttering a word. "Can you be more forthcoming?"

"Slade will meet the same fate as Jonathon."

There were a few moments of silence as both parties glared at one another. Sammy did not know what to expect from his friend and could not gain a sense of what Michael was thinking from the blank expression on his face. He watched as Michael slowly nodded and then took a series of deep breaths.

"Is that your final answer?" Michael asked.

"Yes," Sammy replied, his tone deep and resolute.

A sly smirk appeared on Michael's face. With a suddenness that was surprising even to the other celestial, Michael moved in and forcefully grabbed Sammy by the throat, lifted him off his feet, and rammed his head into the wall with such force that a huge chunk of drywall crashed to the floor.

Michael's angel eyes appeared as his grip tightened. "I am going to speak very slowly so my message will be perfectly clear." He pulled Sammy close and then rammed him against the wall once more. "You are on earth to be among the humans. You will not extract your brand of revenge for Jonathon." Michael released his grip and watched Sammy fall to the floor in a heap. He knelt before Sammy, who was gasping for breath. "If you kill that boy before his time is scheduled to come to an end, there will be a serious price to pay."

"He was my friend."

"He was not your friend!" Michael shouted. "He was a human. You are not a human!" He paused for a few seconds while staring at Sammy with disdain. "You are my friend, but if you break one of the rules that was laid out before you, I will do my duty, and you will not like that."

Sammy struggled to his feet, rubbing and shaking his head in an attempt to regain his senses. He took a few steps, staggering, before falling to his bed. "Your duty?" He rubbed his throat and coughed, struggling to speak. "What are you going to do? Are you going to send that Neanderthal Gabriel after me?"

"No. I will handle it myself." Michael adjusted his overcoat. "And trust me, you will not like me when I am doing my duty as an archangel."

A loud knock on the door interrupted their conversation. When Sammy surveyed the room, Michael was nowhere in sight. He lay on the bed, staring at the ceiling, tuning out the persisting pounding against the locked bedroom door. Despite Michael's harsh warning, his thoughts were on revenge and the myriad ways he could inflict pain on Slade.

His thoughts had turned dark and sinister. The thought of Slade bleeding and suffering brought a perverse smile to his lips. Only Riley shouting his name managed to break his focus. He took a few seconds to regain his composure before finally answering the door.

"Is everything all right?" Riley asked in a tone that dripped with concern.

Sammy stepped into the doorway, blocking Riley's view into his tattered room. He nodded in an effort to save his voice; his throat was still feeling the effects from his encounter with Michael. He stepped into the hall, closing the door behind him, and gave his uncle a hug.

"You have barely eaten anything." Riley gently stroked Sammy's head. "I think we should go get a bite to eat. I don't care where or what. You must eat something."

Sammy agreed and watched as Riley descended the stairs. He did not want to leave the house because of the thoughts that swirled in his mind. He did not know if he could contain his emotions if he crossed paths with the persons responsible for ending Jonathon's life.

Minutes later, Sammy joined his uncle in the car, and the two made their way to grab some dinner. Although Riley made numerous attempts at conversation, Sammy ignored his uncle and stared out the window. The rest of the trip was made in silence.

After a short drive, they arrived at the pizzeria, but before Riley could park, Sammy intervened.

"I do not wish to dine in here tonight." Sammy looked at Riley with tears in his eyes. "I wish to get a pizza and eat at home."

Respecting Sammy's wishes, Riley handed his nephew fifty dollars and waited for him to exit the car before making his way to the store down the road to buy a few essentials.

Sammy stood on the sidewalk and watched as Riley drove away. He struggled to catch his breath as his grief began to resurface. The short time he had been on earth, he had lost the two people he had grown close to, and he was not equipped to deal with such loss or pain. He closed his eyes and tears fell because he could hear Jonathon's voice and his infectious laugh, but he managed to crack a smile as his thoughts veered to their first encounter.

But that soon came to an end, and those pleasant thoughts were replaced by images of Jonathon's mangled face and bandaged body. It was a struggle, but after a few agonizing minutes, Sammy managed to find serenity. He wiped the tears away and took one last deep breath before turning to enter the restaurant. Just as he reached for the door handle, he stopped. He could not believe his eyes as he glared at Slade, who was inside, laughing and joking with his friends.

Sammy's heart began to pound, and his breathing intensified. He grabbed the door handle with such pressure that the metal bent like paper crumbling in his hand. He stepped back, out of the light, because his angel eyes appeared. It was a vision he did not want the patrons to witness.

"No!" he said over and over while clenching his fists so tightly that his human flesh began to bleed. To witness Slade having a merry time while Jonathon lay dead on a cold slab cut Sammy deep. He shook his head a few times, and after his alternative eyes returned, Sammy entered the restaurant. His walk had purpose and determination. His eyes never wavered from Slade as he rapidly approached.

Emily stood at the counter. After grabbing her order, which was a large pizza with all the toppings, she turned and saw Sammy but was alarmed by the disdain lurking in his eyes. She rushed over and wrapped her arm around his neck.

"I was about to come over but stopped and grabbed some food."

Sammy's anger was absolute. He was so focused on Slade that he did not acknowledge her presence. Instead, he brushed her aside and made his way to the superstar. Once he reached his destination, he grabbed Slade by his collar, lifted him out of his seat, and slammed him through the table to the floor.

"You want me so badly, well, here I am." Sammy lifted Slade's body from the floor and then slammed him onto another table, which cracked from the force. He heard Slade whimper in pain as his breath escaped his body. Sammy was prepared to end Slade's existence and deal with the consequences that were sure to come, but a voice—Emily's voice—brought him out of the darkness.

Slade's friends rose to their feet but stopped when Slade began to chuckle. "Why are you so angry?" He laughed, exposing blood-soaked teeth. "I heard your buddy won't be graduating with us."

Sammy placed both hands around Slade's throat and began to squeeze. "Make reference to Jonathon one more time in my presence, and I will end your existence."

"Why are you so mad at me? I didn't do anything to that freak." Slade continued to chuckle, but Sammy's grip made it very difficult.

Ignoring the manager's threat to call the police, Sammy only released his grip on Slade's throat because of Emily. Her pleas and the fact that he did not want her to think of him as a monster were the only reasons Slade lived through the ordeal. After releasing his grip, Sammy watched as Slade fell to the floor. His lackeys rushed to his side.

"One day, you and I will settle this, and you will experience suffering the likes of which you have never known or imagined."

Sammy turned to Emily and placed his arm around her shoulders. He looked at the pizza box in her hand as Riley pulled up to the curb just outside the building. "Let us go back to my place and indulge in that pizza and spend some time together."

Just before exiting the establishment, Sammy took one last hateful look at Slade, and it was returned in kind.

CHAPTER 24

The sun had risen and a new day was born, but that did not matter to Sammy because he had not been to sleep. He had eaten the last piece of pizza from the night before and taken a long walk around the neighborhood. He had intentionally waited to come home until Riley departed for work; he needed to avoid the constant hovering, no matter how well intentioned it was. He grabbed a bottle of water from the kitchen. He was about to head to his room, but a knock on the door interrupted his plan. He was pleasantly surprised to see Emily, and he stepped to the side to allow her to enter.

"How are you?"

"I should be asking you that question," she replied before pulling him into an embrace.

He led her over to the couch after offering her a beverage, which she turned down. He gazed into her eyes and could tell by her expression that something was on her mind.

"To what do I owe the pleasure of this visit?"

"I'm just worried about you." She moved in close. "I saw the look in your eye when you attacked Slade." She paused. "I was afraid you were going to kill him."

Sammy stood and paced the room. He hated that he had allowed her to see him in such a negative light. He approached her and took her hand in his. He got down on bended knee and gave her a soft kiss on the forehead. "I do apologize for my atrocious actions yesterday. I hope you will find it in your heart to forgive my deplorable acts." He turned away, breaking eye contact. "If you do not want to see me again, I understand."

"Stop being so dramatic." Emily laughed, lifting his chin with her bent index finger. "I know you are hurting. Jonny's death has hit us all very hard."

He rejoined her on the couch, but his expression had not changed—a point of concern that did not slip past the attentive eye of Emily.

"Is there something else?" she asked.

"Yes." Sammy took a deep breath and turned away as thoughts swirled through his head. "I have to go over and see Lola at some point. I have to pay my respects."

"I can go with you if you want."

Sammy immediately refused. "I have to go over there alone. I know she is hurting and will say some things to me that I do not wish for you to hear." His expression turned from somber to angry. "Your friend." He scoffed. "I cannot believe she allowed Slade to use her like that. Now he avoids suspicion because of her."

"I'll talk to her." Emily looked away, disgusted and astonished that her friend could be so naïve. "She can't be this stupid."

Sammy stood and then guided Emily to her feet. "I know you have to go to school." He gave her another soft kiss on the forehead. "I will be returning in the next day or two, but my priority today is to go see Mrs. Franks."

He led her to the door, gave her a hug, and thanked her for checking on him. He closed the door after she departed and watched as she drove away. He grabbed his water and, after taking a drink, leaned against the closed door, dreading what came next. The impending visit was the hardest thing he would have to do. Consoling humans was not his forte, and coming face-to-face with Lola would trigger raw emotions. But he also knew it was necessary so the healing process could commence.

Later that day, after cheerleading practice had concluded, Emily made her way to her car with her friend Rose by her side. It had been a grueling session, and both felt sore. Emily had channeled her frustration into the routines and really pushed the other girls. They leaned against the vehicle, rubbing their various bumps and bruises while sharing a few laughs in between moans of pain.

Just as Emily was about to get into her car, a school-girl giggle in the distance caught her attention. Curiosity piqued, she turned and looked over her right shoulder and spotted Joanne and Slade exchanging kisses and playful touches. The openness of their actions on the heels of Jonathon's death angered Emily, so she decided to approach her friend to give her a piece of her mind. She took a few steps but was stopped by Rose, who grabbed her arm. She aggressively pulled away, but Rose grabbed her once again.

"Please don't do this," Rose implored.

"We have not said two words to one another since that day at her house, and a conversation is long overdue," Emily replied, her eyes never wavering from Joanne.

She made her way over to the couple, who could not keep their hands off one another. They did not stop until they saw Emily approach. Even then, Slade continued to examine Joanne's body with his hands, much to Emily's chagrin.

"I need to have a word with you," Emily demanded.

Slade tried to intervene using derogatory language laced with expletives, but Emily ignored him and did not even look in his direction. She made another aggressive request for Joanne's time, and when it appeared to fall on deaf ears once again, she tried a different tactic.

"Either you talk to me right now or I go to Coach and demand that you be kicked off the team since you refuse to talk to the captain of the squad."

Her threat hit its mark. Joanne rolled her eyes and sighed loudly. Emily watched in disgust as the two engaged in yet another deep, passionate kiss as if it were the last time they were going to see each other. The elongated display irritated Emily; her patience came to an end.

"Can you manage to tear yourself away from this clown for a few minutes?" She rolled her eyes. "I was with him before and I know for a fact he isn't all that."

Her scathing words caused the two to abruptly end their affection. With a sarcastic chuckle, Slade made his way back to the locker room, leaving the two girls alone to talk.

"What's so important?" Joanne asked in a tone that reeked with annoyance.

"You know he's using you." Emily frowned as her eyes narrowed, disgusted at her friend's stupidity. "You have to know that you aren't the only female he's seeing."

"Why do you care?" Joanne laughed. "Are you mad that I got someone you pined over, cried about, and couldn't get back?" She slowly shook her head, reveling in the fact that she had gotten someone Emily wanted. "The prettiest girl in the school is mad because I got someone she couldn't."

Emily smirked and rolled her eyes. "Do you think I am jealous?" She laughed. "He's making a fool of you, and you're either too blind to see it or

…" She stopped, knowing her next words would be hurtful, but she could not resist because Joanne's ego needed to be brought down a notch or two. "Or you're so happy that someone is actually paying you attention that you don't care."

Emily knew her words cut deep by the expression on Joanne's face and the tears that welled in her eyes. She did not want to emotionally cripple her friend. Even though they were not on speaking terms, they were still friends. She felt bad and needed to rectify the situation. She moved in for a hug but was met with a slap across the face.

"You are so jealous." Joanne snorted, balling her fist. "You can't stand that someone wants me instead of you. Face it. You're second fiddle."

Emily was shocked as she held her face. Her ears rang, and her left cheek throbbed. Their friendship meant nothing at this point. She looked at Joanne, dropped her purse, and attacked. The two rolled around on the pavement, pulling and grabbing at each other's hair. Their antics drew a crowd, which egged the two combatants to continue their kerfuffle. Rose ran over and tried to break up the fight, but their rage was too much for the slightly built cheerleader to overcome.

Finally, a few members of the basketball team emerged from the school after hearing the commotion. They made their way over and separated the two girls before any of the school faculty could see them fighting on school grounds.

Emily broke away from the jocks and straightened her hair and clothes before grabbing her purse. She looked to her left and saw Slade in the crowd of people, reveling in the fact that they were fighting and that at some level he was at the root of the issue. She gave him the middle finger after receiving a sly wink from him.

She reached her vehicle and slammed her purse onto the hood. She needed Sammy. She needed to talk to him, to hear his calming voice, and to be in the presence of his reserved manner. She entered her car, and even though she saw Rose approaching, she turned the key in the ignition, quickly put the car into gear, and drove away. Emily's only desire and mission was to be in the company of Sammy and no one else.

CHAPTER 25

Meanwhile, across town, Sammy was slowly making his way over to the Franks' household. The cold, brisk air caused his cheeks to flush and his fingertips to tingle. As he turned onto the street on which the house was located, he came to a stop and simply stared. He thought back to the first time he laid eyes on the house and how nervous he had been about meeting Lola. But most of all, he thought about his friend.

Sammy was hesitant to continue his journey because his best friend was not waiting for him to arrive, and he did not want to be inside those walls with that burden resting on his heart. He took a seat on the curb, his eyes fixated on the front door. At that moment, the first snowflakes of the season began to fall from the sky. He opened his hand and watched the flakes land on his palm, causing him to smile.

It was a little early for snow, but his presence brought on a lot of anomalies. He closed his eyes and tilted his head back so he could feel the snow on his face. He wanted to sit on the curb for the rest of the day and lose himself in the beautiful weather, but he knew he was only delaying the inevitable. He opened his eyes as tears ran down his cheeks. Then he slowly made his way to his feet. A massive lump developed in his throat as he placed his hands in his pockets and made his way to the house.

As Sammy advanced, each step was shorter and slower than the last. Even though it took him twenty minutes to walk a half block, he finally arrived. He raised his hand to knock on a few different occasions but could not bring himself to complete the deed. He thought about turning around and going home. He could not face the heartbreak that lived inside this house.

He swallowed the excess saliva that had accumulated in his mouth. At the moment of truth, he could not bring himself to knock. He succumbed to his heartache, but just as he turned to leave, the door opened and Lola emerged. "What are you doing here?" she asked in a tone that was anything but

inviting.

Sammy was at a loss for words, flabbergasted at the sight he beheld. Her clothes were soiled with grit and grime, and by her odor, she had not bathed or brushed her teeth.

"I just wanted." He stopped. "I felt compelled to stop by and check on your well-being, as well as your husband's." He lowered his head, avoiding eye contact. "I cannot begin to imagine the pain you are feeling."

"No, you cannot." Lola stepped to the side, allowing Sammy to enter. "I won't have this discussion in the open. I don't want the neighbors to be in my business."

Sammy nodded and entered, knowing his presence was not welcome. He refused her offer for a beverage and simply sat on the couch. He was uncomfortable sitting in silence, watching Lola indulge in a multitude of alcoholic beverages.

"I can come back another time if you'd like."

"Why?" Lola finished her vodka and then slammed her coffee mug onto the table, shattering the cup. "Are you here to ease your conscience?"

Just as Sammy was about to respond, Lola interrupted, "If you are going to talk with me, I demand that you show your true self. No more facades."

"What do you mean?"

"I want to look the real you in the eye. No one is here. My husband left and won't be back for days. And Jonathon—" She stopped as tears began to flow.

Sammy tried to pull her into an embrace, but she forcefully rejected him. "So you can show your real eyes or you can get the hell out of my house and never come back."

Sammy agreed by simply nodding. He slowly closed his eyes, and when they opened, his angel eyes had appeared. "Can we talk now?" he asked in a deep voice, staring at her with eyes as dark as coal.

At that moment, a barrage of insults and demeaning words commenced from the distraught mother, but Sammy endured it all because he knew she was in immense pain. While the foul language and hurtful words continued, Sammy looked around the room and noticed that the house was filthy. Clothes were scattered everywhere, and soiled napkins lay all around. He noticed bugs flying and crawling over the pile of dishes that littered the sink. He felt sorry for her and knew Jonathon would not want his mother to give up on life.

He interrupted her soliloquy by placing his hand on her leg. "If I could have given my life for his, I would had done it in a heartbeat. I wish it were me that night instead of Jonathon. I can only imagine how scared and confused he must have been." Sammy stood and then helped Lola to her feet. "I would give anything to turn back the hands of time."

The room fell silent. Sammy did not know what to do or what to say next as Lola simply stared at him with a blank expression. He leaned forward but was met with a thunderous slap across the face, halting him in his tracks.

Sammy was at a loss for words. He staggered and then looked at Lola while holding his face. "How dare you strike me."

"How dare you patronize me," Lola shouted, sprinkles of saliva flying from her mouth along with her words. "You're selfish. You came to earth looking for fun, and all you've caused is pain and misery." She slapped him again. "After your little vacation is over, you will go back to your dark existence while I'll be missing my darling son until the day we meet again." She went to slap him once again, but he caught her hand a few inches before it hit its target. Tired of the vitriol, Sammy pushed her hand back to her side. "I am truly sorry for your loss, but I will not be disrespected by you any longer." His voice got deeper with each word as his anger began to rise. "Your grief has consumed you and obviously blinded you." His resolve deepened. "Evidently you have forgotten who I am. You see this human

shell and have forgotten who lies just under the surface."

After hearing her apologies, Sammy's anger dissipated, and his calm demeanor returned. After his eyes returned to their alternative state, he led her back to the couch. He took her by the hands and wiped her tears away. "I loved your son like a brother, and I meant every word I said. If I could have given my life that night, I would have."

The two shared an endearing embrace, but it was soon interrupted by a knock on the door. Sammy was not surprised or curious by the intrusion and leaned back on the couch while Lola went to investigate.

The door opened. Sammy rose to his feet as the visitor stood in the doorway. Mrs. Stevens emerged, approaching the threshold as she waved at Sammy.

He made his way over to the door and introduced the two women to each other. "I asked Mrs. Stevens to come over because you two unfortunately have something in common, and I believe you will help one another though some hard times." He kissed both ladies on their cheeks before departing.

As he made his way down the sidewalk, he stopped and gazed back at them. He watched as they talked and smiled when they embraced. A day he had dreaded had turned into a day that was much needed. All three of them needed to heal, and they needed each other to do just that.

CHAPTER 26

The next morning, Sammy sat in the kitchen and enjoyed a delightful breakfast with Riley. The two engaged in a heart-to-heart conversation that covered an array of topics, including Jonathon's funeral the next day. After the meal and Riley's departure, Sammy remained seated at the table, deep in thought.

He wanted to say his last goodbyes to his friend, but after a conversation with Michael the night before, they had decided it was not wise for him to attend the memorial service. He remembered what happened at Cathy's funeral and knew history would only repeat itself. The two had conversed about alternative ways for Sammy to see Jonathon and settled upon a solution that would keep his true nature concealed.

After placing his plate in the sink, he exited the kitchen and was about to make his way to his room to prepare for school, but there was an unexpected knock on the front door. He was greeted by Emily's beautiful smile, along with a hug followed by a kiss. He led her to his bedroom, where they sat on the bed.

"I am happy to see you," Sammy said with a grin. He hugged her as a tear fell from his eye. "I had a very difficult day yesterday and a harder night, but all that means nothing now that you are here."

They told each other about their arduous days and commiserated about each other's situation.

They did not have to be at school for hours, so they decided to make use of their time by making love and by enjoying one another. Bliss was restored in their minds and hearts.

At lunchtime later that day, Sammy and Emily walked hand in hand as they made their way through the cafeteria to their table. He made light jokes and fed her potato chips as their infectious laughter filled the air. He showed his affection with light kisses on her cheek and hidden touches on her leg and back, but he also noticed a strange expression on her face.

"Is there something wrong?"

"Of course not," she replied. "But there are a few things I wanted to talk to you about."

Sammy's curiosity was piqued, so he slid back in his chair, giving her space so he could give her his undivided attention. "You know you can tell me anything."

"In a couple of weeks it'll be senior sled day. That's where all the seniors get together and go sled riding." She took his hand. "I know that with everything going on, there are some people there that you won't care for. I was wondering, will you put that aside and go with me?"

Sammy chuckled and moved in close to stare into her beautiful gray eyes. "Of course we can go. Is that all?"

"No." She broke eye contact. "My parents want to meet you. They want to have you over for dinner sometime soon."

"Just name the day. I am looking forward to meeting your parents."

Happy, the two shared one last kiss before returning to their meal. But just as Sammy was about to take a bite of his sandwich, he stopped. His elation turned to disgust as he watched Slade and Joanne saunter though the cafeteria like the president and the first lady. His eyes followed them until they reached their destination just a few tables away. He watched his nemesis and knew that Slade was aware of his hateful glare.

Sammy ignored Emily, who was trying her hardest to get his attention, even trying to reignite their playful fight with food, but Sammy rebuffed her attempts. He returned his sandwich back to the lunch tray as raucous laughter erupted from Slade's table, his minions treating him as if he were the funniest man on the planet.

One comment in particular jabbed at Sammy. He heard Slade make a joke about Jonathon that was in very poor taste. He quickly stood to approach his counterpart, but Emily pleaded with him and grabbed his arm.

"Please don't do anything to him." Emily stood and wrapped her arms around his torso. "He is not worth the trouble."

The two adversaries locked eyes. Sammy continued to watch as Slade took Joanne by the hand and exited the cafeteria, leaving his lunch tray behind for his lackeys to clean up. The feelings that stirred within him concerned Sammy. He did not know if he could contain his raw emotions if ever he were alone with the arrogant sports' star. He knew that he would not settle for anything short of death.

After school had concluded later that day, Sammy spent a few hours with Emily alone at his house, but after her departure, he made his way to Wilson's Funeral Home. He easily managed to sneak his way down to the cellar and entered the unlocked room where Jonathon lay peacefully in his coffin.

He slowly approached with his focus on his friend's face. When he stood next to the body, his emotions became too much to suppress. He ran his fingers along the coffin and smiled when he saw the black suit Jonathon wore.

He lowered his head as his angel eyes became prevalent, but he did not care about that at the moment. He cried and apologized numerous times for not being there for his friend when he needed him most. He took Jonathon's cold, stiff hand and caressed it ever so gently. He talked to Jonathon, reassuring his friend that his mother would be fine and telling him not to worry. As he continued to talk, Sammy noticed Jonathon's spirit standing to his left with a huge smile plastered on his face.

Tears of joy fell from Sammy's eyes because this was the happiest he had been to see anyone in his entire existence. They talked uninterrupted for about an hour, and at times, Sammy laughed, especially when Jonathon described the afterlife as being interesting instead of frightening.

At the end of the discussion, Sammy felt better knowing that his friend was not in pain any longer and was prepared to rest in peace.

The moment his eyes returned to their alternative state, Jonathon's spirit exited the room, and Sammy was alone once again. He began to make his way out of the funeral home but stopped when he heard a noise that sounded like laughter.

He examined the corridor and did not see anything, so he made his way toward the door until that familiar sinister laugh echoed through the air. Sammy abruptly spun, and when he displayed his angel eyes, he saw the black cloaked figure standing at the opposite end of the corridor. He took a few steps toward his replacement but stopped when the entity slowly shook his head, discouraging his advance.

"Why are you here?" Sammy asked in a deep tone.

The mysterious entity chuckled in the same tone and replied, "I am here because I can."

Sammy took another step toward his replacement and then another and watched as the entity stood its ground. He took one more step, and then the lights went out and Sammy was surrounded by darkness. Even with his angel eyes, he could not cut through the darkness and find his replacement, but a chilling voice emerged from the distance.

"Do not worry. You will see me soon."

With that, the lights illuminated and his vision was restored. Sammy looked around frantically, but his replacement was gone. He raced back into the room and found Jonathon's body resting peacefully in the casket. He felt uneasy about the appearance of his replacement and knew something more was on the horizon.

CHAPTER 27

The dreaded day had arrived—the day Jonathon would be laid to rest. Sammy had just finished breakfast and was sitting at the kitchen table, feeling numb while staring at his half-full glass of orange juice.

Riley had tried to engage him in conversation and offer his condolences, but Sammy was fixated on the glass, so his uncle's words simply went through one ear and out the other. His heart was pounding on top of being broken, but his thoughts were on Lola, imagining what she was experiencing during this trying time. After finishing his beverage, Sammy walked over and gently placed the glass in the sink. He looked out the window and smiled when he saw the heavy snowfall. He went to exit the kitchen but was stopped by Riley, who gave him a tight hug before offering him a ride and company to the funeral—an offer Sammy politely declined.

Minutes after Riley departed for work, Sammy sat quietly in the living room and watched television. He had never understood the infatuation with sitting in front of a huge square, ogling a screen, but Jonathon had loved it, as did millions of other humans, so he indulged. He became bored with the tedious banter and the pathetic attempts at humor, so he grabbed the remote and turned off the television before heading to his room.

He took a quick shower but felt a bit odd at the end. He wiped the mirror and stared at his reflection. He was startled when he saw a flash of his supernatural face before it turned back to human.

He took a step back and placed his hand on his cheek, but before a thought could enter his mind, he doubled over in pain when a sudden yet violent jolt surged through his torso. The discomfort dropped him to one knee as he clutched his abdomen. He took a series of deep breaths, and within seconds, the pain subsided. Sammy stood and examined his appearance in the mirror once more. He was relieved that his human face was intact, but he knew his time on earth was drawing to a close.

After dressing in jeans and a sweatshirt, Sammy grabbed his jacket and prepared to leave the house. School had been cancelled because of the services, so he decided to go for a long walk and think about his friend to honor his memory.

Sammy exited the house and stopped on the top step. The snow was falling heavily, and when he looked down, he saw two doves standing on the edge of the stair. He sat down beside the two birds and cupped them in his hands. He softly stroked both as they sat as peacefully as infants in the arms of their mothers. He returned the birds to their resting place and watched as they took flight. He saw their presence and the snow as a sign from Jonathon—a sign that he should not be saddened any longer and should spend the rest of his remaining time enjoying the simple things in life instead of brooding about something he could not change.

He decided to walk past the church where the funeral service was being held. He found it odd, considering Lola's family lineage, but since Jonathon's father's roots were steeped in the church, Lola's husband had insisted that his son be laid to rest with a traditional funeral service.

Sammy's journey ended before it began. As he reached the end of the driveway, Emily arrived. He was surprised but welcomed her presence.

He greeted her with a kiss. "What are you doing here?"

"I came to take you to the funeral." She shook her head while looking at his attire. "Why aren't you dressed?"

"I do not like funerals; they make me feel uneasy." Sammy turned away. "I do not wish to see Jonathon lying in a coffin."

"You have to go to the funeral. He was your best friend and this is the last time you'll see him and have a chance to say goodbye." She took him by the hand. "It's too late to get dressed, so this will have to do."

Sammy pulled away. In the past he would have capitulated to her demands, but he remained steadfast this time. "I am sorry, but I refuse to see my friend lying in a casket." He lowered his head. "His life that was so full of promise. He left this earth too soon." He turned to make his way back into the house but was stopped when she wrapped her arms around him.

"I understand and respect your decision." She laid her head against his back. "I want to support you, so I'll stay here with you if you don't mind."

Sammy turned and gazed into her eyes. "I would love for you to stay here with me, but I need to be alone right now." He lowered his head, breaking eye contact. "He was my best friend and I let him down. I need to come to grips with that, and I cannot do it with you here with me."

Even though he knew she was disappointed and somewhat hurt by his words, he knew she understood. He gave her one last kiss and watched as she departed. He changed his mind about walking past the church and decided to stay home to try to make sense of it all. His friend had been brutally murdered by teenagers and without any sign of sympathy or remorse for their appalling actions. He ventured to his bedroom, sat on the bed, and grabbed the picture of Cathy. During his trying time, he needed to talk to the first person he'd made friends with. After a few minutes, his emotions got the best of him and he broke out into tears.

At that moment, he felt a hand on his shoulder. When he turned, he saw Riley. He could not articulate his thoughts, and Riley did not ask him to. Riley just sat on the bed beside his nephew and held him tightly in his arms as Sammy allowed his tears and pain to flow freely.

CHAPTER 28

A few weeks passed, and normalcy had started to resume. Senior sled day had arrived, and Sammy was preparing for the outing while waiting for Emily to arrive. He finished putting on his layers of clothing. Just as he was about to grab his jacket, another violent jolt rocked his body, sending him plummeting to the floor.

He shuffled over and closed the door after hearing Riley rapidly ascending the stairs. The jolt sent what felt like a current of electricity flowing through his body, but unlike last time, it did not go away. Instead, they came consecutively. He writhed in pain as the heat ripped at his abdomen. At the end of each jolt, it felt like he was being cut with razor blades. His angel eyes were on display as he struggled to muffle his screams. He tried to assure his uncle that all was well as the pounding on the door became louder, but Riley did not settle for Sammy's word and kicked the door down.

Sammy closed his eyes and rolled over onto his side, lying in the fetal position. He turned his head toward the floor while Riley cradled him in his arms.

"Are you all right, son?" Riley questioned. He turned Sammy onto his back. "What's wrong?" he shouted.

Sammy was afraid to open his eyes because he did not know if they were alternative or supernatural. He took a few deep breaths in an attempt to calm his emotions. He was sweating profusely. Just as he felt comfortable answering Riley, another jolt slammed his insides.

"I need a glass of water," Sammy managed to articulate. He felt his body return to the floor and heard the water running in his bathroom.

He struggled to his feet and staggered into the hall bathroom. He shut and locked the door. He knew he only had a few seconds before Riley arrived and continued his pounding. He took a deep breath and looked in the mirror, but much to his horror, his angel eyes remained.

He did not know what to do. His skin was hot to the touch, and his eyes would not return to their alternative state no matter how hard he tried. As if on cue, the pounding started on the door, but he could not allow Riley to see him in this condition. He knew he only had seconds, so he closed his eyes and whispered Michael's name. Then he turned on the cold water in the shower.

When Michael arrived, it brought some relief. Michael helped Sammy, still clothed, into the tub of cold water. Sammy listened to Michael's soothing words as the archangel attempted to calm him. Despite the valiant effort, the attempt was futile, so Michael disappeared. At that moment, a knock was heard at the front door.

The archangel had bought Sammy some much needed time. Instead of checking on Sammy, Riley went downstairs to answer the door, which relieved some pressure and allowed Sammy to focus on his breathing. A few seconds later, his eyes returned to their alternative state and his pain disappeared.

Relieved, he emerged from the tub. His clothes clung to his body. He quickly shed the wet garments and hurried to his room just as he heard Riley close the front door. He rushed to put on some clothes as he heard Riley race up the stairs. Just as he donned his last piece of clothing, Riley stood in his doorway with concern etched on his face.

Sammy did his best to assure his uncle that all was well and gave excuses about eating bad food to explain his adverse behavior. Despite Riley's skepticism, he had faith in his nephew, so he believed the bogus story. Sammy pushed his damaged door back onto its hinges. He looked at the clock and knew Emily would be arriving in a matter of minutes, so he quickly ran into his closet and grabbed a winter hat to finish his ensemble. After applying some cologne, he heard Emily honking her horn outside and raced downstairs, but he stopped at the front door when he noticed Riley sitting on the couch, wearing a somber expression.

"Is something wrong?"

"I know you're about to leave, but I wanted to see what you wanted to do about tomorrow." Riley lowered his head. "It's that time again."

Sammy was puzzled. He did not know what to say or what to do as he gazed into Riley's eyes. He noticed from the tears that his uncle was on the brink of breaking down. He wanted to ask about the issue that was plaguing Riley but did not want to seem insensitive. Whatever the issue was, Sammy should already know.

He decided to ask the tough question instead of standing there, clearly lost, but just as he was about to inquire, a series of beeps blared through the air. He looked at the door and then at Riley. He did not know how to proceed as the noise from the car horn became more frequent.

"Can we talk about this later?"

"Sure, kid," Riley answered softly and took a drink of his alcoholic beverage before staring at a blank space on the wall.

Sammy departed but stopped just outside the closed door. He turned and wondered what was ailing Riley. Part of him wanted to go back inside and ask, but when he saw Emily's beautiful face sitting in her car, waiting patiently with her smile that melted his heart, he decided to go with her instead.

As the couple drove down the street, Sammy's thoughts were with his uncle. He wondered what was making him so sad. He knew Michael would know, but there was no way he could conjure the archangel while he was with Emily, so he reluctantly dismissed the thought.

Minutes later, the couple arrived at their destination. Sammy exited the car and was met by a swirling wind and gusts of snow that blasted his face and body. They made their way through the snow, which had accumulated six inches, and toward the hill littered with high school students exuding jubilance by yelling, screaming, and laughing. He surveyed the crowd and within seconds spotted Slade and his friends. This was not a school- sanctioned event, so no faculty were in sight. If anything occurred between the two, no one was there to intervene.

Emily's friend Rose spotted the couple approaching, so she broke away from her college boyfriend and dashed over to Emily and greeted both with a hug. Sammy flashed a smile, but it was a façade. His gaze rarely wavered from Slade, and he could feel his anger beginning to brew. He placed his arm around Emily, and they continued to make their way toward the rest of the students.

Once they reached the top of the hill, Sammy noticed its steepness and marveled at the students as they recklessly slid down the snowy slope, some using torn cardboard boxes in place of sleds.

"I see you guys didn't bring a sled," Rose said as she retrieved her sled from her boyfriend. "If you guys want to tackle the hill, you are more than welcome to use mine."

Just as Sammy was about to respond, the moment he knew was unavoidable had arrived. He heard loud shouting from Slade before the arrogant star made his way through the crowd with a beer in his left hand and his right arm firmly around Joanne's shoulders and neck. Sammy gritted his teeth and stood his ground as he came face-to-face with Slade and, of course, three of his cronies who were close behind him.

Sammy felt Emily tugging at his arm, but he ignored her. His focus was on his latest confrontation with Slade, and with no adults around, he could finally put him in his place and embarrass him at the same time.

"You do not have your weapons." Sammy looked at Slade's side and then at his friends. "You are not so tough unless you have some wooden sticks to inflict harm."

Slade emitted a sarcastic chuckle, but after a few seconds his expression turned dead serious. Without warning, he reared back and punched Sammy on the right side of his face, just above his jaw. Of course, Sammy was not fazed by the blow, but he had to play it off. He had to make it believable because someone of Slade's size and muscle mass would be able to knock him to the ground with a single blow.

Sammy lay face down on the ground while the crowd's laughter filled his ears. He heard Emily's cries as she knelt by his side. He grasped the earth and snow beneath him as he listened to the students' ridicule. He was ready to eradicate Slade and everyone within eyesight. Just as he was about to stand, he caught a glimpse of Michael standing at the edge of the hill with his wings spread wide and his angel eyes illuminating as white as the snow on the ground.

He knew at that moment if he took action against Slade, his existence would end on that snow-covered hill in Virginia, so he lowered his head and endured the mockery.

Sammy closed his eyes and rolled over onto his back. Once his eyes opened, he saw Emily, who was hysterical. He rubbed his face as Slade stood just over her shoulder, peering down at his fallen adversary with a devious smirk. Sammy watched as Slade motioned to his friends to depart, but before doing so, Slade delivered a playful wink before wrapping his arm around Joanne's neck and leading her away.

He made his way to his feet and then made a move toward Slade, but Emily stopped him. He heard her tearful pleas not to seek revenge but questioned her reasons, especially when he noticed the look in her eyes that screamed fright.

"I need you to step aside."

"Please don't," she said as tears rolled down her cheeks. "Why?"

"I just don't want you to get hurt or worse." She pulled him into an embrace. "I know you can take care of yourself but—"

"But what?"

She squeezed him tightly. "I don't know what I would do if something bad happened to you like it did with Jonny."

He paused as her words managed to cut through his anger and touched his heart. He took a breath and held her just as tightly. Then he closed his eyes and relaxed, resting his cheek on top of her head. He could hear her heartbeat; its steadiness gave him solace, and her tears gave him humanity.

"I love you," he whispered ever so slightly.

Despite the cold weather, they remained on top of the hill even after everyone else had departed.

CHAPTER 29

The next afternoon, Sammy arrived home to an empty house, which was nothing new because Riley was never home to greet him after school. He placed his bag on the floor and slowly moved about the house, wondering what his uncle was going through. Most days when he woke for school, he usually had breakfast with Riley or they would have some sort of conversation before his uncle departed, but that had not happened that morning, which was cause for concern.

He made his way into Riley's room in search of some clues about his mood, but it was futile, so he decided to call Michael. But before he could, he heard a knock on the door. It would have to wait once again. He raced down the stairs and opened the door to find Emily. He did not waste time with greetings. Instead, he peppered her with tender kisses before scooping her off her feet and bringing her inside. He knew Riley would not be home for hours, so he wanted to take advantage of the time. He took her to his room and closed the door. He gently placed her on his bed and looked into her gray eyes. Sammy was captivated by her beauty. Butterflies fluttered in his stomach. He quickly joined her on the bed, and after a long, deep, passionate kiss, they made love.

A short time later, Sammy sat back in the bed and watched Emily as she reapplied her makeup and teased her hair so there would be no indication that they had just had sex. The big day had arrived; the big dinner with her parents was that night. A smile graced his face just thinking about how much he loved and adored Emily—a love that grew stronger each day.

Suddenly, he experienced another violent jolt. The pain started in his abdomen, surged through his limbs, and ended at his phalanges. Tears formed in his eyes. His time on earth was drawing to a close, and the thought of leaving her was devastating.

He wanted to give it all up for her. He desired to stay human and build a life with Emily. He had found his slice of happiness and did not want to leave it behind, but he knew it was a pipe dream and there was nothing he could do about the situation.

Once she emerged from the bathroom, looking as beautiful as she had the first day he'd laid eyes on her, he reached for her and pulled her back into bed. The two shared a laugh as she playfully begged for him to stop, but they both knew she did not wish for his advancements to cease.

After a few minutes of frolicking, they lay in each other's arms, gazing into one another's eyes. They professed their love and shared some tender moments, which included touching and more kisses.

"I could stay here in your arms all day, but we have to get ready to go over to my house. My parents hate for anyone to be late," Emily said.

"I am looking forward to meeting them. I just hope they like me."

"Just be that charming person I fell in love with, and they will love you too." She smiled. "Don't be intimidated by my father. He may come on a little strong, but it is all show. He is a teddy bear." She kissed him. "You'll be fine."

Minutes later, they made their way down the stairs to the door. Being a gentleman, he opened the door for his love. Just as he was about to exit, he stopped. He saw Michael standing by the fireplace, staring at a picture of Riley, and instantly knew something was awry.

He went to approach the archangel, but Emily's voice derailed his journey. He had other engagements but knew he had to make a point of getting to the bottom of this mystery.

For the entire ride, his thoughts were occupied by Michael. He wondered why the archangel felt the need to make his presence known at that particular time and why he was strategically placed in front of the fireplace, staring at that picture.

"What was he trying to tell me?" Sammy asked aloud. "Who are you talking about?" Emily asked.

Sammy quickly dismissed her question with a simple shake of his head and a hand placed on her thigh. He changed the subject by talking about her parents once again, but his thoughts remained on Michael.

Minutes later, the couple arrived at their destination. As they exited the car, Emily raced over and surveyed Sammy's attire for any flaws. She brushed lint off his shoulder and tried to wipe away some wrinkles at the base of his polo shirt.

He grasped her hands and then gave them a soft kiss before pulling her close. "You seem a little nervous, my love."

"I just want you to be perfect." She continued to search for any discrepancies. "I love my parents, but they're perfectionists, and they notice the slightest things and focus on them." She rolled her eyes. "At times they will blurt out those things, which embarrasses me."

"Everything will be just fine," Sammy said, chuckling.

He gave her a soft kiss in an attempt to calm her nerves. He stroked her arms and took her by the hand, and they made their way to the front door. Just before entering, Emily stopped once again. She asked about her appearance, and of course, Sammy was very complimentary, which made her smile. In the next breath, she returned the compliment in kind.

Sammy moved behind Emily as she opened the door and was surprised to see her parents standing a few feet away, smiling, seemingly waiting on their arrival.

The father slowly yet deliberately moved forward. The smile fell from his face and was replaced by a stern expression. He extended his hand. "My name is Roy." His voice was dry and deep. He turned to face his wife. "This lovely lady's name is Donna."

Sammy accepted the handshake and was surprised by its firmness.

His eyes wavered from her parents to the expensive paintings that littered the walls and the vases from different time periods that were meticulously placed in different areas of the house. After introductions were complete, Emily excused herself to freshen up for dinner, which meant Sammy was left alone with the doting parents. He was in awe; everything about their house was immaculate, including their attire.

Roy had donned a black pinstripe suit, while Donna wore a full-length white gown with matching evening gloves that extended to her elbows. She wore pearls around her neck, and her wrists were laced with diamond bracelets.

A feeling of nervousness began to build within Sammy—a feeling that was baffling. He had been in rooms with kings, queens, and dignitaries from around the world at their most vulnerable times, but Roy and Donna's presence seemed daunting. Sammy's palms began to perspire. To stop that process, he repeatedly wiped them on his pant legs. He took a few deep breaths to calm his nerves, but his heart began to pound. The moment Roy approached, a huge lump developed in his throat.

"Would you like something to drink?" Roy asked, placing his arm around Sammy's shoulders. "I have beer, wine, soda, or water." A sly smile appeared. "What do you fancy?"

Sammy was dumbfounded by the assortment of beverages offered, but he quickly replied, "I would love a glass of water."

"Good answer." Roy slapped him on the back. "If you would have gone for the beer or wine, I would've shown you the door."

Sammy shared a laugh with the Keeles as Emily's parents escorted him to the dining room. He took a seat at the table, grazed his fingers along the expensive tablecloth, and admired the fancy silverware. He watched Roy pour two glasses of wine and hand one to his wife while sipping out of the other. His gaze continued to follow Roy until he took a seat at the head of the table. The moment Roy turned his attention to Sammy, Sammy quickly turned away, avoiding eye contact.

He looked over at Donna, who was staring at him with a creepy grin—a sight that instilled fear even in the angel of death. So he had no choice but to turn his attention back to Roy, who seemed as if he were patiently waiting for that very moment.

"So what's your opinion on our home?" Roy asked before slowly taking a sip of his wine.

"Ah, I think you have a beautiful home, sir," Sammy replied as sweat began to form on his forehead.

"Thank you very much." Roy took a deep breath and leaned back in his chair, basking in the glory of his accomplishments. "It took a lot of time and hard work to acquire such nice things." He leaned forward after taking another sip of wine and stared hard into Sammy's eyes. "Speaking of hard work, what are your plans for the future and, most importantly, for my daughter?"

Stumped, Sammy was at a loss for words. He had never been asked that question. He had no clue how to answer and felt immense pressure to provide a suitable answer as both parents waited with bated breath.

At that moment, the dining room door opened and Emily entered, bailing him out of the awkward situation. He was elated by the sight of her. If her parents had not been around, he would have given her the biggest kiss imaginable. She took her seat by his side, and under the table, he took her hand and gave it a slight squeeze.

"Thank you," he whispered.

The conversation immediately changed from future plans to the dinner menu—a change that was greatly welcomed by Sammy.

"I hope you like beef Wellington," Donna said.

"I have never tried it before, but I am sure it will be delicious," Sammy replied.

He leaned back in his chair as Roy grabbed and shook a small bell. Within seconds, the maids brought out a feast that included a plethora of fruits and vegetables, along with the main course.

After a scrumptious meal accompanied by scintillating conversation that covered myriad topics ranging from future plans to politics and everything in between, a series of dessert options were brought to the table. The cherry cheesecake caught Sammy's eye, but he was so full from the beef Wellington that he could not eat another bite, so he regretfully declined.

Everyone moved to the living room and took seats on the couch. Sammy held Emily's hand just out of sight of her parents, but the more minutes that passed, the more he felt at ease because her parents seemed to have taken a liking to him.

Just as the evening seemed to be winding down, Roy rose to his feet and approached Sammy. He had just poured a glass of brandy and, while swirling the drink, stood staring down at him. "I would like to have a few words with you in private out back on the patio."

All the good feelings that had begun to sprout within Sammy disappeared in an instant and were replaced by terror. A massive lump developed in his throat as his heart skipped a beat. He looked at Emily, hoping she would intervene, but much to his chagrin, she remained quiet. So he looked down at the floor and nodded.

"Splendid. I will meet you out there in two minutes." Roy finished his drink and set the glass on the dining room table. He walked over, gave his wife a kiss, clasped his hands behind his back, and sauntered off as if he were a member of the royal family, making his way out the back door.

Sammy took a few deep breaths as his palms began to perspire once again. He swallowed the massive amount of saliva that had accumulated in his mouth, and his stomach began to turn. He leaned back against the couch and closed his eyes, but a soft kiss on the cheek brought his nerves back to their center. He turned and looked at Emily. Once he saw her smile, he knew everything would be just fine. He made his way to his feet, took one last deep breath, and exhaled. He gave his love a wink before slowly making his way to the patio where Roy waited.

Sammy took a seat across from Roy, who was indulging in an expensive cigar, with his legs crossed. He held his custom-made solid gold lighter engraved with his initials.

"It is a nice night," Sammy said, trying to lighten the mood, but his attempt was futile.

"You can relax. I just wanted to talk to you man to man." Roy took a puff and blew out smoke in the form of circles. "You're a far cry from that jerk she used to go out with."

Sammy was at ease as he watched Roy sit back and continue to puff on his cigar. He breathed a sigh of relief at the compliment from patriarch of the family concerning his daughter. It felt good to have his approval.

"My daughter has gone through a drastic change after the unfortunate passing of her cheerleader friend. She used to be really superficial. I think that Slade Connors boy had a lot to do with it." He puffed his cigar once again. "But since she has been with you, she is a joy to be around, and I want to thank you for that."

"I had nothing to do with it. She just had to go through maturation."

"She told me you're very modest." He smiled. "A true gentleman to the end she says." He took another puff. "You're nothing like these moronic young boys running around here thinking they are God's gift to this planet. You're a breath of fresh air."

"Thank you, sir, for the compliments. My uncle raised me the right way."

Roy dropped his cigar to the ground and smashed it with his foot. He placed his hands in his pockets and then went toward the door but stopped before entering. "He did a good job." With those words, he entered the house, leaving Sammy on the patio.

A huge smile graced Sammy's lips after the delightful conversation with Emily's father. He felt relaxed and was looking forward to the rest of the evening now that the hard part was out of the way. Just as he was about to enter the house, a violent jolt reverberated through his body, bringing him to his knees.

He struggled to catch his breath, and just as he thought the worst had passed, two more jolts followed, each worse than the one prior. His breathing became labored, and his shirt became saturated with sweat. He crawled on the ground, clutching his stomach. His insides were on fire, and as hard as he tried, he could not catch his breath.

He made his way over to the glass door and peered in at the family, hoping no one was wondering about his absence or could see him in such a dreary state. He managed to make it to his feet just before Emily joined him on the patio. He avoided physical contact, not wanting her to ask questions about his wet clothing. However, more concerning was the frequency and the severity of the jolts. He knew his time on earth was drawing to a rapid close and that his affairs needed to be wrapped up, including leaving behind the love of his life.

Later that evening, after the violent jolts and more intriguing conversation with Emily and her parents, the couple made their way to her car. Sammy was ecstatic at the way the night had gone. He had garnered the approval of her parents, which meant the world to him. His smile could not be removed. He leaned back in his seat and gazed at the full moon that illuminated the sky. He took Emily by the hand and softly kissed its back and then her palm. Everything was perfect, and he wished he could stay in this moment forever, but the second they reached his neighborhood, his thoughts turned to Riley, who had completely escaped his mind.

Within minutes, they arrived at his house, and he immediately noticed something was wrong because the car was parked on the front lawn instead of in the driveway.

He slowly exited the car and ordered Emily to remain in the vehicle despite her request to accompany him into the house. He approached with caution, ignoring her pleas to remain with him. He knew her presence would be distracting if something egregious was occurring inside. His heart was pounding once he reached the door and dropped when he saw it was ajar. His breathing intensified as terror surged through his body. His hand trembled as he reached for the knob.

He quickly turned and faced Emily when he heard her car door slam. He did not want any harm to come to her or to subject her to the potential horror that waited on the other side of the door. Once she had safely returned to her car, he returned his attention to the door. He stepped back and took a deep breath but knew he could not focus until she had departed.

He jogged over to her and gave her a peck on the cheek. "I need you to trust me." He looked at the door as his insides churned with fear and then back at her. "I cannot have you here right now. I need you to leave."

"No!" she said emphatically. "I won't leave you here all by yourself."

He admired her zest and courage, but her presence was a distraction. He could not show his real self if she was around. After minutes of pleading, she capitulated and left.

With Emily safely away from the premises, he turned back to the house. His angel eyes surveyed the area but found nothing out of the ordinary and no signs of foul play. He reached the door once again, and after taking a series of deep breaths, he finally found the courage to push it open and enter the house.

His stopped after a step because of the sound of glass being crushed under his feet, but what he saw in the living room was much more disturbing.

CHAPTER 30

The image of Riley passed out in his favorite recliner with numerous empty bottles of tequila on the floor broke Sammy's heart. The total number of bottles was unclear because some were shattered from being thrown against the wall. He approached his uncle as tears flooded his eyes. He brushed back Riley's sweat-soaked hair, and the strong scent of alcohol turned his stomach.

Just as Sammy lowered his head, something caught his attention. Riley had something clutched in his arms, nestled close to his heart. He relieved his uncle of the object, and much to his surprise, it was the picture Michael had been staring at earlier above the fireplace. It was a framed portrait of Riley and his deceased sister, but Michael had been shielding her, so all Sammy had seen in the photo was Riley.

It was all starting to make sense. The empty liquor bottles, Riley requesting to speak with him, and Riley clutching the portrait. He wiped the tears from his eyes as a deep voice radiated from behind him. He turned to find Michael nonchalantly leaning against the fireplace with an expression of disgust. Sammy watched helplessly as Michael retrieved the portrait and returned it to the mantle.

"I am highly disappointed in your actions." Michael shook his head in disapproval. "You ignored Riley's request on the anniversary of his sister's death." He glared at Sammy. "The lady who is your mother on earth."

"How was I supposed to know?" Sammy asked.

"If you were not so wrapped up in your own life and opened your eyes, you would have seen that he was in pain." Michael sighed, staring at the portrait. "You are acting very selfish."

Insulted, Sammy gritted his teeth and snarled. "How dare you."

"How dare I?" Michael rolled his eyes and approached Riley, gazing down upon the man's face as drool seeped from the corners of his mouth. "You are so caught up in that girl that you are neglecting every other aspect of being human." He ran his fingers along the photo frame. "Being human entails all aspects of life. That includes being there for others, not just you." Sammy knelt down in front of Riley and stared at his face. He noticed the dried tears just below Riley's eyes and on his cheeks, along with the crumpled tissues that rested on his lap. He felt his uncle's pain at that

moment and began to weep.

"I am so sorry," he said repeatedly. He rested his head on Riley's lap. "I should have been there for you. I am so sorry."

Sammy leaned back on his knees, knowing that his words fell on deaf ears. His insides filled with heat, but he did not know from where. Could it be the sorrow or something else that was causing the discomfort? He moaned as he rubbed his abdomen. The moment he took a deep breath, he felt a hand on his shoulder. He sat back on his rear end in severe pain and looked up at Michael.

"Get your affairs in order because your time as a human is coming to a rapid conclusion," Michael said and then calmly walked out the front door.

Sammy closed his eyes and breathed deeply until the pain subsided. He did not want Riley to see the condition he'd left the house in while commiserating over the loss of his sister, so he decided to clean. When he was done, he retrieved the picture from the mantle and placed it back where he had found it. He hugged his uncle one last time and promised to be a better person before heading to his room. Once inside, he got a call from Emily and assured her that all was well before he went to bed.

Midway through the night, Sammy sat up in his bed after hours of looking at the ceiling, unable to sleep. He got dressed and decided to take a walk to clear his head, but he wanted to check on Riley before departing. He descended the stairs and, as he had expected, found Riley in the same chair and same position, holding the portrait near his heart. He approached slowly, trying not to make any noise, and spread a blanket over his uncle. He was racked with guilt because he'd not been there for Riley, especially since every time Sammy had gone through a hard time or a tragedy, Riley had been by his side, even when he did not want his presence. He grabbed his coat, but before he headed to the door, he kissed Riley on the top of his head and apologized one more time. Then he exited to go on that much needed walk.

He strolled down the street as the brisk wind blew in his face. A few thoughts flowed through his mind, ranging from Emily and their relationship to Riley and how he would get him through this tough time. He walked and talked while being very animated with his hands. Even though he was getting strange looks from people passing in their cars, what a bunch of strangers thought of him was the least of his concerns.

As the time and miles passed, he was still without peace of mind, but when he looked up, he smiled. Sammy was standing directly in front of Jonathon's house—a revelation that made him chuckle. No matter how lost he was or devoid of answers, he managed to find his way to his best friend's house. He did not know what to do. It was three in the morning, and the last thing he wanted was to disturb Lola and her husband, but the lights were on downstairs, so he decided to take a chance and see if she was still awake.

He approached the front door and gave a few soft knocks. He smiled when Lola answered. He gave her a hug, holding her tight, and began to cry as his emotions overflowed. The culmination of events that had occurred, good and bad, hit him at that moment, and he just needed to let his feelings show. After entering the house, Sammy made a request that Lola pondered and then questioned but ultimately answered. He wanted to spend some time in Jonathon's room so he could feel close to his best friend.

Upon entering, he could still smell Jonathon and sense his presence. He moved meticulously around the room, knowing that this could be the last time he would be there. He took the time to touch certain items like clothing and notebooks that contained drawings and poems. He lay down on the bed, and for the first time since returning home from dinner at Emily's, his mind was at ease. He closed his eyes and felt his body relaxing, drifting off to sleep, but was wakened by Lola's request for him to join her in the living room.

Sammy sat beside her on the couch, examining the area. It was much cleaner compared to the last time he had visited, and by her looks, she was in a much better frame of mind, which was a welcomed sight. But one thing was missing.

"Where's your husband?"

"We just couldn't survive after Jonathon's death."

"I am so sorry to hear that." Sammy placed his hand on her shoulder, giving comfort. "How are you taking it?"

She slowly nodded and then smiled, but it was a façade that didn't fool Sammy for one second. She took a sip of her tea and peered at Sammy. "Your time on earth is about to end."

"Yes, it is," Sammy replied in a somber tone. "I have found love, I have lost loved ones, and even though it is very hard being human, I would not give it up for anything in the world."

"How much time do you have?"

"I do not know." Sammy looked down at the floor. "But not very long." He felt his emotions begin to swell once again but managed to hold back his tears.

Starting to become depressed, Sammy quickly changed the subject. The two shared pleasant memories of Jonathon and spoke about Riley's issues with dealing with his sister's death. After receiving advice, Sammy decided it was time to return home to provide Riley with the comfort he'd received just a short time ago.

CHAPTER 31

The next morning, Sammy woke early after about an hour of sleep. He emerged from his room and ran downstairs to talk to Riley, but when he arrived at the recliner, he was surprised to see that his uncle was gone; the only thing left behind was the portrait.

He decided to search for Riley, scouring every room of the house, including the backyard. But much to his dismay, Riley was nowhere to be found. Sammy grabbed the phone and called his uncle but did not get an answer. He was worried, on the brink of becoming frantic. He ran upstairs to get dressed, determined to find Riley, but he had no idea where to search. So, he did the only thing he could do at this point: he called for Michael.

The archangel appeared within seconds, and Sammy was very happy to see his old friend.

"Where is Riley?" Sammy was antsy and kept rubbing his hands together. "I have searched high and low for him. I have called and called and have not gotten an answer."

"Calm down," Michael said. "He just went for a drive and is now sitting at his sister's grave." He paused for a moment. "He is really hurting and just needs some time. He will come back when he is ready."

Sammy breathed a sigh of relief and then sat down on his bed. "I was so worried." He clutched his chest, trying to catch his breath. "I do not know what I would had done if something happened to him."

Michael smirked and shook his head. "You treasure him now that you are about to depart from being human but ignored him this entire time."

Sammy was shocked at Michael's cold response, but when he was about to reply, the archangel was gone. He sat there for a few seconds pondering his next move, and a thought occurred to him. He could not do anything about Riley's mood at the moment, so he decided to do something that was long overdue. He grabbed his phone and dialed the number of one of the last people he could have ever imagined calling.

A short time later, a series of light knocks pelted the front door. Sammy ran downstairs and stopped just short of the door. He paused for a few seconds and closed his eyes, centering his emotions. He straightened his clothes before grabbing the knob. He opened the door and found Joanne waiting on the other side.

He flashed an uneasy smile in an attempt to put her at ease before stepping aside and allowing her to enter the house. The mood was awkward because of their history. In his mind, she'd had a hand in the deaths of both of his closest friends, but he had to put those feelings aside. He offered her a drink and, after she declined, led her to the couch to have a seat.

"I was shocked when I received a call from you," Joanne blurted out. "Are you having problems with Emily and want to use me to make her mad?" She rolled her eyes. "Because if that's the case, I'm not in the business of being used anymore."

Sammy was shocked by Joanne's declaration and decided to put his intentions for her visit off for a few minutes to explore her feelings and to get to the bottom of her issue. "Emily and I are doing well." He paused, searching her face for any expression. "May I ask why you would make a such statement or ask such a question?"

He watched as she squirmed in her seat. By the expression on her face, he knew she was not comfortable discussing anything about her personal life.

He gazed into her eyes and saw pain and anguish. He placed a hand on her shoulder in an effort to provide comfort.

"You do not have to open up to me, but I do think you should talk to someone because it is obvious that something is on your mind."

He gave her a few minutes because he could see her conflict. He knew she did not want to talk to him, but whatever was on her mind was weighing her down. After some awkward silence, his patience was rewarded.

"A few days ago, I was hanging out with Slade and his friends." She paused. "He had a few beers, probably a few too many, and he admitted that he got with me to make Emily mad and to provide him an alibi." She broke down in tears. "I suspected he had something to do with it, but I was so happy that he was with me that I ignored my intuition and kept my mouth shut." With her eyes full of tears, she looked Sammy in the eye. "I'm so sorry that Jonathon suffered. I'm so sorry that I was so stupid and selfish and he paid the price."

He watched as she broke down. He hesitated to provide solace for a few seconds. Listening to her words opened up a wound that had not healed, but he knew he could not carry around anger. His time was short, and he did not want to leave earth and humankind being angry. He dug deep, swallowed his contempt, placed his arms around her, and held her close.

"It is okay." He closed his eyes, and an image of Cathy and Jonathon smiling came into his mind. "Everything will be all right. All is forgiven now."

Flummoxed, Joanne broke the embrace and forcefully wiped the tears from her eyes. "How can you be so forgiving?" Amazed at the gesture, she shook her head. "I would hate you if the roles were reversed."

Ever the gentlemen, Sammy offered her a tissue and smirked. "I was very angry with you, but to heal, I have to let it go or it will consume me." He clasped her hands in his. "You have been in Emily's shadow, and the moment the popular boy in school wanted you, well, you jumped at the chance." He saw that she was turning away to break eye contact, but he would not let her. He gently placed his finger on her chin and turned her head back toward him. "You know he is using you." He paused for a moment, trying to be careful with his next words to keep from hurting her feelings. "You deserve much better than that loser, but you have to realize this."

"I know," Joanne said softly. "He only wants to deal with me when he wants sex." She chuckled in an attempt to mask her pain. "Ain't I pathetic?" "Not at all." Sammy smiled. "You are human, and we all make mistakes."

Joanne's tears continued to flow. "I have alienated my friends." She blew her nose. "I don't know what to do."

"Well, I spoke to Emily, and she is waiting for your call," Sammy said. "What!" Joanne shouted, quickly rising to her feet. "What are you talking about?"

A warm, fuzzy feeling radiated through Sammy as he stood and approached Joanne. He smiled as he looked into her eyes, which looked desperate, and prepared to bestow good news that would change her spirits.

"Emily wants to sit down with you and clear the air. She wants to fix your friendship, but I implore you to end things with Slade Connors."

Joanne was ecstatic after hearing those words. It was music to her ears, and she hugged Sammy, thanking him repeatedly. "I will go to the school right now and end this farce with him and then go make up with my best friend."

"School?" Sammy asked with a raised eyebrow.

"Yeah. He has a key to the gym at school and goes there to shoot between practices and games." Her smile broadened. "I can't wait to see the look on his face when I dump his sorry behind."

At that moment, a sly grin materialized on Sammy's face. "Do not give Slade Connors another thought. You focus all your energy on hashing out your issues with Emily and Rose at some point in the future." He guided her to the door and then escorted her to her car. After wishing her luck, he watched her drive away. Once she was out of sight, his thoughts turned to Slade and a much overdue dose of revenge.

A short time later, Sammy arrived at Princess Anne High School with a duffel bag slung over his left shoulder. He made his way to the outside door of the gym.

He turned the handle, but it was locked. He peeked over his shoulder, and when he was satisfied that no one could see him, Sammy ripped the handle off the door and placed the tattered metal in the bag before entering the facility. The corridors were pitch-black because all the lights were out. It seemed like no one was in the building, but as he moved forward, the sound of a basketball bouncing guided him to where he needed to go.

Sammy saw Slade alone in the gym, practicing his shooting and running wind sprints. He made sure to stand in the shadows, just under the bleachers, out of sight. He thought back to all his encounters with the high school superstar, going back to their first meeting in homeroom. His anger continued to rise just thinking about Slade, and it reached its apex when he envisioned Jonathon lying in that bed, welcoming death because the pain was too much to bear. He was fixated on Slade, watching his every move, while Michael's warning played over and over again in his head. But the moment of truth had arrived, and he had come too far not to have his one- on-one confrontation with his best friend's killer.

While Slade stood at the free throw line, making shot after shot, Sammy retrieved a few slender sticks from his bag and snapped them in half. He stood in silence as Slade quickly turned around, searching for the cause of the sound. He repeated this process a few more times. When Slade ended his session and went to depart, it was time for Sammy to reveal his presence.

"I am truly sorry for the intrusion," Sammy said, emerging from the shadows.

He made his way onto the floor as Slade watched from the foul line on the other side of the court. Sammy retrieved an ax handle from his bag and tapped it on the floor each time his right foot hit the ground.

"I told you we had a score to settle, and the time has finally come."

His focus was steadfast, his anger absolute. Thoughts of Jonathon swollen and covered in bandages burned in his mind. Lastly, the memory of his friend lying in a casket sent his rage over the top. He stopped at half-court, tapping the handle on the floor. He was silent, and his expression was stoic as he waited for a snide comment from his prey so he could attack.

"You need a weapon to beat me?" Slade tossed the basketball into the bleachers off to the side. "You come here to attack me with an ax handle?"

Sammy chuckled, holding the ax handle in the air and gave Slade a condescending stare. "Oh, you thought this was for me?" He tossed the handle in Slade's direction. It landed at his feet. "Using wooden weapons is your thing. I do not desire such primitive means to dispatch a punk like you."

"You must be out of your mind," Slade said as he laughed. "We're alone in this place, and if I pick up this ax handle, I will kill you."

Sammy took a few more steps toward Slade, very slowly and methodically. "Then I suggest you pick that piece of wood up because you will need it."

Sammy proceeded to mercilessly ridicule Slade. He questioned his intelligence, but the moment the subject moved to the superstar's manhood, it was the final straw. Sammy achieved the reaction he wanted. He watched Slade grab the ax handle, but he continued so Slade's rage would be blinding. When Slade attacked, a perverse grin appeared on Sammy's face. Slade swung with bad intentions but hit nothing but air, which further enraged the superstar.

Sammy's movements were like the wind as he dodged Slade's attack with ease, mocking him with each miss. Fifty swings, each harder than the last, all missed their target, but strike fifty-one was caught by Sammy.

He ripped the handle from Slade's grip and aggressively tossed it to the floor, causing a loud thud to echo through the gym. Flashing a smile, he went on the attack. He hit Slade with powerful punches to the face and body, causing his adversary to gasp for breath and then whimper in pain, before hurling him to the floor. He grabbed Slade by the throat and lifted him off the ground. But just as he was about to continue his assault, a violent surge flowed through his body, causing him to drop Slade as he grabbed his torso and cried out in agony. He fell to his knees. His insides felt like they were on fire, and his head felt like it was about to explode.

He saw Slade stumble to his feet after regaining his composure and then slowly make his way over to grab the ax handle, but there was nothing Sammy could do. The pain was debilitating. He watched Slade approach with a sinister laugh. He tried to throw a punch but failed.

"You made a huge mistake coming here." Slade coughed, and blood flew from his mouth. He gently ran his fingers over the handle, admiring its thickness. "Now you'll meet the same fate as that freak you called a friend." He reared back and struck Sammy several times in the face and body and finally to the back of the head, sending him to the floor in a heap.

Sammy lay motionless for a few seconds listening to Slade's banter as he basked in his own glory. The strikes did very little harm, but surges continued to rack his body, causing Sammy to curl into the fetal position.

A few seconds later, the surges subsided, and just in time. Slade lifted the handle high above his head, preparing to deliver what he thought would be the coup de gras. Slade's eyes widened, and a devious grin appeared as he was just about to drive the handle into Sammy's head, but Sammy caught it inches before it struck. He snatched the wood from Slade's hand and made his way to his feet, displaying no sign of injury to any part of his body, which baffled Slade.

"What the heck are you?" Slade demanded as fear coursed through his heart. "You should be dying right now."

Sammy belted out a deep laugh before displaying his angel eyes, which caused Slade to urinate in his shorts. Sammy broke the ax handle over his knee and then slammed the splintered wood to the floor.

"I am death."

The beating Slade endured for the next five minutes was unimaginable, and even though he begged Sammy to stop, the violence continued. When Sammy finally ceased, Slade was unconscious, battered and bloodied, lying in the center of the court.

Sammy collected the wood and returned the two halves to his duffel bag. He stood over Slade's body, and while he stared down at him, heinous thoughts entered his mind. He wanted to end his pathetic life, but Michael's presence in the bleachers deterred him from doing so.

"I cannot take your life in the literal sense, but I can take your life without ending it." He viciously stomped on Slade's lower leg several times, hearing the bones snap with each blow. "Good luck living a long life without the one thing that brought you joy, superstar."

He felt vindicated. He had gotten revenge on the person behind Jonathon's death and the bane of his existence. He gazed at Slade's battered face, admiring the damage he had inflicted. Both eyes were swollen shut, while blood seeped from his nose and mouth. Sammy turned to depart, but before doing so, he delivered one last kick to Slade's groin and then winked.

"You will not be able to reproduce either, you waste of life."

Satisfied, he tossed the bag over his left shoulder and whistled a tune as he headed for the door. He had not felt such elation since falling in love, and only being with Emily gave him more pleasure.

CHAPTER 32

After changing out of his blood-stained clothes, he stuffed them into the duffel bag, boarded a public transportation bus, and made his way home. He leaned back in his seat and closed his eyes, wearing a huge grin. He rubbed his hands together and reminisced about punching Slade and the moans that had come from the not-so-tough bully who had gotten away with murder.

He wanted to call Emily and tell her all about it but thought better of it. The less others knew about his exploits, the more likely they would remain a secret, and he wanted her to keep him in highest esteem rather than thinking of him as a person who settled his issues with his fists. He exited the bus a few blocks shy of his house, deciding to walk the rest of the way to enjoy the weather. Along the way, he thought of Emily and wondered how her reunion with her friend had transpired, so he called but did not receive an answer.

He thought nothing of it, figuring the newly reunited friends had a lot of catching up to do, so he returned his phone to his pocket and continued on his journey. Once he turned onto his block, all his great feelings quickly dissipated. He noticed that his uncle had returned. Now he had no choice but to come face-to-face with him. He approached the door, and with each step, his insides churned because he knew that what lay inside was nothing good.

Sammy made his way into the house to find Riley calmly sitting in his recliner with his legs crossed, staring at the front door. He tried to gauge his uncle's mood by reading the expression on his face, but it was blank, cold, and unfeeling.

He sat down on the couch and softly spoke Riley's name but did not receive a response of any kind, not even a look acknowledging his presence. He leaned forward and placed his hand on Riley's leg, but his uncle quickly rejected the gesture by standing and walking away. Sammy would not let Riley ignore him. He felt compelled to clear the air, so he followed his uncle into the kitchen.

He noticed Riley sitting at the kitchen table, enjoying a glass of milk and a bagel covered with cream cheese, so he decided to join him. He cautiously sat across from his uncle, trying to make eye contact, but it was futile.

"Are you going to talk to me?"

Silence continued to fill the room as Riley looked straight ahead, glaring at the wall. He did not blink, and his eyes did not waver. Once he finished his snack, he calmly stood and placed his plate and cup in the sink and then departed.

Sammy had had enough of the silent treatment. Feeling angry, he abruptly stood and exited the kitchen, stopping Riley before he walked out the front door. He grabbed his uncle by the arm and pulled him back, swinging him around so they were face-to-face.

"You are not leaving until we talk."

"Now you want to talk!" Riley shouted, ripping his arm free. "Every time I came to you wanting to talk, you blew me off, and now you want to talk." Sammy tried to respond, but Riley interrupted, "Your mother loved you like no other. She lauded over you, made sure no harm came to you, and for you not even acknowledge the anniversary of her death ..." He seethed as saliva accumulated in the corners of his mouth. "You are so wrapped up in your own life that you could not even take the time to mourn your own mother!"

He shoved Sammy against the front door. "I don't even know who you are anymore. You are not the little boy that cried every day for two months after your mother died."

Sammy remained firmly against the door. He saw the anguish in Riley's eyes and did not want to add fuel to an already volatile situation by trying to justify his actions. He paused for a few seconds in an attempt to calm things down. He stepped forward without saying a word but maintained eye contact. He moved slowly toward his uncle because he was familiar with the look in Riley's eyes. Sammy had the same look every time he saw Slade after Jonathon's death.

He slowly placed his hands on Riley's shoulders and then guided him over to the couch. He noticed Riley's eyes had gone from unrelenting anger to insufferable sorrow. He handed his uncle some tissues and then ran to the kitchen to grab a bottle of water. After returning, he sat across from Riley in a position to listen and provide comfort. He handed Riley the water and then sat back.

"Tell me more about my mother and you."

"I practically raised your mother." Riley took a sip of water. "I taught her how to ride a bike. I protected her from bullies. I walked her to school, fixed her lunch in the morning, and helped her with her homework." Riley wiped a tear from his eye and then chuckled. "I taught her how to drive a car. I was her big brother, and that was something I took very seriously." He turned to face Sammy. "When she got married, she wanted me to walk her down the aisle, but she didn't want to hurt our dad's feelings."

Riley stood, walked over to the fireplace, and picked up the portrait of him and his sister. "When she was pregnant, she made me your godfather. She knew I wouldn't let harm come to you because I wouldn't let any come to her." He returned the portrait to the mantle. "She was very special to me, as are you." He returned to the couch, sat next to Sammy, and gazed into his eyes. "You are too young to remember, but I was married once." Riley smiled. "We were so happy together and so deeply in love."

"What happened?" Sammy asked.

"When your mother died, it broke me." Riley leaned back on the couch and stared at the ceiling as tears formed. "I was so depressed and could not recover; grief would not let me go." He wiped his eyes. "I didn't know how to help myself, let alone care for you in your time of need, and it became too much for her. We, ah …" Riley paused as his emotions began to stir. "I wasn't the same man she fell in love with. That man was gone and never returned."

"You marry someone for better or for worse," Sammy said.

"I don't blame her for leaving. I think it was for the best." Riley smiled. "She remarried and had three kids." He wiped his eyes once again. "We became friends and speak from time to time. She's happy, and seeing you prosper, so am I."

Hearing those words broke Sammy's heart. He knew Riley carried a huge burden and was condemned to a lifetime of hell because he would never recover from his sister's death. He was reminded of her every day when he looked at her son. Sammy leaned over and hugged Riley, and the gesture was returned.

No words were spoken, just tears shed. One for the loss of Riley's world the day his sister died and the other for understanding once again the joy and heartache that went along with being human. They laughed and cried into the morning hours as Sammy listened to stories about Riley's sister and the life he inherited when he requested to become human. He enjoyed the stories and the way Riley's face lit up as he reminisced about the great times he and his sister shared.

A few days later, Sammy walked through the doors at school. The building was abuzz about the brutal attack Slade had endured that left him hospitalized with several broken ribs, a broken orbital bone, a leg broken in three places, along with major damage to his knee. Lastly, the football star was in a coma.

Sammy was greeted at his locker with a kiss from Emily, who filled him in on her reconciliation with Joanne. While listening to her stories, Sammy filled his bag with books, but out of the corner of his eye, he noticed Alex and his friends approaching with looks of disdain. Not wanting Emily to see the altercation, Sammy gave her a kiss and then sent her on her way. Then he closed his locker and waited for the gang to arrive.

He displayed a huge grin as Alex and the two huge linemen he had fought earlier in the year defending Jonathon stood before him. "I heard about your friend; it is so sad that a person is not safe in the school gym."

"I know it was you that jumped my boy," Alex said.

Sammy smirked and leaned in next to Alex's ear. "I will make a deal with you. If you go to the police and admit what you did to Jonathon, I will go to the police and tell them I beat Slade within an inch of his life."

Sammy took a step back and waited for a reaction to his comment. He recognized the look in Alex's eyes; it was full of anger and a lust for revenge. He knew Slade's lackey wanted retribution. It would have given him great pleasure to put all three in the hospital, but instead, he pointed to his left at the principal, who was walking down the hall. He gathered his book bag and taunted them by winking, leaving the trio fuming as he made his way to homeroom.

Before entering the room, he spotted Emily standing outside the door, awaiting his arrival with a huge smile. He gave her a soft kiss but was taken aback when he saw Emily wince and then place her hand on her head.

"Are you alright?"

"Yeah," she replied, rubbing her forehead and eyes. "I haven't slept that much lately hanging with the girls." She retrieved a few aspirins from her purse. "I'm sure I'll be fine with some medicine and sleep."

Sammy gave her a soft kiss on the head and then pulled her into an embrace. While doing so, he looked up and saw Alex and his friends watching intently, which brought him great joy. A short time ago, he'd been lurking around as Slade and his friends laughed about their dastardly deed. Now the shoe was on the other foot, and he was loving every second of it.

Later that day, Sammy arrived home after another uneventful school day. He dropped his bag by the door and, after hanging up his coat, made his way into the kitchen to get a snack. After grabbing an apple and a bottle of water, he was about to head to his room and rest before going to the park, but an unexpected guest was waiting by the kitchen door. He locked eyes with Michael, and based on the archangel's expression, he knew this was not a social visit.

A few things raced through his mind as the two stood in silence. Was the archangel there to admonish him for what he did to Slade? Or was he there to inform him that his time on earth had come to an end and it was time to resume his duties as the bringer of death?

"I need to have a word with you out back," Michael stated in a very low tone.

Nervous, Sammy tried to open the bottle, but because his hands shook, the bottle fell unopened to the floor. His heart rate increased as fear flooded his body. He knew what his friend was capable of, and in human form, he was no match for Michael.

"Why do you need to speak to me outside?"

"We are just going to talk. It is of utmost importance," Michael said in a calming voice.

Convinced of his friend's intentions, Sammy walked over and opened the back door. As they made their way outside, the brisk air greeted them. Usually Sammy found something so simple delightful, but his curiosity was piqued. In the back of his mind, he knew that whatever it was that Michael needed to discuss, it was not good.

CHAPTER 33

As they continued into the yard, Michael shortened his strides, falling behind Sammy—a move that did not go unnoticed. Sammy was suspicious of this action, and even though Michael had given his word that no retribution was forthcoming for his actions against Slade, an uneasy feeling overshadowed his every step. He peeked over his shoulder and saw that Michael had stopped just a few feet from the house, while he stood in the middle of the backyard.

Sammy came to a stop and then lowered his head. He took a deep breath, preparing for a physical confrontation with his best friend, but just as he was about to turn and face Michael, that familiar sinister laugh radiated through the air. It was very close. He quickly turned to find the culprit standing beside his friend. He was dressed in a black cloak and holding a scythe in his right hand, no doubt mocking Sammy. Sammy's eyes bulged, and his heart raced. He began to move closer to the mysterious imposter, but his steps were slow because even though he was curious, the unknown made Sammy apprehensive.

The cloaked figure stepped forward, away from Michael, when Sammy was a few feet away, which caused Sammy to come to a halt.

"Reveal yourself at once," Sammy demanded.

A deep laugh radiated from the mysterious entity. "I see why the humans fear you." He removed the hood and revealed his identity; it was none other than Gabriel. "This outfit instills terror even in me, and that is not easy." He shivered as though he were afraid.

Speechless, Sammy stared at Gabriel and then at Michael, who immediately broke eye contact by looking to the ground. Sammy stepped toward his friend as his anger rose. "How could you allow such an egregious act to occur?"

"Know your place and show respect before I put you down, dog," Gabriel shouted. He drove the scythe handle into the ground. "Nothing would bring me more pleasure than to destroy you." He smirked and then stood face-to- face with Sammy. "Michael and I came here for a reason, so I suggest you shut your mouth and take heed to what he has to say."

Sammy shoved Gabriel aside and approached Michael, waiting with bated breath for the words that were to come.

"As you know, your time on earth is drawing to a close." Michael paused as he tried to contain his emotions. "It would have ended weeks ago, but something was brought to my attention, and it was best that you got a slight extension on your time."

"What is going on?"

"I will be more than happy to answer this one," Gabriel said, exuding pleasure.

"Silence!" Michael shouted.

Michael placed his hands on Sammy's shoulders as a single tear fell from his eye—a show of emotion that struck fear in Sammy's heart.

"What is it?" Sammy asked in a low tone.

"I do not know how to say this." Michael paused. "We have been friends for a very long time, and this is the hardest conversation I have ever had to have in my entire existence. It pains me that it has to be had with you." He closed his eyes and then looked down once again before reestablishing eye contact. "The reason for your time being extended was that he thought it would be extremely cruel for you to have to perform your duties and take this person's life."

Sammy's heart dropped as he broke away from Michael. "Riley has been through so much." He swallowed the excess saliva that had accumulated in his mouth. "Please, talk to him and spare his life. Riley is a good man and does not deserve this."

"Who said anything about Riley?" Gabriel said and then chuckled deeply. Sammy stood in shock as Michael tried to silence Gabriel, but it was too late. He realized to whom Michael was referring. He looked at his friend in

disbelief. "Emily?"

While Michael tried to console his friend, Gabriel reveled in Sammy's misery. He stepped forward, disobeying Michael, pushing him to the side and standing face-to-face with Sammy. "Your girlfriend's pathetic life is coming to an end, and after I claim her life, you will be able to go back to your mundane existence surrounded by death."

Sammy was lost. He did not hear a word Gabriel said. He fell to his knees and stared at the ground while the two archangels bickered. Their voices had faded until it was silence all around. He closed his eyes, and the moment he saw Emily's face, tears rolled down his cheeks and fell to the ground. He felt as if his heart were being ripped out of his chest. Despite Michael standing a few inches from his head, saying his name repeatedly in his ear, he could not hear anything. All his focus was on Emily. How he could exist in a world that she no longer occupied?

Sammy crawled on the ground because he could not muster the strength to stand. He leaned against a tree and stared straight ahead but saw nothing. "How?" he muttered, his insides sinking at the mere thought of the question. "How does she die?"

He saw Michael cross his path and take a seat to his right. He heard a bunch of meaningless words in an attempt to provide comfort, but the answer to his question was nowhere to be found in Michael's soliloquy, which tested his patience. The last straw was the moment Michael placed his arm around Sammy's shoulders. Sammy's temper flared, and he harshly shoved Michael's arm away.

"Can I get an answer to my question?" Sammy slid to his right, glaring at the archangel with his angel eyes on display. "The only thing I want to hear is the how Emily dies."

"Brain aneurysm," Michael said in a low, somber tone.

Even though Sammy had the answer he required, it only caused the pain to intensify. He opened his mouth to scream, but the air had left his body, so no sound was emitted. He returned to the tree and rocked back and forth, trying to wrap his mind around the fact that someone else he cared about was about to perish in their teenage years. He refused Michael's predictable attempts at comfort and fixated on Gabriel, who was approaching with a huge grin on his lips.

"You know, you are to blame for these kids' misfortunes," Gabriel revealed.

"Quiet!" Michael shouted.

Sammy wiped his eyes and continued to focus on Gabriel. "What are you talking about?"

"You do not find it odd that three kids who attend the same high school in their formative years all die within a year?" Gabriel placed a finger on his chin. "Do you not see what all three kids have in common?"

Sammy slumped back against the tree as his insides sank. He turned to Michael because he knew his friend would be honest without taking pleasure in his misery. "You mean to tell me that these kids are dying because of me?"

Michael noticed the broken spirit behind Sammy's saddened eyes. He wanted to find a way to lessen the pain but needed to be candid. "He allowed you to be human, but you needed to know all aspects of being human." He paused. "You wanted the joy but had to feel the heartache. You cannot have one without the other."

Sammy was speechless. The gravity of his request broke his heart. His need to be loved had greatly affected the lives of countless people for the worse, and three people he cared for immensely were or would be in their graves prematurely. He could not conceal his pain as his tears fell freely. The sounds of Gabriel's laughter cut deep and could not be ignored.

"What is so funny?"

"You are truly pitiful!" Gabriel replied. "You cry for these humans like you are one of them. It is like you desire to be an ant instead of the boot." He clasped his hands behind his back as though deep in thought and paced in front of Michael and Sammy. "There is a way you can save her."

Despite Michael's objections, Sammy was intrigued at the mere mention of a way to save Emily from a doomed fate. "I have never heard of any way to stave off death."

"There is a lot that your arrogance would not allow you to know." Gabriel shook his head. "Let me draw you a picture." He slowly placed the hood on his head, covering his eyes, and grabbed the scythe. "I will come for her. She will plead and beg, but I will chuckle because I know she means so much to you." He smiled while staring at Sammy. "To save her life, all you have to do is confront me. All you have to do is defeat me. If you do, her life will be spared, but if you do not and die …" He chuckled. "There is no coming back, Mr. Angel of Death."

Sammy rose to his feet with malice in his heart. He glared at Gabriel with his angel eyes and clenched his fists so tightly that blood trickled to the ground. He could no longer contain his rage because of the perverse pleasure Gabriel took in the prospect of taking a young, vibrant girl's life. Just as he was about to unleash his venom, Michael intervened, stepping between them. Sammy pushed his friend to the side but could not escape his grip.

"I will tell her. I will warn her of what is to come so something can be done."

"You will do no such thing," Michael quickly replied. "The moment the words flow from your lips, Gabriel will immediately take her life, and I will be forced to end your existence, and that is something I do not wish to do."

Sammy felt helpless. He took a step back as his eyes returned to their alternative state. He stumbled until the tree stopped him from falling to the ground, while Michael pelted Gabriel with stern words and then ordered him to depart. Sammy continued to take deep breaths as Michael approached.

He aggressively grabbed the archangel by the shoulders and pleaded, "You have to do something. You have to go talk to him. I cannot lose her."

"The decision has been made. There is nothing I can do," Michael said and gave his friend a hug. "I am so sorry, my friend."

Sammy broke the embrace and watched as Michael spread his wings and took flight. He turned and punched the tree, sending a huge part of the trunk flying across the yard. He could not believe how everything had changed so fast. The best time of his life had quickly turned into his worst nightmare.

CHAPTER 34

Days turned to weeks, and weeks turned to months. What should have been a joyous time for Sammy was agonizing because of the unknown. The weather had turned from brisk to comfortably warm, so Sammy spent every waking moment he could with Emily, doing a myriad of things, from walks on the beach to picnics in the park. Events at school were back to normal, even though a buzz circulated when Slade woke from his thirty-day coma. Even though he was slated to make a full recovery, he could not remember anything about his encounter, so Sammy was in the clear.

The week was coming to an end. After Emily departed for the evening, Sammy lay on his bed, staring at the ceiling. Every time she was with him, he wrestled with telling her the truth. But he knew the consequences for her and did not want her life to come to an abrupt end, ignoring the fact that he would meet the same fate. A light knock on his bedroom door interrupted his thoughts, but he was pleasantly surprised when Riley entered the room. Sammy sat up on his bed and noticed the huge smile on Riley's face.

"Why are you so happy?"

"I saw Emily leave a few minutes ago, and I think it is wonderful to see my young nephew in love." He sat on the bed and gave Sammy a hug. "To see you happy makes me happy."

Sammy forced a smile, but Riley recognized it was not genuine. "Is something wrong?"

Sammy wanted to open up and tell Riley everything. He wanted to reveal his true nature and everything about Emily dying. He needed to talk to someone because it seemed like the weight of the world was on his shoulders and it was becoming too much to bear.

He took a deep breath, and just as he was about to come clean, something inside instructed him to do otherwise. Instead, he decided to search for information. "Can I ask you a few questions?"

"Anything," Riley quickly replied.

"Do you believe in angels?" Sammy positioned himself so he could look into Riley's eyes. "Do you believe in the angel of death or the grim reaper?"

The room fell silent for a few seconds. "Where is this coming from?"

"Jonathon used to talk about the angel of death at times, and I wondered if you believe in such things."

"I never gave it much thought," Riley answered, but after a few seconds of thinking, he continued, "I guess I do believe that there are angels that watch over us, so I can say that there is an angel that takes our lives as well."

"If you were face-to-face with the angel of death, what would you say to him?" Sammy moved in closer. "Are you angry with him for taking your sister's life?"

"I'm not angry at him." Riley's smile disappeared. "I'm sure it was not his call. It was a higher power, and death was just doing his job."

Sammy breathed a sigh of relief. This time his smile was sincere instead of a façade. "Let me ask you something else." His smile disappeared. "If there was any chance you could have saved her life, even the slightest chance …" He took a deep breath. "Even if it meant your life would have ended, would you have done it?"

Without hesitating, Riley gave an emphatic yes. He then placed his arm around Sammy. "You know how much I loved your mother, and if there was any chance I could save her, no matter how bad the odds, I would. Even if it means my life would come to an end." He pulled Sammy in and kissed the side of his head. Then he stood and went to depart, but he stopped. "I notice that you've been watching a lot of cooking shows. Do you plan on cooking for Emily?"

"I actually plan on cooking for her tomorrow night. I would love it if you could join us."

"I would like that very much, but I have one request." "What?"

"I would like to bring a guest."

Hearing those words brought excitement to Sammy. His eyes lit up like lights on a Christmas tree. "Who are you bringing?"

"You will just have to wait and see." Riley winked and closed the door behind him.

Some of the weight Sammy had been carrying lifted because Riley did not blame him for his sister's death. He had also finally started to date again.

Sammy did not want Riley to spend the rest of his life alone, mourning. Seeing his earth uncle happy and smiling brought Sammy some joy, even if it would be short-lived.

The next day, after another uneventful day at school filled with the same veiled threats from Slade's minions, Sammy arrived home to prepare for the evening's meal. He grabbed pots and pans as his favorite cooking show played in the background. All the while, he racked his brain for clues about the identity of Riley's new love interest. A short time later, Emily arrived, and the search and prep work came to an end as the couple took advantage of their alone time by making love.

After they concluded, they held each other and closed out the rest of the world. Sammy leaned back against the headboard as the covers covered his lower body. Emily's head rested on his chest. He kissed the top of her head and relished in her delectable scent, which brought to mind fresh roses. He listened to her sweet voice as she spoke about how happy she was and how much she was in love. The moment she began to speak about their future together, Sammy succumbed to his emotions. He held her closer and tucked his head behind hers to shield his teary eyes from her vision. He lied multiple times when she asked about his emotional state. He could not let her know how much pain he was in. He could not break her heart, even though his was shattered. He gave her one more tender kiss on top of her head, but their moment was interrupted by the sound of a car door slamming outside.

Terror struck his heart like a bolt of lightning. They looked at each with fear in their eyes. Sammy leapt out of bed and tossed Emily her shirt. He quickly grabbed a pair of sweats and a T-shirt and raced down the stairs and into the kitchen just as the front door opened.

He was able to don his clothes just before Riley entered the kitchen, unaware of what he would have seen if he had entered a few seconds earlier. Sammy's heart was pounding as he mustered a smile.

"Hey, Uncle Riley," he uttered between attempts to catch his breath. "I was about to start preparing dinner. I hope you are hungry."

Sammy was perplexed because Riley did not provide his usual immediate response. Instead, his uncle just stood and looked around the room. He watched as Riley exited the kitchen and returned a few seconds later with an inquisitive expression.

"I saw Emily's car parked on the street, but there's no sign of her." Riley placed his jacket on back of the dining chair. "Where is she?"

Sammy struggled to produce an answer, as his heart was in his throat. He stuttered for a few seconds and felt Riley's eyes pierce through his head as he waited for an answer. As sweat formed on Sammy's forehead, the kitchen door opened and Emily appeared with a huge grin. Sammy was relieved at the sight of her. She looked immaculate. Not a single hair was out of place, and her makeup was flawless. There was no evidence that they had just made love.

He watched as she turned on the charm and said all the words that Riley wanted to hear, excusing her absence from the kitchen. Sammy happily accepted her kiss on the cheek and then turned his attention back to Riley. "So who is your date?"

"You'll see when she gets here." Riley looked at his watch. "I have to go get cleaned up so I can go pick her up." He walked over and gave Emily a hug. "You are perfect for my boy. You put a smile on his face and a light in his eyes, and that brings me joy." He kissed her cheek. "I think of you as a daughter. Thank you for loving my nephew." After waving

CHAPTER 35

Sammy stood in the kitchen, applying the finishing touches to his masterpiece of a meal. His dish was top secret, so much so that he made Emily wait in the living room, refusing to give her a hint of what was in store. He was excited and anxious because Riley had called to inform him that he was en route with his surprise friend in tow. Sammy wanted everything to be perfect and yearned to make an impeccable first impression.

Minutes later, the meal was complete and just in time. He heard the front door open and Riley's voice reverberating from the living room. He removed his apron and gently placed it on the counter. Then he rushed into the living room, searching for the woman who had returned the smile and light to his uncle. But he didn't see her anywhere.

"Where is this special lady?"

"She's outside by the car making a phone call." Riley winked. "Be patient."

Sammy tried to sneak a peek through the window on the door, but Riley led him away. Riley wanted this person's entrance to be grand. Sammy rolled his eyes, as the anticipation was becoming too great, and returned to the kitchen amid snickers from both Riley and Emily.

They tried to enter his domain because the scent of his creation was alluring, but Sammy quickly halted their advances by pushing on the other side of the door.

"If I have to wait, you too shall wait." He extracted his revenge by mimicking their laughter before returning to the stove to check on his entree.

Seconds later, Sammy was summoned into the living room by Riley. He dropped his cooking spoon and rushed through the doorway toward Riley, who was waiting by the front door with a huge grin plastered across his face. The moment had arrived. Sammy's eyes never wavered from the door. He grabbed Emily's hand, holding her close. He heard the woman's heels pounding the cement outside and saw her silhouette as she approached the house. His eyes lit up like fireworks exploding in the night sky once she made her way into the house. The mystery was finally solved, as Riley's friend was none other than Lola.

Sammy's mouth gaped as he approached Lola and gave her a hug. "I never saw this coming." He turned to Riley. "How and when did this come about?"

Always the gentlemen, Riley took Lola's jacket and purse and hung them on the coatrack just to the right of the front door. "I was sitting in a diner a short time ago, thinking about my sister, when I saw this beautiful lady sitting a few tables down." He pulled Lola close and lovingly gazed into her eyes before returning his attention to Sammy. "I recognized her from the hospital that awful day Jonathon was … injured." He paused and took a deep breath. "I went over and sat with her, and we started talking." He smiled. "She informed me that she was divorced, and I decided to take a chance and ask her out." He kissed her. "She made me the luckiest man on the planet when she agreed, and I have spent every waking moment trying to show her that she didn't make a mistake."

Sammy gave his congratulations and well wishes on their relationship, and after informing everyone in the room that dinner was finished, he led them into the kitchen and sat them down before making his way over to the stove to retrieve the food.

"So my secret has been revealed. It's time for you to reveal yours." Riley rubbed his hands together. "What's for dinner?"

Sammy set the table, playing up the suspense as Riley had earlier. After Emily ordered him to reveal, he did so with a huge grin. "We are having spaghetti and meatballs." He placed a plate beside Lola. "For my brother whose spirit is with us tonight."

He catered to everyone by filling their plates with food and providing them with refreshments before taking a seat. He graciously accepted everyone's praise for his culinary skill and took a drink of orange juice after a job well done.

As the evening progressed, Sammy sat back and observed the interactions between the other three. He listened to their banter and marveled at how easily they meshed. They laughed at Riley's bad jokes and listened to more stories about how he and Lola met. At one point, Sammy leaned back in his chair and gazed at everyone, his heart aflutter. Everyone who meant the most to him sat at that table. At that moment it hit him; it was like a family. He promptly excused himself from the table as tears welled in his eyes. After assuring everyone that all was well, Sammy made his way outside to avoid any further questions about his emotional state.

He slowly sat on the top step of the back porch and gazed up at the full moon, which had provided him solace during his toughest times as a human. Many thoughts ran through his mind, ranging from Emily to what life would be like for Riley after his departure. He took several deep breaths and continued to bask in the brightness of the moon until something across the yard caught his attention.

The mysterious figure lurked behind the tree in the middle of the yard, but it was too dark to see who it was. When he used his angel eyes, the identity of the figure was revealed. It was none other than Gabriel. Sammy clenched his fists as his heart raced. He could not believe Gabriel's audacity, besmirching Sammy's moment of solitude. He rose to his feet. Just as he was about to confront the archangel, he heard the back door open. His heart jumped into his throat out of fear that it was Emily. He quickly turned, preparing to warn his love no matter the consequences, but was relieved when he saw Lola emerge into the night air.

He smiled, but it was a façade. He did not want her to see Gabriel. When he turned his attention back to the tree to check on Gabriel's whereabouts, his nemesis had disappeared, leaving behind only his maniacal laugh, which lingered in the air. Sammy breathed a huge sigh of relief as his nerves began to calm. He returned to his seat on the top step as Lola joined him, placing a hand on his back, providing comfort.

"You stormed out of the house, and everyone is concerned," Lola revealed. "Emily rushed to check on you, but I managed to talk her down, convincing her you needed a few minutes." She leaned in his direction. "Do you want to talk about what's on your mind?"

Sammy sat in silence for a few seconds, debating whether to share his woes, but he needed to talk to someone, so after taking another deep breath, he decided to open up. "You know my time on earth is drawing to a close, but it was extended." He paused. "I should have left a while ago, but they decided to keep me on earth to spare me from what is to come."

"She's going to die, isn't she?"

Sammy looked at Lola with an expression of disbelief. "How did you know?"

"You're a celestial being, and celestials aren't supposed to be on earth for an extended amount of time, interacting with humans without repercussions." She smiled, but her grin was racked with pain. "I knew my son could be in danger hanging around you, but before you entered the picture, he was lost and miserable." She wiped her eyes. "But when you became his friend, he came alive. He enjoyed life instead of just existing." She turned away as thoughts of her son experiencing good times entered her mind. "His time on earth was cut short, but he was happy, and that's all that mattered."

He apologized as tears formed in his eyes. He looked away because maintaining eye contact after hearing her words was too difficult a feat. He felt her arms wrap around his torso and heard the words of forgiveness she whispered in his ear, but that still did not take away the sorrow.

"I cannot exist knowing that she is not living life to the fullest. I cannot do my duties knowing that every person I take from this planet will be joining her in the afterlife."

"What do you plan to do?"

"I was told that I could face my replacement and if I defeat him, she will be spared." He sighed. "I will not have the luxury of my powers. I will be stronger than a human but nowhere strong enough to take down an archangel."

"I remember telling you about my great-great-grandmother being murdered." She paused. "The being that killed her was an archangel."

Flummoxed, Sammy shook his head. "Why?"

"She was mastering the dark arts and was becoming powerful." She slowly shook her head. "She had a husband she was teaching witchcraft to, and that was a no-no." She paused again. "The archangel descended upon my ancestor and killed her, along with her husband. He was ordered to kill her bloodline but did not." She smiled. "He still checks in on me from time to time, and we have nice conversations."

"Michael?" Sammy asked. "Yes."

Sammy looked up at the moon and wiped the tears from his eyes. "I have to face Gabriel and save her life."

"Killing an archangel is virtually impossible."

Sammy turned to face her with a huge grin. "The key word is virtually, but not impossible." He chuckled. Then his half-hearted laughter gave way to a serious expression. "It breaks my heart that when I leave no one will remember me."

"I won't completely forget," Lola revealed. "I'll have times that I'll remember fragments, sort of like déjà vu." She turned to him, matching his serious expression. "Are you really going to face him?"

"I have no choice. I love her too much to allow Gabriel to end her life."

"I would not expect anything less from you, Sammy." She kissed him on the cheek and then entered the house.

Sammy closed his eyes and was about to stand and follow Lola into the house, but the door opened once more. This time Emily emerged. He did not say a word. He simply stood, pulled her close, and hugged her as if it were the last time he would have her in his arms. He assured her that all was well and reiterated it after she did not believe him. After a passionate kiss, she was convinced. He took her by the hand and led her into the yard. He gazed into her eyes and then expressed his love before humming a song and leading her in a slow dance.

As her head rested against his chest, just over his heart, he rested his head on top of hers. They swayed in unison, not uttering a word.

Unbeknownst to the lovebirds, they were being watched from the doorway by Lola and Riley. Their love melted the adults' hearts. As they continued to watch, cuddled in one another's arms, Lola turned to face Riley. "I need you to go upstairs and pack a bag."

"Why?" Riley asked.

"We're going away for the weekend and hopefully will find something special like they have." Lola smiled and softly kissed Riley on the lips. "Can we?"

Riley simply smiled. "You bet your life we can."

CHAPTER 36

" Ah!" was the sound Sammy let out with his hands folded behind his head early Monday morning. He lay in bed, leaning back against his headboard. He had offered to accompany Emily so she would not face the wrath of her parents alone for staying out all night long, but she declined. So he was left to reminisce about their magical weekend alone. He listened to the birds chirping just outside his window, and his mind went to the moment that he and his beloved had sat in the backyard and fed the birds while having a picnic. He heard the front door open and close and knew the coast was clear. His uncle had left for work.

Unclothed, he leapt out of bed and ventured to the kitchen to indulge in a glass of orange juice. Midway through, he smiled at the thought that in a matter of minutes, he would be seeing Emily's beautiful face once again. He returned to his room and sat on the bed. He could still smell her perfume in the air, which made his smile broaden. He donned his clothes and raced down the stairs to grab his book bag just in time to hear the car horn honking. His heart fluttered at the mere thought of Emily waiting in the driveway. He could not wait another second to see his love, so he opened the door and raced out, but he stopped abruptly when he spotted the foreign car that waited for him.

His heart sank, fearing the worst. He dropped the bag that was draped over his right shoulder. "Where is Emily?" His stomach turned as he waited for the response. He watched as Joanne turned off the engine and emerged from the car with a blank expression.

"She isn't feeling well, so she asked if I could pick you up and take you to school," she answered.

Sammy quickly retrieved his phone and called Emily. It seemed like an eternity as he waited for her to answer. His angst grew with each ring. On the fifth ring, just as full panic was about to set in, Emily answered, which provided much needed relief because his thoughts had escalated to morbid. He leaned against the front door as he listened to her words assuring him that all was well. Hearing her voice managed to calm his heart rate and breathing. After the phone call concluded, he grabbed his bag and headed toward Joanne's car.

They made their way to school mostly in silence, but that was broken when Joanne decided to open up and reveal some things to Sammy, who turned to face her, giving her his undivided attention.

"I visited Jonathon's grave last week." Joanne pulled the car over so she was not distracted. "My heart was heavy, and I felt the need to apologize to him for the part I played in his death." She wiped the tears from her eyes. "I wanted to go over his mother's house and apologize to her also."

"I do not think that is necessary." Sammy placed a hand on her knee. "His mother is healing, and even though she will never get over the loss of her son, she is finding happiness and putting her life back together."

"We haven't talked as much since the whole thing that happened with Slade, but it's no coincidence that he was beat up after I left you that day."

His curiosity piqued, Sammy leaned back in his seat. "Where are you going with this?"

"Slade had whatever he got coming." She smiled. "It couldn't have happened to a nicer person." She rubbed Sammy's arm. "Emily is so lucky to have a standup person in her life; I just wish you had a brother who looks and acts just like you."

Sammy was pleased by the compliment and thanked her before leaning over and giving her a hug. The two then continued their way to school, enjoying a few laughs while engaging in light conversation. Even though the laughs were plentiful, Sammy's thoughts never wavered too far from Emily. He knew he would not feel fully satisfied until he saw her beautiful face.

Shortly after arriving at school, Sammy grabbed his books and headed to homeroom. He took his seat but not before directing his daily taunts in Alex's direction. He checked his phone and found a text from Emily, letting him know that she was on her way, but he was still nervous because he knew a lot could happen to her between her house and school.

Meanwhile, high above the clouds, Michael was preparing to embark on his duties, but things seemed out of sorts. His fellow archangels were nowhere to be found. An uneasy feeling settled over him, so he felt the need to do some investigating. He checked on Gabriel's duties and raised an eyebrow when he discovered that he was going to be in the Virginia area. Michael dug deeper by checking the human lives ledger and gasped when he saw Emily's name. He became frantic. The first thing that entered his mind was to get word to Sammy. He tried to depart, but his access to earth had been restricted. When he tried to communicate with Sammy, he found it to be futile.

The deed was going down today, and he was stuck high above, unable to warn or provide any assistance to his friend. Sammy was truly on his own.

Back at school, it was shortly before ten o'clock, and Emily had just arrived. She parked her car, retrieved her phone from her purse, and sent Sammy a text that included lines laden with affection. She entered the building and headed straight to her locker. She gathered her books, but in doing so, she noticed that the halls were uncommonly empty and extremely quiet. The hallways had turned grayish in color, and when she grabbed her phone, she noticed that even though it was on, the screen was blank.

A chill ran down her spine. She was frightened. She did not know what to do. Her first instinct was to run to her car and drive away as fast as she could, but Sammy entered her mind. She did not want to run away and leave Sammy to fend for himself. She could not live with herself if something happened to him while she was safe and sound far away from school. She decided to go find him and get him to safety, but the moment she returned her phone to her purse and turned to head to his class, her worst fear came to stand directly in front of her face.

She took a step back as fear radiated through her body. Gabriel stood before her wearing a cloak and holding a scythe; the silver blade cut through the dull gray light. She questioned if she was dreaming. At that point, a dream would be welcome over reality. Her heart pounded, and her mouth was devoid of saliva. She took another step back, but Gabriel stood his ground. She dropped her books and her purse and finally found the courage to ask the question that needed to be answered: "Who are you?"

"That is a complicated question but a very simple answer," Gabriel said in a very deep tone followed by an even deeper sinister laugh. "Who do you think I am?"

Emily shook her head, refusing to answer, because if she was correct, she knew what it meant for her. So, she shook her head and closed her eyes, hoping that when they opened, he would be gone and everything would be back to normal. She turned away and was about to run, but in an instant, Gabriel closed in and stood so close that she could feel his breath against her face and neck.

"I asked you a question, and I expect an answer." He removed his hood and glared into her eyes. "Who do you think I am?"

"I'm too afraid to say."

"Say it!" he shouted so loudly that his voice echoed throughout the halls.

She felt helpless and looked down at the floor. She knew it was in her best interest to answer him because she did not want to suffer through the alternative. "I think you're the grim reaper."

She watched as he slowly circled her, taking perverse pleasure in her misery. She tried to be brave in the face of fear as he removed his cloak and tossed it and the scythe to the floor. He stood before her with his muscular frame and his mace attached to his belt. With a sudden move, she felt his hand wrap around her neck and give it a tight squeeze. Then he pulled her close.

"That is what I thought you were going to say." He tossed her to the floor and laughed once again. "I told you it was complicated, and it is." He moved in close and knelt before his fallen prey. "I am filling in for the grim reaper while he is off doing whatever." He phased, exposing his beautiful white wings and then glared at her with disdain. "If I were that pathetic excuse for an angel, do you think I would have exquisite wings like these?"

He retracted his wings but kept his smug smirk. "The funny thing is the grim reaper has been among you guys for months now and you have been none the wiser."

"Who are you talking about?"

"That is not important." He ran his sharp nail down the side of her face. "There is one person here that can save your life." He grabbed her by the back of the neck and hoisted her into the air. "You will yell his name. He is the only one that can hear you." He squeezed tighter. "Yell his name at once."

She thought about it for a few seconds and did not want to involve Sammy, but she knew Sammy wanted to protect her, just like she would do everything in her power to protect him. As the pressure mounted around her neck, Gabriel left her no choice. With everything deep inside her, she closed her eyes and screamed Sammy's name. Then she lowered her head, hoping he would come to her rescue.

CHAPTER 37

Meanwhile, Sammy was sitting in math class, enduring another tedious day of school, oblivious to the events happening two floors below. He leaned back in his chair and nonchalantly provided the correct answer to the equation written on the chalkboard after his classmates failed miserably, yelling out incorrect answers. He reached into his jacket pocket to retrieve his cell phone in the hopes Emily had attempted to get in contact, but he stopped when he heard Emily's voice reverberating in his ears. She was calling his name.

His world came to a stop. He felt that Emily was in danger and immediately stood and exited the classroom, despite the teacher calling his name and ordering him to return. The command was inconsequential. He made his way down the hallway, following the echoes of her voice like bread crumbs. He reached the end of the hallway and turned right as the echoes became louder. As her voice elevated, the voices of the people in the school faded. The moment he reached the top of the staircase, all outside noise completely disappeared. The only sound he could hear was the continuous echo of Emily calling his name once.

He stood there for a few seconds as the unknown became very unsettling. He could hear the distress in her voice, and because he did not know what was happening, nervousness and fear racked his stomach and heart. Fear was a foreign emotion to him, but now he had someone for whom he cared deeply and could not imagine his existence without her, so the feeling was apropos.

He needed answers, so he decided to call for Michael. When his friend did not appear, he knew something was amiss, he was on his own. He made his way down the stairs, and with each step, her voice became louder. As he reached the final step before landing on the ground floor, he exposed his angel eyes to assess his surroundings. He noticed the ground floor was gray in color. With that clue, he knew who was behind this sinister plot. His eyes returned to their alternative state. He took a deep breath before reluctantly taking the final step down. He slowly turned the corner, and what he saw rocked him to his core.

He was witnessing his worst nightmare as he saw Emily, terrified, in Gabriel's clutches. His first instinct was to charge his nemesis and save the woman he loved, but the expression on Gabriel's face—the smirk with a malevolent gleam in his eye—made him think better. Sammy took a step forward, and Gabriel pulled her back slightly, mimicking Sammy's movement.

"Ah ah ah!" Gabriel said, followed by a wink. "I would not do whatever you are thinking." He chuckled while gazing at Emily. "I would hate to snap her neck; that would take all the fun out of this encounter."

"What are you doing?" Sammy asked, taking slow steps toward the archangel in an effort not to incite his adversary. "You are supposed to be better than this. You are supposed to fight for the humans, not to torture them."

"Look who is all high and mighty now." Gabriel rolled his eyes. "You have been torturing humans your entire existence and now you want to look down your nose at me?" He held her high once again. "You knew this day was coming, but before the deed is done, I thought I would have some fun first."

Gabriel phased, spread his wings, and levitated. "You know the only way to save her pathetic life." He tossed her in Sammy's direction. "The moment of truth has arrived; it is time to choose."

Sammy rushed to his beloved's side and cradled her in his arms. "Are you alright?" He brushed her hair away from her face. "He did not harm you, did he?"

"I'm fine." She broke away from Sammy and shuffled behind him. "What's going on? Who in the hell is he?"

"His name is Gabriel," Sammy said. "He is an angel."

He kissed her on the cheek and lips, assuring her all was well, but deep down he needed to be convinced also. Gabriel was an imposing specimen, and without his powers, Sammy would be full of hubris if he thought taking on the archangel would be a walk in the park. He turned his attention to Gabriel and saw that he was still in the air, slowly flapping his wings while smiling.

The archangel's arrogance angered Sammy. He clenched his fists. Just as he was about to make his way toward Gabriel, he felt Emily's hand on his forearm, stopping his advancement.

"Please don't go." A tear formed in Emily's eye. "You don't have to do this. We can run. We can go far away from here and make a new life somewhere he can't find us."

Sammy wiped the tears from her eyes and gave her an endearing kiss on the forehead. "There is no running or hiding from him. He is here to carry out a mission, and nothing will deter him from that but me."

"How do you know so much about him?" Emily asked.

"We will talk about it later. I promise." He gave her one more kiss before rising to his feet.

Sammy made his way toward Gabriel despite Emily's pleading. He stared his nemesis down, refusing to break eye contact. He stopped when he was twenty feet away. His heart pounded, and his mouth was dry as a nervous feeling that bordered on fear washed over him. He watched as Gabriel retracted his wings and returned to the floor. They stood across from one another as if they were preparing for an old-fashioned gun fight at the O.K. Corral. Sammy was ready, even though he heard

Emily crying, which caused his heart to break. For a moment, hearing the pain in her cries took him back to the hut in Colombia. He equated her anguish with Carolina's family's when she passed away, but he had to find a way to block all that out and remain focused.

"I see you have not been forthright with the so-called love of your life," Gabriel said. "You have not told her who you really are. She believes you are some punk high school kid instead of a celestial being here searching for love." He wagged his finger. "You claimed to love her, yet honesty seems to have escaped you, Samael." He chuckled. "*Tsk, tsk, tsk*." He clasped his hands behind his back. "Do you want to tell her who you really are, or should I?"

Sammy turned to face Emily, who bombarded him with questions about Gabriel's words. He knew it was a ploy to cause conflict between him and Emily and to distract him, rousing his anger. The latter was successful.

"I have had it with your petulance. If we are going to fight, let us begin," Sammy said in a deep voice that frightened Emily.

"The girl wanted to know who the grim reaper was. I think you have answered her question," Gabriel said.

Sammy exposed his angel eyes as he prepared for combat, but he was not immune to Emily's cries. He peeked over his shoulder and made eye contact with her. The look on her face was a sight that would be etched in his mind for the rest of his existence. The horror and dismay she exuded broke his heart, but he also knew explanations and apologies would have to wait. Standing a few feet away was the biggest threat to both their lives, and no apologies were going to make the archangel disappear.

CHAPTER 38

Sammy glared at Gabriel, trying to figure out an effective attack that would defeat his adversary. He endured the archangel's ridicule and maintained his composure even though Gabriel's words exacerbated his anger. He searched Gabriel's frame for a weakness, a point upon which to focus his offense, but alas, there was none.

"You know you do not have a chance against me." Gabriel smiled. "Even in your previous state I would vanquish you, but in this form, you do not stand a chance." He rubbed the handle of his mace. "I am going to give you one last chance to save yourself, but you have to watch her die. I insist on that part."

"It is funny. You call yourself an angel but harbor so much malice in your heart."

"You are right, Samael. I do have malice in my heart when it comes to these humans." A look of disgust appeared on Gabriel's face. "He loves them so much that he has given them everything; he has blessed them with life and the ability to create life." He began to pace back and forth. "He has given them the world, and how do they repay him? How do they act?" Gabriel spit and then aggressively wiped his mouth. "They do senseless acts of violence against one another, and why? Because one group does not share the same beliefs as others or because one group of people has different skin color." Gabriel slowly approached Samael. "These vile humans love money, and most refuse to use that money to help others unless it benefits their own cause. When things are going well, they forget all about him, but when things turn for the worse, they quickly call out for his help."

He panted, staying focused on Samael. "If it were up to me, I would eliminate every single one of these ungrateful miscreants and just allow the beautiful animals to roam the earth." He drew within a few feet of Samael and glared into in his eyes.

Gabriel gazed over Samael's shoulder and made eye contact with Emily, who was curled up against the wall on the right side of the floor. "Your girlfriend was so in love with herself that she constantly disrespected an educator and made the woman's daughter's life pure hell." He turned his attention back to Samael. "But what sickens me more is that you want to lower yourself and be one of them. You want to be loved by these pathetic ingrates instead of being a higher form."

Gabriel turned his back to Samael in the ultimate show of disrespect and began to walk away. "So what is it going to be? Are you going to step aside and live but watch her die, or are you going to join her in death?"

Samael stayed silent for a few moments as Gabriel's words swirled in his head. He knew there was finality to this, and the moment of truth had finally come. Even though he could not summon or communicate with Michael, he knew his friend would beg him to back down, allow Gabriel to do his duty, and leave earth. His eyes returned to their alternative form as he slowly turned and looked at Emily. He saw she was afraid and gave her a wink as though to say everything would be okay. He told her how much he loved her and then turned his attention back to Gabriel.

He exposed his angel eyes once more, and his smile quickly disappeared and was replaced by a look of disdain. "If you are done bloviating, we can finally get down to business."

Sammy stood at the ready with his fists clenched as a fiendish smile graced Gabriel's lips. The moment the archangel exposed his angel eyes, Sammy took a deep breath and charged, going on the offensive. He bombarded Gabriel with a barrage of thunderous punches to his face and torso, but they had little effect. The archangel laughed in a mocking manner, but that did not deter Sammy as he continued his attack.

Growing tired of Samael's futile attempts to harm him, Gabriel drew back and swatted him away like a gnat, sending him hurtling back twenty feet to land hard on the floor.

Samael recovered quickly and went back on the attack, throwing more punches at Gabriel, a number of which were easily dodged.

Gabriel pushed Samael back, quickly phased, and wrapped himself inside his wings. Despite being feathery and soft, when used in combat, his wings became hard and could be used for protection and as a weapon.

A few seconds later, Gabriel emerged from his shell and spread his wings with such force that the wind pushed Samael back a few feet. Samael stood, preparing for what came next. When Gabriel began to spin in a circle like a top, trying to cut Samael with the sharp edges of his wings, Samael leaned back and was barely able to avoid the onslaught.

Once Gabriel came to a stop, Samael saw his chance and recklessly rushed in, but he was stopped when the archangel grabbed him by the throat.

"My turn!" Gabriel said in a deep tone as a sinister smile appeared on his face. He lifted Samael off the ground and stared into the eyes of his prey. He punched Samael in the stomach, forcing the breath from his body, and then punched him in the face before tossing him to the ground like a bag of trash.

Samael grabbed his midsection as pain radiated through his body. He gasped, trying to recapture his breath, but Gabriel went on the attack before he could do so.

The archangel violently snatched him off the ground. He punished Samael with bone-breaking punches to the torso and then tossed him through the air. While Samael flew, Gabriel spread his wings and took flight. He grabbed Samael by the throat and drove him into the floor, leaving a deep imprint in the marble.

"I am not finished with you yet," Gabriel said in a frighteningly deep tone.

He yanked Samael off the floor as he gasped for air, defenseless. The archangel threw him against the wall. Just as Samael was about to slump to the floor, Gabriel retrieved his mace from his hip. He turned the handle, exposing the spikes, and with a mighty upward swing, he struck Samael, shattering the bones on his left side and mangling his face. He slammed Samael to the ground and stood over him, watching as blood poured onto the floor.

"I tried to tell you that you did not stand a chance against me." He kicked Samael's hand to the floor as it reached for his leg. "I have waited a long time to kill you, and I will do it slowly to savor the moment." He kicked Samael in the face, displacing four teeth, and then turned his attention to Emily. "Now we have time to play."

Meanwhile, high above, Michael watched helplessly as his friend lay on the ground as the life force drained from his human shell. He tried numerous times to break the invisible barrier that kept him from descending to earth but was unsuccessful. His frustration grew. Not only was he unable to help his friend in his time of need, but Gabriel had ignored his pleas and allowed his personal hatred for Samael to usurp his celestial duty.

Michael paced for a few seconds as his irritation turned to anger. He decided to take it out on the barrier. He kicked, screamed, and punched the barrier with all the force he could muster, and in the end, he noticed something: a foot high and foot wide crack that lasted only a few seconds. He knew he would not be able to fit through the crevice, but his sword could, so he repeated his attack and then sent his sword plummeting down to earth, hoping it was not too late.

Back at the school, Samael tried to make his way to his feet, but even the slightest movement was a chore because of the pain that ravaged his body. Blood leaked from every orifice, five of his ribs were broken, his left eye was swollen shut, and the skin hung loosely from the bones of his face. He managed to roll over to his side and caught a glimpse of Gabriel taunting Emily. He took a deep breath and tried to stand, but it was futile. His spirit wanted to continue the fight, but his body was too battered. He felt his life slipping away.

Tears rolled down his cheek, as defeat was imminent. His thoughts returned to the millions of people's lives he had taken through the years.

Now that his was slipping away, it reaffirmed how precious life was and that no moment should be wasted. He apologized to those faceless, nameless people as he stared at his blood on the floor. Just as he rolled over onto his back, he heard a loud crash from the ceiling.

His gaze shot upward, where he saw Michael's sword rip through and plunge into the floor just to his right. Total despair was replaced by a single shred of hope. He prayed Gabriel had not heard the ruckus. When he turned his head to see if the archangel had noticed anything, he saw Gabriel taunting and toying with Emily, completely unaware of the new turn of events. He closed his eyes and took a few deep breaths, searching for the strength to make one last stand. When he heard Emily's pleas for mercy, it was all the motivation he needed. Sammy made his way to one knee and then spit out a mouthful of blood. He grabbed the handle of the sword, pulled the weapon from the ground, and laid it flat on the floor before collapsing.

"I am not finished with you yet, Gabriel," he shouted and grimaced before clutching his abdomen.

Sammy lay on the ground, struggling for every breath, but he took solace in the fact that his words had hit home. Out of the corner of his eye, he saw Gabriel stop just short of taking Emily's life and turn his attention back to him. Sammy grabbed the handle of the sword and hid the weapon behind his right leg as he continued hurling insults, knowing they would pick at the archangel's ego and drive his fervor to attack, diverting his attention from Emily.

He continued his banter, even throwing in a smile. Though he was weak, his plan was working. He knew he had one shot at this, so he watched Gabriel intensely as he approached. When the archangel grabbed his mace and raised it above his head, Samael saw the hate in his eyes and his trademark sinister grin. His grip tightened on the sword as Gabriel phased and took flight. His heart pounded as fear coursed through every nerve in his battered body.

Samael's eyes widened as Gabriel neared. He struggled to keep his focus, stay conscious, and block out Emily's blood-curdling screams. He locked eyes with Gabriel, who was now within fifteen feet of him.

The angel let out a dreadful roar, which gave Samael the indication that he was ready to deliver the death blow that would undoubtedly give the archangel indescribable pleasure. Samael's eyes turned toward the mace, in particular its thick, sharp points. It was now or never. He closed his eyes and dug deep to muster the strength he needed to lift the sword. At the last second, he thrust the weapon upward as a strong force emitted from Gabriel came his way.

Samael heard a loud thud just inches from his head, but when he opened his eyes, what he saw was a thing of beauty. The blade was plunged in the left side of Gabriel's abdomen, about a foot deep. He smiled as he saw Gabriel's eyes bulge. When he noticed the archangel's wings slump until the tips rested on the floor, he finally let out a sigh of relief. Victory was within his grasp. Samael could smell the stench of fear emanating from Gabriel and saw the look of despair on his face. He took time to bask in the moment as he watched the life force drain from his adversary.

"Everything that lives can and will die." He pushed the sword deeper. "Even an archangel."

Gabriel belted out a loud yelp but somehow found the strength to dislodge himself from the sword and quickly departed by busting through the ceiling. Sword still in hand, Samael's arm fell to the floor. He heard Emily rush over to his side, and that gave him proof that she was well and her life had been saved. He let go of the sword and slid it under his leg. He turned and gazed at her as the weapon disappeared then exhaled allowing himself to be

cradled in her arms.

He closed his eyes and took in the smell of her sweet perfume. Tears rolled down his face as he reached up and touched her cheek and then her lips. "You are alive," he whispered.

"You did it. You defeated him." She looked around. "We have to get you *outta* here and to a hospital." She kissed his forehead. "I don't know where we are, but it looks like school."

"I guess with everything going on, I never told you where we are." He struggled to take a breath. "We are in the crossroads of your life, an in- between of life and death. You were not supposed to be transported here; he was supposed to take you beyond this place."

"Why didn't he?"

Sammy gazed into her eyes. "Because he wanted to goad me into a confrontation and take both our lives." He looked to his side and saw the sword had vanished, and then turned his attention back to Emily. "He was so arrogant and thought he was going to kill both of us, but he was sorely mistaken."

"Why would you risk your life for me?"

"You already know the answer." He smiled even though he felt the life force leaving his body. "I love you more than anything. I could not exist if you did not."

"We have to get some help. I have to get you to the hospital." Emily ran her fingers though his blood-soaked hair. "You saved my life. Now it is time for me to save yours."

"No hospitals." Samael coughed, and blood flew out of his mouth and nose. "There is nothing they can do for me; there is nothing that can be done for me now."

"Don't talk like that." She held him close. "We have a long life to build together."

Sammy's eyes returned to their alternative state as his breathing began to slow. "You want to build a life with me even though I was not completely honest with you about my true self?"

"I know who you are. You're Sammy Angel. The new kid that came along and stole my heart, the one I'll always love." She ran her fingers over his swollen face. "I want you to look at me with your natural eyes."

Sammy exhaled heavily and closed his eyes. He did not want to show her his dark eyes; he wanted her to see the beauty and not have the darkness be her last memory of him. He reluctantly displayed his angel eyes and then gazed at her. He looked over her right shoulder and saw the auras of his friends, Jonathon and Cathy, so he knew his time was coming to an end. He turned his attention back to Emily, caressed her face, and forced a smile even though sadness and pain overwhelmed him.

"I want to thank you for showing me the meaning of the word *love*. I want to thank you for loving me and showing me the best time that anyone could ever have." He coughed once more as tears continued to fall. "You were the calm in the storm; you were the bright light in an existence ruled by darkness. Words cannot do service to how I feel about you; love is not a strong enough word to describe my feelings. It would take me an eternity to find the words to describe what I feel in my heart for the most beautiful woman I have ever seen."

He lowered his head. "I hate that you will never remember me after I leave, or our time together, but I know your heart will always remember me."

"I'll never forget you." She placed her hand over her stomach. "This bundle of joy will always remind me of you and our love." She smiled.

"I'm pregnant."

CHAPTER 39

I*mpossible* was the word that went through Sammy's mind on a continuous loop. He looked at her face in an attempt to read her facial expression. Her smile was too broad to be a lie, even though her eyes were filled with tears. He separated from her and then examined her body, starting with her head. He searched for injuries inflicted by Gabriel and was relieved to find none, but when he got to her stomach, he paused.

His heart filled with joy as he saw his child. He was at a loss for words. He turned away as his emotions overflowed. He managed to hold back his cries as he struggled to breathe, but he had to remain strong because so much needed to be said. He placed one hand over her stomach and wiped the blood from his mouth with the other.

He smiled even though the pain warranted a grimace. "It is a boy."

"I'm only eight weeks; it's too early to tell the sex of the baby."

He smiled. "It is too early for humans and their technology, but not for me." He reached over and took both her hands in his. He kissed the back of each and then lowered his head. "This is a miracle, an unprecedented feat." He looked into her eyes as his joy dissipated. "Life will be very hard for him; you need to protect him. Celestials will be coming for him from both sides."

"You'll be here with me to raise our son." Emily began to cry. "You can't put this all on me; I can't do this alone."

Sammy took some quiet and subtle breaths, trying to stave off death for as long as possible. He looked around, searching for Cathy and Jonathon, and was pleased when no sign of their auras were present. He knew he had more time. He slid beside her and wrapped his arms around her, showering her with tender kisses on her cheek while caressing her stomach.

"You will never be alone. I will always be with you." He looked down at her stomach. "I will always be with both of you."

He began to feel weak and lightheaded. He laid his head in her lap, positioning his ear next to her stomach. He closed his eyes and focused his hearing on his son. He heard the heartbeat and smiled as if the child were talking to him. Afterward, he looked up at her and gazed into her tear- reddened eyes.

"You are going to make a wonderful mother." He removed the angel necklace from around his neck and placed it around hers. "I told you that you would forget me, but this necklace will ensure you remember everything." He winced in pain. "I need you to tell him about me. I need you to tell him how much in love we were." He coughed, spewing more blood. "He will be confused and probably shy because he will not know how to handle the changes he will be going through. You need to be patient with him and let him know that he can talk to you about anything and everything, no matter what."

Sammy paused and winced as the pain intensified. He gazed into her eyes. "No one else will remember me, but Lola will have faint memories. You can trust her. Think of her as an emissary of sorts. She has knowledge of the supernatural and will be very helpful."

He looked at her stomach, staring at his son. "I want you to name him Azreal. He will want vengeance. I want you to steer him away from that destructive path. With his power, he could leave this planet in ashes." He kissed her stomach. "Show him there is another way; teach him how to love just like you taught me." He placed both hands on her face after wiping the blood from his lips. He gave her a soft, tender kiss and then proclaimed his love for the last time.

He smiled and took a deep breath as a bright light glowed, and within seconds, Sammy was gone.

The late bell rang—a sound that brought Emily back to reality. She was on her knees just outside the closed door of her history class. She was bewildered as she looked around the empty halls, feeling like she was experiencing déjà vu. She inspected her hands and clothes, but there were no signs of blood. There was also no sign of Sammy. Her heart was heavy as she placed her fingers on the angel pendant that hung from her neck. Every memory the two had shared raced through her mind, and as her emotions swelled, she let out an ear-piercing scream.

She placed her face in her hands and began to cry. She felt a hand on her shoulder and jumped back, scooting along the floor until her back was against the wall. She had flashbacks of Gabriel taunting her about ending her life and felt that she was about to relive that ordeal. But when she opened her eyes, she was pleased to see Mrs. Stevens's face.

"Are you alright, Emily?" Mrs. Stevens asked.

Emily was still in a daze. She looked at Mrs. Stevens but also noticed that the hallway had quickly filled with students and other teachers because of her outburst.

"Do I need to call your parents?" Mrs. Stevens asked.

Emily slowly stood and shook her head. She stared into the faces of some of the students, who were mumbling inaudibly, but she knew it was about her.

"Where's Sammy?" Emily asked. "Who?" Mrs. Stevens responded.

Emily placed her hand on her stomach as tears rolled down her cheeks. Sammy was gone, and Mrs. Stevens's response made it real for her. She spotted Rose and Joanne quickly approaching and gave them both a hug when they arrived.

After the embrace, she turned her attention back to Mrs. Stevens. "I'm not feeling well, but there's no need to call my parents. I'll just go see the nurse and then go home for the day."

She slowly made her way down the hall, feeling everyone's confused glares. She placed her hand on the necklace once more and at that moment, she heard his soothing voice, his euphoric laughter, and lastly; she could smell his invigorating scent. She stopped at the locker he had once used and grazed her fingers down the metal door. She did not want to go forward, didn't know how she would be able to, but placing her hand on her stomach was all the inspiration she needed. The love of her life was gone, but at least she had a piece of him to love and watch grow. She kissed the locker and then softly placed her head against the metal. She knew going forward would be hard without Sammy by her side, but she had to be strong because he would not want it any other way.

Later that day, Michael sat high above the clouds, still in the same spot, not moving an inch. He was still in shock and disbelief that his friend had perished.

Memories of the times they had shared, the good and the bad, along with thousands of years of conversations played over in his mind. Their bond was everlasting, and the fact that he would never speak to his friend, his brother, again was beginning to resonate. His heart was extremely heavy.

His thoughts were interrupted by a noise that could only be described as both a moan and a whimper. Michael turned his head slightly to the right. Over his shoulder, he spotted Gabriel. His fellow archangel was still in very bad shape; his wound was not healing, and his wings, which were usually bright and breathtaking, were dull and losing feathers. Michael gritted his teeth at the sight of him. Thoughts filled with malice began to creep into his mind as he touched the sword that had caused Gabriel's discomfort. But he quickly retracted his hand because he knew acting on such thoughts would make him just like the angel he had come to dislike.

"This wound is not healing," Gabriel said as he stumbled toward Michael. "I think I am about to die."

"You deserve whatever you get. Do not look my way for any sympathy," Michael said with scorn.

Gabriel pressed on his wound in an attempt to stop the bleeding. "I see you are mad that your friend is no more." He chuckled. "It is ironic that the angel of death is dead."

"He is not pleased with your actions, and you will have to face him because he is the only one that can heal your wounds and save you at this point." Michael rose to his feet and turned to face Gabriel with an expression filled with contempt. "Part of me hopes you do not go see him so you can meet the same fate as Samael."

"Do not be mad at me because your friend could not stand aside."

"Do not act like you are innocent; you could have just done your duty and gone on to the next stop, but you baited Samael. I wish he had his powers so he could have survived the encounter." Michael glared at Gabriel with clenched fists. "You went at him when he was stripped of his abilities; that made you feel powerful!"

"It would not have made a difference if he had his powers; he still would have lost," Gabriel said and then fell to one knee, capitulating to his pain.

"Lost?" Michael laughed. "How do you think he lost?" He shook his head. "He went to earth and made friends and found a love that he deemed worthy to give his existence for. He loved that young lady so much that he would rather die than have an existence in which she was no longer breathing. That is the complete opposite of losing. He won, my ignorant brother."

Michael turned his back, not wanting Gabriel to see him getting emotional. He wiped the tears from his eyes and then turned to face his fellow archangel. He focused on the wound that Gabriel was trying so hard to heal. He watched as drops of blood seeped between his fingers and colored the cloud red. "You need to find the gumption to face him so he can save your life, and be prepared for the punishment that you will surely face."

After Gabriel departed, Michael walked over to the spot where Sammy had made his initial request. He smiled when he thought back to the moment Sammy's request was granted; the pure joy he had exuded was priceless.

He peered down upon the earth, at Emily's house, to be exact. He saw her lying peacefully in bed, sound asleep, but something shining brightly caught his eye. He looked over both shoulders, and when he was satisfied that he was alone, he spread his massive wings and descended to earth with great speed.

Within minutes, he landed on the street where she lived with such force that a huge crater formed in the street and the windows of each vehicle parked on the block shattered.

The carnage he left in his wake was of no importance. He was on a mission for answers, and nothing else mattered, certainly not some property damage that could be repaired by the well-to-do residents of the neighborhood. He made his way into the house and into Emily's room. He stood at the foot of her bed and stared at her; he admired her for the courage she had shown in the face of certain death and sympathized for the love she had lost.

Michael moved to the side of her bed and spotted the trinket that had caught his attention. Once he saw the wings and the way the angel illuminated in his presence, he knew her memories had not been taken the moment Sammy died; the question that needed to be answered was why. He paced the room for a few seconds, pondering why Sammy would need her to remember his existence and the painful memories of his final moments. After a few more seconds, the answer dawned on him, but he needed confirmation.

He took a step back and examined her body with his angel eyes. When he reached her stomach, his hunch was substantiated. He reached for his sword, knowing something so powerful could not live among the human race. He knew a half human, half celestial would be a king living among mice and would be a threat to all living beings, angels included. He knew what must be done, but he could not bring himself to complete the deed.

His love for his best friend would not allow him to end the lives of Sammy's child and the young lady he had adored more than anything. Instead, Michael knelt beside the bed and gazed through her stomach directly at the baby.

"He would have made a wonderful father. He loved your mother to no end, so I know he would have loved you the same." He placed his hand within an inch of Emily's stomach. "I promise to watch over you and protect you as if you were my own son. I will guide you and help you harness your immense power and do my best to shield you from all supernatural beings that will come for your life." He stood and placed his hand over his heart to solidify his vow. Then he gave the baby a loving wink before departing.

Shortly after Michael's departure, Emily woke from her sleep feeling like something was awry. She surveyed the room but found nothing to support her hunch. Unable to dispel her notion, she got out of bed, looked out the window, and spotted a winged entity flying through the sky toward the bright full moon. She placed her hand on her stomach.

"Everything will be all right, Azreal. Everything will be all right."